Urban Fantasy

Urban Fantasy

EXPLORING MODERNITY THROUGH MAGIC

Stefan Ekman

Lever Press (leverpress.org) is a publisher of pathbreaking scholarship. Supported by a consortium of higher education institutions focused on, and renowned for, excellence in both research and teaching, our press is grounded on three essential commitments: to be a digitally native press, to be a peer-reviewed, open access press that charges no fees to either authors or their institutions, and to be a press aligned with the liberal arts ethos.

The complete manuscript of this work was subjected to a fully closed ("double-blind") review process. For more information, please see our Peer Review Commitments and Guidelines at https://www.leverpress.org/peerreview

DOI: https://doi.org/10.3998/mpub.14414299
Print ISBN: 978-1-64315-064-2
Open access ISBN: 978-1-64315-065-9

Library of Congress Control Number: 2023952399

Published in the United States of America by Lever Press, in partnership with Michigan Publishing.

This book is typeset in Calluna and Mr Eaves XL Mod OT.

To the memory of Lillemor Ekbom,
who always listened.

Contents

published in English, but I have used some texts written in other languages as well.

. . . a relationship between modernity and the fantastic, a core concern with the unseen, and a combination of traits from other genres.

Rather than defining urban fantasy by either specifying necessary and sufficient conditions or anointing a prototypical text around which the genre crystalizes, I consider it in terms of an idealized cognitive model. The model (in fact a cluster of models) structures the various dimensions—of content and form as well as production, marketing, and consumption, in the present and over time—of the mental space that is *urban fantasy*, and it can be summarized by the following three points:

1. The world of an urban fantasy story contains a nonnegligible number of supernatural elements that are placed in some sort of relation to expressions of modernity in that world.
2. The story involves as a core concern spaces (settings) and/or beings (characters) that are in some sense unseen by the members of the fictive world's mainstream society.
3. Story or world combines genre characteristics from two or more different genres.

These three points are not necessary and sufficient conditions for the genre. They can be true to various extents and in different ways: a "nonnegligible number of supernatural elements" can be one or two such elements, if they dominate the narrative, or it can be a different world, brimful of gods, magicians, and strange beasts while still being distinctly modern. China Miéville's *The City and the City* (2009) exemplifies the former, with its two interlaced city-states whose inhabitants "unsee" anything belonging to the other city. An example of the latter is Max Gladstone's Craft Sequence (2012–present), in which both demons and student loans can kill you, and living skeletons enjoy drinks by the pool. The three points above are not features that set up a boundary around the urban fantasy genre, but they help in deciding what texts can be considered typical. They emerged from my readings of criticism and descriptions of urban fantasy, as well as from my own analyses of a significant number of texts, but at the end of the day, they capture my own idealized cognitive model. They also require some elaboration on a few key points.

Supernatural. The term *supernatural* is here understood broadly as comprising fantastic elements that can be described as "impossible" according to the rules of the actual world. Urban fantasy has borrowed a number of supernatural elements from, for instance, fantasy, folklore, and the Gothic. Common examples include magic powers and wielders thereof; creatures from folklore, fairy-stories, and ghost stories; and hidden places that are ontologically complicated, for instance present and not present at the same time. They are all forms of "the impossible," signaled by the text not to be read as part of the consensus reality of the writer or reader, indeed, not even possible as part of consensus reality.[22] Fantastic elements that do not yet exist but could conceivably be invented or discovered are not absent from the genre—particularly not in near-future settings or alternative histories—but they are much rarer than the supernatural. These supernatural elements combine, mix, or otherwise interact with some of the many expressions of modern society, the most common of which is the city itself.

Modernity. Urban fantasy is not the only fantastic genre to deal with modernity in various ways. Science fiction could be considered a genre of unfolding modernity, in which the development of modern society and its resilience (or lack thereof) to external shocks provide key themes. Fantasy, on the other hand, has largely displayed skepticism regarding modernity and relied on worlds that are in some sense premodern. In urban fantasy, modernity is brought to the fore by its relation to the supernatural and is occasionally cast as either villain or hero but is mostly given more complex roles. In some urban fantasies, for example Kate Griffin's Matthew Swift series (2009–12), the supernatural arises out of the modern itself, but more often, the supernatural and modernity have to contend with each other. The close connection between urban fantasy and modernity has been observed by other critics as well, from various angles. Farah Mendlesohn and Edward James connect urban fantasy with the notion of modernity when they describe Diana Wynne Jones as an urban fantasy writer because of her mostly "post-eighteenth-century-style" and occasionally industrialized settings.[23] Siobhan Carroll reads modernity as a threat to place in urban fantasy,[24] and Viviane Bergue and Arno Meteling both point out the combination of modern and fantastic as typical for urban fantasy.[25] Urban fantasy is a genre of questioning, contemplating, and debating modernity, not just condemning or commending it.

Cities, one of the foremost expressions of modernity, are not a necessary requirement for urban fantasy, despite the word *urban* in the label. It is common to insist that urban fantasy is by necessity set in a city, but I would argue that given how the genre has developed over the past few decades, this is not true; it is too easy to find counter-examples. Some series include novels that are set away from cities, such as Ben Aaronovitch's *Foxglove Summer* (2014; Rivers of London #5), in which the protagonist leaves London for rural Herefordshire, and Kevin Hearne's *Tricked* (2012; Iron Druid Chronicles #4), in which the main characters leave the Phoenix Metropolitan Area to hide in the Arizona desert. Other urban fantasies are primarily set in and around small towns, or on the road, like Gaiman's *American Gods* (2001), Charlaine Harris's Sookie Stackhouse novels (2001–13), and the Engelsfors Trilogy (2011–13) by Sara Bergmark Elfgren and Mats Strandberg. Helen Young also observes that modern suburbia can provide urban fantasy settings.[26] This insistence on city settings derives partly from a misunderstanding of the label *urban fantasy*. The *urban* has been taken by some to indicate a strict requirement rather than an early descriptor, a descriptor that might have been appropriate when the genre formed but that has come to be less appropriate over time. Partly, however, the insistence on city settings comes from the fact that the city *is* a very frequent setting. The genre has increasingly come to set the modern in juxtaposition with the supernatural, and since one of the foremost, and certainly most easily identifiable, expressions of modernity is the modern metropolis, it becomes a simple feature to identify.[27] The urban setting is used as a convenient shortcut to categorize a text, even when the city itself has less to do with the story than do other expressions of modernity. Examples include Aaronovitch's Rivers of London series (2011–present), in which reliance on expert systems and a reflexive approach to knowledge in the face of the supernatural is more prominent than the urban environment; Hearne's Iron Druid Chronicles (2011–19), in which modernity is primarily considered in terms of its convenience and entertainment value; and Gladstone's Craft Sequence, in which the conflict between modernity and tradition is expressed through the problems caused by global capitalism.[28]

In brief, the *urban* in *urban fantasy* is like the *science* in *science fiction*, not a required feature for a given story. It is an acknowledgement of how frequent stories about cities and science are in the respective genres and a reminder that the stories are set in a modern world defined by urbanity (for urban fantasy) or a universe of science (for science fiction).

The unseen. Urban fantasy's concern with the unseen can take a wide variety of forms. The societies of urban fantasy are often divided into a social mainstream, which generally provides a substitute for the reader's perspective, and one or more other social groups—for instance the less fortunate, the criminal, or the excessively powerful and wealthy. The term *unseen* covers the full range of reasons for which people, objects, and places are out of the sight (and mind) of mainstream society. The most obvious explanation is that there is a supernatural reason for why mainstream people do not see something, such as the magical invisibility of the Shadowhunters in Cassandra Clare's Mortal Instruments series (2007–14) and any number of mythical and fairy creatures in different stories. Invisibility is often explained through an unconscious (and often metaphorical) effort by people in the mainstream society to ignore something, for instance, anything that contradicts their consensus reality in Charles de Lint's Newford stories (1987–present) or characters associated with social outcasts and marginalized groups, such as the denizens of London Below in Gaiman's *Neverwhere*. Protagonists are generally special in that they have or gain the ability to see through invisibility. Other unseen creatures intentionally stay out of sight of the mainstream. These creatures include supernatural folk that hide from humanity, including vampires, werewolves, and fairy creatures but also more mundane people, such as criminals. Occasionally the groups overlap, setting up vampires as lords of organized crime, for example. Finally, there are the things that are unseen because they are hidden, obscured, or living in darkness. Labyrinths and dark underground tunnels as well as roofscapes and other places that are unvisited and ignored abound in the genre.

The various forms of the unseen found in urban fantasy have been brought in from other genres.[29] The monsters that lurk in the darkness and the dark places that hide them come from the Gothic. Invisible fairies and equally invisible magicians are fantasy fare, previously introduced from folklore and fairy stories. From crime fiction come criminal organizations and shady operators. In urban fantasy, the many unseen beings and spaces have adapted and developed to fit their new generic home, turning into a core concern for the genre and a key component in its social commentary.[30]

Hybridity. The are several genres that meet and mix in urban fantasy. One thing that distinguishes urban fantasy is its genre hybridity, the fact that it not only allows the introduction of traits from other genres but is built around such inserted traits.[31] The most obvious genre to make a substantial contribution is fantasy, and it is not uncommon to find claims that urban fantasy is "only" a form of fantasy in early[32] as well as recent[33] scholarship (the similarity in names is partly, but not wholly, to blame for this). Fantasy features that appear in urban fantasy include magic and magical creatures, a quest-like narrative, and possibly a fictive world distinct from our own. Another oft-cited contributor to urban fantasy is, as mentioned, the Gothic, and a third genre that contributes to much to the genre is crime fiction. The basic detective plot, figuring out the solution to a mystery, is understandably useful in stories where something magical suddenly shows up to surprise the central characters, but urban fantasy often goes further than that. The prevalence of the crime fiction plot and the investigator figure in urban fantasies has been pointed out before,[34] and private investigators, police officers, and other crime-solving characters are exceedingly common. A sample of private investigators includes Kim Harrison's Rachel Morgan, Tanya Huff's Vicky Nelson, Mike Resnick's John Justin Mallory, and Simon R. Green's John Taylor. Aaronovitch's Rivers of London series could be read as police procedural just as well as an urban fantasy story.[35] Science fiction has contributed settings to urban fantasies, where the supernatural in some form has come to dominate the modern world: in Liz Williams's franchise city Singapore Three, from her Detective Inspector Chen series (2005–15), people in the afterlives can be emailed or telephoned, and Hell's demons employ high-tech devices in their plotting; in Harrison's alternative history, a genetically modified virus nearly wiped out humans in the 1960s and paved the way for magical species to run society; and both Ilona Andrews (in the Kate Daniels series, 2007–present) and Suyi Davies Okungbowa (in *David Mogo, Godhunter*, 2019) set their stories in future worlds to which the supernatural returned and brought enormous change. Building fictive worlds by exploring how the introduction of one (or a few) supernatural elements would transform society is urban fantasy's version of the kind of extrapolation of social changes found in much science fiction from the introduction of a *novum*—a scientific discovery, technological invention, or alien encounter, for example. Harris provides a good example in her exploration of the various effects that the invention of artificial blood and revelation of vampire existence have on the people in and around the small town of Bon Temps. The vampires perform the function of a *novum*, and Harris sets her stories in a world where society has had to adapt and people relate to the new state of affairs.

Fantasy, the Gothic, crime fiction, and science fiction are not the only possible contributors to urban fantasy, although they are all common components in the genre hybrid. Depending on what one considers a genre, it would be possible to name other components as well, such as the fairy tale, the romance, the adventure story, the vampire story, and the story about the modern city. This is not an exhaustive list, and an attempt to create such a list would miss the point: that urban fantasy has developed into a form that not only accepts the introduction of traits from other types of stories but demands it.[36] Reading a text as urban fantasy thus requires awareness of what other genres have been combined to create that text. It also explains why novels that can all fruitfully be read as urban fantasies might still appear superficially quite dissimilar.

• • •

Genres are complex categories, both personal and cultural, and that complexity is reflected in the cognitive models that underlie them. The cognitive model that I suggest as a basis for urban fantasy is, despite my best efforts, biased and subjective. As has been mentioned, genres are social constructs, created by actors such as writers, publishers, readers, and even critics, but they are also personal constructions. We group texts together if we feel that they resemble each other in a (for us) meaningful way. The cognitive model that we construct and revise combines properties from our own urban fantasy experiences with properties from what others call urban fantasy. It is partly our own and partly something we share with others. The cognitive model for urban fantasy described above has influenced my analysis, and although it is an attempt to describe the genre in a broad sense, it is also a model that looks beneath the surface, beyond particular settings and characters. Others might employ a cognitive model that looks to such formal descriptions (what types of characters are involved, what plots are enacted, where do they take place). They will disagree with some of my findings in the following chapters, but probably not all. More than one cognitive model can determine a category, and context lets us decide which model is most useful in a given situation—most of us know, for instance, when it is appropriate to refer to bananas and strawberries as berries and when it is not. This goes for genres, too: the many models that determine what fantasy is provide a good example of this. A genre's cognitive model could vary between groups—publishers could use a different model than readers, scholars could use a different model than fans. It could also differ depending on when you began to form ideas about the genre (in the 1980s, 1990s, or 2010s?) and from which other genre you came to urban fantasy. Someone whose cognitive model of urban fantasy is based on de Lint's Newford stories, which largely concern fairies and mythic beings, would have different ideas about the genre than someone who constructed their cognitive model based on Hamilton's Anita Blake, Vampire Hunter and other vampire-dense urban fantasy.

The three-point cognitive model for urban fantasy has led me to read some unexpected examples in terms of the genre and compare them to other, possibly more typical, examples. It is not only the genre hybridity that determines a text's typicality. Each of the three main points of my idealized cognitive model allow for a wide range of expressions in the genre's many stories, and to what extent each point is in focus can differ between stories. The model's three points interact and interfere with each other, and although I suggest that a text that conforms to all three of them would come across as more representative of urban fantasy, less emphasis on one point than another would still not disqualify the text from the genre. The cognitive model also explains why a role-playing game world such as Eberron (an official Dungeons & Dragons campaign setting since 2004) can feel like urban fantasy even if it is not marketed as such. The basic assumption in Eberron is that magic has developed in a similar way to technology in our world and is now ubiquitous and commonplace. Eberron thus treats the supernatural (magic) in a modern and mundane, rather than an arcane, fashion. The world is also explicitly set up to mix the genres of fantasy, noir, and adventure stories in a post- (or inter-) bellum world reminiscent of the 1920s.[37] When considered as fantasy, certain features stand out more clearly than others; when examined with an urban fantasy lens, other patterns emerge, suggesting different adventures for the players to engage in. Eberron might be ranked as less typical than the otherworldly urban fantasies of Miéville's *Perdido Street Station* (2000), K. J. Bishop's *The Etched City* (2003), or, for that matter, Michael Swanwick's *The Iron Dragon's Daughter* (1993), but it still fits within a category structured by the cognitive model I have proposed. It is quite possible to analyze these four worlds in relation to each other and learn something about the genre.

URBAN FANTASY WORLDS

Urban fantasy is not limited to a particular setting or a particular world. When I first set out to examine urban fantasy, I kept coming across the opinion that setting defined the genre. I have explained why I do not consider a city to be a necessary setting for the genre; in this section, I argue that neither is urban fantasy limited to a particular kind of world. For this, I need to introduce some terminology related to fictional worlds, however, terminology that is used throughout the rest of the book.

Some World Terminology

The most basic distinction in discussing a fantastic world is whether it is a *primary* or *secondary* world, that is, how it relates to *the actual world*. The first two terms come from J. R. R. Tolkien's "On Fairy-Stories" (1947), in which he refers to the fictional world as a "Secondary World." The reader's mind enters this world and, inside it, what the writer relates is "true." The "Primary World," according to Tolkien, is the world of the reader.[38] This distinction remains important to fantasy theory, but the terms have been qualified over time. Where Tolkien used *secondary world* to refer to all fictional worlds, the term has come to mean more specifically a fantasy world that is different from our own.[39] Because the conflation between a literary construction and the world of the reader and writer is potentially confusing, I use *primary world* for a fictional world that, at least on a macro scale, looks like and works like ours.[40] For the world inhabited by the reader and writer, I use a term that I have borrowed from possible-world semantics: the *actual world*.[41]

Primary and secondary worlds should be considered as the opposite ends of a spectrum rather than as distinct and separate categories. The terms are useful as shorthand descriptions of whether a fictional world looks like the actual world or is something obviously different, but there is no clear line separating them. As with the mimetic and fantastic modes, the extremes (completely secondary and completely primary worlds) would not be useful as story settings. If the world imitated the actual world down to the smallest detail, the story would end up being a documentary. If there was nothing about the world that resembled the actual world, we would not understand the story. Mark J. P. Wolf suggests that fictional worlds should be considered in terms of degrees of "secondariness," "the extent to which a place is detached from the Primary World and different from it, and the degree to which its fictional aspects have been developed and built"[42]—he does not differentiate between the actual and primary worlds. There is a spectrum of fictional worlds, which differ from our world to varying degrees and in different ways. On this spectrum, trying to draw a line between primary and secondary worlds is hard and often irrelevant.

A world—not least in urban fantasy—can also be divided internally into different *domains*, that is, parts in which reality behaves differently or follows different rules. Fictive worlds can be what Lubomír Doležel refers to as "dyadic worlds," that is, split into two domains with "contrary modal conditions."[43] Depending on modality, these domains can have, for example, contradictory value systems, knowledge, or social or natural laws. Nancy H. Traill discusses fantastic worlds as being dyadic, with a *natural* and a *supernatural* domain. She defines the former as having "the same natural laws as does the actual world,"[44] however, which makes the definition too narrow for most urban fantasy purposes. I therefore use the *mundane domain* to signify the broader concept of a domain in which the supernatural might exist, as in, magic might work and supernatural beings may move around unrecognized, but the general population assumes that the same natural laws apply as in the actual world. In the other domain, the supernatural exists and is generally *known* to exist. There is not necessarily a sharp distinction between the two domains, and they might even just be social constructions, or, conversely, they may split the world into two distinct, geographical parts.

Types of Urban Fantasy Worlds

When describing urban fantasy, it is common to insist that stories predominantly or even necessarily are set in the primary world, a claim with which I disagree. Mendlesohn and James equate urban fantasy with "low fantasy," a term that Kenneth J. Zahorski and Robert H. Boyer introduced for fantasy set in the primary world.[45] In *The Encyclopedia of Fantasy* (1997), John Clute claims that an urban fantasy story is "significantly *about* a real city," although he allows for the possibility that the city could be set in a secondary world as well.[46] A fantastic city is appropriate for the genre only if it "alludes to a real one," according to Elber-Aviram,[47] and Leigh M. McLennon claims that the urban fantasy worlds "closely mimic our contemporary reality."[48] This assertion, that only stories set in primary-world cities or in secondary-world cities that allude to actual-world counterparts qualify as urban fantasy, excludes a great number of stories that in other senses can be read as typical urban fantasies. It also requires one to determine the degree of secondariness that makes a setting "too secondary" for urban fantasy or to identify allusions to actual cities without fail. Since urban fantasy writers appear to enjoy writing worlds that are just enough secondary to clearly not mimic the actual world, and their allusions are not necessarily obvious, I disagree with the insistence that urban fantasy is tied to the primary world. Instead, I suggest that urban fantasy can be set in worlds of all degrees of secondariness.

To demonstrate the variety of worlds in the genre, I briefly present a number of examples of what urban fantasy worlds can look like. In order to facilitate presentation, I have divided them into five clusters, loosely ordered from least secondary to most. There is a measure of subjectivity in my selection, and I encourage the reader to rearrange or substitute examples if they feel that they have better alternatives. My point is only to show why I see urban fantasy as a genre that is not tied to a particular kind of world.

Cluster 1 (least secondary): fictional versions of the actual world, with only a few or very restricted supernatural elements. These worlds are often contemporary, and the settings are mostly locations that exist in the actual world.

- Miéville's *The City and the City* introduces two fictional, superimposed city-states, in which people actively "unsee" that which belongs to the other state. Its fantastic elements are supernatural only in the sense that they are impossible in a psychosocial sense.

- The TV series *Lucifer* (created by Tom Kapinos; 2016–21) focuses on supernatural characters from the Christian belief system: apart from the Lord of Hell, various demons, angels, and, as the series progressed, other celestial and infernal characters. The supernatural focus remains on Lucifer Morningstar, in Los Angeles, with the suggestions that although some supernatural individuals, like Lilith and Cain, have moved around in the world, it is mainly a mundane world inhabited by normal people.
- De Lint's Newford story "The Wishing Well" (1993) leaves the reader wondering whether the protagonist's experiences have a natural (psychological) or supernatural explanation. Rather than presenting itself as a world of ghosts and magic, it builds on what Tzvetan Todorov calls "the fantastic" (orig. "le fantastique"), characterized by a hesitation between a natural and a supernatural explanation.[49] While many Newford stories, and thus Newford interpreted as a complete storyworld, portray clearly supernatural events, occasional stories are less obviously supernatural.

Cluster 2: worlds that are more secondary in that they are dyadic. These worlds are more common in the urban fantasy genre and are divided into a mundane and a supernatural domain, although the domains differ in how they are constructed. They range from being entirely social constructions to being (almost) magical divisions into (nearly) separate worlds. The supernatural domain can be a secret that most people do not know about, but magic and magical beings mix freely with the society at large, keeping some hidden areas more or less to themselves. Examples include:

- Aaronovitch's Rivers of London series, in which magic is not really kept very secret; people just prefer to not talk about it for the risk of appearing weird or feeling uncomfortable; and

- the *Grimm* television series (created by Stephen Carpenter, Jim Kouf, and David Greenwalt; 2011–17), in which mythological creatures, so-called *Wesen*, hide in plain sight in human society. *Grimm* edges up on the worlds in which the supernatural domain exists "invisible or undetected [. . .] in the interstices of the dominant world," a "wainscot society,"[50] but in these, there is a greater degree of separation between the two domains.
- In Martin Millar's *The Good Fairies of New York* (1992), there is a multiethnic fairy-community in New York, invisible to the human occupants. The fairies and humans exist in the same physical spaces and can interact in some ways, but their domains are clearly separated.
- Huff bases her supernatural domain on hiding rather than invisibility in her Blood Books (1991–97; 2006): creatures such as vampires and werewolves conceal their supernatural nature from people in the mundane domain. The difference between the Blood Books and *Grimm* is that the *Wesen* constitute a significant community that also makes up a part of human society, whereas Huff's supernatural beings keep more to themselves, alone or in small groups.
- A final type of these dyadic worlds are those where the domains almost constitute separate worlds. It is difficult to interact across the domain borders, and events in one domain rarely affect the other. A typical example is the dyadic London of Gaiman's *Neverwhere*, where people in London Below can barely interact with those Above, and the domains are mostly separated physically. Movement between the domains is depicted as nontrivial, much like moving through a magic portal into a different world, although, as Mendlesohn points out, "we [the readers] are never fully in the other world."[51]

Cluster 3: worlds that, although they are similar to the actual world, have been transformed on a macro level. These include alternative histories, where the world's past has been radically changed (usually to allow for a supernatural presence), but it might also involve changes to the world's present or portray a version of its future. Whatever change has been made, it is clear that this is not our world. This cluster includes what Wolf calls "overlaid worlds," in which "fictional elements are overlaid onto a real location" in a way that would be conspicuous to the world's inhabitants.[52]

- The smallest degree of secondariness in this cluster can be exemplified by Tom Pollock's *Our Lady of the Streets* (2014; final part of the Skyscraper Throne trilogy), in which London is entirely reshaped in terms of topography and living conditions. The government and most of the inhabitants are forced to flee, and attempts to take back the city by military force fail.
- More global changes are introduced in Harris's Sookie Stackhouse series, where the invention of artificial blood allows vampires to live alongside humans, and other supernatural creatures are introduced as the series progresses. Hamilton's Anita Blake, Vampire Hunter series similarly presents a seemingly contemporary world in which supernatural creatures live alongside humans in society. In the Hollows series (2004–present), Harrison alters the world's history by advancing biotechnology faster during the twentieth century. This advancement caused a plague that nearly wiped out humanity, and supernatural creatures (immune to the virus) came out of hiding to save society.
- Even more profound transformations are possible. In the Kate Daniels series (2007–present), Andrews builds a version of the primary world in which magic comes and goes in waves, destroying much of what relies on technology and allowing supernatural beings to become both a major problem and a significant power factor. Aliette de Bodard sets her Dominion of the Fallen series (2015–19) in a turn-of-the-century Paris struggling after a destructive arcane war, with fallen angels ruling the great Houses of the city, and Liz Williams's Detective

Inspector Chen series (2005–15) is set in a future in which the celestial and demonic realms regularly interact with the domain of living mortals, although not always in legal ways.

Cluster 4: settings that consist of two, or occasionally several, distinct worlds, with protagonists who travel from one (usually the less secondary) to the other. In this cluster, there remains a connection between the worlds. Such otherworlds can be reflections of the more primary world:

- Most obvious are the fantastic, distorted versions of actual cities, such as London in Miéville's *Un Lun Dun* (2007) and Pollock's *The Glass Republic* (2013), New York in Resnick's Fables of Tonight (1987–2012), and Malmö in Helen Ekeroth's Silver Ring duology (2022).
- Other worlds are types of heavens or hells; Williams's Detective Inspector Chen travels to both Heaven and Hell in the line of duty, and Richard Kadrey's Sandman Slim series (2009–21) opens with the protagonist's escape from Hell, after having been trapped for eleven years.
- Fairy or spirit realms provide otherworlds of a variety of forms. De Lint offers spirit realms that are closely connected to and affected by the mundane world in, for example, *Moonheart* (1984) and *The Onion Girl* (2001; a Newford novel). Fairy lands inspired by Celtic folklore can be found in Butcher's Dresden Files and Seanan McGuire's October Daye novels (2009–present), and Hearne offers a "multiverse" of otherworlds from different belief systems in the Iron Druid Chronicles. Tad Williams's industrialized Faerie is distinctly separated from the human world in *The War of the Flowers*.
- Finally, the protagonists can travel to worlds that are unlike anything in the primary word, for instance, the surreal world in Catherynne M. Valente's *Palimpsest* (2009), which can only

be reached through sexual intercourse with someone who has already visited it.

Cluster 5 (most secondary): worlds with no, or a very slight, connection to the primary world. These are worlds in which modernity and urbanity are expressed in widely different ways. The greater a world's degree of secondariness, the greater can its conception of modern society deviate from the actual world. In these worlds, modernity is portrayed through various features that are meant to make them recognizable as modern, but often they come across as pseudomodern instead. At the same time, the modern features used to create an impression of modernity are generally revealing of a particular stance to our modern world and its problems and benefits.

- In Terry Pratchett's Ankh-Morpork, in the Discworld series (novels and adaptations: 1983–2015), modern ideas and inventions are reinterpreted in traditional high-fantasy terms and applied to a pseudomedieval fantasy setting.
- In Miéville's *Perdido Street Station*, the modernity of nineteenth-century industrialism is intertwined with later forms and transplanted to a world of rulebound thaumaturgy, fantastic creatures, and workers struggling against brutal capitalism.
- In Gladstone's Craft Sequence, modernity has mostly defeated the traditional, religious society in a war in which human wielders of magic fought deities and their priests. The result is a world in which the power behind magic functions as the main currency and resource, and globalization disrupts local communities.[53]

As can be seen from the spectrum described above, there is no distinctive break between various types of worlds, nor should we expect there to be one. Authors build their worlds to fit the stories they want to tell, and stories can twist and turn as they are being told, requiring new additions to their worlds. Pollock's Skyscraper Throne trilogy provides an interesting example, where the story of the first novel (*The City's Son*, 2012) is set in the supernatural domain hidden in the wainscots of London. In the second novel (*The Glass Republic*), the setting is mainly that of a secondary world found on the other side of mirrors, and in the third (*Our Lady of the Streets*), London of the primary world is significantly reshaped by the supernatural powers that rule it. Each book in the series thus fits into a different cluster of the world spectrum.

Long series consisting of several books also tend to change over the course of the series, transforming the fictional world as the extended story progresses. Particularly novels that begin with a protagonist's first encounter with the supernatural tend to introduce more supernatural elements in each instalment. In her discussion of intrusion fantasy (many urban fantasies can fruitfully be read as such), Mendlesohn observes how "the [fantastic] intrusion wins [. . .] by fundamentally remaking the world into one that can be sited within the immersive fantasy."[54] In other words, fantastic elements that are introduced as something previously unknown to the protagonist (and the reader) are, by the end of the story, accepted as part of the world. For each story, new fantastic elements are added, increasing the degree of secondariness of the world step by step, siting it "within the immersive fantasy" rather than the intrusive. In Rivers of London, Aaronovitch even doubles this transformation: it is a process of the protagonist (and the reader) finding out more about the world as well as a story of a world which itself is changing as magic returns. In this way, the storyworld undergoes a significant change over the course of the series, almost as enormous as that in Pollock's world.

This chapter has presented my basic understanding of urban fantasy literature and what the corpus of texts on which I base my analyses in the remaining chapters is like. The interlude that comes next is a brief overview of modernity and how the concept is understood in this book, followed by a chapter that presents an overview of the historical development of urban fantasy and of urban fantasy scholarship.

INTERLUDE ONE

AN INTRODUCTION TO MODERNITY

Modern life can be many things: fun, exciting, stressful, predictable, comfortable, safe, boring . . . but it is rarely magical. A central characteristic of urban fantasy is that the genre combines fantastic ingredients with modern life. The mundane urban existence that we, as readers, are familiar with is combined with mythical objects, faerie creatures, and magic. This combination of the fantastic and modernity is an underlying reason for urban fantasy's social commentary. The concept of modernity—and related expressions, such as *modern society*, *modern civilization*, and *modern life*—is used throughout this book. It is therefore briefly introduced in this interlude, including some structural and historical perspectives. A short note on urbanity and modernity is also added at the end. This is an introduction to modernity in general and how the concept is understood in this book, not to modernity in urban fantasy in particular. The many ways in which urban fantasy valorizes, comments on, and criticizes modernity are dealt with in the main chapters, and particular aspects and details on modernity are presented more fully in their respective contexts.

What modernity is cannot be described quickly or precisely. Numerous scholars have applied, developed, and theorized the concept for more than two centuries, and there is no lack of definitions and descriptions of what it means. I share Marshall Berman's view of modernity as not only a historical period but as a particular mode of experiencing our life and environment.[1] This mode is largely the product of processes that arose in Europe and then influenced and were influenced by the colonialization of large parts of the world, and the twentieth century saw features of modernity spreading widely also to societies outside the Western cultural sphere.[2] It is also important to recognize that *modernity*, as a stage in the history of Western civilization, is not to be confused with *modernism*, an aesthetic concept arising largely in opposition to what the former stood for.[3]

Modernity developed through processes in Western cultures and societies over time. Although there is no exact date or event that marks its appearance, modernity is still seen as what Anthony Giddens describes as "an extended period of change [which is] discontinuous with previous forms of society."[4] The notion of discontinuity, between modern and premodern (or traditional) societies, is central to the idea of modernity—at some point in time, there was a distinct break. The time of that break with premodern society has come to be identified with the period around 1500,[5] although others suggest later dates.[6] Modernity then developed through a number of stages, the exact dates of which depend on the scholar who describes them. Berman divides modernity into three phases.[7] His first phase (*early modern times*) begins in the early sixteenth century and lasts until the late eighteenth, a period which contains the Enlightenment. His second phase is the nineteenth century, which begins with "the great revolutionary wave of the 1790s"[8] and lasts until 1900, largely coinciding with the industrialization of the Western world (*classical modernity*). During Berman's third phase, the twentieth century, he claims that modernity spreads to the entire world (*late modernity*). (A fourth phase of modernity provides a central theme in Max Gladstone's Craft Sequence and is addressed in chapter 8.)

The overarching characteristics of modernity can be described in terms of four types of modernizing processes. Political processes include the rise of secular power, the notion of sovereignty, and the idea of the modern nation-state. Economic processes include the maturation of monetized trade and exchange of goods, the emergence of large-scale production and consumption, and an increasing focus on private ownership of property. A decline of a traditional social order, formation of new social classes, and changes in the division of labor between the sexes are examples of social processes. Finally, cultural processes include a turn toward a secular, materialist culture informed by individualist, rationalist, and instrumentalist values.[9]

The modernizing processes have been abstracted into various defining features of modernity. One such feature, which often clashes with the fantastic elements in urban fantasy, is what Max Weber calls the "specific and peculiar rationalism of Western culture"[10] and which Kenneth H. Tucker, Jr., goes so far as to refer to as "the master process of modernity."[11] This "master process," Tucker argues, resulted in religion being separated from a number of social spheres, and the subsequent development of these spheres according to their own inner logics and standards of evaluation.[12] To Weber, "rationalism" has two connected yet distinct meanings that have also come to inform later conceptions of modernity. It refers to an understanding of the world in increasingly formal, mathematical, abstract ways; and it describes the rise of principled reasoning in various areas of social life, such as systems of law and morality.[13] Rationalism has shaped the development of modern civilization, turning it toward secularism and science as well as capitalism and a bureaucratic administration. In urban fantasy, modern rationalism is frequently called into question in encounters with the supernatural, for instance, by proving insufficient to deal with the existence of magic, to provide mental tools well suited to dealing with supernatural entities, or to require amendments in order to fit a supernatural world.

Another central feature of modernity is a drive for order and for ordering the world. This is one of the perspectives that Zygmunt Bauman employs in his analysis of modern civilization. Modernity, Bauman explains, set itself "the task of order,"[14] and the underlying drive in much of modernity is a striving for order and a reduction of chaos. Bauman also contends that the very dichotomy of order and chaos is a modern conception, that "the divinely ordained world" of pre-modernity simply was the way it was supposed to be.[15] Bauman's view of order as the distinction between the modern and premodern worlds is similar to Stephen L. Collins's perception of a shift from a "Tudor" (premodern) to a "Hobbesian" (modern) idea of order. The Christian, Tudor worldview saw a natural (and divine) order, which was thus threatened rather than improved by change, whereas the Hobbesian order is created by humans, a restraining of natural flux that takes the world from disorder to order.[16] The attitude to order constitutes a fundamental part of the worldview in many urban fantasy stories, either portraying the supernatural as threatening chaos or representing modernity as ignoring a higher order either natural or divine.

A feature of modernity that is related to the idea of ordering and rationalism is the related concepts of professionalism and expertise, and it has a particular position in discussions of magic-wielding characters in urban fantasy. Premodern social life was dominated by uncontrollable natural processes and ruled by traditions that determined present actions on the basis of the past. Modernity brought with it an increasing understanding and command of the natural world and erosion of traditions. Part of the shift away from the dominant position of tradition is the advancement of professionalization and the rise of expertise.[17] There is, Giddens argues,

> a difference between expertise and the traditional claims to knowledge of religious officials, witch doctors, spiritual leaders or

whatever, because expertise depends upon knowledge which, in principle, anyone could acquire, and without having to perform specialized, arcane rituals to do so.[18]

Whether or not magic is governed by logic and rationality is one way to think about whether it is part of a traditional or modern system of thought. Another is through Giddens's separation of who has access to knowledge. The ways to access magical knowledge runs the gamut from mysterious, possibly innate, gifts to the result of diligent studies. In Lauren Beukes's *Zoo City* (2010), people inexplicably acquire minor magical talents as a result of causing another person's death, and these talents resist all attempts at scientific, rational explanation. Druids in Kevin Hearne's Iron Druid Chronicle (2011–19) and wizards in Ben Aaronovitch's Rivers of London series (2011–present) learn by study and practice, and their magic can be understood in rational terms. Between these extremes, of the premodern and modern magic-users, lie all the modern and traditional ways to magic, "in principle" possible for anyone to acquire or accessible only through "specialized, arcane rituals"—or as a supernatural but inexplicable gift. Magic is a key element in the vast majority of urban fantasy stories, and whether it is part of a modern system of expertise or a traditional claim to knowledge is one way of approaching the portrayal of modernity.

Modernity can also be understood through a wider set of features. Giddens characterizes modernity through four "basic autonomous institutional dimensions."[19] These institutional dimensions are *capitalism*, or the accumulation of capital in the context of competitive markets; *industrialism*, taken broadly to mean the use—in production as well as other areas of social life—of machinery driven by inanimate power-sources; *surveillance*, by which he means direct or indirect supervision and control of information (including bureaucratic administration); and *military power*, the state-monopoly on violence in the context of industrialization of war.[20] According to Giddens, these institutional dimensions combine or interact to give rise to Western modernity, driven by social and technological developments that de-emphasize local and personal contexts and allow for reflexive considerations of social practices and knowledge. (Modernity's sources of dynamism are addressed further in chapters 6 and 8.) These developments make it possible for modernity to depart from the traditional orders rapidly and radically,[21] resulting in the modern experience being one of a society in which everything is sped up and displaced, transformed and reshaped, even if that experience of acceleration is unevenly distributed over time spans and social groups.[22] Different institutional dimensions are challenged or foregrounded by the supernatural in different urban fantasy stories, thus drawing attention to various aspects of modern society.

It should be pointed out that modernity as it is described above mainly captures modernization in western Europe, but that it never developed in separation from other parts of the world. The modernizing processes in the West did not develop in a vacuum. Several European countries set themselves up as colonial powers, and modern life in Europe both affected and was affected by what happened in the colonies. The exact relationship between colonialism and modernity is still a matter of debate among sociologists, however. Some go so far as to claim that "[c]oloniality [is] the underlying logic of the foundation and unfolding of Western civilization [. . .] of which historical colonialism have been a constitutive [. . .] dimension"[23] while others argue that colonialism is only a highly significant element of modernity.[24] Regardless of which position one adopts, colonialism has played a significant part in the modernization of many Western countries. In his overview of empires, Richard Lachman emphasizes the need to take into account how "dominant societies benefit from and are shaped by their efforts" to control and extract wealth from other parts of the world, as well as the need to pay attention to how former colonies "continue to be shaped and limited by the ways in which they were exploited in the past."[25] Many urban fantasy writers grapple with or outright challenge the effects of a past or present colonialism, through narrative friction,[26] conflicts, or alternative histories. Examples include the looming war between the native animal people and the European fairies in Charles de Lint's *Widdershins* (2006), the relation between a war-torn France and its South-east Asian colonies in Aliette de Bodard's Dominion of the Fallen series (2015–19), an early twentieth-century Egypt that rises to power when magic returns to the world in P. Djèlí Clark's *A Master of Djinn* (2021), and the struggle for control over physical reality between colonizers and colonized in Gladstone's *Ruin of Angels* (2017).

Colonialism is not the only way by which modernity has spread to the world beyond Western Europe. Giddens calls modernity "inherently globalising"[27] and Ulrich Beck makes a point of distinguishing between the notion of an international capitalism and (borderless) global markets, on the one hand, and, on the other, a more multidimensional process that comprises the spreading of cultures, the development of international organizations, and the growth of transnational forms of life.[28] Because of my own limitations in what I have been able to access (for practical as well as linguistic reasons), the vast majority of my urban fantasy examples are written in, and portray societies of, the West, however. Moreover, an extensive colonial and postcolonial analysis of the urban fantasy genre deserves a book-length study of its own. I have therefore decided to address colonialism and the global dimensions of modernity first and foremost in chapter 8, in relation to Gladstone's Craft Sequence, as they are central themes in this series.

Urbanity and modern civilization have developed in tandem to the point where it is hard to imagine one without the other, and in chapter 1, I explain that I consider urban fantasy to be a fantastic genre of the modern rather than (just) of the urban. The proliferation of urban forms of life is one of many processes of modernization,[29] and the modern metropolis offers a site from which modernity can be investigated.[30] "The metropolis," Helen Young observes, "is understood as both symbol and manifestation of the problems of modernity,"[31] and urban fantasy addresses these problems—for instance, "loneliness, isolation, fragmentation, alienation"[32]—on both the symbolic and the concrete level. It is, I would argue, a genre that deals with a modern civilization that expresses itself through its relation with the urban. Even if a story is set in a small town, it is a small town that is specifically not a city. Siobhan Carroll observes how J. R. R. Tolkien's concern with modernity and "the threat posed by late capitalism to place"[33] is inherited by urban fantasists such as de Lint and Megan Lindholm. She also notes how that threat is self-consciously articulated in Neil Gaiman's *American Gods* (2001), an urban fantasy story set mainly in small-town United States. The threat to place at the heart of Carroll's analysis is only one of many concerns that urban fantasy articulates; by relating the supernatural with the modern and urban, the genre draws attention to a wide variety of issues within our society.

The portrayal of modernity in urban fantasy is one in which strengths and weaknesses are brought into relief through meetings between the modern world and the supernatural fantastic. But modern society is also depicted through the contrasts between actual modern life and fantastical modernity, which emphasizes problems and offers alternatives. Together, those visions of modernity provide a frame for the genre's widespread comments on our society, a frame examined in more detail in the rest of the book.

CHAPTER TWO

A SHORT HISTORY OF URBAN FANTASY

While the rest of this book takes a largely synchronous look at the urban fantasy genre, the present chapter focuses on the way the genre has developed. I argue that urban fantasy can be understood as a form of literature that has been transformed by distinctive sets of additions over time. The way in which someone describes and understands the genre depends on which sets they combine. Over the decades, urban fantasy writers have had a greater selection of such additions to pick from and have learned to combine them in more elaborate ways. Note, however, that although these additions have become part of urban fantasy, they have also existed and developed outside of the genre, as part of other genres.

Already in the first paragraph, I have run into a terminology problem. *Sets*, *additions*, *combining* . . . these words do not quite capture how I envisage this process. The process has rather been like *braiding*: over time, new strands have been added to the urban fantasy bundle, and authors can select those they prefer to braid together for the story they want to tell. Each strand goes back into history but was added to the bundle at some particular moment in time. Each strand comes with its own narrative features and possibilities. These features and possibilities include, for instance, motifs, tropes, plot and character types, settings, and story and world structures. My argument, in other words, is that urban fantasy is a bundle that has gained an increasing number of such strands over time and that authors have used different combinations of strands to braid together their stories.

After a brief discussion about when the genre can be said to have begun, I address the major strands of urban fantasy, including some thoughts about how urban fantasy has changed in the past ten or fifteen years and what that might mean for the future. These strands are (the decades are only approximate):

Proto-urban fantasy (from the 1840s):

- the Gothic romance
- tales about the modern[1] city
- supernatural stories.

Fantasy (as popularized by J. R. R. Tolkien) encounters modernity in the 1960s and 1970s:

- combinations of mythical and pseudomedieval fantasy with modern society
- the development of a modern, secondary fantasy world.

Cities develop as fantasy settings in the 1980s:

- the cities themselves emerge as sources of the fantastic
- fairies and other mythic beings migrate into cities.

The investigators, vampires, and women of the 1990s:

- the investigator plot
- vampires and other monsters become allies
- tough female protagonists.

Making things weird again in the 2000s:

- the New Weird—modern, urban, secondary-world settings.

• • •

The issue of how and when urban fantasy began has been debated by readers, writers, and critics, but claims have often simply been stated rather than argued. The lack of agreement partly depended on a lack of consensus regarding what urban fantasy is. Available criticism should be read in terms of when it was published but also what strands have been chosen by the critic to make up their particular urban fantasy braid. This chapter contains some observations on how the critical view of the genre has developed along with the genre itself.

Almost as complicated as the how and the when of the genre is the where. My perspective in this book is Anglocentric. That is perhaps even more noticeable in this chapter, and my only excuse is that I consider urban fantasy to have developed from and as part of an anglophone literary culture. It does not mean that no urban fantasy stories have been written in other languages but that I think that they have had comparatively small effect on the genre as it developed in English and that they have often evolved under the influence of English-language urban fantasy stories.

HOW DOES A GENRE START?

Pinpointing when a literary genre started is fraught with difficulties. Once we have come up with a definition of and term for a particular type of stories (say, urban fantasy), we could, for instance, go through the entire literary history and include all other stories of similar type. Depending on our definition, that could mean adding to the genre texts from centuries or even millennia ago. In popular culture, this method has been used to "claim" canonical or critically acclaimed texts for one's "team." This has the advantage that, because of the genre label, readers can discover earlier texts that they might enjoy but have previously overlooked. A disadvantage is that the genre can grow ever more vague. On the other hand, it is never easy to draw the sharp line that proclaims that "This is the first urban fantasy (or whatever) text. Anything before this is not urban fantasy." Scholars (and fans) will forever argue about which is the first science fiction novel—is it really Mary Shelly's *Frankenstein, or, The Modern Prometheus* (1818)?—or the first fantasy novel—could it be George MacDonald's *Phantastes: A Faerie Romance for Men and Women* (1858)?

An alternative way of thinking about a genre's beginning is to look at when the genre was first thought of as "a commercial category or a self-conscious tradition"[2] rather than as a collection of texts that just happen to have some features in common. This is not an easy moment to identify: not everyone involved comes to that realization at the same time or about the same texts. We can find written evidence of when the genre label was first used to refer to a particular type of fiction, though. Before *urban fantasy* became a compound word, it was used as a combination of adjective and noun: an *urban* fantasy as opposed to a *rustic* one, for instance. In fact, this is how *urban fantasy* is still used beyond the confines of literary discussions and popular culture. Fanciful architecture and cityscapes could be referred to as urban fantasy, for example, as demonstrated by *Venice, California: An Urban Fantasy* (1972) by Horst Schmidt-Brümmer (a book that tends to crop up in searches for early usages of *urban fantasy*). Before the late 1970s, this is how *urban fantasy* seemed to be used: as a way of modifying *fantasy* to express a connection to the city environment. In 1971, Uri Shulevitz's *One Monday Morning* (1967) is described as an urban fantasy.[3] Shulevitz's illustrated children's book tells the story of a boy who imagines that a royal entourage visits his inner-city apartment. The following year, John Rechy's (mimetic) novel *City of Night* (1963) is called an urban fantasy in *Contemporary Novelists* (1972), because New York, in which the novel is set, is "a metaphor city, a fairy city [. . .] where anything might happen."[4] In another text from 1972, surrealist painters like René Magritte, Paul Delvaux, and Paul Klee are referred to as "sources of urban fantasy."[5]

By the end of the 1970s, this had changed and there are indications that urban fantasy had begun to be recognized as something particular. According to some critics, urban fantasy emerged during the 1970s and 1980s, and I agree.[6] Trying to find really early examples of *urban fantasy* being used in a sense similar to current usage, I used the Google Books corpus. Searching for the phrase "urban fantasy" between 1940 and 1990 yielded three relevant instances from 1978. Two of these, from *New York Magazine* and *Ebony*, come from magazine articles about *The Wiz* (1978), Sidney Lumet's film version of the 1974 musical based on L. Frank Baum's novel *The Wonderful Wizard of Oz* (1900). The *New York Magazine* piece focuses on the urban design of setting and costumes, referring to the film as "Oz as urban fantasy."[7] The production designer, Tony Walton, is quoted as explaining that they wanted to "create a level of fantasy that could incorporate an urban texture of reality. [. . .] Fantasy with the city as focal point."[8] This is beginning to sound like what we understand as urban fantasy today, and although not evidence of anything, the fact that both magazines decide to describe the film using the same term is at least noteworthy.

Together with the third example from 1978, the pieces about *The Wiz* suggest to me that the starting point for urban fantasy was in the latter half of the 1970s. In the September 1978 issue of *The Magazine of Fantasy and Science Fiction*, there is a review column written by the science fiction author, editor, and critic Algirdas Jonas "Algis" Budrys. Budrys offers a brief summary of the "tried and true elements" of urban fantasy:

> the desuetudinous old rooming house and its counterculturish residents, the bit of old wilderness rising atop its mysterious hill in the midst of the city, and the strangely haunted, bookish protagonist who gradually realizes the horrible history of the place where he lives.[9]

Budrys's view of urban fantasy appears to be consistent with what I call *proto-urban fantasy*, supernatural stories that draw on the Gothic and are set in a city, but the "counterculturish residents" and "bookish protagonist" recall the artists, musicians, and scholars that have become common among the genre's cast members.[10] The old house and the old wilderness in the midst of a city suggest the resurfacing of suppressed history that Helen Young connects with the strain of urban fantasy she calls the "sub-urban."[11] The book Budrys reviewed was Fritz Leiber's *Our Lady of Darkness* (1977), and the fact that it fit so neatly with Budrys's urban fantasy description suggests that he may have adapted his description to Leiber's novel. It is clear that "urban fantasy" was a label that Budrys expected his readers to be familiar with, however. "[W]hen we speak so glibly now of 'urban fantasy', we pay passing homage to the man who invented it . . . in a 1941 story called 'Smoke Ghost' by Fritz Leiber,"[12] Budrys asserts, and "Smoke Ghost" certainly could be read as an urban fantasy even by today's understanding.

Personally, the earliest text that fits my cognitive model of urban fantasy is Leiber's *Conjure Wife* (1943), in which a university professor discovers that his wife has defended him from magical attacks.[13] That does not make it the *first* urban fantasy story or even *an* urban fantasy story (although it can certainly be read as such). Judging from Budrys's remark, the label formed and spread during the 1970s, and I have found no earlier indication that it was widely used. The strands that make up the genre today had begun to come together, and by 1978, the label was established, even though it signified something somewhat different from its later incarnations.

PROTO-URBAN FANTASY: THE GOTHIC, THE CITY, AND THE SUPERNATURAL FANTASTIC

Some central strands of the genre were braided together long before urban fantasy was thought of as a particular category in the

1970s. I refer to the many forerunners that combined the first three strands as *proto-urban fantasy*, because I think it makes sense to see them as works that together gave rise to urban fantasy. Other critics have considered them as early urban fantasy.[14] The three strands that constitute proto-urban fantasy are Gothic fiction, with its origin in the mid-eighteenth century Gothic romances; the story about the modern city, which arose in the early nineteenth century; and tales of the supernatural fantastic, such as ghosts, monsters, fairies, and magic. Not until these three were braided together could a text be considered specifically urban fantasy—it would be too far beyond the category otherwise. An early example of proto-urban fantasy is Charles Dickens's *A Christmas Carol* (1843), in which the miserly Ebenezer Scrooge is visited by spirits of Christmases Past, Present, and Future and is transformed into a better man.[15] It is of course possible to claim earlier works, such as "The Vampyre" (1819), John William Polidori's short story about a naive young man who befriends but is deceived and eventually killed by the vampire Lord Ruthven; or *Les mystéres de Paris* (1842–43; trans. *The Mysteries of Paris*), Eugene Sue's story about Rodolphe, a noble in disguise who tries to find a boy who has disappeared in Paris. Rodolphe's compassion for the poor and disadvantaged and his search for the boy leads him into several adventures in various parts of the metropolis. Although John Clute calls Sue's work "a full-fledged [urban fantasy]," he admits that a supernatural element is missing.[16] In Polidori's story, on the other hand, London and other cities are only flimsy backdrops. While important texts leading up to proto-urban fantasy, they fall far outside my cognitive model of urban fantasy.

Addressing the entire history of the first three strands is beyond the scope of this chapter, and I will only briefly sketch the development from when the Gothic, the city, and the supernatural first came together. The Gothic romance, when it arose in the second half of the eighteenth century, was set in ancient castles and monasteries, out in the wilderness, but in the 1830s and 1840s, the Gothic moved into the cities. The dark, labyrinthine passages of old buildings and the distant past were swapped for the dark, labyrinthine alleys of the urban centers of the present.[17] Sue's *Les mystéres de Paris* led to the development of the city mystery genre during the nineteenth century, stories that explore the social misery of many major cities, including George W. M. Reynolds's dark *The Mysteries of London* (1844–46; by other writers until 1856). As Gothic features were combined with the urban setting, "[t]he city, a gloomy forest or dark labyrinth itself, became a site of nocturnal corruption and violence, a locus of real horror."[18] Already a genre open to occult motifs, the Gothic romance also brought supernatural, including infernal and divine, influences and agents into the urban forests and labyrinths, and the history of proto-urban fantasy is largely the history of that portion of Gothic fiction that remained in cities and other modern environments and concerned itself with the supernatural and occult. The development of the Gothic strand will therefore be given a little more attention.

As it entered the cities of the nineteenth century, the Gothic romance of the eighteenth century began to transform into something more lasting. Alastair Fowler explains that "the gothic romance [. . .] yielded a gothic mode that outlasted it,"[19] and Fred Botting calls it a "Gothic strain" of motifs, figures, and strategies.[20] Fowler and Botting both point out how Gothic influences reached into the twentieth century and spread over aesthetic forms, media, and genres. There is

> a diffusion of Gothic traces among a multiplicity of different genres and media. Science fiction, the adventure novel, modernist literature, romantic fiction and popular horror writing often resonate with Gothic motifs that have been transformed and displaced by different cultural anxieties. Terror and horror are diversely located in alienating bureaucratic and technological reality, in psychiatric hospitals and criminal subcultures, in scientific, future and intergalactic worlds, in fantasy and the occult.[21]

Botting's list of literary forms in which the Gothic has survived for more than two centuries is both an example of how a literary form can adapt and a demonstration of how certain ideas prove to be so useful that they become almost ubiquitous in our culture. It also explains why the Gothic strand manages to remain so prominent in contemporary urban fantasy. Botting's "Gothic strain" seems to be able to handle any cultural anxiety by clothing it in darkness and labyrinths, making it irrational or incomprehensible, or dwarfing us with the ancient and enormous. The strain's connection to death and the ancient past makes it particularly suited for stories about the never-dying vampire or ghost, with an occasional werewolf thrown in—creatures that have made a career for themselves in urban fantasy as well. In his analysis of late-twentieth-century Gothic literature in an intermedial context of film, rock music, and role-playing and computer games, Mattias Fyhr demonstrates how the Gothic has turned into a pervasive form of portrayal rather than a collection of props, motifs, or themes to be added to a story.[22] From this perspective, the presence of a Gothic strand in urban fantasy is not surprising: not only has the Gothic become common in most popular culture, it is also adaptable and suited to portray that which we do not know, do not see, and do not understand. If anything, its contribution to the formation of urban fantasy as an identifiable category is amplified because, according to Fyhr, from about 1970 and for a couple of decades, there was a Gothic wave in various media.[23] Urban fantasy can be considered part of, or shaped by, this wave.

The three-strand braid that makes up proto-urban fantasy developed but remained easily identifiable until the 1970s, when new strands were added. Proto-urban fantasy changed as its constituent strands developed: the modernist portrayals of the city of the twentieth century, the aforementioned development of the Gothic, and the changing fashions in supernatural fiction also affected writers who combined these strands. Viviane Bergue observes how proto-urban fantasy has combined with other urban fantasy strands from the 1980s, including fantasy in modern settings and investigation plots (Bergue reads these in terms of "the Gothic," "fantasy," and "thriller plot").[24] This first bundle of strands remains a mainstay of the genre, and provides a core around which many other strands have been twined.

In children's literature, a parallel tradition with magical events in modern cities emerged around the turn of the previous century with writers such as E. Nesbit and J. M. Barrie. Barrie's *The Little White Bird* (1902; some chapters were later published as *Peter Pan in Kensington Gardens*, 1906) is set in a contemporary London with some fantasy elements, with a middle section that portrays Kensington Gardens as a place of fairies and magic once the park closes for the night. Nesbit wrote several books in which modern children experience magical episodes. *Harding's Luck* (1909), a sequel to the time-travel fantasy *The House of Arden* (1908), is probably the most urban fantasy-like. Dickie Harding is an orphaned boy from a poor area of London who ends up in a magical time-travel adventure only to discover his real identity. These texts can be considered early urban fantasy[25] but did not establish a distinct strand. Their influence can still be seen in occasional later texts, however, and they deserve a mention in the history of urban fantasy.

THE 1960S AND 1970S: MODERN FANTASY MEETS MODERNITY

This section traces the main development of two strands that contributed to the formation of urban fantasy during the 1960s and 1970s, both of which concern the fantasy genre as it was popularized by Tolkien's *The Lord of the Rings* (1954–55). These strands emerged from experiments in combining the mythical and pseudomedieval fantasy with modern society, and from the development of a modern, secondary fantasy world.

After *The Lord of the Rings*, fantasy appeared to develop in reaction to Tolkien's novel, and Alan Garner's stories offer an illustration of different ways in which a Tolkienian kind of fantasy can be combined with modern society. There were three general types of reactions among writers: the urges to imitate, to improve, and to experiment. The imitations (attempts to write another *The Lord of the Rings*) and improvements (by including, for instance, underrepresented groups or social and psychological realism) are of less concern here than the experiments. Some of these consisted of confronting the magical, mythical, premodern brand of Tolkienian fantasy with modernity to see what happened. A good example is Garner, who published three such experiments during the 1960s. His first novel, *The Weirdstone of Brisingamen* (1960), describes a magical and mythical quest in a fantastic landscape that "overlies" the nonmagical landscape of Alderley Edge in modern Cheshire. The atmosphere of myth and magic that suffuses the setting is similar to that of Tolkien's Middle-earth, while remaining grounded in the everyday of the physical place. The technique is one that later urban fantasy writers have employed to transform well-known cities into sites of myth and magic. Garner's second experiment was *Elidor* (1965), in which a group of children enter a secondary world and help save it from a dark power. The children return home but have unwittingly connected the two worlds and find themselves besieged by the forces of darkness in their house outside of Manchester. The modern world and the fantastic forces of a magical otherworld clash in ways recognizable from numerous later urban fantasies. Garner's third experiment was *The Owl Service* (1967), where pre-Christian powers erupt into a modern world, as pointed out by Farah Mendlesohn and Edward James.[26] In this tightly woven story, present-day characters find themselves tangled in a mythical tale, their modern mindsets in conflict with the forces that drive the myth. Modern rationality breaks against the power of story. Each of Garner's experiments differs somewhat from the others, but they all share a curiosity about what happens when the myth and magic of fantasy is combined with the everyday of modern life. They provide early examples of what has become a part of the urban fantasy genre: the juxtaposition of the supernatural and the modern.

Where some fantasy writers experimented with inserting the fantastic into our modern world, others brought modernity to secondary worlds. Garner's three experiments from the 1960s all added a fantastic component to a version of our modern world. At about the same time, other writers created modern otherworlds for their stories. Mervyn Peake introduced a modern but fantastic city in the third of his Gormenghast books, *Titus Alone* (1959), but it would take a few more years for the idea to really catch on. Randall Garrett set his stories about Lord Darcy, criminal investigator, in a twentieth century based on the rule of magic rather than science. The stories about Lord Darcy, the first of which is "The Eyes Have It" (1964), flamboyantly bring together alternative history, fantasy, and crime fiction with allusions to several well-known crime fiction characters and motifs. Roger Zelazny created a world that very literally juxtaposed science and magic in *Jack of Shadows* (1971): an unspinning world with a dark side, where magic works, and a light side, which is run by science. The eponymous Jack derives his power from the shadow between the two sides. German writer Michael Ende built a world in which he stages a conflict between the little girl Momo and the sinister Men in Grey, who steal people's time under the pretense of saving it for them for future use. Ende's *Momo* (1973) is a powerful critique of modern capitalist society, and its message is perhaps even more relevant today than when it was written. These three examples illustrate how writers experimented with building secondary worlds that still included a significant measure of modernity. Such modern otherworlds would increase both in number and complexity and have been an important part of urban fantasy since the 1980s.

Zelazny's Chronicles of Amber (1970–91) also foreshadow much of what would become urban fantasy, especially in the first five books of the series. "The premise [of the Chronicles of

Amber] is loosely science fictional but the execution is affiliated with fantasy and with the trappings of the Gothic (castles, dungeons, magical artefacts, family secrets)."[27] To this mix of genres can be added the distinct crime-fiction opening of the first novel. The main character wakes up from a coma without memories and has to figure out who he is and what has been done to him. The first-person voice recalls that of hardboiled detectives such as Raymond Chandler's Philip Marlowe. Modern society and magical realities are blended together. The fifth and final book of the first part of Zelazny's series was published in 1978, by which time several strands of urban fantasy had begun to come together, and Budrys thought the label in need of no explanation. It was in this year that Lumet's movie *The Wiz* demonstrated how the classic fantasy land of Oz could be turned into a modern, urban space and still retain its magic. But there still remained strands to be added to the urban fantasy braid, and the 1980s would provide two key ones.

THE 1980S: THE MODERN AS A SOURCE OF MAGIC, AND FAIRIES MOVE INTO TOWN

The 1980s is a popular starting point for many who have written the history of urban fantasy, possibly because of the popularity of the two strands that were added during this decade. One of these strands also drew more attention to urban fantasy than did any previous strand. The two strands were the various attempts to create modern settings that themselves gave rise to the fantastic and the introduction of fairies and other mythical beings into modern cities.

The fantasy experiments of the 1960s and 1970s continued during the 1980s. Of particular interest for urban fantasy are the stories with fantastic elements that emerged from the modern—often urban—environment itself. Alexander C. Irvine captures this impulse, describing how the city

> animat[es] the narrative and determin[es] its fantastic nature. [. . .] [T]he city creates its own rules, independent from existing canons of folklore. In the purest examples of these stories, whatever fantastic elements exist derive from the nature and history of the city. These are stories of the fantastic city, distinguishable from stories of real or almost-real cities in which fantastic events occur.[28]

Rather than transplanting fantastic elements from existing mythic and folkloristic sources or even from previous fantasy stories—today, there is no shortage of stories about Tolkien-inspired elves, dwarves, and orcs in modern or even futuristic cities—the city itself gives rise to the fantastic. *The Wiz* demonstrates how this can work, by turning New York into a modern Oz, but during the early 1980s, other writers began to create fantastic modern places from whole cloth.

Earlier authors had begun building fantastic cities to some extent, but in the 1980s, we find examples that connect more distinctly to urban fantasy. Sylvia Kelso sums up this strand when she describes how a particular type of fantasy fiction of the 1980s "turns from denying industrial reality toward a determined initiative to make that industrial world not only numinous, but worth fighting for."[29] Instead of denying modernity like much Tolkien-inspired fantasy does, the modern world is given value through an infusion of myths and magic. Fantasy reclaims modernity. In John Crowley's *Little, Big* (1981), the City (New York) is a place of crime and poverty but also a place of story, in which the protagonist suffers events as part not of life but of a Tale. The urban setting becomes charged with meaning. In Mark Helprin's *Winter's Tale* (1983), New York provides the main character with a mysterious white horse for a guardian, sends him through time via a cloud wall, and eventually gives him enormous powers. In the unnamed town that serves as the setting for Diana Wynne Jones's *Archer's Goon* (1984), the modern systems of power, control, and surveillance are embodied through seven siblings with tremendous magical powers. Megan

Lindholm presents a wizard who lives outside of domiciled society and derives his magic from the city of Seattle itself in *Wizard of the Pigeons* (1986).[30] Terry Pratchett developed a distinctly personal flavor of urban fantasy in the satirical Discworld books even though the earlier books fall fairly far from the genre. In the first book, *The Colour of Magic* (1983), Ankh-Morpork is satirically portrayed as a (premodern) fantasy city that suffers a terrible conflagration as a result of a (modern) tourist introducing the idea of insurance. By the end of the decade, in *Guards! Guards!* (1989), Pratchett has turned Ankh-Morpork into a modern city in pseudomedieval garb, and this and the following stories about the City Watch can easily be read as urban fantasies set in an "increasingly nineteenth-century city."[31]

Several critics have argued that urban fantasy came into being when a group of writers began to write stories about fairies and other mythic beings in urban settings. Fairies took their time to confront modernity and have a long tradition of departing the modern world instead. The 1970s saw a few stories where fairies and modernity meet but usually in attempts to resist change wrought by modern society. Poul Anderson sets fairies against the advancing disenchantment of an early Industrial Revolution in *A Midsummer Tempest* (1974). The novel takes place in a parallel world in which William Shakespeare was a historian (what we know as plays of fiction actually happened there) and Oberon and Titania interfere in the English Civil War. Jones's *Power of Three* (1976) is the story of two types of fairy-inspired people who have to join forces with a couple of "giants" (humans) in order to prevent their home moor from being flooded by the establishment of a water reservoir. A similar story is told in *Blodwen and the Guardians* (1983) by David Wiseman, in which humans and fairy creatures band together to prevent a highway from being built through a small village. From the mid-1980s, the fairies moved into the cities of North America, at least partly as reclamation of a Western society reeling from the decade's many challenges.[32] Charles de

Lint's *Moonheart* (1984) is a story about ancient myths, ageless bards, and a portal to a spirit world, set in contemporary Ottawa. The first two anthologies in the Borderland series were published in 1986 (*Borderland* and *Bordertown*, edited by Terri Windling and Mark Alan Arnold), each containing four short stories set in Bordertown, a city on the threshold between the Elflands and the primary world. An additional three Borderland anthologies (1991, 1998, and 2011) and three novels (Will Shetterly, 1991, 1993; Emma Bull, 1994) have been published so far, demonstrating a continued enthusiasm for the shared world. The following year, Emma Bull published *War for the Oaks* (1987), and de Lint published *Jack, the Giant-Killer* (1987). De Lint's first story set in the city of Newford came out a year or two later.[33] The Borderland anthologies, de Lint, and Bull have often been proclaimed to be the origin of the genre[34] while others identify them only as early examples of a particular type of urban fantasy.[35] Of the three, de Lint has made the greatest mark on the genre, and Newford has come to represent a particular view of the genre as defined by a vast array of mythical and magical beings living (mostly) unseen in a modern metropolis. The first collection, *Dreams Underfoot* (1993) was edited by Windling, and the blurb proclaims that "[l]ike Mark Helprin's [. . .] *Winter's Tale* and John Crowley's *Little, Big*, *Dreams Underfoot* is a must-read book not only for fans of urban fantasy but for all who seek magic in everyday life."[36] The blurb's explicit connection to Crowley's and Helprin's novels seeks to establish urban fantasy as a distinct category to which Crowley, Helprin, and de Lint belong.

The Windling/Bull/de Lint type of stories have also been referred to, not least by themselves, as *mythic fiction*. In *The Urban Fantasy Anthology* (edited by Peter S. Beagle and Joe R. Lansdale, 2011), de Lint describes his development as a writer up to the point where he published *Jack, the Giant-Killer* and how he and Windling came up with the term *mythic fiction*.[37] Citing Windling, he explains that that term covers a somewhat different type of text than does *urban fantasy*: "novels and stories [. . .] that make conscious use of myth, medieval Romance, folklore and/or fairy tales, but that are set in the real world, rather than in invented fantasy landscapes."[38] He also notes that the subtitle of *Jack*, "A Novel of Urban Faerie," somehow translated to "urban fantasy" in subsequent references to the novel.[39] While mythic fiction remains a valid category and is occasionally used in de Lint's and Windling's original sense, most texts that include fairies and other mythical and magical beings in modern cities (Newford is teeming with all kinds of creatures, including ghosts and vampires, fairies and animal people, even the living embodiment of the city) are also seen as urban fantasy today. The fact that the blurb of *Dreams Underfoot* places the Newford stories in the urban fantasy bracket has no doubt contributed to this.

THE 1990S: CRIME FIGHTERS, VAMPIRES, AND THE TOUGH FEMALE PROTAGONIST

Three more strands were added to the urban fantasy braid in the 1990s: the investigator figure,[40] the vampire (and to a lesser extent the werewolf and other "monster") companion or protagonist, and the tough female protagonist. Each of the first two strands requires a brief historical recapitulation.

The combination of the supernatural and detective stories is not a recent phenomenon, having been around at least since the mid-nineteenth century, but although it occasionally touched proto-urban fantasy, it did not really enter the urban fantasy genre until the late 1980s. Maurizio Ascari explores the relation between crime fiction, the supernatural, and the Gothic, and observes how "detection and the supernatural combined to form 'the story of psychic detection'" in the late nineteenth century.[41] He discusses some supernatural sleuths from the late nineteenth and early twentieth century that, I would argue, find their descendants among recent investigators of the urban fantasy genre. Among early examples of detectives involved with supernatural crimes are Fitz James

O'Brien's Harry Escott (1855 and 1859), E. and H. Heron's Flaxman Low (1898–99), and William Hope Hodgson's Thomas Carnacki (1910–12). Garrett's Lord Darcy stories also combined the crime genre with a secondary-world fantasy in the 1960s. In de Lint's *Moonheart*, the Royal Canadian Mounted Police has an operation for documenting "psychic resources" that plays a central role.

By 1987, crime fiction and urban fantasy have become fully braided together in two novels by Mike Resnick and Glen Cook. Resnick's *Stalking the Unicorn*, the first novel in the Fables of Midnight series (based on a 1986 short story), tells the story of when private detective John Justin Mallory is contracted to find a stolen unicorn in an alternate New York. Resnick did not produce a sequel to *Stalking the Unicorn* until 2008, by which time private detectives, supernatural police, and other investigator figures were firmly braided into the genre. Cook's *Sweet Silver Blues* is the first story in the series about Garrett P.I. (1987–2013), a private investigator in a secondary fantasy world. Cook's prose and settings draw on the hardboiled detective story. Pratchett's City Watch books are other early examples, inspired by the police novel rather than the hardboiled private eye.[42] Then, in the early 1990s, two urban fantasy series established the detective character as one of the genre's strands, but because they also included the two other 1990s strands, Tanya Huff and Laurell K. Hamilton are addressed after the vampires and tough female protagonists have been introduced.

A second strand added to urban fantasy in the 1990s was the human vampires and other monsters. In the 1960s and 1970s, the nonhuman monster of the horror genre began to shift away from a monstrous Otherness toward a more human portrayal. In 1967, the vampire Barnabas Collins entered the American soap opera *Dark Shadows* (created by Dan Curtis, 1966–71). Over the course of the show, Barnabas develops from a sinister monster to what amounts to the hero, who repeatedly risks himself to save others. Robert Aickman won the 1975 World Fantasy Award for his novelette "Pages from a Young Girl's Journal" (1973), in which the female protagonist describes her fascination with what turns out to be a vampire and her desire to become one herself. The mid-1970s saw the publication of Fred Saberhagen's *The Dracula Tape* (1975), in which Bram Stoker's novel is told from Dracula's point of view, followed by Anne Rice's immensely popular *Interview with the Vampire* (1976), in which a vampire gets to tell his own story. These four works indicate how the vampire took on a new role, transforming from the antagonist and monster seen from outside to a possible ally, romantic object, or even protagonist with its own perspective. Anna Höglund suggests that Aickman's story can be considered an early example of the later quite popular vampire romance,[43] and she identifies a split of the modern vampire character into what she calls *monster vampires* and *human vampires*. The latter struggles to keep its humanity in control over its dark, monstrous side, and it often provides the narrative perspective.[44] Not only the vampire changed, however. Other monsters were given a voice and a point of view, or were at least treated as companions rather than dark threats. Science fiction writer Clifford D. Simak published a story about a werewolf-as-alien that comes to Earth by sharing the body of a human astronaut (*The Werewolf Principle*, 1967). Peter S. Beagle's "Lila the Werewolf" (1969) relates the problems of having a werewolf for a girlfriend in a story that would feel familiar to many readers of more recent urban fantasy.

After *Interview with a Vampire*, the vampire character kept evolving before it was braided into urban fantasy. The 1980s saw two more installments in what has come to be referred to as Rice's Vampire Chronicles (1976–2018): *The Vampire Lestat* (1985) and *The Queen of the Damned* (1988), both of which explore the vampire perspective further. Chelsea Quinn Yarbro's *Hôtel Transylvania* (1978) contains the first appearance of the aristocratic vampire St. Germain and moved the vampire romance along another step; and the therapy sessions of the vampire Dr. Weyland in *The Vampire Tapestry* (Suzy McKee Charnas, 1980) helped develop the human vampire's self-reflective side further.[45] By the 1990s, vampires and other monstrous beings had apparently become self-reflective and "human" enough to pull them into the urban fantasy braid. Vampires and werewolves showed up not only in the traditional role as monstrous antagonists but as romantic objects and allies, and even as protagonists, often playing several roles in the same story. The line between contemporary Gothic fiction, the vampire story, and urban fantasy became indistinct, something that is particularly apparent when urban fantasy is compared to the heavily Gothic and Rice-influenced role-playing game *Vampire: The Masquerade* (Mark Rein-Hagen, 1991). Michał Wolski observes that the game portrays vampires much in line with previous vampire fiction, such as Rice's books,[46] but also claims that urban fantasy writers like Hamilton, Huff, and Patricia Briggs conform to the *Vampire* game over time.[47] At the same time, the game world, the World of Darkness, changed, with the addition of wizards (1993) and fairies (1995) as well as werewolves (1992) and ghosts (1994). So while urban fantasy writers moved toward the World of Darkness, that world also became more like urban fantasy.

The romantic aspects of the vampire strand brings urban fantasy close to what has become known as paranormal romance, to a point where some readers and critics find it difficult or unnecessary to separate the two. According to Leigh M. McLennon, urban fantasy and paranormal romance are one genre, and she claims that it arose in the 1990s.[48] In line with Clute and David Langford,[49] I would rather argue that a category of writing arose that braided together certain strands of urban fantasy and a version of romance, with focus on the relationship between human protagonists and supernatural characters. This category, paranormal romance, shares many of urban fantasy's character types, settings, and motifs but has been marketed (and is seen by many readers and writers) as its own type of fiction. Many texts can be read as either urban fantasy or paranormal romance, resulting in different emphases on particular story themes. The cognitive models for these respective categories are distinctly different, with the model for paranormal romance stressing the relationships and sexual encounters of the protagonist far more than does the model for urban fantasy. A key discrepancy is that the removal of the romance strand would cause a paranormal romance story to collapse, which would not necessarily be the case for urban fantasy.

The third strand added to the urban fantasy braid in the 1990s was the tough female protagonist. Although previous urban fantasies have often centered on female characters, and these characters have often been portrayed as strong and self-reliant (Bull's Eddie and de Lint's Jilly Coppercorn are two examples from the 1980s), the 1990s brought female protagonists who are not afraid to use, and often encounter, physical violence. Despite their initial carefulness—Huff's Vicky Nelson is aware of the limitations caused by her weak eyesight, and Hamilton's Anita Blake knows that her black belt in judo is of little use against a much larger opponent[50]—their kick-ass attitude and abilities are evident. The tough female protagonists who emerged in urban fantasy in the 1990s arose in parallel with the series *Buffy the Vampire Slayer* (created by Joss Whedon, 1997–2003; the 1992 film directed by Fran Rubel Kuzui) and *Xena: Warrior Princess* (created by John Schulian and Robert Tapert, 1995–2001). I share Mendlesohn and James's ambivalence regarding the influence of *Buffy* on urban fantasy;[51] it seems reasonable to assume that the fighting female characters of books and screens (including video games[52]) came from a growing interest in seeing women portrayed as martially proficient heroes, and that the various stories fed into each other over time.

Huff's Vicky Nelson and Hamilton's Anita Blake both capture urban fantasy's transformation in the 1990s by incorporating all three of the new strands. The tough female investigator characters who work with vampires (albeit in somewhat different ways) became immensely popular. Vicky Nelson, in Huff's Blood Books (1991–97; 2006), is a former police officer who has had to leave the force due to her failing eyesight. She works as a private detective and teams up with the vampire Henry Fitzroy. Together, they solve supernatural crimes in five novels and a collection of short stories. Hamilton's stories about Anita Blake (1993–present) are set in a world in which vampires live alongside humans, and some magic, such as reanimating the dead, is commonplace (certain other beings, such as shapeshifters, keep a lower profile). Mendlesohn and James describe the first books as

> essentially detective novels, but running through them are romantic complications. [. . .] The books lose interest in the detective element and are increasingly concerned with the politics of the paranormal denizens of [St. Louis], which just happen to play out in Anita's bed, often accompanied by whips and chains.[53]

They observe how the readership began to change around book ten as "[m]any early fans simply could not handle the quite explicit descriptions of consensual sadism and also sexual abuse in the later books."[54] Perhaps Hamilton's series no longer fit the cognitive model of urban fantasy of its original readers. Both she and Huff combined earlier strands of the genre with tough female investigator characters and vampires and other monstrous beings as their allies or partners, and their series established a particular tone for urban fantasy.

Previous urban fantasy strands also kept developing during the 1990s, and not all writers added all the available strands to their works. De Lint published three Newford collections and six novels, dominating the "mythic fiction" braid of urban fantasy strands (and there would be numerous more Newford stories published in the 2000s, advancing that particular combination of strands). Two novels from the 1990s that provide interesting examples of the possibilities offered by the genre are Michael Swanwick's *The Iron Dragon's Daughter* (1993) and Neil Gaiman's *Neverwhere* (1996). Swanwick tells the story of the human changeling Jane in a very modern Faerie. Jane teams up with a dragon-cum-fighter jet to escape her indentured labor in a factory that builds such dragons. The story follows Jane's time in school, university, and high society, combining traditional fairy and fantasy tropes with an often scathing indictment of late-modern society. Swanwick's rationalized version of a modern Faerie might not be typical for the urban fantasy genre, but it illustrates the extent to which the genre's strands can be used to create stories that tightly combine political and mythical themes. Gaiman's novel, originally a short television series that he wrote for BBC Two (1996), has become one of the genre's more well-known examples. It relates how Richard Mayhew finds himself stuck in an alternative London, unseen by mainstream Londoners and populated by people at or beyond the margins of society as well as by various magical beings. Although Richard's story follows a typical quest trajectory rather than an investigation plot, Gaiman has tied in many other strands, including a tough female warrior and the vampiric Lamia. A mythical being (an angel from Atlantis) is central to Richard's quest, but much of the fantastic emerges from the modern city, to the point where the magic is often based on puns or literal readings of the names of London's various areas and underground stations. The popularity of *Neverwhere* has resulted in it being highly representative for urban fantasy to many readers, not least because it braids together several of the genre's strands. Its literalization of the metaphor of an unseen social margin, that it shares with earlier works by, for instance, Lindholm and de Lint, sets it in a group of works that have influenced the general cognitive model of the genre.

Urban Fantasy Research in the 1990s

One of the most influential studies of fantasy, Brian Attebery's *Strategies of Fantasy* (1992), includes a chapter on a type of fantasy that could be considered urban fantasy today. These fantasies describe "settings that seem to be real, familiar, present-day places except that they contain the magical characters and impossible events of fantasy."[55] Attebery wrestles with what to call these stories, rejecting "low fantasy," "real world fantasy," and "modern urban fantasy" before settling for "indigenous fantasy" because it is "fantasy that is, like an indigenous species, adapted to and reflective of its native environment."[56] Occasional critics have made use of this term, notably Mendlesohn and James, who decided to use Attebery's term rather than "urban fantasy" when they write about the 1990s and later,[57] but it never gained the popularity of "urban fantasy." It has been pointed out that the connotations of the adjective "indigenous" make the term problematic, and Attebery now discourages the use of the term.[58] Nevertheless, Attebery's chapter discusses how the strands that developed during the 1960s through 1980s work; contains insightful readings of Lindholm's *Wizard of the Pigeons* and Crowley's *Little, Big*; and could be considered the first broad analysis of some of the urban fantasy genre's central strands.

The mid-1990s saw two other critical overviews of urban fantasy, one well known and the other less so. The latter is Faye Ringel's article "Bright Swords, Big Cities," published in *The Year's Work in Medievalism X* (1995). Ringel discusses the postmodern approach taken to medievalism by urban fantasy and how "the trappings of medievalism [. . .] collide head-on with those usually associated with science fiction."[59] She considers urban fantasy writers to be "heirs of Tolkien and Morris" and identifies as a common theme that "in the city, the magic is real and necessary for the right maintenance of the contemporary world."[60] Her examples were published between 1984 and 1994, but because of the focus on medievalism, works like Huff's and Hamilton's are excluded. Ringel's analysis thus concentrates largely on the strands that arose from fantasy in the 1960s and 1970s, along with the urban fairy strand of the 1980s, but as an analysis of those strands, this is a valuable text. Ringel is also among the first to point out the importance of the poet, visionary, and homeless characters to much urban fantasy.

The second critical text from the 1990s, and one that has been far more cited than Ringel's, is the entry on urban fantasy that Clute wrote for the *Encyclopedia of Fantasy* (1997). Clute's entry was first published, together with the entry for "city," in the journal *Paradoxa* (2:1) in 1996, making it roughly contemporary with Ringel's. Where Ringel includes the urban fairies strand and largely ignores proto-urban fantasy, Clute mainly sees urban fantasy as the strands that have come together by the mid-1980s. The description and analysis of the category—he refers to it quite specifically as a "mode"[61]—starts with the Gothic romances in the eighteenth century. The importance of the city story comes through in the insistence that urban fantasy "is significantly *about* a real city" and that the city has been "created not just as a backdrop but as an environment."[62] Few examples given were published after 1990, and using this entry as a means to understand post-1985 urban fantasy requires awareness of what strands are being excluded by Clute's perspective. For the strands that he does address, however, Clute has much of value to say.

THE 2000S: NEW WEIRD MEETS URBAN FANTASY

During the first decade of the new millennium, urban fantasy's popularity increased, in terms of reading, writing, and publishing, and the most recent strand of the genre was added, the so-called New Weird. This label was first introduced by M. John Harrison in 2003, who claimed to have heard it in a conversation with China Miéville,[63] and it was hotly debated at the time. New Weird has had an entry in the online version of *The Encyclopedia of Science Fiction* since at least 2012.[64] In 2008, the anthology *The New Weird*, edited by Ann and Jeff VanderMeer, presented a multifaceted view of this type of writing: what it was, where it came from, what it looked like, and whether the label was acceptable. Among works claimed for the New Weird in the introduction to the anthology are *Perdido Street Station* (Miéville, 2000), *City of Saints and*

Madmen (Jeff VanderMeer, 2001), *A Year in the Linear City* (Paul Di Filippo, 2002), and *The Etched City* (K. J. Bishop, 2003).[65] Di Filippo's novella does not fit the urban fantasy model particularly well, but the other three books have also been referred to as urban fantasies.

As is clear from the four examples that Jeff VanderMeer provides in his introduction, the New Weird contains an urban streak. His working definition similarly stresses that aspect: "New Weird is a type of urban, secondary-world fiction that subverts the romanticized idea about place found in traditional fantasy, largely by choosing realistic, complex real-world models as the jumping off point for creation of settings that may combine elements of both science fiction and fantasy." He then mentions the use of elements from horror and the influence from New Wave writers and notes that "New Weird fictions are acutely aware of the modern world."[66] From this definition, it is possible to question whether the New Weird is a new strand at all or simply a developed version of some previous strands. The modern secondary worlds of fantasy go back to the 1960s and 1970s, urbanity and the influence from horror further than that.

New Weird was not an offshoot from urban fantasy but rather a case of parallel evolution. Many of the building blocks are the same, but, according to VanderMeer, it also had two specific "stimuli" that distinguished it from the "old" weird fiction of writers such as H. P. Lovecraft and Clark Ashton Smith: the genre mixing, formal experiments, and political point of view of the New Wave of the 1960s; and a repurposing of transgressive horror from the 1980s, to "focus on the monsters and grotesquery."[67] Those stimuli were the nerve of the New Weird. When writers such as Miéville, Bishop, and VanderMeer produced works that to a great extent looked like—and could be read as—urban fantasy, they also attached themselves to the urban fantasy braid, as another strand for writers to employ.

The 2000s was a decade during which urban fantasy gained a firm foothold, even though no consensus was established about exactly what it looked like. All the strands developed in their own directions, while still being available to writers of urban fantasy. Certain combinations achieved brief recognition, occasionally dominating the market and discussions. Depending on which strand or strands one focused on, it was possible to claim that there was only one type of urban fantasy, or two, or three, but because writers kept creating combinations that fit their particular stories, there were always exceptions. Depending on whom you ask, typical urban fantasy from the 2000s could contain strands mainly from the 1980s, from the 1990s, or from the 2000s. Major titles include Gaiman's *American Gods* (2001), Miéville's *Perdido Street Station* and *Un Lun Dun* (2007), Catherynne M. Valente's *Palimpsest* (2009), Jim Butcher's *Storm Front* (2000, #1 in the Dresden Files series), Charlaine Harris's *Dead Until Dark* (2001, #1 in the Sookie Stackhouse series), Kim Harrison's *Dead Witch Walking* (2004, #1 in the Hollows series), and Cassandra Clare's *City of Bones* (2007, #1 in the Mortal Instruments series).

Urban Fantasy Research in the 2000s

The 2000s was a decade of very little urban fantasy scholarship, largely because urban fantasy was mainly considered a subgenre to something else: fantasy, romance, or vampire literature, for example. Clute updated and expanded his thoughts on urban fantasy in *The Greenwood Encyclopedia of Science Fiction and Fantasy* (2005),[68] but although the examples now included de Lint's Newford, Gaiman's *Neverwhere*, and Miéville's *Perdido Street Station*, his perspective remained essentially the same as in the earlier encyclopedia. The main strands were the city story and the fantastic emerging from the city, but city fairies and Gothic traits are mentioned as well. Robin Anne Reid also included an entry on urban fantasy in *Women in Science Fiction and Fantasy* (2009)[69] in which she elaborates on Clute's idea that urban fantasy is a mode. "Considering urban fantasy as a mode allows useful discussion of works" in various other genres, according to Reid, and she describes the mode as a filter that can be placed over a text.[70] Despite its brevity, Reid's entry manages to address an urban fantasy braided together by all the strands mentioned in this chapter, and it marks an important, and undeservedly disregarded, contribution to urban fantasy scholarship.

Academic research that engages with urban fantasy beyond analyses of one or two texts remained scarce during this decade, although the category garnered interest by fans and writers. Two of the rare examples of academic attention to urban fantasy more broadly are Kelso's "*Loces Genii*: Urban Settings in the Fantasy of Peter Beagle, Martha Wells, and Barbara Hambley" (2002) and Allan Weiss's "Destiny and Identity in Canadian Urban Fantasy" (2006). Kelso does not refer to what she examines as urban fantasy, but describes it as examples of texts that present "non-realist elements, particularly magic" in cities.[71] The trend that she identifies (emerging in about 1986) is made up particularly of the strands of the 1970s and early 1980s, and she concludes that by moving fantasy into the "Here and Now," we are forced to recognize that we are personally responsible for saving the things we value.[72] Weiss draws on Clute but also on nonacademic, online sources in order to cobble together a definition.[73] Such sources were generally where discussions about the nature of urban fantasy could be found during this time. Lazette Gifford's piece in the online magazine *Vision* is an early example, but Gifford defines the genre so broadly that it includes both *Alice's Adventures in Wonderland* (1865) and *The Wonderful Wizard of Oz*, as well as any story in which magic exists in our world.[74] To support librarians who encountered a demand from readers for urban fantasy books, Nanette Wargo Donohue published an article in *Library Journal* with an overview of the genre. Donohue considers urban fantasy to have its roots in the late 1980s and early 1990s and divides it into two branches: "traditional" and "contemporary." The former centers on the two strands of modern fantasy and the urban fairies strand while the latter combines the three strands of proto-urban fantasy with the tough female protagonists and the vampires and investigator figures.[75] N. K. Jemisin proposes an alternative division, between "structural" and "contextual" urban fantasy, in a blog post that sparked some debate. Contextual urban fantasy is roughly the same as Donohue's contemporary, but by "structural, " Jemisin means texts that exhibit "better writing" and concern themselves with "*the city* or society."[76] From her examples, including works by VanderMeer, Gaiman (*Neverwhere*), and Miéville (*The City and the City*, 2009), it is clear that the New Weird is a part of her urban fantasy braid. She ends by "hypothesizing" that there is no real difference between the two types. A further demonstration of the genre's popularity was the 2009 publication of an urban-fantasy-themed *Locus* issue (issue 62, no. 5), with several short pieces on various aspects of the genre (focusing largely on the strands of tough female protagonists and vampires.)

THE 2010S: EXPANSION AND IMPLOSION

By 2010, the urban fantasy genre had established itself as a distinct marketing category and as a well-known literary category among its readers. The variety of strands available had prevented it from turning into a homogenous form, although certain combinations (investigating, tough female characters with bloodsucking and shapeshifting allies in particular) tended to dominate. New writers found new ways to use the available strands, and the 2010s saw some authors use urban fantasy in radical ways.

The way the genre changed from around 2010 can to some extent be thought of in terms of what Gary K. Wolfe calls "evaporating genres." Wolfe suggests that the readers of science fiction, fantasy, and horror, respectively, came to identify writers that served as the genres' "central ideological lynchpins," writers whose worldviews came to dominate the genres.[77] Urban fantasy, because of its addition of new strands over time and the way readers and writers modeled their understanding of the genre on particular configurations of strands, lacks a single monumental writer that serves as ideological lynchpin—there is no urban fantasy equivalent to Tolkien, Lovecraft, or Robert Heinlein (to use Wolfe's examples). Instead, a number of writers have emerged and provided worldviews around which parts of the genre have formed—possible candidates could be de Lint, Hamilton, Gaiman, Butcher, and Miéville. This adds to the impression that the genre is divided or—since these worldviews overlap to a considerable degree—exists on some sort of spectrum (see, for example, Irvine's spectrum outlined below).

As a genre develops, writers have to relate to the genre worldview in some way. In his discussion of the other three genres, Wolfe observes that

> the dialectic of the relevant genre seemed to define itself in recapitulation of, or reaction against, the world-views of these central figures, [offering] two possible routes for later writers: expansion of discourse to the edges of genre and beyond, or collapsing of the discourse into an increasingly crabbed and narrow set of self-referential texts.[78]

New writers are not only faced with the possibility of braiding the available strands into new combinations; they have to decide whether they will follow in the footsteps of the defining figure or turn their back on the ideological lynchpin and forge their own path. Miéville's *The City and the City* is an example of a novel that, to use Wolfe's words, expands its discourse to the edge (and possibly beyond) of fantasy and urban fantasy by situating the fantastic doubleness of its interlaced city-states in the active unseeing and political reality of its citizens: instead of being supernaturally separated, the cities are kept apart by fiat. The pervasive feeling of magic comes from very peculiar social rules, in a novel that can be read as either fantasy or urban fantasy. The notion of two city-states being able to exist geographically interlaced while separated by the inhabitants' ability to willingly unsee the other city is fantastic, impossible, and yet Miéville crafted an elegant murder mystery based on that premise. Ben Aaronovitch took the strand of the investigator and wrote a series of police novels in which the hunt for criminals and the workings of magic are both subjected to an utterly modern, rational, and scientific approach (the Rivers of London series, 2011–present). Max Gladstone created a secondary world which displays all the problems of late modernity and global capitalism while brimming with fantasy features such as magic, demonic contracts, enslaved gods, undead vampires, and living gargoyles (the Craft Sequence, 2012–present). At the same time, the book market remained full of novels published in urban fantasy "uniform" over this period: novels with covers that look if not identical then at least very similar. An image search for *"urban fantasy" cover* yielded page after page of book covers in dark shades of purple, blue, and green with predominantly dark-haired female figures armed with swords, guns, or magic, suggesting a narrow view of what urban fantasy should look like and deal with. (The pattern was striking when I first tried this in 2013. Ten years later, the tendency is weaker but remains much the same.)

The genre has reached for the borders and experimented with its many possibilities, while maintaining a hard core of "self-referential texts."[79] Not all writers have either expanded or collapsed their discourse as far as possible; much of urban fantasy exists between the two extremes, exploring the many ways that the strands of the genre can be braided, knotted, and woven together. Wolfe describes a spectrum of genre writers, ranging from authors who "strive to free genre material from genre constraints" to those who "recycle familiar tropes and effects" not in an attempt to enter into dialogue with previous writers but "simply [to] echo them." Between these poles are the vast majority of writers who test the possibilities of a genre without "contesting its terms."[80] Urban fantasy has not quite reached that stage yet, but the past ten or fifteen years have seen a movement in that direction. What "true" urban fantasy is still depends on whom you ask, on what part of the spectrum they are familiar with, on what strands and combinations of strands they prefer.

Urban Fantasy Research in the 2010s

Scholars began to take real interest in urban fantasy from the early 2010s, an interest that quickly exploded. 2012 saw the publication of a book on spirituality in science fiction, fantasy, and urban fantasy (based on a doctoral thesis)[81] and a journal article on urban fantasy and place, focusing on Gaiman's *American Gods*.[82] Clute's *Encyclopedia of Fantasy* entry was updated,[83] and an essay on urban fantasy was published in *The Cambridge Companion to Fantasy Literature*.[84] In this essay, now a frequently cited source in urban fantasy scholarship, Irvine presents urban fantasy as a spectrum that stretches between two poles: the stories of "the fantastic city" and the stories of "real or almost-real cities in which fantastic events occur."[85]

Other noteworthy scholarly texts from the years that followed include Young's chapter on urban fantasy in her *Race and Popular Fantasy Literature* (2015), in which she introduces the idea of "sub-urban fantasy" in which the supernatural might come from what lies underneath the city or in its past;[86] and my own "Urban Fantasy: A Literature of the Unseen" (2016), in which I analyze various ways of describing or defining the genre and identify what they have in common.[87] In 2019, the first scholarly anthology on urban fantasy was published. *Gender Warriors* (edited by U. Melissa Anyiwo and Amanda Jo Hobson) analyzes gender roles in the genre, with contributions slanted largely toward the proto-urban fantasy strands and the strands of vampires, investigations, and tough female characters. The editors nominate Hamilton's

Anita Blake series as the "foundation of contemporary urban fantasy" and describe it as a blend of horror, detective/crime fiction, romance, and fantasy.[88]

Urban fantasy research began to explore a number of angles during the decade, such as urban fantasy for children and young adults,[89] the use of space and place,[90] and the relation between urban fantasy and paranormal romance.[91] Not least, urban fantasy set in London has received critical attention.[92] Further doctoral theses have been defended, at least one of which has so far been published.[93] Research into urban fantasy has, in other words, blossomed during the last decade. Whether this will continue and develop in the same way that research into its sibling genres has remains to be seen.

CHAPTER THREE

UNSEEN PEOPLE

Fantastic literature is full of creatures that stay out of sight. Vampires, werewolves, fairies, and ghosts move among the members of mundane society, invisible, in disguise, or hiding in the dark. They are common characters in urban fantasy stories, which reveal glimpses of their unseen lives. Other unseen characters are not as magical: the people who are mostly ignored, passed by, quickly forgotten. These are the homeless, disenfranchised, and outcast, who live on the fringes of modern society;[1] but they are also the secret rulers of society, those powerful and influential enough to reign unknown. This chapter focuses on unseen social groups that are constructed as part of the supernatural domain, mainly concentrating on people on society's unseen margins but also addressing the unseen masters that control society in secret. Whether the magical reality is situated with the poor and powerless or with the rich and influential, urban fantasy tends to build part of its supernatural world in a way that draws attention to social hierarchies and inequalities. The unseen people of the genre are thus a key aspect of its social commentary.

The supernatural domain is often kept out of sight from the inhabitants of the mundane domain. A common way to describe the domains is in terms of what John Clute calls "wainscots" or "wainscot societies" in *The Encyclopedia of Fantasy*.[2] The supernatural domain "occurs under our floors, behind our skirting boards (hence wainscots) or in the margins of our lives."[3] It is predominantly related to the mundane domain in one of three main fashions, according to Clute: (1) the nature of the wainscots' inhabitants may distinguish them from the mundane domain; (2) they "may *seem* visible to the world, but in fact conduct their true lives in private"; and (3) the wainscots can, for all intents and purposes, constitute a separate space from the mundane domain.[4] The first way in which the wainscots can be related to the mundane domain include beings that are not seen because they are, for instance, tiny, or fairies, or ghosts. Examples include Mary Norton's The Borrowers series (1952–82), in which families of small human-like beings live hidden in an English house; Charles de Lint's *Jack of Kinrowan* (1995; consisting of *Jack, the Giant-Killer*, 1987, and *Drink Down the Moon*, 1990), in which the cap from a fairy creature gives the protagonist the ability to see the fairies who live in modern Ottawa; and Paul Cornell's Shadow Police novels (2012–16), in which a group of police officers accidentally develop the ability to see supernatural creatures. Creatures who seem visible but hide their true lives (the second way wainscots can be related to the mundane domain) include supernatural beings who look like ordinary people: any number of vampires and werewolves pretending to be humans fall within this category, as do magic users who keep their magic secret. Examples are numerous and range from J. K. Rowling's Harry Potter books (1997–2007) and Cassandra Clare's Mortal Instruments (2007–14) to Jim Butcher's Dresden Files (2000–present) and Tanya Huff's Blood Books (1991–97; 2006). These forms of secret organizations of supernatural beings also constitute the premise for the World of Darkness role-playing games (White Wolf Publishing, 1991–2004[5]), in which vampire clans, werewolf tribes, and mage factions vie for influence over the world without being noticed by mainstream society. The third and final of the main fashions that Clute lists comprises the many examples of supernatural domains that are almost or entirely separated from the mundane domain.

Cases when the supernatural domain is situated within the context of society's outsiders can be read in terms of social fields. In such cases, the "wainscots" do not constitute the "interstices in the dominant world"[6] so much as they are segments of society that the mainstream does not see. One way of gaining a deeper understanding of such social divisions is to adapt Pierre Bourdieu's concept of social fields. In sociology, the social field is a unit of analysis when working to understand an empirical material and can be understood as a system of relations between groups of people and institutions in competition for something they have in common.[7] Fields are generally smaller than an entire society, although Bourdieu also suggests that there is a "social field in its entirety."[8] They can vary in extent and complexity; since Bourdieu introduced the concept in the 1970s, studies have been carried out on, for example, the field of economic power, of religious power, of university professors in Paris, of authors, of politics, and so on.[9] Societies in fiction, such as those in urban fantasy, can likewise be read in terms of their social fields, but they have to be analyzed with the understanding that a fictive society can (and likely does) differ drastically from actual societies and social fields. The concept still provides a tool for exploring the social structures and relations in the story.

A common social structure in urban fantasy is to have a field of society's mainstream culture set in opposition to a field of social outcasts. Being unseen by the mainstream society means having little or no so-called *capital* in the mainstream social field, thus having no power and position within that field. Capital is a characteristic of Bourdieu's social fields that makes them particularly useful when discussing unseen people in urban fantasy. Different types of capital are relevant for different fields. In short, Bourdieu postulates that apart from economic capital (wealth in terms of money, income, property, and so on), there are also specific forms of capital that have value within each given field. Capital has a double function: it is what people in a field compete for, and it is what they compete with, and one form of capital can be translated into another. In the readings below, I will focus mainly on two types of capital that characters have or lack and how that positions them in relation to the field of the mundane mainstream society. The types are *cultural capital*, that is, knowledge, culture, and educational credentials (in particular the knowledge required to survive in a particular field); and *social capital*, that is, networks, friends, and contacts.

In the following section I address three ways in which unseen and outsider groups in urban fantasy stories can be used to comment on society and the ways in which we lead our lives in modern society. The first text shows how dividing society into two fields makes it possible to criticize the mainstream way of life and offer a positive alternative. The second example looks at how the seen and unseen fields follow different rules and value systems and the challenges involved in entering the mainstream society. In the final text, the supernatural domain consists of seen outcasts, but the focus on it draws attention to other, unseen, groups.

THE UNSEEN MARGINS OF SOCIETY

Since the 1980s, many urban fantasy writers have moved their narrative focus to the vulnerable members of society. Authors such as de Lint, Neil Gaiman, and Mercedes Lackey (with various coauthors) have offered fantastic perspectives on the homeless of our modern world, while, for instance, Tad Williams, K. J. Bishop, and Catherynne M. Valente have provided views of the poor and underprivileged in secondary worlds.

Brian Attebery proposes a possible fantastic foundation for fantasy set in the modern world, locating it in a tendency to "unsee" street people,

> those people with too many layers of clothing, who launch into improbable conversations with strangers or with the empty air, who make us uncomfortable without threatening us, so that our usual response is to avert our eyes and walk past. In that averting of eyes is the rationale for [claiming that a contemporary city can also be a fantasy world]. Why can't an invisible person be doing impossible things?[10]

Out of sight is out of mind. As we avert our eyes, we perform an everyday act of magic by bestowing invisibility upon these people. Behind Attebery's suggestion lies one of the most intriguing features of fantastic literature, the ability to turn a metaphor into something actual: the metaphorical invisibility of the unseen street person turns into magical invisibility. And, in urban fantasy, these invisible people often do a great many impossible things.

Creating a supernatural domain by turning people with little standing in mainstream society invisible is one of the most direct ways of commenting on society in urban fantasy. There is a tendency to take no heed of and look away from people who are positioned at the bottom of a social field, who lack any type of capital in it and are therefore "considered a negligible quantity."[11] In urban fantasy, this tendency is used to open up a space for the fantastic in a modern environment, a space where impossible things can happen. This space for the fantastic also draws attention to the characters at the bottom of—or even outside—the field that constitutes mainstream society, as well as to the social fields in which they exist. The following three analyses use Bourdieu's fields to demonstrate ways in which urban fantasy stories about society's outsiders can contribute to the social commentary of the genre.

Through a Social Mirror in Seattle

Megan Lindholm's *Wizard of the Pigeons* (1986)[12] is a story about having different identities in different social fields, and it offers a harsh criticism of mainstream society as a field of conflict and violence. In the novel, the unseen field of social outsiders is a domain in which magic is possible, and it is characterized by cooperation and support. The protagonist, the eponymous Wizard, finds himself beset by forces that attempt to trap him in the mainstream field, bereft of his magic as well as of any social position or power.

From its outset, the novel presents the supernatural domain as the default perspective for the reader and then pairs the supernatural with the field of outsiders. The very opening sentence of the novel establishes Seattle as a fairy-tale or fantasy setting, estranging the city for the reader: "On the far western shore of a northern continent there was once a harbor city called Seattle." The paragraph then mentions that it is called "The Emerald City" (recalling its namesake in the Land of Oz) and concludes with "In that city, there dwelt a wizard" (1). The reader is invited to interpret descriptions and events that follow as supernatural rather than mundane. "Details that could be arranged into a sociological study of the homeless," Attebery observes, "contribute to the fantasy because they are interpreted as magical."[13] These details still describe a field of social outsiders (not all of them are homeless, and some have chosen this field over mainstream society), but the field is intertwined with magic. Wizard sleeps in a squat together with pigeons and stray cats; relies on dumpsters for food, clothes, and other possessions; and thinks about these aspects of his life in terms of magic. His contentment with this existence reinforces the identity between the supernatural domain and the field of outsiders. When people in the mainstream field fail to see him as someone who lacks capital in their field, this is similarly described in terms of, and thus ascribed to, Wizard's magic.

The perspective changes when Wizard is drawn into the mainstream field by a combination of the malevolent force called Mir (named after the initials MIR, found on a footlocker hidden in Wizard's squat) and the attention of the waitress Lynda. As Lynda brings light to his squat, it exposes the squalor there (132). The mainstream perspective reveals that his ability to pass as a member of the mainstream field is not a magical power at all but simply his ability to dress, behave, and speak in a way that makes him accepted. This ability to negotiate a social field is what Bourdieu terms *habitus*, "a system of structured, structuring dispositions [. . .] which is constituted in practice and is always oriented towards practical function."[14] Wizard has simply learned, in his previous mainstream life as Mitchell Ignatius Reilly and as the outsider Wizard, a system that helps him produce the correct practices for the field; there is no magic involved. The two social fields offer two opposing perspectives on Wizard's life—as a wizard with magical powers and as a homeless Vietnam veteran—but also on the world, as supernatural or as mundane. In one field, Wizard has cultural and "magical" capital and a position near the top of the field; in the other, he has virtually no capital apart from what little social capital his relation with Lynda provides.

The social field of outsiders in Lindholm's novel is characterized not only by the supernatural but by giving and trust. To Bourdieu, social fields are arenas of conflict or struggle over control of capital,[15] but the outsider field to which Wizard and his fellow Seattle wizards—Rasputin, Euripides, and the powerful Cassie—belong is not characterized by struggle. It is a field based in trust, gifts, and helping others. From that perspective, it is a city that boasts "a great friendliness that fell upon strangers like its rain" (1), and Cassie tells Wizard that "[t]he city will take care of you. And you take care of the city" (61). In the field of outsiders, Seattle provides what Wizard needs in its dumpsters, even though its gifts should not be taken for granted. Wizard knows "never [to] quite trust all [his] weight to it. Nor lose faith in it" (13). There is a sense of responsibility in Wizard's trust: as long as he does not grow complacent, does not expect or demand, the city's magic will provide. Its favor is a gift freely given, not something to control or force. The wizards' magical capital is similarly a magic of giving and of trust. Cassie imparts wisdom through stories; Rasputin can tell a wizard what rules govern their magic; and Euripides can play the tunes that run through people's heads. His power also lets him give a magic wish to a little girl with leukemia in the hope that she will remember it when she needs it (46–48). Wizard has a paper bag that never runs out of popcorn to feed his pigeons. He mysteriously receives knowledge that has value to other people and must convey this knowledge to them whenever they are moved to find him (5–7). The wizards also support and help each other, beyond their magic, members of a social field of giving.

Wizard's view of how cultural capital is related to economic capital is the opposite to how these kinds of capital are seen in the mainstream social fields. To Bourdieu, "[t]wo major competing principles of social hierarchy [. . .] shape the struggle for power in modern industrial society: the distribution of *economic capital* [. . .] and the distribution of *cultural capital*."[16] The distribution of economic capital is the "dominant principle of hierarchy" and the distribution of cultural capital is the "secondary principle of hierarchy."[17] In other words, modern people judge social standing by money and wealth as well as education and cultivation, but wealth is more important. This is not how Wizard sees the hierarchies. In the field of outsiders, survival requires appropriate knowledge and practices (cultural capital and mainstream habitus) rather than money (economic capital). Cassie has shown him how to pass as a member of mainstream society, and he observes how other street people fail in this regard (43). Wizard considers them "not too bright" but, he reflects, if someone has to be *taught* the strategies required to pass in the mainstream, they would not be able to learn them (43). They lack the cultural capital required to be a successful "scavenger," the habitus that allows one to spend a day browsing in a bookshop or have a cup of coffee in a café. Whether they have the money to buy a cup of coffee is of less interest to him—in fact, Wizard never allows himself to carry more than $1 in change. Knowledge rather than money is important in the outsider field; cultural capital is "the dominant principle of hierarchy" in the field.

The central conflict in *Wizard of the Pigeon* is the combined attempts, by Mir and Lynda, to force Wizard into the field of mainstream society. After Mir's first attack, Lynda sees Wizard as a homeless person, causing him to abandon the trust his field requires and doubt himself and his magic. This doubt, and Lynda's encouragement, sets off his shift into the mainstream field, in which his cultural capital is not acknowledged and his magic does not work. Instead of having a high position in the social field, he finds himself at the bottom. Lynda presents him with a future in mainstream society:

> You could stay with me [. . .], get your head straight, and then you could look for work. Or sign up for unemployment or welfare or something. Honey, I look at you and I can see you weren't made for this kind of life. You're the steady, reliable type. (159)

She paints a picture of a life conforming to the "doxa"—Bourdieu's term for the often tacit and unquestioned rules that govern the struggles in a field[18]—of the mainstream field, a life as a couple living together in an apartment, in which economic capital is key. Her list of possible sources of income reveals her hierarchy of preferences: income from being employed, benefits for being unemployed, or support from a social welfare system. First, however, he must "get [his] head straight," that is, accept the field's doxa and forget about the outsider field. Her argument is insidious: he did not belong to his former field because he was not suited to it; he is the kind of person suited to the mainstream field, being "the steady, reliable type."

The dominance of economic capital in the mainstream field emphasizes Wizard's position at the bottom of that field. Lynda's description of the mainstream field parallels Bourdieu's portrayals of a field as an "arena of struggle."[19] Any "arena of struggle" has two distinct dimensions: a struggle over the distribution of capital and a struggle over the definitions of what form of capital is most legitimate for a particular field.[20] Lynda gives the impression that economic capital is the most valuable resource in the mainstream field, and other descriptions in the novel contribute to that impression. From his perspective as street person, Wizard observes numerous examples of how economic capital is made the requirement for entry or participation. A restaurant requires a minimum expenditure per patron (8), but the understanding is always that you must have more economic capital than you are required to spend; for all that Wizard claims that "the price of survival is the price of a cup of coffee," being recognized for having no more than that, he is not even allowed to buy the coffee (13, 101–2). Since Wizard has "withdrawn from the major economic system [. . .] a long time ago" (102) to live in a field which prioritizes cultural capital and gift-giving, he is devoid of the field's dominant type of capital.

In Lynda's words lies the power to define what kind of capital is of greatest value in the field, to convince Wizard of the mainstream doxa. *Symbolic power* allows her to "impose classifications and meanings as legitimate."[21] It is through this symbolic power that she redefines the worth of Wizard's squat and possessions, reducing the place and things that he values to something unwanted and unwantable. She calls the cat that keeps Wizard company "a nasty looking animal" (133) and when she suggests he move in with her, tells him that he could leave most of his possessions behind "and not take a loss" (159). This power to decide what has value and what does not "creates a form of *violence* that finds expression in everyday classifications, labels, meanings, and categorizations,"[22] and

Lynda uses this symbolic violence to persuade Wizard to accept the doxa of the mainstream field.

In her application of symbolic violence, Lynda defines the mainstream field not only as an arena of struggle but as an arena of *violent* struggle. Bourdieu points out that symbolic violence is not secondary to physical violence[23] and refers to it as "the gentle, disguised form which violence takes when overt violence is impossible."[24] Wizard lacks the symbolic power that symbolic violence requires and must resort to overt violence, encouraged by both Mir and Lynda. Mir attempts to bring back Wizard's memories as a former Vietnam soldier, feeding him violent dreams and luring him into a series of fights with armed opponents. Lynda manipulates him into a confrontation with her former lover, to improve her own standing and social capital, and possibly—Wizard is uncertain—to find validation in having two men fighting over her (123, 137). Without any other resources, Wizard has to rely on the combat skills of his former life, almost letting them turn him into a killer again, underscoring how violence is necessary to survive in the mainstream field.

The field of mainstream society thus comes across as brutal and cold, in its focus on economic capital and violence as well as in comparison to the field of outsiders. The nonstruggle and focus on trust and giving practiced by Wizard and his fellow wizards accentuate how ungenerous and socially impoverished mainstream society is, and how easily manipulated by Mir's evil. Attebery summarizes the core challenge of the plot: "Instead of being Mitch Reilly, whose past is unbearable and whose future is hopeless, he must find a past and future for Wizard."[25] To do so, Wizard must break free from the mainstream field and its restricting doxa of modern capitalism, violence, and the struggle for dominance, and instead commit to the generosity and trust that is the field of outsiders. It is in this fight for freedom that we find the novel's biting criticism of modern society.

Shifting Fields in Newford

De Lint's Newford stories comprise more than a score of novels, short-story collections, and chapbooks, published since the late 1980s. The stories are set in a fictive North American city afflicted by the social failures of Western modernity and home to a wide range of fantastic beings. Its supernatural domain covers everything from "the clearly impossible to the almost possible"[26] and includes a significant element of indigenous characters and mythic beings.[27]

One of the many recurrent characters in the Newford stories is Maisie and her family, which consists of several rescued dogs and Tommy, a man with an intellectual disability whom she has also "rescued." In a suite of three short stories—"But for the Grace Go I" (1991), "Waifs and Strays" (1993), and "The Pochade Box" (1994)[28]—Maisie makes a challenging transition from living in a squat to being employed, in education, and domiciled. Her perspective reveals strengths and weaknesses with both the mainstream social field and the field of social outsiders, or, as she calls them, the people of the day and the night.

Maisie explicitly constructs a binary society with two main social fields. She offers different descriptions of these fields, referring to the inhabitants of mainstream society for instance as "regular citizens," "straights," or "taxpaying citizen[s]" ("Grace" 327, 328; "Waifs" 15), while the people in her field are "down-and-outers" ("Grace" 328). Her social construction casts the field to which she belongs as a dominated group, even though her tone is partly ironic, suggesting an ambivalence with regard to the fields' hierarchy. Her most distinct formulation of Newford's social fields is in terms of night people and day people:

> You could say it's divided up between the haves and the have-nots, but it's not that simple. It's more like some people are citizens of the day and others of the night. Someone like me belongs to the night. Not because I'm bad, but because I'm invisible.

> People don't know I exist. They don't know and they don't care [. . .]. ("Grace" 326)

Maisie overtly denies that the important distinction is access to economic capital, and in "Waifs and Strays," she stresses how it is not just a question of homelessness, even if that is part of it. It is a cultural division, with a "subculture [. . .] of street musicians, performance artists, sidewalk vendors and the like" ("Waifs" 34). To the "straights" of the day field, people in the night field are "invisible"—ignored and unseen.

This social invisibility is both metaphorical and magical in Newford. In "The Invisibles" (1997), the narrator sees people whom others cannot see. He reflects that "[t]he world is full of invisible people and our not seeing them's got nothing to do with magic. The homeless. Winos. Hookers. Junkies. [. . .] The list is endless."[29] These people are unseen, like Maisie and the people in the night field, but in Newford, perceived and literal (magical) invisibility shade into each other. Unseen is unseen regardless of reason. Literal invisibility in Newford is never far from the unseeing to which people without capital in the mainstream field are subjected.

This construction of Newford society as divided into the fields of day and night captures de Lint's concern with social issues of modern, urban society. His focus is almost entirely on how the night field is "populated" as a result of society's many ills, such as poverty, drug addiction, child abuse, and lack of care for the mentally impaired.[30] Maisie ran away from home as a result of abuse, Tommy was discharged from a mental institution because no one would pay to keep him there, and other Newford characters suffer or have suffered similar hard fates. The stories try to offer glimmers of hope in this urban darkness, but unlike Lindholm, de Lint does not construct the night field as preferable, only more magical. I have argued elsewhere that the division into day and night people captures the overall social structure of Newford and overlaps with two other divisions, between magic and mundanity as well as (wild) nature and culture[31]—the supernatural domain is mostly physically located to urban wilderness and inhabited by night people.

The arc that runs through the three short stories about Maisie traces her attempt to rejoin the day field, with the help of a social worker. The texts establish as Maisie's core value the happiness she experiences with Tommy and the dogs and how this value comes into conflict with the doxa of the day field. The central story, "Waifs and Strays," tells of her failure to integrate her pride and self-sufficiency with what she misinterprets as a required habitus for the day field. Each story opens with Maisie having problems but being too prideful to ask for help: in "But for the Grace Go I," she receives what she interprets as a supernatural death threat; in "Waifs and Strays," her day field life makes her and her family miserable because she has too little time and energy left for them; and in "The Pochade Box," she wrestles with how to give a person with an intellectual disability the time, energy, and attention they need without having time on her own to recuperate.

Both fields share the hierarchy that ranks economic capital above cultural capital. Maisie explains how valuable the right cultural capital is to make it in the night field. She knows how to get hold of discarded books and free food ("Grace" 323, 333) and, like Lindholm's Wizard, she keeps clean and well dressed enough to be accepted in "places where they don't let in bums" ("Grace" 330), aware of the advantage it means to be accepted by day people. Knowing how to scavenge only gets her so far, however. Cultural capital has to be transformed into economic capital (money) because unlike Wizard, Maisie is part of the mainstream economy. She must pay for things such as clothes, a post office box, and magazine subscriptions (Tommy enjoys playing with figures cut out of magazines). Her money comes from using her knowledge (cultural capital) to find discarded items and identify those that she can sell—she has learned this "cash for trash" operation from the "bag lady" who took care of Maisie when she first entered the night field.

The day field requires different cultural capital than the night field, and its doxa, in particular the rule that people have a formal place of abode, requires more economic capital. The night field requires some money to get by, but Maisie has cultural capital enough to exchange for the necessary funds. The day field, however, is portrayed as a space of productivity, in which the accumulation of economic capital is required to maintain even a minimum position in the field.

> We've got a real place to live in—a tenement on Flood Street just before it heads into the Tombs, instead of a squat. I had a job as a messenger for the QMS—the Quicksilver Messenger Service [. . .]. Evenings, four times a week, I was going to night school to get my high school diploma.
>
> But I just didn't see it as being better than what we'd had before. Paying for rent and utilities, food and for someone to come in to look after Tommy, sucked away every cent I made. Maybe I could've handled that, but all my time was gone too. ("Waifs" 21)

Maisie's division of society is evident from the opposition between the "real place to live" and the "squat" and is underscored by the spatial difference; they do not live in the Tombs, the place of the night field, anymore but outside it, if only just. In fact, they still live on the same street as before, only a minimal distance, spatially as well as socially, from their old life. Her job gives her the economic capital required to stay in the day field, and the evening classes allow her to gain the symbolic capital a high school diploma provides. (The text is vague about the exact value of this diploma in the day field, but it is implied to have importance to maintaining or advancing one's position in the field.) The conflicts between the different values of her current and previous life are then introduced in the second paragraph. The day field values a "real place to live," including the ability to pay for food and utilities, over time spent with one's family; Maisie feels that she has to choose between the values, the doxa, of the day field and her own need for family and self-reliance.

Part of Maisie's portrayal of the day field as having doxa emphasizing values such as a "real place to live," utilities, and food that has been bought rather than donated—and the ability to pay for these—over time with one's family comes from her need for self-reliance. This need runs through all three stories, but she expresses it most succinctly in "The Pochade Box": "It's hard [. . .] Always asking, always standing with your hand out" ("Pochade" 300). In the night field, she had the capital required to keep her family alive as well as together. In the day field, the energy and time required of her to even manage to stay in the field leaves too little to satisfy her family's needs. Each story teaches Maisie that it is acceptable to ask for and accept help. A social field does not have to be (just) an area of struggle. "If we're not here to look out for each other, then what are we doing here?" the artist Jilly Coppercorn asks Maisie ("Pochade" 300). It is a caution against a modern society in which self-reliance is more important than solidarity and empathy.

It is no coincidence that it is Jilly who delivers this central message. Artists, musicians, and writers are given a special place in the Newford stories, on the border between night and day. These types of characters are common in urban fantasy[32] and I have previously observed how art spans the domains of night people, magic, and wild nature in Newford.[33] Ultimately, Maisie's stories suggest that constructing a binary opposition of night field and day field is a mistake. This is foreshadowed already in the first story, when Maisie realizes that conforming to the day field will not be easy because "I'd probably never fit in completely, and I don't think I'd want to" ("Grace" 338). The solution to balancing her need for time with her family and earning the economic capital required by the day field is to cut down on working and studying and instead utilize her cultural capital from the night field, taking up the "cash for trash" operation together with Tommy and the dogs. "We're spending a lot more time together," Maisie explains, "and everybody's happier" ("Waifs" 45). She has realized that happiness can lie in accepting that she has access to more than one field, and through Jilly, de Lint suggests that a social field does not have to be an area of struggle.

Seen and Unseen Outcasts in Johannesburg

Zinzi December, the protagonist and first-person narrator of Lauren Beukes's *Zoo City* (2010),[34] is a "zoo," a person who is magically connected to an animal (in Zinzi's case a Sloth—animals are capitalized, their species is also their name). As a zoo, she is a social pariah, forced to live in an inner-city slum in Johannesburg, called Zoo City. The novel's central plot concerns Zinzi's being hired to find a missing teenage starlet and the complications that ensue.

Critics have read *Zoo City* in terms of its comments on various aspects of contemporary South African society, including issues such as post-apartheid inequalities,[35] hydrological and other urban infrastructures,[36] and social marginalization and invisibility.[37] They have mainly focused their analyses on the important connection between the fiction and the actual society by which it is inspired and on which it comments. In contrast, my reading addresses the construction of seen and unseen social fields in the novel, with much less emphasis on the connections to actual South African society.

Lindholm and de Lint place the supernatural domain within groups at the margin of society but in *Zoo City*, Beukes uses the supernatural to create the novel's marginalized people. They are the zoos, people who have caused another person's death and are now inexplicably and inextricably connected to an animal. This global phenomenon began thirty years before the novel's present, but the text provides no definitive explanation, although it is made clear that extensive research has been carried out. The animals appear to be of all species—various types of mammals, insects, reptiles, and arthropods are mentioned in the story—and beyond a certain distance, physical separation of animal and human causes them both unbearable pain. Killing the animal leads to the person's death within seconds, by the incomprehensible and inescapable effect called the "Undertow." Because the reason for becoming animalled is having caused someone's death, however, zoos are easy targets for discrimination and social exclusion.

The zoos constitute their own social field of outcasts in *Zoo City*, rejected by mainstream society and forced to live together, spatially and socially, regardless of their social background, nationality, and reason for being animalled. The animals are visible expressions of guilt, "personal scarlet letter[s]" (60), and therefore grounds for mainstream prejudice and exclusion. Before she acquired Sloth, Zinzi was a well-educated young woman from an upper-middle-class family. Her substance addiction resulted in her brother's death during a drug deal gone wrong, and even though she served a prison sentence and went through rehab, being a zoo prevents her from re-entering the social field of the mainstream. Zoo City, a slum with run-down apartments and dilapidated buildings, is the only place where she can find a place to rent, regardless of her cultural capital and appropriate habitus.

Being animalled is to belong to a group that mainstream society feels justified to shun and mistreat. The South African setting invites a parallel to apartheid,[38] but zoos can be read as any group that is socially excluded on the basis of identifiable characteristics, something that various episodes in the novel demonstrate. Zinzi describes several episodes of "animalism" (a term created to provide a parallel to "racism"), ranging from "aggressive hoots from passing cars" whose drivers are "so cloistered in suburbia that they don't get to see zoos" to restaurants with anti-animal policies (18, 115, 127). The situation in other countries is reported to be even worse: in India, zoos count as a caste below untouchable, and in China, they are executed "on principle" (99, 15). In one instance, zoos are even proclaimed not to be human (76). Animalled people are not just ignored in the mainstream field; they are actively and occasionally aggressively excluded.

Instead of employing fields that situate an unseen fantastic domain in a (largely) unseen social field, Beukes creates an entirely fantastic and very much *seen* field. Unlike the mainstream citizens of Lindholm's Seattle and de Lint's Newford, the inhabitants of Beukes's Johannesburg are all well aware of the supernatural presence in the world. The zoos are presented as a high-visibility group.[39] The consequences of this high visibility can be seen, for example, in the various ways in which Zinzi is treated by non-animalled people, including pity, condescension, and countercultural "adoration" by rebellious "Goth kids" (127). Other reactions to the zoo visibility come across through the different voices and text types that are interspersed in Zinzi's narrative. These alternative voices show the fascination zoos hold for members of the mainstream field. Documents from a variety of sources provide alternative perspectives on the zoo phenomenon, including an excerpt from a book of interviews with animalled prisoners in different countries; an entry from an online database for documentaries ("Get Real: The Online Documentary Database") on a film about an animalled warlord; an abstract from a scientific paper about the Undertow; and an entry from a dictionary of "animalled terms." These inserts reveal strong anti-zoo sentiments (a particularly vehement example can be found in a comment to the "Get Real" entry), but they also illustrate the considerable social awareness of and interest in this group. These alternative voices build a larger social world, and their perspectives are invariably from the mainstream. From these perspectives, zoos are the targets of curiosity, hostility, or contempt, but they are not dismissed or ignored. Animalled people might be excluded from the mainstream field, but unlike Lindholm's wizards and de Lint's night people, they are certainly not unseen.

By connecting the zoos with other marginalized groups, *Zoo City* calls into question what it means to have caused another person's death and, by extension, cautions us to judge anyone too quickly. Surrounding and overlapping the zoos' field are several other fields of marginal or excluded people, and the high visibility of the zoos draws narrative attention also to these other fields. Refugees and immigrants from other African countries are portrayed as being afforded little capital and no acceptance in the mainstream field. The field is represented by Zinzi's Congolese lover, Benoît, and his friends, many of whom are also animalled and live in Zoo City. The story of Benoît's attempts to find his lost wife and family bookends and weaves through the main narrative, and through him, the conditions of refugees gain narrative prominence. Zinzi describes how his feet look like "knots of driftwood" when she introduces him in chapter one. "Feet like that, they tell a story. They say he walked all the way from Kinshasa [to Johannesburg] with his Mongoose strapped to his chest" (7). Even before Zinzi tells her own story, she starts telling Benoît's, and it is a story that invites the reader to consider what being animalled says about a person. Because of the Mongoose, the Congolese man is forced to be a resident of Zoo City, marked as a killer, but his gnarled feet tell a story about a man who has undergone great hardships to find a place where he can make a safe life for himself. Jocelyn Fryer observes how the reader is encouraged to empathize with Benoît and suggests that imagining his hardships makes it difficult to see him as an outsider.[40] Eventually, he reveals why he was animalled. His family was attacked by the Forces démocratiques de liberation du Rwanda. Benoît fought off the attackers, killing two of them, while his wife and children escaped into the forest, before he was subdued and subsequently tortured. What it means to be animalled, never a straightforward issue in the novel, becomes impossible to say. Is Benoît's Mongoose a scarlet letter of guilt or a red badge of courage? Is he simply a refugee, or is he a strong, resourceful person who keeps fighting, against all hope, to reunite his family, despite having been tortured and shunned by mainstream society? Through his story the reader is asked to reevaluate the equation of animal and guilt and is encouraged to reevaluate any judgment passed on refugees.

Refugees are not the only marginal fields that are made visible to the reader through their connections to the zoos. To work off her drug debts, Zinzi is coerced into using her writing skills, acquired at university and in her former job as journalist, to create advance-fee scams for a criminal organization. She takes a certain pride in her work as the scams strike at people in the mainstream field and the global North, explaining that she has become "a master builder in the current affairs sympathy scam." Her scams are "all topical. All rooted in the hard realities of the world" (37). One of these scam letters, constituting the novel's second chapter, details the hardships of children working in a Congolese coltan mine. Although the details are invented, there is truth to the situation, something emphasized in the text as the email appears without previous context. The reader does not know in what way the email is part of the diegesis, at what level of fictionality it exists. The explanation is withheld for another two chapters before it is revealed as a fiction within the fiction, but a fiction with a kernel of truth, rooted in current affairs. Despite its double fictionality, the plight of the children forced to work in coltan mines calls attention to the actual situation. Coltan, the email explains, is used for the production of cell phones, computers, video games, and other electronics for the people in the global North (25–26). The field of coltan production and its powerful and powerless actors is put under a spotlight, exposing it as a system of oppression in which everyone who uses electronics, everyone in a modern society that relies on electronics, is implicated. Zinzi's email scams also expose a field of scammers, a criminal system with people who ruthlessly try to benefit from their marks' compassion or greed. It is a field in which the scammed are only a resource, drawn in by wanting to do the right thing for the wrong reasons. The American couple who want to help a victim do so in the hope of a massive reward but lose all their savings. A journalist who wants to write a story about the fictitious coltan mine would be "milk[ed] [. . .] for visa application fees" had not Zinzi intervened (184). Neither the criminals who scam nor the people who fall for their scams are cast in a positive light but are held up for the reader to see and reflect upon them.

The refugees, enslaved children, and scammers are only some of the many unseen groups that constitute social fields within and around the zoo field and made visible in Beukes's novel. The text shows us a field of drug abuse, including the sellers and the users; criminals, people in prison, and ex-cons; the homeless and street people, sleeping rough or in shelters; and all those involved in the "hustle economy" of uncertain, irregular, often informal, employment.[41] At the same time, the text reveals how this visibility is an illusion. Lisa Propst persuasively argues that there are limits to what the reader knows about the characters and cautions against reading the setting of *Zoo City* as a "knowable space."[42] The multiplicity of voices in the text helps set limits to what the reader can know; the narrow narrative focus of Zinzi's perspective and the viewpoints of the many inserted documents never coalesce into one picture. They do not explain the world, but, as Andy Sawyer puts it, they "[show] us how it feels to live there."[43] Ultimately, making the unseen parts of society seen might not mean that they become known to the reader, but through the stories that are told, stories such as Benoît's, at least they might be felt.

• • •

When the mundane mainstream field is contrasted to a supernatural field of outsiders, it says something about modern society. Urban fantasy needs somewhere to situate the supernatural in the modern city society, and the invisible outsiders provide one possibility, regardless of the author's ideological or political agenda. Each of the three authors above construct their mainstream somewhat differently, with different agendas. Lindholm portrays it as violent, selfish, and greedy, de Lint warns against the dangers of self-reliance and promotes solidarity, and Beukes challenges its prejudices and ignorance. What they have in common is a shifting of perspective and focus. The reader is asked to see the socially unseen and to pay attention to, reconsider, and ponder modern society. Because any details that are actually true can be ignored as fiction, however, the readers are above all encouraged to feel for people who belong to other fields than themselves and, perhaps, see the unseen people around them.

In the next section I turn to four ways in which unseen masters in urban fantasy stories can be used to address social problems by concretizing their causes and ascribing them to individuals rather than to abstract forces of modernity. In the first text, an unseen struggle for control of a city reveals social forces that threaten the cohesion of urban society. It is followed by three shorter readings of varieties of secret masters. The first is an example of how unseen rulers can be used to represent the repressive power of late-stage modernity. The second demonstrates how the unseen field can represent wielders with so much power and wealth that they can control society without really having to care about it. Finally, I briefly address a role-playing game in which the world is constructed with ruthless, supernatural beings who run it in secret and where the natural domain is portrayed as being kept in the dark and deprived of power and influence.

UNSEEN DOMINATION

Not all unseen people lack capital, position, and power in the mainstream field; some actually dominate it in secret. According to Clute, wainscot societies that "*seem* visible to the world, but in fact conduct their true lives in private" are connected to the "notion of the secret organization which covertly governs the world."[44] Wainscots are thus linked to a group of other concepts, such as "Fantasies of History,"[45] "Secret Masters,"[46] and "Immortality."[47] Together, these entries paint a picture of stories in which powerful, often immortal, beings run society behind the scenes, manipulating society for their own benefits or toward their own goals. This form of unseen domination of society can be found to varying degrees in several urban fantasies. It occasionally provides the very foundation for the plot, such as in Diana Wynne Jones's *Archer's Goon* (1984) or Tom Pollock's Skyscraper Throne trilogy (2012–14) but is often just one small facet of the urban fantasy world.

In Bourdieuan terms, these unseen masters have a large amount of power within particular fields or even in the entire social field. This power is commonly wielded indirectly through representatives in key positions, especially when economic capital provides the main basis for power. Immortal or long-lived beings, such as vampires and werewolves, as well as ancient organizations can amass enormous wealth by just investing their money over many decades or centuries. Some stories present beings with power to directly influence people and events, through mind control or the ability to change reality itself to their liking. Such powers can be coupled with the ability to erase the memory of those who come into contact with them, thus maintaining the unseen status. These secret masters may already have won the struggle in the social field without anyone noticing, or they are part of a field of their own, in which stakes are higher and the resources required to participate in the struggle are beyond the mundane (and mortal) members of society. In the first example, however, the unseen control of people is part of an attempt to dominate a city, a piece of a greater conflict.

An Unseen Battle for (and against) Control

The City We Became (2020)[48] by N. K. Jemisin is a tale about the struggle for control over people but also over forces that could tear apart the fabric of urban society. The novel is the first instalment of Jemisin's Great Cities Duology (followed by *The World We Make*, 2022) and tells the story of how New York City awakens as a living city. This awakening turns a handful of people into avatars, living embodiments, of the city's boroughs and of the totality of the city itself. They have to fight the extradimensional (and more than a little Lovecraftian) Enemy that tries to kill the infant city as it comes alive. The plot centers on the attempts by the Enemy—manifested in the form of the Woman in White—to gain control of New York and on the avatars' attempts to understand and accept what is happening while defending themselves and the city.

The Enemy's key strategy is to gain control of the city's inhabitants and spaces by planting white, tendril-like growths on people and in various places. These tendrils affect people's behaviors, and sites where they grow become favorable for the invader. The white, almost translucent, tendrils are imperceptible to normal people but visible to the avatars. Their increasing presence in the city is likened to a spreading infection (353, 366) or infestation (40, 364). Through the tendrils the Enemy can see and hear what goes on in the city (107, 330, 365), but the way they exert control over people is by making them compatible with the Enemy's agenda. The Woman in White explains that the "guide-lines," as she refers to them, "don't *control* people, not precisely. They just . . . guide. Encourage preexisting inclinations, and channel the energies from same into more compatible wavelengths" (331). These "preexisting inclinations" and "compatible wavelengths" prove to be dispositions that drive people apart rather than bring them together, such as racist, xenophobic, and homophobic stereotypes. The Enemy seeks to shatter the city's sense of unity and of being special. White tendrils also attach themselves to spaces that are generic and general (and use them to attack the avatars) in its fight to wreck the city's identity. Enemy control thus emphasizes aspects of modernity that drive uniformity and decrease a sense of community.

The novel uses the police force as a vivid example of how certain people are easier for the Enemy to "guide." From the very beginning of the novel, the police are portrayed as largely racist. All the avatars except Aislyn, the avatar of Staten Island, are people of color, and the distrust between the police and people of color is a recurrent theme. Bronca (the Bronx) and her colleagues do not expect the police to help them in a case of breaking and entering (263–64), and the primary avatar of all of New York City repeatedly voices his fear about being harassed or worse because he is Black (e.g., 2, 3–4, 5, 9, 11). The inside perspective offered by Aislyn's police officer father displays similar distrust. He has arrested a Puerto Rican man who was just sitting in a car ("I figured he was dealing") and admits to having invented an assault charge because he "needed something to run him in on" (92–93). The Enemy's physical attack on the primary avatar, by monstrously merging the bodies of two officers, eventually results in its "taint" spreading through the city (12–16). But it is also made clear that the Enemy's control does not extend to the entire police force. A dispute between police officers with and without tendrils demonstrates how the city has its own champions on the force, and its own ability to control them, by affecting how the officers see the avatars (393). The dispute captures the struggle between the forces that hold the city together and those that tear it apart. It also reminds the reader that police officers should not be prejudged, either; not every officer is a racist or under the Enemy's influence.

The Enemy tries to gain control over the city by directly confronting and attempting to win over the avatars, with only limited success as their boroughs' natures carry over into the avatars' habitus. The avatars act as embodied metonyms for their respective borough—or, in the primary's case, the entire city—each standing for its borough as a whole. The stereotypical behavior of a borough's inhabitants, the borough's quintessential nature, expresses itself as the habitus of its avatar. Bourdieu's habitus, the system that structures someone's behaviors, could be thought of as "a 'sediment' from the past that functions to make practical 'choices' that are 'non-conscious.'"[49] The Bronx, for example, is described as the part of New York that "gets hit the hardest by everything. Gangs, real estate scams, whatever. Hard people, too, if they came through any of that . . . so in a lot of ways, this is the heart of

New York. The part of itself that held on to all the attitude and creativity and toughness that everybody thinks is the whole city" (135). This description—attitude, creativity, and toughness—aptly captures Bronca's disposition, and like the borough she embodies, that disposition—her habitus—is the result of past life-experiences that determine her reactions and choices. This habitus centered around creativity and toughness makes Bronca impervious to the Enemy's attempts to convince and threaten her—Bronca refuses to compromise with her artistic principles and will not let herself be intimidated. In a similar manner, the nature of Staten Island is portrayed as fearful and alone, and thus open to being influenced and eventually controlled by the Woman in White. Aislyn's habitus is the most detailed, showing how her current actions are determined by the "sediment" from her past:

> everything in her life has programmed her to associate evil with specific, easily definable things. Dark skin. Ugly people with scars or eye patches or wheelchairs. Men. The Woman in White is the visual opposite of everything Aislyn has been taught to fear, and so . . . even though intellectually Aislyn now has proof that what she's been seeing is just a guise, and that the Woman in White's true form could be any*thing* . . .
>
> . . . Aislyn also thinks, *Well, she looks all right*. (333)

Aislyn's habitus is repeatedly summarized as nothing being more important to Staten Island than *belonging* (e.g., 287, 409). It also comprises a deep-seated feeling that the borough is not really a part of the city, is not wanted by the rest of the city, and does not want to be a part of the city (e.g., 105, 134, 286). The avatar's behavior and choices are based on insecurity, fear, resentment, and self-sufficiency, already inclined to prejudge by "easily definable" criteria. This habitus does not only embody Staten Island but represents insularism, narrow-mindedness, and bigotry. Despite the compassion and empathy with which Aislyn is presented (her habitus is a result of being "programmed" and "taught" rather than some innate ill will or small-mindedness), the borough and its avatar are nevertheless easy prey for the Woman in White. The whiteness of the Enemy merges with the idea of whiteness as a culturally valorized category.

By accentuating whiteness, and the valorization of whiteness that is part of the Staten Island habitus, the text suggests that whiteness could be read as a form of capital. The avatars are endowed with a range of different forms of capital. Both the Manhattan and Brooklyn avatars have significant economic capital, but the avatars' main power lies in various forms of cultural capital. Brooklyn is a well-connected politician with a past as a popular rapper, the Queens avatar is a skilled mathematician with an advanced degree, Bronca is an artist, runs an arts center, has a doctorate, and teaches at a community college. Their positions in various cultural fields are mostly good. The only avatar presented as having no capital, no position in any social field, is Aislyn. The thirty-year-old woman has no degree, a job "off the books" in a local library, and still lives with her parents. And unlike the other avatars, she is white. Whiteness has been introduced in Bourdieu's theories in different ways, for instance by arguing that whiteness is somehow intrinsic to the concept of cultural capital.[50] This does not fit Jemisin's novel; apart from Aislyn, the avatars are people of color and are presented as having access to cultural, economic, or social capital. But whiteness could also be considered as a form of capital in its own right. Berndt Reiter proposes that there is "racial capital" to be added to forms of capital described by Bourdieu and that in, for instance, the United States, a "white" person holds more racial capital.[51] Seung-Wan (Winnie) Lo similarly extends cultural capital to race by what she calls "white capital," the power that comes through the norms and privileges of whiteness.[52] To the extent that Aislyn holds any capital at all, it is capital that is similar to the racial capital described by Reiter and Lo. She belongs by virtue of being white, of having white capital. In this, she is similar to the Woman in White. This form of the Enemy also appears to possess "white capital"—enough to gain Aislyn's trust but also to have influence over the rightwing "artists" that visit Bronca's arts center. Through their visit and subsequent social-media campaign, the Enemy seeks to undermine the artistic capital of the center (and of Bronca) by exchanging their white capital into artistic capital: maneuvering the center into exhibiting pieces that are "racist, misogynistic, anti-Semitic, homophobic" as well as really bad art (141) would mean that artistic capital would be transferred from Bronca to the Enemy's representatives. They ultimately fail, a reminder that "racial capital is not as fungible as the other capitals"[53] and cannot easily be translated into cultural capital. Bronca and her colleagues refuse to exhibit the group's works, thus refusing to accept that racial capital has value in the field of art. The Enemy's attacks through racial capital eventually come to naught, although its whiteness proves valuable on Staten Island. Instead, its most successful strategies rely on economic capital.

The greatest threats against the New York avatars come from indirect attacks against them and their boroughs, attacks using economic capital and the power conferred by such capital. As mentioned, Bourdieu argues that the distribution of economic capital is more important than the distribution of cultural capital in determining social hierarchies.[54] In *The City We Became*, this economic dominance is put to the test. The two main attacks leveled against the avatars themselves are the attempt to buy influence at Bronca's arts center and the attempt to have Brooklyn evicted from her home. The Woman in White offers a major donation to Bronca's arts center, a donation that comes with two conditions: the center must provide exhibition space for some of the bigoted "art" that the rightwing group has produced, and they must remove all works featuring art by the primary avatar (photographs of his graffiti). The sum is large enough to convince the center's board members to accept the conditions, and only a social-media campaign mounted by Bronca and the center's staff—a display of social capital—forces the board to change their minds. The second indirect attack is aimed at Brooklyn and her family. By creating an administrative loophole, the Enemy, under the guise of the Better New York (BNY) Foundation, manages to buy Brooklyn's two brownstone houses and then seeks to have her and her family evicted. Drawing on her political acumen and connections—her political and social capital—Brooklyn manages to stay the eviction process. Her victory is only partial, however, and the legal battle over her houses becomes a central plot thread in the duology's second novel. She counters the first blow but the fight is not over.

These two attacks are part of a greater strategy to defeat not only New York but all living cities by destroying the unique character of cities and thus weaken and even kill them or prevent them from awakening. Behind the economic attacks on Brooklyn and Bronca is the BNY Foundation. This organization is a front for the Enemy, acting out long-term economic strategies to destroy New York's special identity and the particular identities of the boroughs. In the Bronx, the avatars discover how a building that housed not only an iconic burger restaurant but also dozens of apartments has been bought and demolished by the BNY Foundation, in order to build "overpriced, ugly-ass *condos*" (356). The foundation is a subsidiary to the international company with the candid name Total Multiversal War, LLC (360). Through this company the Enemy has been able to use economic capital to set "[l]ittle corporate traps in every city, in case it comes to life. Infusions of cash here and there to weaken cities before they're born—maybe keeping them from being born?" (361). The Enemy has amassed worldwide economic power, which not even the combined cultural and economic capital of the New York avatars can withstand, even though they manage to dodge the attacks against themselves. At the end of the first novel, New York has not fallen, but the Enemy is still present, powerful, and dangerous.

Jemisin's novel establishes an unseen social threat defined by a habitus characterized by ideas of belonging and fear of people who are different; whiteness as capital; and the dominance of economic capital over cultural capital. It also celebrates the notions of community, diversity, and uniqueness. As such, it encourages readers to consider the often unseen mechanisms that have impact on society and its development and thus demonstrates how urban fantasy can draw attention not only to the unseen people of our cities but also to the unseen forces that shape those cities.

Harassed by Late-stage Modernity

Archer's Goon[55] constitutes an example of how unseen masters control society through their supernatural powers. Referred to by Farah Mendlesohn as "one of the most complex and sophisticated of Jones's novels,"[56] it is similar to several other of Jones's stories in that it deals with secret rulers of the world (e.g., *The Homeward Bounders*, 1981; *Hexwood*, 1993; and *Deep Secret*, 1997). The Sykes family discovers that their town is controlled by seven siblings with immense magical powers. These siblings have divided the various areas of society between them: Archer, the eldest, controls electricity, gas, and banking, Shine controls crime, Dillian law and order, and so on.

Their power is the power of modernity and its systems and they wield it with complete control. The siblings do not merely influence or rule society; they have total control over their particular areas, to the point where Archer can spy on the Sykeses through lightbulbs and the television set, and Torquil, who controls music, can cause the instruments in their home to play music. They bring their powers to bear on the Sykes family in an attempt to coerce the father to do what they want. In a dystopian display of how modern society can harm its citizens, each sibling uses the capital they have in their respective areas to bring the family to their knees. Mendlesohn observes how "the siblings exercise their power by exaggerating the impact that the modern world can have on an individual's quality of life. When the siblings attack the Sykes family they do so through the power of the modern world."[57] The family is deprived of electricity and gas, is subjected to ceaseless musical noise, has its bank accounts frozen, and the street outside is turned into a trench. The children are harassed by a band of hooligans, the mother is threatened with being fired, and the father receives a demand for thirteen years' worth of unpaid taxes. The siblings may have powers akin to magic, but they attack through their control of modern society, not with magic per se.

Through the unseen rulers in *Archer's Goon*, Jones turns the hierarchies and hidden power structures of modern society into a fantastic world. It is not only a world in which "the fantastic and the urban mundane are interwoven";[58] it is a world in which the fantastic arises from the urban mundane. The siblings' control is unknown by the town's population, with a few exceptions. Archer and his siblings have been read in terms of totalitarian control, not least in Kyra Jucovy's well-argued parallel between *Archer's Goon* and George Orwell's *Nineteen Eighty-Four* (1949)[59] but also, perhaps more chillingly, as a description of our modern society. Rather than interpreting the siblings as an authoritarian regime with sophisticated surveillance equipment, they can be read as "bureaucracy [as] the agent of magic,"[60] but, I would argue, they represent more than that. Together, the seven siblings control all four of modernity's institutional dimensions—bureaucratic surveillance, capitalist production, industrial manufacture, and the means of violence.[61] Marilynn S. Olson claims that Jones's work "captures the postmodern condition of life in Britain's cities, where few know why they are doing certain things, where elected authorities have merely the illusion of power, and where magicians (central government) appoint quangos to make disruptive magic in our streets."[62] And this is not just Britain's cities, nor a postmodern condition; I would suggest that the unseen rulers in *Archer's Goon* embody the complex systems of power, control, and surveillance that constitute late-stage modernity.

Unseen Power Struggles

Kat Howard's *An Unkindness of Magicians* (2017)[63] offers a different kind of unseen magical people with great supernatural, financial, and social power. The novel is set in the magical wainscot society that exists on Manhattan ("the Unseen World") and describes "the Turning," a recurrent event in which magical duels determine future standing in the field's hierarchy. The duels of the Turning redistribute power and influence among the Houses of the Unseen world, deciding which House rules, which new Houses can be established, and which Houses should be unmade. It is a story about the power struggles over economic and "magical" capital in a social field only seen by and accessible to people with such capital.

At the center of the social structure of the Unseen World are the Houses, which act as expressions of capital as well as of position in the social field. A House is a combined social, familial, and organizational construction, referring to the actual buildings and to the families that own them, as well as to people accepted as House members. The established Houses are described as nexuses of economic, magical, and cultural capital. Most Houses are committed to tradition, carrying names that evoke great magicians of story and history: Merlin, Prospero, Dee, and so on. The environments are described in terms of great wealth, emphasizing the various forms of capital available to them.

> House Dee in its architectural incarnation was old and elaborate, the kind of space meant to remind people that it, and its inhabitants, had been here a while and were likely to remain. Set-dressed to exude power and wealth, it was warm and baroque. Light glinted off crystal glasses and chandeliers. It shone on wallpaper rich in texture and color; it warmed the beeswax polish on the furniture. Establishment and tradition perfumed the air. (51)

This description does not only convey the appearance of wealth and power; it portrays a place that performs a role through its appearance. It is "meant to remind people" about its age and strength. It is "[s]et-dressed" to give an impression of having influence and economic capital. It is an environment that in itself is part of position-taking in the field, creating a particular atmosphere by "exuding" and "perfum[ing] the air" with the desired impression. Markers of affluence and tradition are combined, consciously avoiding the appearance of being vulgar or nouveau riche. This combination of power, money, and tradition pervades most homes of the Unseen World that are described, not only the Houses. The few exceptions are of central importance to the plot.

The behavior and value systems of the Unseen World mirror the economic, cultural, and magical capital expressed by their homes. The magicians' main concern is with their position in the social field of the Unseen World, that is, with power. The field's types of capital—economic, cultural, and magical—can be exchanged for one another depending on what resources the struggle requires. The right background, behavior, and connections are as important as how good you are at magic, and although you can buy a first-rate champion to fight your magic duels for you, no amount of money can compensate for having no magic, nor can it quite compensate for not coming from the right background. Laurent, who was born mundane but discovered that he could do magic, is acceptable (but barely) because he "came from money" and is friends with a Prospero (52). His is the role of the underdog, who struggles to attain a position in the field, something his background combined with his unexceptional magic skills makes difficult. The fact that he is Black does not help; the Unseen World is cast as conservative and with a racist slant: Laurent is the only Black person in the Turning, and he believes himself to be the first Black man allowed to establish a House (65–66).

The magicians of the Unseen World see themselves as so far above the mundane domain that they pay almost no attention to it, despite the fact that they depend on and remain part of it. Laurent asks a friend why the "Unseen *World*" is so small. "All of you live in the same few blocks, pretty much, and I'm the only new guy since I don't know how long. Aren't there other magicians anywhere?" (99) His friend's reply dismisses the rest of the world as unimportant, confirming an inward focus that sits at the core of the Unseen World as well as the novel at large. This confined world recalls the world of the unseen rulers in *Archer's Goon*, which Mendlesohn refers to as small and enclosed.[64] The two worlds differ in that Jones's world is a totality, with both the mundane and supernatural hemmed in together. Howard's world is one in which the supernatural domain of the rich and powerful turns its back on the much larger world around it. The plot does not affect the mundane population of New York (except for a bus accident when a spell goes wrong), and the worst crime that can be committed is to reveal the Unseen World's existence to the mundane domain. At the same time, the domains exist as part of each other, and magicians use mundane technology, ride in mundane cabs, and eat at mundane restaurants. It is also implied that they earn their money from mundane investments, becoming wealthy by combining magic and mundane skills (8), splitting their portfolios between "Unseen World concerns" and mundane investments (128). Mostly, however, the wealth of the Unseen World is simply there, neither questioned nor commented on, somehow seen as the magicians' due.

The Unseen World is framed as a social field of the powerful and affluent and can easily be read as a symbol of the super-wealthy of modern society. Although magic supplies a fair bit of their creature comforts, it does little to affect the mundane world. Instead, the magicians are the unseen privileged of society, endowed with limitless power and resources, moving and living among us but still entirely cut off from mainstream society. They are the people with impossibly expensive properties, involved in their private power struggles, and with almost absolute control of a mundane world that they mostly ignore, except when they need a taxi or good food. Ultimately, Howard's novel uses the unseen masters to criticize a modernity that created and accepts that the richest one percent of people hold almost half the world's wealth.[65]

Vampire Rulers in a World of Darkness

A more brutal form of capitalist power and explicit social influence by an unseen group can be found in the urban fantasy in which vampires are cast as secret masters of society. Vampires have been portrayed as wealthy and influential at least since Bram Stoker gave Count Dracula a peerage and enough wealth to buy a house near London, and by the 1990s, the idea that they walked among us with the power to secretly control our society had become commonplace. One notable contribution to the vampiric strand of urban fantasy during the 1990s was not fiction but a role-playing game.[66] White Wolf's *Vampire: The Masquerade* (1991)[67] by Mark Rein-Hagen casts the players as vampires in a dark, Gothic version of the modern world, a world ruled by unseen, supernatural beings.

The *Vampire* game is set in a world in which vampire clans strive to remain unseen while simultaneously modifying and controlling mortal society. A core part of the game concerns maintaining "the Masquerade," which consists of two parts. "[R]easonable secrecy and care was required" of all vampires in order not to "betray [their] continued existence," and "active steps must be taken *to change the character of mortal society*, and direct minds away from superstitious thoughts" (8, my italics). Through the concept of the Masquerade, the game establishes the notion of vampires as unseen rulers, hidden as a wainscots in human (urban) society and working to influence it. The rule book introduces seven vampire clans, some of which specifically try to influence mortal society. Examples include the Brujah, who want to overthrow social systems and often live with suburban families they have dominated (68); the Toreador, who specifically turn the greatest artists of all sorts into vampires, making them immortal (73); and the Ventrue, who "believe in good taste above all else," mingle with the mortal upper crust, and control powerful members of mortal society (75). Already these brief descriptions indicate how the game builds a world in which vampires are constructed as secret masters, manipulating the mortal domain from the shadows. (They are not uncontested—Rein-Hagen's book mentions several opposing and competing forces.) Accumulation of power through political, economic, and cultural capital within the mortal fields is not as valuable as capital in the field of the vampiric society, however. The importance of such capital is coded into the game mechanics through the statistic Status, which correlates roughly with age as well as physical and supernatural powers. The game thus combines power struggles in two fields, the mundane and the vampiric, and provides players with a massive advantage in the former.

As the game developed over time, this notion of social influence became more pronounced as part of the game world. Where Howard's magicians seem to keep themselves aloof from mundane affairs, struggling mainly over capital within their own field, the vampires treat mundane society as a chessboard. By the time the game supplement *A World of Darkness Second Edition* (1996)[68] was published, power struggles within both the human and the vampire fields had become central aspects of the game. The supplement describes Earth's continents in terms of what they look like in the game world, mainly focusing on vampire activity and society. Within the fiction, this world has developed largely under the control of the vampires, and they have shaped human history in a wide range of ways. In Britain they controlled Oliver Cromwell, made Aleister Crowley a deranged vampire, and influenced the government to destroy Glasgow's industrial base (54, 56). The ancient vampire Baba Yaga (a character borrowed from Slavic folklore) caused the fall of the Soviet Union and the withdrawal of Russia from the West (83). Mortal affairs become proxy wars for the vampire sects, such as when one sect instigates the military coup in Panama in 1968 and controls the country until an enemy sect manipulates the United States into invading in 1989 (34). Vampires also gain economic capital by controlling resources such as companies and organized crime (11, 15, 128). Few aspects of human society are left in mortal hands; humans are manipulated and controlled at every turn. This is an image of modern society as run by the ultimate conspiracy, where people are at best pawns, at worst nourishment.

To portray unseen vampire control of society as a major conspiracy has become common in urban fantasy. The near-immortality of vampires in combination with their prevalence in many stories have made it easy to cast them as secret masters with little concern for mortals. An example quite similar to the World of Darkness vampires is the Red Court of vampires in Butcher's Dresden Files. They maintain a range of political and financial influence all over the world until they are destroyed.[69] Other urban fantasy vampires have made themselves known to society at large, such as in Laurell K. Hamilton's Anita Blake, Vampire Hunter series (1993–present), Kim Harrison's Hollows series (2004–present), and Charlaine Harris's Sookie Stackhouse series (2001–13). These vampires are not unseen as a whole, although their influence is often hidden or unacknowledged. Their power is largely painted in terms of economic capital accumulated over a long time, a phenomenon arising from their longevity or immortality.

• • •

Urban fantasy's unseen people are groups who can populate the supernatural domain. They can represent the social powers that are imposed upon us from above, incarnations of the intangible and abstract forces that modernity's systems create, the gods (or demons) that we do not see but that appear to hold sway over us. Other unseen groups are those we know are there but often ignore, those who lack the capital necessary to take part in the struggles of our social fields. In urban fantasy, they are brought to the fore, made part of a magical life for better or for worse but always for the story's sake. Both groups offer alternative representations of modern life, new vantage points for us to consider society. What we see from those vantage points is largely up to us.

CHAPTER FOUR

UNSEEN SPACES

Unseen spaces are, in some sense, the most emblematic of urban fantasy's settings, not least because many stories need locations for the supernatural to hide. The bright lights of modern society may illuminate and reveal most of our surroundings—most, but not all.[1] Any modern city has spaces that remain out of sight for the majority of its citizens: dark underpasses and underground sewers, unlit alleys and abandoned factories, secret research facilities and exclusive clubs. In urban fantasy, such unseen spaces are constructed first and foremost as spaces for the supernatural, but as such, they are generally spaces that are also hidden from the mundane. The three types of unseen spaces that are addressed in this chapter reflect three reasons for why members of the mundane, mainstream society do not see them. Each reason, in turn, reflects some aspects of society. Through their constructions, these unseen spaces comment on or criticize society, but they do it in different ways. The fictional world is split not just into supernatural and mundane but into spaces of inclusion and exclusion. And for the stories to take place, there are always some characters who have the ability to cross that border, to see what others do not, and go there.

SOME NOTES ON SPACES

In my discussion of unseen spaces, I use *space* to mean neither just a physical area nor just the mental geography people have imposed on that area but both, a double perspective on social space. Any reading of spaces in fiction requires a brief preamble that deals with the issues of story-space and how spatiality is understood, because there is nothing self-evident about either of those concepts. Even something as basic as the term *space* needs explaining to avoid misunderstanding. In my analyses of unseen spaces, I use *space* to mean the fictional equivalent of what Edward W. Soja calls *Thirdspace*, a social construction of a location.[2] Soja distinguishes between three approaches—*Firstspace, Secondspace,* and *Thirdspace*—depending on what is in focus for the analysis. To think about Firstspace is to privilege the objectivity and materiality of space,[3] that is, to focus on what an area is like physically, in terms of dimensions, topography, hydrology, and such characteristics. Firstspace is the place without meaning and social context, whereas Secondspace comprises the "conceived" or mental geographies we project onto the empirical world (for instance through maps).[4] This is the focus on meaning that is imposed on an area through ideas such as national boundaries or neighborhoods or "usefulness." To understand the world as Thirdspace is to open up the duality of First- and Secondspace, to think of the world's spatiality as a complex of social, historical, and spatial interactions, beyond simply combining or synthesizing the two parts of the Firstspace/Secondspace duality.[5] It is to think of space inextricably linked to its social context. This is how I read the various unseen spaces below, not just as physical locations or social constructions but as both in a complex interaction.

In a discussion of fiction, it should be borne in mind that settings are not primarily depictions of actual spaces but are created as part of the storyworld. Unseen spaces in urban fantasy do not (necessarily) correspond to unseen spaces in the reader's lifeworld—they are constructed to be unseen within the fiction and unseen by a certain part of a fictive society (mostly the social mainstream that constitutes the mundane domain). They are part of the supernatural domain, and as such, they are what Daniela Hodrová calls *místa s tajemstvím* (places with secrets—Hodrová uses *place*, *místo*, where I use *space*).[6] In such places, the connections between characters and place are particularly strong, to the point where the two almost coincide. A *místo s tajemstvím* "carries the memories of all the beings that ever appeared in this place (their stories often make up an important part of the story)."[7] In this sense, the unseen spaces of urban fantasy are spaces with secrets, thick with story and linked to the unseen people who dwell there.

The unseen spaces hold secrets, and stories, and characters, and to read them means to explore them closely, not to gaze upon them from afar or above. Michel de Certeau offers two alternative positions for how to look at a city. The voyeur's perspective is gained by seeing the city from the top of a tall building, the city as totality or panorama or map. It is, to de Certeau, a visual simulacrum, a picture that makes it impossible to understand the practices of those who live down below.[8] It is also a way to ignore the "mobile and endless labyrinths far below."[9] This perspective, along with the maps that so concretely promote it, is uncommon in urban fantasy. Instead, the reader is given the perspective of what de Certeau calls "the walker," the perspective of the ordinary practitioner of the city down in the streets. "These practitioners make use of spaces that cannot be seen," says de Certeau, and although he refers to their failure to "read" the "text" of the city written by all their practices,[10] it also draws attention to how the walker's perspective is restricted, limited, unseeing. The unseen spaces of urban fantasy are largely constructed through the walker's perspective, from moving within the urban labyrinth, experiencing it as a social Thirdspace. In the following readings I therefore walk through the unseen spaces of some urban fantasies, to uncover their secrets and stories.

• • •

The remainder of this chapter examines three types of unseen spaces that are common in urban fantasy. Each type is examined and illustrated through its particular example, which is also discussed in a broader context. The Tombs in Charles de Lint's Newford exemplify spaces that are unseen because they are largely ignored by the mainstream society. For unseen spaces that are located in the darkness underground, Neil Gaiman's London Below serves as a point of departure. The spaces that are unseen because most people are kept out are exemplified by various spaces in Richard Kadrey's *Sandman Slim* (the first book in the Sandman Slim series, 2009–21).

SPACES UNWANTED AND UNSEEN

A certain kind of unseen spaces, the spaces of the poor and outcast, has spread from the nineteenth-century Gothic to urban fantasy. When the Gothic romances entered the cities, authors began to set stories in urban slums, replacing the labyrinthine passages of caves and castles with the mean, narrow streets of the city's unfortunate.[11] According to Robert Mighall, the Gothicizing of the urban environment resulted from a combination of several factors, including the use of unmistakably Gothic imagery and situations but also the application of a social perspective that presents older and poorer neighborhoods as disordered, obscured, and dangerous.[12] "The relocation of the Gothic in the modern city involved the city itself, or at least part of it, being Gothicized, and thus analogous to and appropriate for scenes of terror associated with earlier romance traditions."[13] Urban areas with old buildings, poor illumination, and twisting streets, as well as poverty, crime, and iniquity, were fictionalized (often suitably embellished) and turned into spaces where anything could happen, unseen by the reading middle classes.

The urban fantasy genre inherited from the urban Gothic the proclivity to construct particular areas as unseen spaces outside of the social mainstream and thus as spaces suited to the supernatural domain. Aliette de Bodard's Dominion of the Fallen series (2015–19) provides numerous examples of how urban fantasy can draw upon the urban Gothic. The novels are set in Paris six decades after a devastating magical war. Magical and temporal power rests in the hands of the Houses, social hierarchies as well as large edifices. The first novel, *The House of Shattered Wings* (2015), centers around House Silverspire, once established by the first Fallen angel, Morningstar. Silverspire's Gothic heritage is obvious: a huge complex of unused, abandoned rooms in "a series of buildings joined by a maze of corridors and courtyards, stretching across the entire Ile de la Cité."[14] The House even includes the Notre-Dame cathedral, one of the foremost examples of French Gothic architecture. De Bodard's version of the cathedral has been wrecked by the war, its stained-glass windows broken, and its altar "turned to rubble long ago."[15] Where the Houses, and Silverspire in particular, recall the edifices of Gothic romance, the war-torn city outside echoes the urban Gothic described by Mighall. The skies are perpetually overcast, the river black from ashes, monuments blackened by soot. The Grands Magasins lie devastated since the war, with still-active spells and "the ghosts and the hauntings and the odor of death [still hanging] like fog over the wrecks of counters."[16] The slums of the la Goutte d'Or district, in particular, resonate with the urban Gothic. Scenes of poverty are combined with dirt and disrepair. There are "[d]oors falling into ruin, repaired with flimsy wood; windows taped shut with patchworks or oiled papers; buildings where entire walls had collapsed, and where families still thronged, the wail of babies piercing the air like sword strokes: the misery of the Houseless, laid bare for all to see."[17] This is the unseen spaces of society, brought into view, a tangle of ill-paved streets in a space where human misery and physical decay combine, a space where very real social critique also recalls the dark, urban labyrinths introduced in the Gothic stories of the early nineteenth century.

Several other urban fantasy writers have similarly combined unseen urban spaces with the city's marginalized inhabitants. These spaces include not only inner-city slums but other spaces associated with society's less fortunate, the beggars and the rough sleepers. The Beggar King lives among rough sleepers under an overpass in Kate Griffin's *A Madness of Angels* (2009). Much of the story in Megan Lindholm's *Wizard of the Pigeons* (1986) is centered on the main character's squat on the abandoned top floor of a building. The protagonist in *Zoo City* (Lauren Beukes, 2010) lives in a dilapidated building in the ghetto reserved for the outcast "animalled" people. And in his attempts to shed critical light on the many social failures of Western modernity, de Lint frequently returns to the urban blight called the Tombs, which provides the touchstone for my discussion of unwanted, unseen spaces.

The Unseen Failure of Capitalism: The Tombs

The Tombs in Newford is a space that brings wilderness, magic, and alternative culture together to create one of urban fantasy's most emblematic unseen spaces. In my analysis of the relation between nature and culture in de Lint's Newford stories in *Here Be Dragons* (2013), I found that the domains of wild nature, the supernatural, and alternative culture intersect and overlap.[18] This commingling of domains that are all portrayed as existing somehow beyond the awareness of the city's domiciled, mainstream culture contributes to the construction of certain central settings as unseen spaces. The foremost of these unseen settings is the Tombs. In this inner-city wilderness, runaway children, street people, and drug addicts exist side by side with a range of supernatural creatures.[19]

The Tombs is constructed as a spatio-social divider, a space that is ignored and thus unseen by mainstream society but that provides a place to live for those who, for some reason, are forced to (or choose to) live in the social margin. How someone regards the Tombs—as safe or dangerous, as home or wilderness, as central to the city or not quite part of it—becomes a shibboleth for what group they belong to.

The history of the Tombs is one of unseeing as a result of both physical and social factors. Not all de Lint stories that feature the Tombs outline the history of the area, but some provide a fair amount of detail:

> a bunch of developers got together and planned to give the area a new facelift. I've seen the plans—condominiums, shopping malls, parks. Basically what they wanted to do was shove a high class suburb into the middle of the city. Only what happened was their backers pulled out while they were in the middle of leveling about a square mile of city blocks, so now the whole area's just a mess of empty buildings and rubble-strewn lots.[20]

The Tombs is a gentrification project gone awry, a failed attempt to capture more urban space for the well-off middle classes. This is a sharp warning about what happens when development of the public space is left in the hands of venture capitalism. It is a mistake to entrust what should be a long-term social project to short-term return on investment, because when things go wrong, there is no one there to repair the damage. The Tombs is a reminder for the people of Newford (and the reader) of what destruction can be wrought when public space is turned into an investment. The combination of eyesore ("a mess of empty buildings and rubble-strewn lots") and evident failure of the prevailing capitalist ideology of North America in the 1980s encourages the social mainstream to ignore, turn away from, and unsee the Tombs. The city administration and the domiciled inhabitants abandon the area. It is ignored by the mainstream, an unseen space that can be used for any kind of refuse that the city wants out of sight and out of mind.

Officially abandoned, an area apparently divested from the public spaces of the city, the Tombs becomes a dumping ground for that which people want to get rid of. Anything from broken cars and old car parts to bags of trash and even unwanted dogs are abandoned there.[21] It turns into a space of that which is unwanted, broken, useless, and thus becomes even more unseen, a rubbish heap people are aware of but ignore. But for people who are not part of the mainstream, such a space is also desirable, because it exists outside of the social economy and the social norms that govern most of modern society. The "decaying tenements and rundown buildings" offer

> [t]he kind of place to which the homeless gravitated, looking for squats; where the kids hung out to sneak beers and junkies made their deals [. . .]; where winos slept in doorways that reeked of puke and urine and the cops only went if they were on the take and meeting the moneyman.[22]

The Tombs is a social blindspot, but it also creates a space for a counterculture in Newford. It is not only a space beyond the social economy, where a place to live can be had for free, but also a space where other social norms can be ignored or challenged. It is neither protected by the law nor controlled by it. It is what Cat Ashton calls "the quintessential wilderness in Newford."[23] Rules and laws do not apply, at least not the rules and laws of mainstream society. Its social lawlessness makes it even more ignored, amplifying its unseen quality among certain social groups.

While constructed as unseen for some (large) parts of urban society, it is also constructed as a space distinctly seen by others. For those who see the benefits of the dilapidated area, it has positive connotations. It is described as being "stolen back from the neon and glitter" of the rest of the city,[24] not a friendly or pleasant or safe place but at least a refuge from an urban social space where some feel intimidated, uncomfortable, out of place. The squatter Maisie describes the Tombs as somewhere where people "are just putting in time, trying to make do," and death, whether by overdose, murder, or suicide, is a way to get out.[25] De Lint's stories offer both perspectives. The Tombs is portrayed as unseen by the social majority but also as a space very much seen and known by more marginalized groups, as well as by the reader.

By establishing the area as an urban space both seen and unseen, de Lint can turn the Tombs into a part of the supernatural domain. Magical and mythical beings hide there, beyond the gaze of the social mainstream, still visible to the various point-of-view characters—those who belong to the Tombs as well as those outsiders who dare venture out of the seen city into its unseen space. To one such outsider, LaDonna, the Tombs is a no-man's-land beyond civilization, a place where "[y]ou almost expect some graffiti to say, 'Here there be dragons.'"[26] The Tombs is given an atmosphere of magic, which remains even when LaDonna tries to modify it by referring to a biker gang called the Devil's Dragons. In various Newford stories, sinister or even malevolent supernatural denizens are found in the Tombs, including a group of bogans (fairy-creatures) instrumental in causing a war between Newford's European fairies and the native spirits of the surrounding country.[27] Other supernatural beings are harmless or even friendly but have found a place to exist, unseen by most humans. By constructing the Tombs as both seen and unseen, part of both the mundane and the supernatural domain, de Lint has established a setting where social criticism and urban magic are tightly interwoven.

The Tombs is possibly one of the most developed unseen spaces in the urban fantasy genre. It is predominantly actively unseen by the social mainstream, ignored because of its history, physical undesirability, and the unseen people making it their home. It shares many features with similar unseen spaces in other urban fantasies. Dean-Liathine McDonald makes a case for urban fantasy being a reaction to the widespread disenchantment with Western capitalism in the 1980s,[28] which would explain the many unseen spaces that are the result of capitalism's social failures. China Miéville, for example, describes the history of the suburb/slum Spatters in *Perdido Street Station* (2000) in a manner that recalls the Tombs: the suburb was originally built by "planners and money-men" but before it was finished, "the money had run out. There had been some financial crisis, some speculative bubble had burst, some trade network had collapsed under the weight of competition [. . .], and the project had been killed in its infancy."[29] Like in the Tombs, the mainstream urban society had turned its back while poor immigrants moved in. The area became known as a "ghost sector [. . .] where taxes and laws were as rare as sewage systems," an area disregarded even by the slum-dwellers inside the city.[30] Spatters sits at the edge of the city and establishes its own social services, of sorts, but like the Tombs, it is a final refuge for those who have nowhere else to go. Miéville does not need a particular space for his supernatural domain, but like de Lint, he offers an image of what can happen when urban planning is left to the vagaries of capitalism and what an urban space might look like when the social mainstream turns away, deliberately ignoring it.

The Threat of Unseen Waste

Some unseen spaces are unseen because they are where society leaves what it does not want, urban fantasy settings that are poisonous reminders of the self-destructiveness of modern society. Urban fantasy offers numerous and detailed examples of dumps and their waste that emphasize how society's refuse, when collected, creates spaces that can become obscenely unnatural and inimical to life. The Tombs sits at the middle of a spectrum of the unwanted and unseen, and Spatters, where unwanted people have created their own, unseen, society, exemplifies one extreme of that spectrum. At the other extreme are spaces dedicated to society's refuse. Supernatural encounters are set in waste dumps and scrap-yards, surrounded by that which society has put out of sight and out of mind. The Griss Twist industrial dumps in *Perdido Street Station* are described as beyond natural or human control, their own kind of space, "landscape[s] not urban, not created by design or chance," a "ruinous trashscape" in which the waste spawns its own form of life.[31] This is where the Construct Council came into existence, an artificial intelligence with its own agenda, ready to take up arms against the city's inhabitants. In Griffin's *The Midnight Mayor* (2010), a scrapyard with air that tastes of "salt and dry spilt chemicals, old bleach and broken bottles of things that should not have had the safety cap removed" provides the setting for the first direct encounter between the protagonist and the malevolent Death of Cities.[32] In Robert Weinberg's Horizon War trilogy (#2: *The Ascension Warrior*, 1997), the main characters fight a climactic battle against overpowering odds in a dump for hazardous waste. Weinberg describes a nightmarish hell on Earth, whose very air holds an "ever-present corrosive chemical mist [that] caused horrible damage to exposed skin and eyes."[33] These spaces do not only caution against capitalism but also serve as reminders of how our late-modern economy has become shortsighted and self-destructive and that unseeing is society's way of dealing with the dangers posed by our own waste.

Sometimes ignoring is not enough to unsee the pollution caused by industrialism and capitalism. In the animated series *Arcane: League of Legends* (Riot Games/Fortiche, 2021–present), based on Riot Game's fictional world for *League of Legends* (2009), the city of Zaun is polluted by industries largely owned and operated by its sister city, Piltover. Zaun's dark and dirty slum is unseen by the light, airy Piltover by being located in a deep crevasse, away from the light. The subject for the next section is those spaces that are unseen because they are hidden where they cannot be seen—under ground.

UNSEEN UNDER GROUND

Even though the unwanted unseen spaces might be ignored, they are still significantly present in the cityscape or landscape, visible to de Certeau's voyeur from their panoramic viewpoint. The unseen spaces underground are only visible from within, accessible to the bold or unfortunate walker who ventures down into the dark maze. For everyone else, they are not just unseen but unseeable, unknown as much as ignored. They offer a dark reflection of the domain above ground, impossible rather than possible, more fantastic than modern, a subterranean past to the surface present—a symbolic underworld below the living city. Stories about journeys into the underworld, as a mythical hell or realm of the dead or as an undiscovered, subterranean country, are as old as literature itself, and there is no room here to provide a comprehensive history of the theme.[34] The focus of this section is on the subterranean spaces that are constructed as unseen by and unknown to mainstream people who dwell on the surface and that thus provide space for the supernatural domain.[35] Gaiman's novel *Neverwhere* (1996)[36] is set in what may be urban fantasy's quintessential underworld, London Below, and provides my central case in an examination of the unseen spaces underground.

Some scholars consider subterranean passages and underground tunnels to be prominent features in urban fantasy,[37] and underground spaces are certainly popular settings in the genre. In the first Anita Blake novel, *Guilty Pleasures* (1993), Laurell K. Hamilton locates much of the action in a vampire lair deep underground. The denouement of N. K. Jemisin's *The City We Became* (2020) is set in a chamber off the New York subway system. In Lisa Goldstein's *Dark Cities Underground* (1999), the subway systems of the world's major cities are connected in a World Below charged with myths. The tunnels under Malmö central station are central to the plot in Nene Ormes's *Udda verklighet* (2010), and Finnish supernatural creatures have gone into hiding in caves deep under Helsinki in *Underfors* (2010) by Maria Turtschaninoff. But the single city with the most urban fantasies set in its system of dark tunnels is without a doubt London, and *Neverwhere*'s London Below is probably the most well-known urban fantasy version of the city's subterranean spaces.[38]

Unseen Above, Unseen Below

The unseen spaces underground can overlap with the ignored unseen spaces of the surface, but they are also unknown because they are unknowable and impossible. Hadas Elber-Aviram reads London Below as "constantly shifting and unmappable," thus "[p]itting itself against [the] grid-based version of London" of the Underground map that is reproduced in the novel.[39] The topography is impossible to understand in terms of the "handy fiction" of the map (10) and is located explicitly beyond the possible. *Neverwhere*'s apparently immortal and definitely sinister assassins, Mr. Croup and Mr. Vandemar, live deep underground in

> the cellar of a Victorian hospital, closed down ten years earlier because of National Health Service budget cutbacks. The property developers, who had announced their intention of turning the hospital into an unparalleled block of unique luxury-living accommodations, had faded away as soon as the hospital had been closed, and so it stood there, year after year, gray and empty and unwanted, its windows boarded up, its doors padlocked shut. (71)

The pattern recalls both the Tombs and Spatters, an unwanted and derelict urban space created by public and private failure, a monument to the unreliability of venture capitalism. The narrative then follows the rain water that leaks through the rotten roof and drips through the empty wards, down to the basement, where there are "a hundred tiny rooms" and the floors are "covered with a thin layer of oily rainwater" (71–72). In a rare case of direct address to the reader, the narrator continues the downward movement:

> If you were to walk down the hospital steps, as far down as you could go, [. . .] you would reach a small, rusting iron staircase [. . .]. And if you went down the staircase, and traversed the marshy place at the bottom of the steps, and pushed your way through a half-decayed wooden door, you would find yourself in the sub-cellar, a huge room in which a hundred and twenty years of hospital waste had accumulated, been abandoned, and, eventually, forgotten. (72)

The description makes it clear that the subcellar is an unseen space of waste, forgotten and ignored. It parallels the unwanted and unseen spaces discussed above in that respect. What is different is the journey downward, distinguished by the second-person address. The abandoned hospital is portrayed in great detail before we are invited, in the subjunctive (because it is assumed that we would not go there), to go down into its basement, "as far down as [we] could go." And when we have reached the bottom, as far down as possible, we are asked to proceed. We leave the world of the possible and enter a domain of the *im*possible, going *further down* than we could go. In this paragraph, Gaiman leads us, by means of a rusting iron staircase, from the familiar, mundane domain (in which hospitals are closed down and developers pull out) to London Below, the supernatural domain of *Neverwhere*, a place of the forgotten past further down than we can possibly go.

Descent into Avernus

Descending into the dark maze beneath the cities of urban fantasy can be to descend from the possibilities of the natural domain into an impossible underworld or otherworld. Irina Rață observes how *Neverwhere* parallels a Christian cosmology, associating London

Below with Hell.[40] Not every undercity is as clearly an underworld as London Below is, but they have in common a challenging return journey, and few protagonists come back unchanged. In the ancient stories, a journey into the underworld, *katabasis*, is always complicated and almost invariably comes with a caution: getting down is easy, getting back is hard. Already Virgil's Æneas is warned about the easy descent into and difficult return from the underworld, Avernus.[41] London Below is populated by those who have slipped through the cracks of London Above and have failed to return, and *Neverwhere* is the story of Richard's quest to escape. Once he succeeds, Richard realizes that the perfect life he returns to in London Above no longer interests him, and he descends once more into London Below. Even when he is allowed to return, he has become part of the impossible underworld. Other urban fantasy examples show a similar pattern. In Ben Aaronovitch's Rivers of London series (2011–present), Peter Grant's spirit travels to the distant past while his body asphyxiates in the darkness underground, and he escapes, but mentally scarred and changed by the experience.[42] In the sunless realm under Helsinki in Turtschaninoff's *Underfors*, Alva discovers her true identity as princess of Finland's hidden fairy folk and never returns to her life above. Avernus waits below the city, ready to change those who journey there.

The urban fantasy underworld is entered via some sort of liminal space, part of the surface but still verging on the underworld. The lair of Croup and Vandemar lies below the basement in an abandoned hospital. The alley where Richard first meets the Marquis de Carabas is a liminal space, situated on the border between Above and Below, and the Marquis brings Richard even further down, through a manhole at the edge of the alley. The most typical way of entry into the underworld, in London and elsewhere, however, is the subway system. David Pike argues that the urban transport system, especially in its underground form, plays a large role in fantastic narratives set in versions of familiar (actual) cities as a threshold between natural and supernatural domains,[43] describing the subway as "a prominent, if not the sole, threshold" between the domains.[44] The gaping tunnels that lead off from the subway stations can be portals into the undercity, or mysterious doors can offer passage between the mundane and the supernatural. The subway trains can themselves be supernatural entities, bringing protagonists from one domain into the next, such as in *Stalking the Unicorn* (Mike Resnick, 1987), *Something from the Nightside* (Simon R. Green, 2003), and *Dark Cities Underground*. The urban sorcerer Matthew travels on the *idea* of the last train for the evening to meet with a clan of artistic magicians in their underground demesne in *A Madness of Angels*. The nameless protagonist in "The Third Rail" (Aaron Sterns, 1998) undergoes a gruesome rite of passage on a subway platform, to become accepted by the mysterious, brutal city that takes care of its own. And in *Neverwhere*, the Underground is a zone that exists in both domains, both mundane and supernatural, both above ground and below it. Once he is part of London Below, Richard cannot pay to enter the Underground, nor does the barrier keep him out (59); the caution to "Mind the Gap" is relevant to travelers from Above and Below alike but mean very different things (141); and what are names of stations in London Above are names of perils and entities Below: the deadly Night's Bridge (instead of Knightsbridge), the fallen angel called Islington (instead of Angel, Islington), and the dangerous shepherds of Shepherd's Bush, to name a few. Entering the subway, in London or elsewhere, can be the first steps of a descent into Avernus.

The History Below

Entering the underground domain can also be a journey back into the city's history. Walking down is to walk into the past. Walter Benjamin describes how the city street would take a flaneur into a vanished past that is not their own but that remains a time of childhood.[45] Unlike streets, underground passages do not conduct the walker to innocent childhood times but lead them into the city's past. In London urban fantasies, the various tunnels underneath the streets—old bunkers; covered rivers and sewers; underground train lines, roads, and the subway system—are often used to evoke a sense of London-ness in fictive Londons,[46] but all cities have some of their history underneath the buildings and streets of today. Reflecting on cities and time in *The Culture of Cities* (1938), Lewis Mumford remarks on how cities are a "product of time" and that "[l]ayer upon layer, past times preserve themselves in the city."[47] To Mumford, this layering is the result of the material components of the city being preserved over time with the new being added to the old without completely erasing it. Cities become palimpsests over time, with layers of past under a present surface. Originally referring to the way in which traces from previous texts were left behind when parchments were reused, the term "palimpsest" has come to be employed metaphorically to "describe the partial erasing and constant overworking of sites and buildings over time."[48] Elber-Aviram's suggestion that urban fantasy often adopts a "palimpsestic model of the city as a paradigm for its fictional cityscapes"[49] parallels Helen Young's understanding of (sub)urban fantasy as "suppressed history of modernity resurfacing."[50] Urban fantasy shows how modern society confronts that suppressed, subterranean past in supernatural terms. Actual cities contain layers of their previous incarnations as memories kept under ground, often well known and accessible, but in urban fantasy, the buried past often provides building blocks for the unseen, unknown underground settings.

Neverwhere's London Below is a jumble of London's history. Old structures remain accessible, like Croup and Vandemar's subcellars under the Victorian hospital and the equally Victorian sewers. But bits and pieces of old time also drift down into the underworld. There are Roman soldiers camped out by the subterranean Kilburn River (89–90), the London smog of bygone days remains in pockets of old time (229), and the labyrinth at the bottom of London Below contains "alleys and roads and corridors and sewers that had fallen through the cracks over the millennia, and entered the world of the lost and the forgotten" (308). Divided into baronies and fiefdoms, with people fighting with spear and quarterstaff while wearing old-fashioned clothes and armor, London Below resists the modernity of its Above reflection.

The unseen underground in urban fantasy is the unseen past. The tunnels are the results of a historical need for spaces below ground, but they are also the literary scions of Gothic forbears, such as the labyrinthine tunnels and dark passages of Ann Radcliffe, Horace Walpole, and Matthew Lewis.[51] The underground hides societies lost from the surface, such as the Quiet People, who have lived for generations in deep tunnels under London in Aaronovitch's *Whispers Under Ground* (2012), the mysterious "skookin," inhabitants of the Old City that lies underneath Newford in "The Stone Drum" (De Lint, 1989), and the secret community of New York Downsiders in the novel of that name, who are forbidden all contact with the people of the surface (Neal Schusterman, 1999). In *Lycidas* (Christoph Marzi, 2004), the undercity of London is even called *die uralte Metropole* (the ancient metropolis). The Dungeons & Dragons Eberron setting, arguably the game's most urban fantasy-like setting, makes use of the layering of cities to create underground spaces of the past. Human cities are built on the ruins of previous eras: "Sharn was built on the foundations of an older city, which was itself built atop goblin ruins."[52] These subterranean pasts provide spaces for the supernatural domain, for challenges and adventures, but they are also reflections of the present surface.

The surface and underground are distorted mirror images of each other's social spaces. There is a long tradition of a "schism" between London's surface and hidden depths in English literature,[53] and Paul Kincaid traces the mirroring of above and below from *Alice's Adventures in Wonderland* (Lewis Carroll, 1865) through "A Story of the Days to Come" (H. G. Wells, 1899) to *Neverwhere*.[54] Gaiman's novel certainly establishes London Below as an "unreal mirror" of London Above (122), rife with inversions: old instead of new, magical instead of scientific, and with an inverted value system.[55] This distorted mirror image can be understood in terms of Michel Foucault's *espaces autres* (different spaces), spaces he calls *utopias* and *heterotopias*. The former have no real place but present society in a perfect or inverted form; the latter are real sites that simultaneously represent, contest, and invert all the other real sites of a culture.[56] Foucault uses the mirror as an example: the utopia of the mirror image, the virtual nonspace, is combined with the real space of the mirror surface, the heterotopia.[57] According to Camilla Del Grazia, "most critical investigations of *Neverwhere* have read it as a heterotopic space,"[58] but I would suggest that the (fictive) underground space is in fact a mirror in that it contains both the utopic and the heterotopic within itself. It is a Thirdspace, a complex inversion and reflection of a fictive world's history, society, and spatial practices. This mirroring is not mainly of the actual world (although that can certainly be part of it) but of the mundane domain above. The spaces above and below mirror each other, and through the reflections, they bring each other's details into sharper contrast, a stereoscopic view of the fictive society portrayed—and this reflection works regardless of the world's degree of secondariness

The unseen spaces underground are a complex Thirdspace, a utopic and heterotopic mirror of the surface spaces. They provide a setting for the impossible, hiding in the dark descendants of Gothic labyrinths—both the city's past and the stygian underworlds. While arguably not quite as prevalent as Elber-Aviram, Young, and Alexander C. Irvine would have it, there are still many urban fantasists who make use of the subterranean spaces to provide an unseen supernatural domain. Elber-Aviram argues that in many urban fantasies, "the fantastic city's subterranean history poses a constant danger to the integrity of the present, as its underground layers harbour supernatural forces threatening to erupt onto the surface" and considers the protagonists to be “symbolic archaeologists” who should venture into the underworld “to recover the city’s hidden past and contend with its forgotten monsters.”[59] That is certainly one story, but the unseen underworlds also offer others. The unseen spaces below are gates between the possible and impossible; they need saving from their own, ancient threats; and they ask of the protagonist to understand themselves.

THE INACCESSIBLE UNSEEN

Most urban fantasy worlds are dyadic, divided into two domains, mostly one supernatural and one mundane.[60] Some people have access only to the mundane domain, others to the supernatural, and some to both. There is one type of spaces that are unseen because most mundane people are prevented from seeing them. A person or group actively prevents access by some form of power, such as wealth, physical force, or magic. Other such spaces are simply magical in themselves, accessible and visible only to those who belong to the supernatural domain. Kadrey’s novel *Sandman Slim* (2009)[61] offers a range of inaccessible unseen spaces and provides a touchstone for a look at how such spaces can comment on the society in which they are located.

When James Stark manages to return to Los Angeles after eleven years of imprisonment in Hell, he wants to take his revenge on the people who sent him there. Stark’s quest for vengeance drives the plot of the first Sandman Slim novel and takes him to a number of unseen spaces in the city, the abodes of various actors in the supernatural domain. These spaces are generally accessible only for the select few: the exclusive “gentlemen’s club” Avila, the seemingly abandoned aircraft factory, the old warehouse filled with neo-Nazis, and Mr. Munnin’s store of arcane goods. Each space demonstrates a particular reason for and way of preventing access to it, and thus each space exemplifies a different approach to constructing an unseen space.

Only the Super-Rich and Ultra-Powerful

The club in *Sandman Slim* is the kind of establishment that only the super-rich and ultra-powerful have access to, and it shows how wealth can be used to construct unseen spaces. Avila is located in the hills above Los Angeles, protected by various kinds of security. The club offers eating, drinking, gambling, and an incredibly expensive bordello. Its clientele are men of power in politics, finance, and culture, and Stark's description of the club during his first visit is laced with contempt for the patrons, mixed with social concerns. Extreme wealth is represented as a social evil, without regard for the natural world or other people.

> They must have cut down half the Amazon rain forest to get the dark wood for the bar. The Rolexes in this one room could pay off the national debt. [. . .] Half-naked and just plain naked hostesses serve drinks and tapas and hold out silver trays piled high with white powder, syringes, and glass pipes, whatever the partiers want. (163–64)

The hyperbole notwithstanding, the description addresses hedonism, chauvinism, greed, and blatant disregard for environmental issues among Avila's members. The feeling that this a space beyond the mundane is emphasized by the club's location. It sits physically above the city and lets the wealthy and powerful men look down (quite literally) upon the normal people who live below. These men are their own form of divinity. "Their wealth doesn't insulate them from the world. It creates it" (165). It is a Mount Olympus of amoral debauchery and a kind of unseen space that is constructed as something so far beyond mainstream society that anything can happen there.

Established as an unseen space, Avila is also revealed to be part of the supernatural domain. It is run by a magical adept (allied to the antagonist) and her security magicians. The bordello includes an area in which those rich enough can pay to abuse captive angels.

The debauched gods of wealth are not satisfied with power over the world of humans but want to lord their might over celestial beings as well. The supernatural aspect of the unseen space is used to emphasize the wickedness of wealth. In the world of Kadrey's novels, great power does not come with great responsibility, only great iniquity.

The unseen spaces of wealth appear in various guises in urban fantasy stories, and, as in Kadrey's novel, rarely as indicators of social virtue. The wealthy magicians' Houses in Kat Howard's *An Unkindness of Magicians* (2017) combine the magical power of the Houses with temporal affluence, and mundane people are kept out of the homes and clubs of the magical community as much by that affluence as by magic.[62] The High Council of British mages stages a ball at the top floor of the iconic Canary Wharf building in Benedict Jacka's *Fated* (2012), constructing a space that is inaccessible unless you have access to wealth and influence or belong to the supernatural domain in the novel. The Amiltech company is run by one of the antagonists in Griffin's *A Madness of Angels*, and its offices are protected by mundane and magical security and hide a room full of supernatural creatures used for experiments. Whether personal or corporate, wealth is used to construct these spaces of the supernatural domain to which the general population is denied access and which they therefore cannot see.

Government Facility: Keep Out!

Sandman Slim also provides an example of how the military-industrial complex and government can be used to establish unseen spaces to which people are denied access. When Stark is captured by men from Homeland Security, he is taken to what looks like an abandoned aircraft assembly plant. The plant is surrounded by fences, and there are signs that warn of hazardous material and claim the area for the Department of Defense (217). The space echoes the ignored unseen spaces in its dereliction, but the combined authority of industrial private property and government—with its monopoly on violence—creates an area clearly out of bounds for the law-abiding citizen. On top of that, the warnings about possible health risks from "hazardous material" amplify the inaccessibility of the space. Entering, the visitor appears to be informed, means risking violence, legal action, and health repercussions.

Like Avila, this unseen space is part of the supernatural domain, the local headquarters for the celestial forces on Earth. Protected by the old plant's outward appearance, reinforced by internal illusions of broken machinery, emptiness, and darkness, the local chapter of the Golden Vigil is active. The Vigil is an ancient "coalition of celestial beings and humans, dedicated to protecting the world and mankind from its greatest enemies" (222), which prove not to be Lucifer and his armies but the Kissi, agents of chaos created by divine mistake. The factory complex has been turned into an industrial-scale production of occult weaponry, paralleling its former use as a "Cold War-era industrial assembly line" (219). Its description combines technology and the occult, the modern and the supernatural, to reinforce the impression of hidden forces carrying out a secret war to save present-day Earth. Although Stark directs his overt scorn at the celestial forces and the angel in charge, Aelita, there are some noticeable symbolic parallels between the Vigil and the temporal government. Stark remarks on how he is threatened with execution or imprisonment without due process by the Homeland Security forces that bring him in. Aelita justifies her allies' behavior by her own holiness: whatever she does is right because she cannot do wrong, the ultimate justification of any abuse of power. A final confirmation of that abuse comes in the form of Aelita's sudden (unsuccessful) attempt to murder Stark. Both the heavenly and earthly governments come across as undemocratic, even despotic.

These forbidden unseen spaces can be prohibited by the power of the state or by the violent force of criminals. In Miéville's *Un*

Lun Dun (2007), the elevator between London and its un-city is hidden in the heart of Westminster, in an office belonging to a Secretary of State. The access to the supernatural is a state secret, kept in a space that is inaccessible because it belongs to a government minister. In his *Perdido Street Station*, the spaces where the frightening ambassador of Hell and the alien and incomprehensible Weaver can be contacted are accessible only to the Mayor of New Crobuzon and his staff. In New Crobuzon, there are also secret governmental facilities for biohazard research and production plants for crime syndicates. Both of these inaccessible, unseen spaces are key to the novel's plot: the alien slake moths, the main threat that the protagonists need to neutralize, were meant for the former but were sold to the latter by a corrupt official, resulting in the moths' subsequent escape. Criminal spaces mirror those forbidden by government fiat by promising violence outside of the state monopoly. Thus the Kissi in Kadrey's novel are first encountered in an old warehouse teeming with brutal neo-Nazis, a distorted reflection of the Golden Vigil's factory and their Homeland Security staff.

Protected by Magical Wards

A final and very common form of unseen spaces are those that are inaccessible to mundane people through some sort of mystical or magical force. On the thirteenth floor of a five-story building lies the shop of Mr. Muninn in *Sandman Slim*. Muninn is a trader in the utterly arcane. He has a captured Fury in a jar outside his store filled with curiosities, and narrow stone stairs lead down from the store to an impossibly vast cave of magical wonders. Muninn is an obviously supernatural person. His skin is as black as a raven, and he is (or so he claims) immortal or at least long-lived enough to remember multiple ice ages. His name, which is Old Norse for "memory" or "mind," recalls one of the Norse god Odin's ravens and suggests that his cave, which seems to hold almost anything, can be read as a mind or a memory palace, a spatial expression of memory. (Muninn's exact background and nature are revealed in later books.)

Muninn's store is constructed as a distinct part of the supernatural domain, even spatially impossible in relation to the mundane. The thirteenth floor is not floating in the air far above the building's roof but is a version of the third floor, the shop coinciding with a mundane home-decor shop. It takes a moment for Stark to identify the switch, and inside the store, he still sees people moving in the mundane domain outside the window (157). The "real store" in the enormous cave below, and the stairs leading down, are similarly impossible in the mundane space, occupying a magical elsewhere. This is a space only accessible to people in the know, appropriate since it is at least in some sense a space of the mind. Knowledge restricts access to this space, unlike the two previous spaces, which were restricted because of wealth and power.

Magical unseen spaces are commonplace in urban fantasy and can symbolize many things. The magical college Brakebills in Lev Grossman's Magicians trilogy (2009–14) has wards set about it to prevent access to nonmagicians. The "knowes" or fairy hills in Seanan McGuire's October Daye series (2009–present) are splinters of Faerie that contain the residences of fairy nobility and are accessible only to those of fairy blood. The Institute of the Shadowhunters in Cassandra Clare's *City of Bones* (2007) is hidden behind the illusion of an abandoned cathedral sealed by police tape, keeping out anyone mundane except under very special circumstances. These spaces ultimately divide the world into the worthy few and the unworthy masses. Other examples are meant to keep the mundane and supernatural apart. The fairies in Emma Bull's *War for the Oaks* (1987) ward the spaces where the Seelie and Unseelie courts do battle, as well as the location of a fairy revel. The separation of fairies and humans is not uncommon in fantasy and urban fantasy, and the construction of the unseen spaces can reveal the relationship between the two groups. Humans are, for instance, cast as dupes, threats, or irrelevancies, suggesting that modern society is controlled by secret masters, violently opposed to strangers, or boring and mundane. It is also possible to combine aspects of the underground and inaccessible unseen spaces. In *Udda verklighet*, the main character must travel through layers of time and space to visit the lair of the antagonist. The unseen space that consists of pockets of time brought together can only be navigated with the help of a guide who knows the rituals and routes necessary, and like any guide through the underworld, they come at a price (in Ormes's novel the price is the loss of a valuable memory).

The unseen spaces in *Sandman Slim* reveal a social world divided into various dimensions: on one side, the common inhabitants of the mundane domain, and on the other, the influential few, whether exorbitantly rich, powerful, dangerous, or knowledgeable. Other texts offer other divisions of the world, but they have in common the construction of worlds in which some people have the power to divide the world and decide who is worthy to enter the secret spaces—and who is not.

• • •

To construct a setting as an unseen space is necessarily to make a statement about society, in one way or another. The three ways in which a space can be unseen that this chapter has addressed illustrate some frequent types of settings in urban fantasy, showing how unseeing can be voluntary, physical, or compelled. As the example of the route down to the lair of Mr. Croup and Mr. Vandemar demonstrates in *Neverwhere*, the types can overlap and combine; authority restricts access to the abandoned hospital, but it is also an ignored space with a passage down to London Below. The many factors that make this an unseen space—historically, economically, socially, even topologically and ontologically—stretch out to the surrounding world, revealing behaviors, ideologies, and mindsets of a modern society. The weaknesses of venture capitalism and failures of public management, the modern propensity to be wasteful and leave waste out of sight, the problem with private ownership, and our fear of what lurks in the darkness below are all brought to the fore by Gaiman's unseen space. Other spaces show us other things about modern society, but they all show us something.

CHAPTER FIVE

INVESTIGATING THE UNSEEN

Most of modern life, actual and fictional, can be seen and understood, but in urban fantasy, there is also a great deal that stays out of sight and, once it is seen, is incomprehensible.[1] Upon those who see lies the burden to investigate. Whether because of unbridled curiosity, twisted fate, or professional duty, these investigators have to find explanations, reveal secrets, and solve mysteries. In crime fiction, such investigations are related to crimes, but a plot based on how an inexplicable transgression is, eventually, explained by following clues and drawing conclusions can be adapted to other genres as well. This is not a recent discovery: John G. Cawelti discusses at length the application of the detective formula in other fiction in *Adventure, Mystery, and Romance* from 1976.[2] The investigation plot has proved to be very useful for dealing with encounters with and explorations of the supernatural in the urban fantasy genre. It has become a common urban fantasy component and brings with it much of crime fiction's particular focus on society and its various issues. This chapter discusses how the investigator characters and investigation plot contribute to the social commentary of urban fantasy.[3]

The investigator figure in one form or another is a frequent cast member in urban fantasy stories. Regardless of whether a supernatural crime has been committed or whether there is simply something strange going on, urban fantasy involves a striking numbers of investigators and investigations. The private eye, police officer, journalist, or freelance guardian of the law may simply stumble across some "weird bollocks" (the term of preference in Aaronovitch's Metropolitan Police) in their mundane line of duty, but often they specialize in crimes related to the supernatural. Several of these investigators even belong to the fantastic domain themselves. Examples include private investigators such as Derek Landy's Skulduggery Pleasant, Mike Resnick's John Justin Mallory, Glen Cook's Garrett P. I., and Simon R. Green's John Taylor, as well as specialized police units, for instance, in the books by Liz Williams, Ben Aaronovitch, and China Miéville. Less typical investigators can also be found. P. Djèlí Clark's Fatma el-Sha'arawi is a former police officer who works as an agent at the ministry for the supernatural. Aneta Jadowska's Dora Wilk is a primary-world police officer who uses her skills as investigator in a parallel, supernatural world. In the television series *Grimm*, Nicholas Burkhardt is a homicide detective who finds himself to be a guardian of the balance between mythological creatures and humanity.[4] Trying to list all investigator figures in the genre would be futile, because it is such a common type of character, versatile and variable. The central examples in this chapter are drawn from novels by Kim Harrison, Jim Butcher, Terry Pratchett, and Paul Cornell.

I refer to the character type specifically as *investigator* rather than *detective*, *private eye*, *police officer*, or something else.[5] The investigation plot is often populated by characters that solve crimes or mysteries professionally. The private eyes and police officers are frequent in urban fantasy, but they are not the only investigators around. A detective story does not need a detective, as long as a character takes on the role of (successful) investigator.[6] Laurell K. Hamilton's Anita Blake starts out as a person with supernatural skills who occasionally consults with the police. Zinzi December, in Lauren Beukes's *Zoo City* (2010), is a former journalist with a supernatural ability to find lost things. Charlaine Harris's Sookie Stackhouse is a waitress who can read minds and finds herself involved in criminal investigations. Aaronovitch's Abigail is a teenager with supernatural contacts and a penchant for untangling mysteries. Other characters find themselves caught up in mysteries that they have to unravel in order to understand themselves and their new circumstances. Not all of them are professional detectives, but they are all investigators.

In chapter 1, I explain why I see urban fantasy as a genre of the modern rather than of the urban, but the city is a major setting for crime fiction, and the investigator plot thus introduces a bias toward urban environments into urban fantasy. The city has been an important milieu for detective stories since Edgar Allan Poe's "The Murders in the Rue Morgue" (1841),[7] a point likewise raised by Peter Messent.[8] Messent also notes that "the traditional connection between crime and urban space has been rendered—to some degree at least—obsolete."[9] Urban fantasy investigations can be set in areas that are more rural than urban, as demonstrated by various novels in the Hollows (Harrison), Rivers of London (Aaronovitch), and Sookie Stackhouse (Harris) series.[10] In urban spaces, crime thrives, however, as the city creates a "manifold opportunity for crime."[11] Building an urban fantasy story around a supernatural crime plot does not require a city setting but makes that setting more suitable. And with an urban environment suited to a crime story comes social criticism because, according to Peter Clandfield, the "connection between dysfunctional social systems and menacing urban environments is a foundational convention of crime fiction."[12] The usefulness of a detective story to deal with the unseen in urban fantasy thus explains the prevalence of both urban settings and social commentary.

One reason for why the investigation plot is so well suited to urban fantasy is that much urban fantasy is structured in terms of so-called *intrusions*. In *Rhetorics of Fantasy* (2008), Farah Mendlesohn describes the trajectory of intrusion fantasy as a disruption of normality by an intrusion, which then has to be dealt with—negotiated with, defeated, sent back whence it came, or controlled.[13] Mendlesohn parallels intrusion fantasy with the crime novel,[14] and I agree: there are some striking similarities between the two, most noticeably the aforementioned trajectory. Like intrusion fantasy, the typical investigation plot constitutes a disruption of normality by some kind of mystery, and the plot revolves around dealing with the disruption. The most basic form is the murder or other crime, perpetrated by person or persons unknown. The investigator must figure out the who, why, and how of the crime in order to deal with it. This similarity in trajectory makes the intrusion variety of urban fantasy and the investigation plot easy to bring together. Let the mystery be something fantastic and have an investigator figure solve it, and the genres are combined.[15]

Another reason for the prevalence of the investigation plot in urban fantasy is that it provides a plot structure that drives the protagonists to explore the world. Part of the work that a story must do is to show the reader what its setting is like. Brian Attebery points out how a fictive world that looks like the actual world can be extended outward because we make assumptions about similarities between the worlds—if there's London, we assume Paris; if there are cars, we assume traffic lights.[16] This is similar to what Marie-Laure Ryan refers to as "the principle of minimal departure": readers assume that the fictive and actual worlds are the same and make adjustments when prompted by the text.[17] Once we pick up a book in the fantastic mode, however, we also assume that the worlds—the fictive and the actual—are significantly different, and we expect the story to tell us about and make use of those differences. An investigation sparked by a mystery is an effective way to convey information about the world within the framework of the story because solving the mystery requires moving from location to location. The "city's secrets must be exposed through the mapping of the urban space if the crime narrative is to fulfil its truth-seeking agenda,"[18] and much urban fantasy has a similar agenda: the supernatural provides mysteries that need to be revealed, and the revelations are partly spatial. Through the "mapping of the urban space," the world, whether primary or secondary, is revealed to the reader. The investigation is, in fact, a particularly useful way to reveal the world, because investigators have incentive to go everywhere and talk to everyone. Ian Rankin remarks that the police detective has "open access to all layers of society, from the oligarchs to the dispossessed,"[19] and although the access may be less open for other types of investigators, they will certainly try—if nothing else, they have a motive to visit all parts of society. A police officer solving a case or a journalist investigating some supernatural weirdness both have reasons to interview anyone, from street people to captains of industry, introducing the reader to a wide range of settings and characters in the process.

The investigation does not only provide a route through the urban spaces; it can also constitute an epistemological path, a structure for revealing knowledge about the larger context of the fictional world. Clark's *A Master of Djinn* (2021) exemplifies how the investigation of a murder requires the uncovering, for the investigator figure Fatma as well as for the reader, of the world's history and prehistory, international relations, magical nature, and gender politics.[20] The story is set in Cairo in an alternative version of 1912, in which magic and djinn have returned to the world. Egypt is at the epicenter of this re-enchanted, modern world, a great power envied not least by the European nation-states and declining empires. The mysterious murder of a British businessman obsessed with Al-Jahiz, the mystic who once brought back magic to the world, brings Fatma into an ever-growing investigation. She must take into account Al-Jahiz and his strange disappearance, take part in a conference between European heads of state meant to preserve the continent's fragile peace, achieve a better understanding of the djinn that live among the mortals in Cairo and their cultural history, and ultimately discovers that treating women as inferior to men can lead to the destruction of the world. Step by step, Fatma puts together pieces that lead to a denouement in which her world faces an apocalyptic war that may result in the extinction of all humans. Like the epic quest that ends with the hero having to defeat an existential threat, often to the entire world, the investigator plot in Clark's novel brings the protagonist (and with her, the reader) from the small and local scale to universal danger. Clark stresses this parallel by repeatedly alluding to not least *The Lord of the Rings* (1954–55) in the novel's climactic scenes. At the end of the novel, the investigation has uncovered murderer, means, and motive but has also presented many of the physical and social spaces of Fatma's Cairo and has left the reader with much knowledge about her alternative world.

Even something as self-contained as a locked-room mystery relies for its solution on a deeper understanding about the world. Michael Swanwick's "A Small Room in Koboldtown" (2007) demonstrates how a problem and its solution can be used to shed light on the social dynamic of a city.[21] A corpse is found in a room locked from the inside, and the mystery is solved through the revelation that the victim can be resurrected: the "murder" (actually a less-than-permanent suicide) is meant to frame the one person in the building who can pass through a locked door. Once the protagonist investigator discovers this, the mystery is solved. There are similar examples of locked-room mysteries explained by a broader understanding of the supernatural world. In Aaronovitch's "The Domestic" (2012), a ghost's behavior reveals how a woman can be involved in a loud fight while apparently being alone in her home. In Pratchett's *Feet of Clay* (1996), the fact that golems do not have any scent explains how an old man can be murdered without anyone apparently having entered his museum. A few small details about the world are required to explain how the apparently impossible is possible. Through the investigation, readers and characters can learn something about the supernatural but also about society.

Swanwick's story is one about racism, not least among the police; Aaronovitch and Pratchett both write about the loneliness of the elderly members of the community.

Crime fiction is a genre suited to commenting on modern society. Lee Horsley observes that it is fiction with "a capacity for socio-political comment [. . .] facilitated by the very nature of crime fiction" and that it "contains characteristics that lend themselves to political and oppositional purposes."[22] That nature and concomitant capacity remain when crime fiction is combined with urban fantasy. To demonstrate how the investigation plot contributes to the overall social commentary, I delve deeper into two particular forms of crime fiction types that are both frequently employed in urban fantasy: the hardboiled detective story and the police novel.

THE HARDBOILED DETECTIVE: MAGIC IN THE GREAT WRONG PLACE

Many urban fantasy stories have incorporated both the wretched urban settings and the grittiness of the hardboiled detective story. Raymond Chandler concludes his seminal essay "The Simple Art of Murder" (1944) with a detailed description of the private eye as a man of (rare) integrity in a society of (ubiquitous) crime. Chandler portrays an urban society in which crime is commonplace and organized and law enforcement is corrupt and feckless. It is such a bleak (or, as Chandler puts it, "realist") portrayal that W. H. Auden famously refers to the setting as "The Great Wrong Place."[23] "[D]own these mean streets a man must go," Chandler declares, "who is not himself mean, who is neither tarnished nor afraid."[24] This brave, untarnished man is the detective who has come to be known as *hardboiled*. Urban fantasy has its own fair share of Great Wrong Places, with people who, like Chandler's hero, search for hidden truths while maintaining a measure of honor and integrity. They go by names such as Vicki Nelson (Tanya Huff) and John Taylor; John Justin Mallory and

Ivy Granger (E. J. Stevens); and the examples under discussion, Rachel Morgan and Harry Dresden.

The "realism" that Chandler advocates is a critical portrayal of modern urbanity. The Great Wrong Place was originally an image of the United States in the 1940s, but although society changed over time, the bleakness remained. "The crime novel became," in Messent's words, "a tool to dissect society's flaws and failures, and to expose the wrong turns that a capitalist economy, and the political structures to which it was allied, had taken."[25] Hardboiled crime fiction, in particular, was set in "a complex and labyrinthine urban world."[26] This modern urbanity and the hero in search of a hidden truth are highly compatible with the urban fantasy genre, and along with hero and setting came the social criticism implicit in that setting. The bleakness of the Great Wrong Place, already detectable in Charles de Lint's early Newford stories (1987–present), established itself in the urban fantasy world in the 1990s.

My two examples of how the hardboiled-detective form can be combined with the urban fantasy genre have been selected because they illustrate how the form can be adapted while still contributing to the social commentary of the genre. Both examples are the beginning of longer series: *Storm Front* (2000)[27] is the first book in Butcher's Dresden Files (2000–present), featuring Harry Dresden, freelance wizard and consultant with the police.[28] *Dead Witch Walking* (2004)[29] is the first book in Harrison's Hollows series (2004–present) about Rachel Morgan, witch and private investigator ("runner").[30] Harry becomes involved in a case with a murderous and powerful sorcerer-cum-drug dealer, whom he must find and defeat before Harry himself is killed; Rachel, in an attempt to evade assassination, tries to find evidence that a powerful, mysterious businessman and politician is also a drug lord. Each story is set in an interpretation of the Great Wrong Place, Harry's in Chicago and Rachel's in Cincinnati in an alternative timeline.

The combination of hardboiled-detective story and urban fantasy draws attention to the ills of the fictive society, locating some of those ills at the center of the setting. Butcher's and Harrison's investigating heroes live in cities dominated by organized crime. In *Storm Front*, Chicago has just undergone a gang war, with the winner, Johnny Marcone, controlling all crime in the city. Marcone makes sure that freelance criminals either are handed over to the police or go missing, but keeps his own operations shielded by a team of lawyers. According to Harry, the police seem reluctant to chase Marcone, preferring his rule to "anarchy in the underworld" (25). The criminal scene in *Dead Witch Walking* is more complex, which partly depends on the setup of the fictive world. Although identifiable as a version of present-day Cincinnati, the series is set in an alternative timeline in which supernatural beings such as vampires, were-creatures, and witches (collectively called "Inderlanders") came out of hiding and kept civilization running when a self-inflicted pandemic almost wiped out humanity. There is a mélange of criminals at large. At the top end are Trent Kalamack, politician, businessman, and producer of illegal drugs, and Piscary, ancient vampire and crime lord. Toward the bottom are, for example, a vampire who feeds without consent and a leprechaun who illegally fabricated a rainbow to get the gold at the end of it. Society is mostly segregated along human/Inderlander lines, and there is a certain tension between the groups, geographically visible in humans living mainly on the Ohio side of the river and Inderlanders living in the Hollows, on the Kentucky side. Both settings recall the image of the United States society that dominated the early private eye stories. "Urban blight, corrupt political machines, and de facto disenfranchisement of significant sections of the population through graft and influence-peddling were part of the background in which crime of a new and organised kind was becoming endemic."[31] Harrison clearly echoes this kind of Great Wrong Place, and Butcher's setting has distinct similarities.

Both authors portray societies that have gone wrong not only because of organized crime but also through problematic law enforcement. The social segregation in Harrison's Cincinnati is mirrored in a divided, corrupt, and ineffective law enforcement. The police are split into the humans-only Federal Inderlander Bureau (FIB) and its Inderlander-run counterpart, Inderlander Security (I.S.). The competition between the two police forces is fierce, verging on open animosity. The FIB's human officers are all but incapable of dealing with Inderlander lawbreakers, such as an angry vampire (343), and deal predominantly with human criminals. I.S. is a more efficient organization but corrupt, brutal, and with little regard for the rule of law. Rachel is not surprised to find colleagues who work for external interests, and it is taken for granted that employees who quit their jobs at I.S. risk assassination. When Rachel resigns, even her final pay check has a death curse put on it (49–50). Corruption is so endemic that even Rachel and her friends have no qualms about letting captured offenders go if the price is right. Butcher's police force is less corrupt, although there are apparently officers feeding information to Marcone. Their main inefficiency lies in an inability to accept the magical reality. The Special Investigations unit keeps swapping directors, and the unit's current second-in-command does not believe in magic (158, 15). In both novels, the police force ultimately has to rely on the hardboiled freelancers (Harry and Rachel) to save the day, because the police are incapable of dealing with the problems. Ultimately, the police contribute to the wrongness of the Great Wrong Place, down whose streets the heroes walk.

The setting itself is part of defining the protagonists, offering a contrast between the iniquity of society and the integrity of the hero. In lieu of Dark Lords and dragons, the Great Wrong Place can make urban fantasy heroes appear heroic. "The Great Wrong Place suits the tough detective, giving him something to be tough about," Tony Hilfer explains, a description that fits Butcher's and Harrison's protagonists well. Through their first-person narration, they set themselves up as points of light in a dark, hard world. Rachel makes it through the story despite numerous assassination attempts (courtesy of the I.S.), captivity by a drug lord, and a demonic attack. Harry survives despite being attacked by a vampire, demons, giant scorpions, and a powerful sorcerer, and being in the crosshairs of both the police and the White Council (the governing body of wizards that protects humanity from magic abuse). Both get severely beaten up, demonstrating the private eye's ability to "take the occasional beating [that is] ritualised proof of a private eye's power to survive in a tough world."[32] This toughness is common to hardboiled urban fantasy investigators but perhaps more prominent when it comes to those who, like Rachel, are women. According to Dennis Porter, it was long seen as unsuitable to have female private investigators, but, he claims, this trend broke in the 1970s, and the 1980s saw a new generation of female PIs.[33] The "[f]it, self-contained, and street-wise" female PIs of Marcia Muller, Sara Paretsky, and Sue Grafton[34] are able to handle guns and face threats and attacks,[35] much like the tough female protagonists of urban fantasy that appeared in the 1990s, such as Huff's Vicky Nelson, Hamilton's Anita Blake, and, for that matter, Harrison's Rachel Morgan.

Honor is an important trait to the hardboiled investigator, but the urban fantasy investigator is not untarnished. Chandler describes his hero as a man of honor but not as a saint, descriptions that fit both Rachel and Harry. Rachel's weapon of choice is nonlethal magic, and although she finds herself expanding her magic use and combat techniques during the course of the series, she is cast in stark contrast to the violent police force she has quit. Where Kalamack lets the end justify the means, and her former I.S. colleagues are stupid, greedy, and spiteful, Rachel comes across as a paragon of virtue (if not of forethought). She fits the image of a hardboiled investigator who serves as an example of "(by and large) honesty and integrity in a modernized urban world generally associated with greed, chicanery, and political corruption."[36] When Kalamack attempts to buy her loyalty, she resolutely responds that "I quit my job [. . .], not my morals" (168)—forgetting that in order to quit, she released a criminal in exchange for three wishes

(25). In *Storm Front*, Harry appears as less resolutely honorable. He describes himself as an old-fashioned gentleman who "treat[s] women like something other than just shorter, weaker men with breasts," and he "enjoys treating a woman like a lady, opening doors for her, paying for shared meals, giving flowers—all that sort of thing" (11–12). When coerced into making a love potion, he feels that such a potion would be taking advantage of a woman (an understatement, since the potion invalidates any notion of consent), but appears just as concerned about the implication that he could not charm a woman without magic (99–100, 350). When he is about to die, he wishes that he could apologize to the victims of the evil sorcerer for failing to protect them (343). Once through the ordeal, he makes good on his promise to reward the fairies that assisted him. On the other hand, he is no knight in shining armor. He follows the Laws of Magic but regards human laws as negotiable: breaking into a crime scene and lying to the police gives him no qualms. When threatened, he tends to do violence to whatever scares him (82). And in his past, he has committed a magical crime—albeit in self-defense—for which he has been given the equivalent to a suspended sentence: one minor transgression of the Laws of Magic and he will be executed by the White Council.

Harry and Rachel share the same need for autonomy, but Rachel has to learn, already in the first installment in the series, to temper that need. Autonomy is a central driving force for a number of male and female detectives.[37] Throughout *Storm Front*, Harry remains a loner, set apart from both the magical and the mundane community. His story is one of self-sufficiency and distrust of others (with the exception of his cat and a memory spirit), including the police lieutenant who heads Special Investigations. This autonomy complicates his case and puts others at risk, and in the end, he needs to be saved by a White Council wizard. Independence, while desirable, is suboptimal. Rachel displays an equally fervent need to be autonomous, and the story springs from her struggle for independence, to rid herself from the I.S. and then survive their assassination attempts long enough to buy her contract. Her deep-seated distrust of people partly stems from the betrayal that killed her father, but eventually she also begins to fear that she might put her friends in danger. Over the course of the novel, however, her fairness, self-sacrifice, and integrity earns her the loyalty and friendship of many of those she comes into contact with, and this fuels an internal conflict in Rachel. "'I owe Nick and Jenks my life,' I said, hating it. 'What's so great about that?'" (323). She fails to realize, at first, how her friends have become her greatest assets because they are also the greatest challenge to her independence, and this becomes a focal point for conflicts in the novel.

Rachel's role as hardboiled private eye creates a story-driving conflict with her role as typical fantasy hero. Like so many heroes on fantasy quests and protagonists in various urban fantasies, she finds herself the leader of a motley crew of companions whose loyalty she commands. As the plot progresses, Rachel is forced to change from lone wolf figure to the center of a traditional fantasy fellowship. "Looks to me like you've become the leader here," the guide figure Keasley tells her at a pivotal moment. "Accept it. People will be doing things for you. Don't be selfish. Let them" (323). Grudgingly, she does, thus beginning to consolidate the roles of fantasy hero and independent PI, a character development that progresses over several books.

The urban fantasy version of the Great Wrong Place is not the easily condemnable place that the hardboiled detectives grew out of, however. Neither Harrison's nor Butcher's setting ends up as singularly dismal as the society described by Chandler. Rachel's perspective is skewed by the history of her world and the segregation between Inderlanders and humans that she has grown up with. Her relentless hunt for Kalamack ultimately leads to the capture of biodrugs that he attempts to smuggle into the city. Through Rachel's narration, these drugs are described as highly illegal contraband, but the reader can see them for what they are: medicines to treat diseases such as Huntington's, cystic fibrosis, and diabetes, banned by a human society that almost exterminated itself through its own biotechnology. Protagonist, antagonist, and setting all dissolve into shades of gray as Kalamack's criminal, humanitarian efforts are brought to naught by Rachel's efforts on behalf of a nation that has outlawed and murdered its own bioengineers. Through Harry's actions, the evil sorcerer is killed by his own creations, thus returning full control of the illegal drug trade to Marcone. A magical threat is dealt with, but organized crime remains very much organized, and Harry does not bother to deny the rumor that he was hired by Marcone to remove the competitor. At the end of the novel, Harry laconically accepts that "[t]he world is getting weirder. Darker every single day" (351). He claims that he tries to maintain order "in [his] corner of the country" and establish a world where "trolls stay the hell under their bridges [. . .] elves don't come swooping out to snatch children from their cradles [. . .] vampires respect the limits, and [. . .] faeries mind their *p*'s and *q*'s" (351–52). As the mundane Chicago falls under a crime lord's dominion, the only light that shines in the deepening supernatural darkness is a flawed loner. Whatever hope there is for society, it is slight.

THE POLICE NOVEL: A FRACTURED COMMENTARY ON MODERN SOCIETY

A particular set of urban fantasy stories have made use of the broad, fragmented view of urban society common in the police novel (including the police procedural). These stories, about police officers at work trying to solve crimes, share some features with the hardboiled detective story, but the fact that they are told from a multiple, rather than single, perspective offers greater possibilities for portraying society. Both the British and American police novel have been increasingly influenced by the American "hardboiled tradition of gritty realism and (to varying degrees) social disarray."[38] Those urban fantasy writers who have made use of the police investigation have similarly been influenced—to varying degrees—by the hardboiled tradition and have located the "gritty realism" and "social disarray" to different areas of modern life. Aaronovitch's first-person police narrator is mainly concerned with issues of race and migration whereas Williams uses her urban Hell to address an array of social problems. Specialist police forces, such as Project Mindreach of the Royal Canadian Mounted Police (de Lint, *Moonheart*, 1984) and the Fundamentalist and Sect-Related Crimes Unit of the Metropolitan Police (Miéville, *Kraken: An Anatomy*, 2010) occasionally present a view of the supernatural as criminal, or at least antisocial, activity. The two examples under discussion here, *Feet of Clay* by Pratchett[39] and *London Falling* (2012) by Cornell,[40] offer a normal police force that solve normal crimes in a supernatural secondary world, on the one hand, and, on the other, a squad of London police officers who have thrust upon them the ability to perceive the supernatural domain.

Neither Cornell's London nor Pratchett's Ankh-Morpork are really the Great Wrong Place of the hardboiled detective story, but they are both examples of imperfect and problematic urban settings. Their shortcomings and failures are communicated from the perspectives of their respective police teams and provide a social context to the criminal investigations that drive the two plots. Messent observes that "[t]he police novel is a form that, at its best, has mutated into an ongoing (serial) enquiry into the state of the nation, its power structures and its social concerns."[41] The police novel structure used in *Feet of Clay* and *London Falling* offer such enquiries, even though the former dresses its social critique about race, gender, and power in the concerns of various fantasy species, and the latter has its officers wrestle with racism, organized crime, and collapsing local communities while trying to deal with the challenges of a (to them) previously unknown supernatural reality.

Both books are clearly identifiable police novels, and could be read both as crime fiction and urban fantasy. *London Falling* is the first book in Cornell's Shadow Police series (2012–16[42]), featuring a police team in the London Metropolitan Police who gain the ability to see the supernatural. Their investigation of the inexplicable murder of the leader of an organized crime syndicate leads to their discovery of a serial killer, who turns out to be a five hundred-year-old witch. The novel tells the story of their parallel attempts to understand their new reality and bring the witch to justice. *Feet of Clay* is the third of eight Discworld novels about the Ankh-Morpork City Watch,[43] in which several murders prove to be connected to a plot to remove the Patrician (the city-state's ruler) from power and replace him with a puppet king. The murders are also related to an attempt by the city's enslaved golem population to find some measure of sovereignty for themselves.[44] The novels are distinctly different in that Pratchett leans into the motifs, settings, and creatures found in much Tolkienesque secondary-world fantasy whereas Cornell draws on supernatural horror and London as an ancient city.[45] They include clear examples of police investigations, are narrated from several different characters' perspectives, and provide a distinct and critical commentary on modern society and the people who live within it.

Like police novels in general, Pratchett's and Cornell's respective novels share a keen concern with the state of the societies in which they are set. *Feet of Clay* is a novel that personalizes major social issues through its narrative structure. It draws attention to a number of social and political questions, including whether there is equality before the law, whether the dehumanizing (and concomitant slavery and lynching) of golems is morally acceptable, and whether there is racism and sexism in the police force. *London Falling* is less explicit in its interrogation of its social context. Like in the City Watch novel, racism within and outside of the force is addressed, but it is treated even more as a personal matter. The setting is one in which local communities are collapsing under the weight of poverty, crime, and government cutbacks. The failures of society are (mostly) taken for granted and (largely) accepted but reside beyond the perimeter of the criminal investigation.

The police novel brought with it a shift in focus from the single detective to the police as a team, which also broke apart the narrative perspective. Unlike the hardboiled detective's generally single, unifying viewpoint, the police novel's focus on the investigation as a group effort produces a narrative perspective that is fragmented and occasionally contradictory. Both *London Falling* and *Feet of Clay* are told as a patchwork of perspectives from various members of the respective police groups and, in particular in Pratchett's novel, with additional perspectives from other characters. The use of such "criss-crossing" narratives, Messent notes, undermines the single or shared perspective of the private eye or single investigator and downgrades their narrative authority, something that he finds to be "increasingly common in contemporary crime fiction."[46] Ankh-Morpork is described with a constantly shifting narrative focus, including not only several members of the Watch but also victims, witnesses, conspirators, even an anthropomorphized Death—to name a few. London is predominantly described by the four members of the police team, with some exceptions (including a few key passages from the killer's perspective). The result is a broad portrayal of urban life, with a narrative that moves its points of view from the pinnacles of society to its lowest depths, from bystanders to victims to police to perpetrators. Rather than having a detective move around, providing a varied but coherent path through the city, the narration switches from focalizer to focalizer. A city "cannot be known as a panoptic whole";[47] through the men and women of the force, the reader is presented with a fragmented albeit wide view of city life with a decidedly personal perspective.

Not all police novels construct their narrative focus in a similar fashion, something that also influences the way in which a story enquires into various social concerns. Lee Horsley observes that there is a common overlap between the investigative team and the individual investigator who "often retains considerable autonomy" within the police force.[48] Messent takes this further, suggesting that police novels fall on a spectrum between, on the one hand, police officers who carry out their duties without qualms about the law that they represent, and on the other, stories about the individual law enforcer whose social values lead to a questioning of the system and a distancing of the larger policing group.[49] He also suggests that the mostly team-focused stories are less likely to question the dominant social system than those that feature one or two individuals.[50] (Messent admits that there are some exceptions, however, notably the Martin Beck stories by Maj Sjöwall and Per Wahlöö, 1965–75.) While *London Falling* is a largely team-focused story, *Feet of Clay* lies somewhere in the middle of this spectrum, offering a double perspective on policing that provides a social critique on both a political and a personal level. The prominent perspective of the largely autonomous Commander Vimes is combined with the multiple, less obtrusive, viewpoints of other City Watch members. Pratchett's novel thus brings together the two perspectives described by Messent, resulting in a social critique that adds the individual officers' personal perspectives to Vimes's more general, critical opinions about society. Cornell's novel lacks a similar, strongly autonomous voice, resulting in a much less general social commentary, dominated instead by the team's personal viewpoints and experiences. Both the general and personal perspectives on society's shortcomings are addressed below.

Commander Vimes provides a distinct, political critique of society. Unlike his counterpart in Cornell's novel, Detective Inspector James Quill, Vimes maintains a large degree of autonomy in his policing. He largely occupies a narrative position that Horsley relates to "narratives that move towards an exposure of the injustices and failures of the official machinery of law and order,"[51] with the added complication that he represents both social privilege and legal influence—he is married to one of the wealthiest women in the city and is head of the police force. Vimes feels himself bound by the law while recognizing its inadequacies. When he finally arrests the culprit, his internal monologue reveals that he is under no illusions that they will soon be released because they are necessary for the workings of the city, that politics in Ankh-Morpork is a game of chess, and no one cares if a few pawns die. There is not even enough evidence for a conviction, and Vimes alone knows the whole truth (392–93). He is the character most prone to criticize the sociopolitical system of Ankh-Morpork, if from a somewhat awkward position. He has risen from poverty to become a member of the establishment and is therefore stuck in a social no-man's-land, "[a] jumped-up copper to the nobs and a nob to the rest" (16). When someone attempts to poison the Patrician, it is his sense of duty and an awareness of the damage such a murder would cause the city that prompt Vimes to try to save the ruler and solve the crime. The collateral deaths of an old seamstress and her grandchild upset him much more, partly because the victims lived in his old neighborhood and partly because the perpetrators did not care about their deaths. Through Vimes's character, the point that people, as individuals, matter is forcefully made; they are always more than *only* collateral damage or *just* pawns in political power games; they are actual people.

London Falling provides a dispersed, general criticism of its social context but through occasional comments rather than a single, distinct voice. Once the police officers realize that powerful supernatural entities are real, they consider whether those entities control the world. "Maybe they're the reason why the banks got fucked up, and politics is corrupt, and there's war all the time, and the frigging global warming, and every year a new epidemic" (165). The officer's desperation is prompted by the suspicion that whatever humanity does, they will lose to this unknown, unseen enemy. Quill turns it around, suggesting that *if* this is the case, they finally have a chance to fight back. Neither officer questions the description of the world, however: theirs is ultimately a world that has failed. This impression is supported, for instance, by the supernatural entity that blames humanity and modernity's grand narrative of eternal economic growth for overpopulation, resource depletion, and global warming (342). Repeated observations are made regarding the hydra nature of organized crime (e.g., 46), and occasional comments address, for example, the problems faced by print media and the cutting of public spending (157, 221). Having defeated the witch, Quill informs the supernatural community that they are now subject to "the same law as [. . .] everyone else" (404). He echoes Vimes's desire for equality under the law but reveals a similar frustration with the conflict between effective policing and citizens' rights. Because his team alone can see the supernatural creatures, the law will in fact *not* be the same as for everyone else. Their policing of the supernatural domain will include foregoing paperwork, not worrying "too much about the rights and needs" of supernatural creatures, not "watch[ing] our Ps and Qs with the cautions," even physically abusing miscreants (404). Where Vimes accepts some overstepping of the thin blue line, Quill intends to clean up in supernatural London, with or without legal equality.

In the two novels, society's problems are mainly portrayed through the people who investigate crimes as a collective effort and through their personal experiences. "[C]rime and police work," Leroy L. Panek claims, "have a unique impact on the way men and women work as well as the way they live."[52] The investigations in both novels are related from individual points of view, centering on personal concerns. Sociopolitical issues remain mostly people-sized. Crime fiction scholarship "holds that the genre meets head on bitter racial, ethnic, class, and gender conflicts without providing easy answers,"[53] and these urban fantasy novels are no exception, neither when it comes to the meeting head on nor to the absence of easy answers. In *Feet of Clay*, racial and gender issues are of particular prominence, and through its characters, *London Falling* concentrates on how race, class, and sexual orientation can create a sense of alienation.

In the City Watch novels, racial and ethnic issues are conflated through the various species in the City Watch books, and dwarfs in particular provide fodder for Pratchett's satire on ethnicity. The subject of race is dealt with in many Discworld novels, but it is often done so in general terms, by portraying the conflicts between different species rather than different races. “Racism was not a problem on the Discworld,” one of several explanations goes, “because—what with trolls and dwarfs and so on—speciesism was more interesting. Black and white lived in perfect harmony and ganged up on green.”[54] The *Feet of Clay* narrator valorizes Vimes for his accepting as watchmen a wide range of beings, including not only dwarfs but trolls, a werewolf, a gargoyle, and, at the end of the novel, a golem. Golem rights are a central issue in the novel: the text argues against the enslavement of intelligent beings and clearly condemns the persecution and killing of golems, even though it allows characters to hold a range of views on the subject. In his discussion of racism in the City Watch texts, Edward James points out how Pratchett maintains the complexity of the issue by having even sympathetic characters harbor prejudices against one species or another.[55] *Feet of Clay* sports several such prejudices among sympathetic Watch officers: against vampires, golems, werewolves, and the generally undead. Prejudice becomes something to be confronted on a personal level, a case in point being the friendship between the newly recruited dwarf Littlebottom and Constable Angua. The dwarf fails to recognize that her newfound friend is a werewolf, and dramatic irony mounts as Angua suffers Littlebottom’s anti-werewolf sentiments in silence. Eventually, however, Angua is forced to reveal her secret in order to save the dwarf’s life. Littlebottom then has to reconcile her prejudicial stereotype with what she feels about an actual person and friend.

Racism in *London Falling* is more recognizable from the actual world. Two of the police officers in the team, Detective Sergeant Costain and Detective Constable Sefton, are Black, but they wrestle with this in different ways. Both see their race as an advantage to their work as undercover detectives, because “so many of the [organized crime networks] were of African ethnicity,” although Sefton adds that his race is also a disadvantage in all other police careers (15). Sefton sees his entire identity as complicated, however.

His upper-middle-class background means that he must hide his accent to fit in when undercover, but he cannot hide the color of his skin among his (mostly white) police colleagues. He even expects people in his old neighborhood to call Neighborhood Watch when they see him in the street (335). His dilemma is similar to Vimes's: as Black, he is not accepted by his upper-middle-class peers; as upper-middle-class, he will not pass in a Black criminal network. Costain's background makes him suited to his undercover work, but he is acutely aware of the racism within the police force. He has been stopped and searched on multiple occasions, and it is implied that his race was partly the reason why. A young patrol officer even "called him 'nigger' and slapped him on the cheek" (26). Costain intends to report the officer (he carries that officer's identity number in his wallet), suggesting that the police at least pay lip service to a nonracist policy. The perspectives of Sefton and Costain show a society in which being Black signals alienation at best and criminality at worst but also a society which is aware of the problem and (perhaps ineffectually) is trying to deal with it.

A second prominent issue raised through Littlebottom is that of gender expression. Pratchett employs the well-established fantasy trope that dwarf men and women look the same in order to have the female dwarf critique a concept of equality that requires everyone to behave like men.[56] Angua discovers, from the dwarf's scent, that Littlebottom is female and then supports the dwarf's desire to express her female nature in contravention of dwarf culture. Step by step, and encouraged by the werewolf, Littlebottom "comes out" as female by beginning to wear makeup and high heels and finally changing her first name from Cheery to Cheri (245, 338), much to the confusion of her colleagues. Triumphant at last, the dwarf spreads her idea of feminine expression among the other female dwarfs in the Watch (411), forcing her colleagues to accept that knowing that someone is a woman does not mean that you should treat them differently (358). The dwarf's struggle to express and be accepted in her female identity can be read as a broad critique of any social denial of identity expression. Pratchett's critique is a gentle one, however, as he reminds the reader that both support and acceptance can be found among friends and colleagues. Through Littlebottom's attempts to assert her femininity as dwarf and as police officer, identity issues are made both personal and social.

In *London Falling*, the officers' reflections on their own identities, backgrounds, and history also present various social issues. Sefton's sexual orientation and the family history of the analyst Lisa Ross both contribute to their sense of loneliness and alienation. They make assumptions about others' reactions and behavior, based on their previous experiences of being bullied and ostracized. Even the negative development of local communities is connected to personal history. When the four officers visit the area of Willesden, Costain's reverie is similar to when Vimes ponders his childhood in Cockbill Street. Vimes sees a community stuck in virtuous poverty, where people refuse to acknowledge that they are poor (232–34). Costain sees a "rotten black and Irish" community that had briefly nudged into middle-class acceptability before sliding back again, without quite passing "decent black and Irish" (68). He remembers deciphering the signs during his first time on a police beat, reading the shopping street in terms of who paid for protection and where drug-dealer lookouts hid. Then, there had been traces of community and "black grannies who kept those sociable gardens nice, and owned their own houses" (68). Now, even that was gone. Costain feels his sense of belonging slipping; Willesden, where he feels some sense of belonging, is threatened by gentrification; a London only for the white, the well-to-do, establishes itself in a slow spread from its center and outward.

The police novel may not be set in the Great Wrong Place, but it is not set in a particularly good place, either. It is a society with many problems, presented through the fragmented perspectives of the men and women involved in investigating its mysteries, as a team and as individuals with their own quandaries. This form of investigation plot establishes a social context in which crime and poverty belong but also a context in which people can feel alienated as well as at home. It is an imperfect place that provides urban fantasy with a flawed world and a society in need of improvement.

• • •

The introduction of the investigation plot in urban fantasy brought with it crime fiction's portrayal of a modern society that is damaged and broken, a world in which crime belongs. The hardboiled detective story and the police novel are not the only types of investigation stories to be found in urban fantasy, although variations on these are common. Crime and intrusions of the supernatural can produce plots that are similar in structure and require ways to deal with the unseen and unknown. "[C]rime fiction confronts the problems of the everyday world in which we live as directly as any form of writing can," Messent suggests. "It allows its readers—though sometimes indirectly and obliquely—to engage with their deepest social concerns, their most fundamental anxieties about themselves and their surrounding world. This engagement, though, can vary in intensity and vary too in explicit recognition by the reader of its presence."[57] Crime fiction's confrontation of problems and engagement with social concerns is made part of urban fantasy as well. It is one of the key components that explain how social commentary has become an obligatory part of the genre.

INTERLUDE TWO

SOME NOTES ON FOCALIZATION

The blend of the modern and the magical can take many forms, but what they all have in common is that they provide the reader with a possibility of seeing modernity from new perspectives.[1] This could be the perspective of someone who suddenly comes across the magical domain and, like Richard Mayhew in Neil Gaiman's *Neverwhere* (1996) or Clary Fray in Cassandra Clare's Mortal Instruments series (2007–14), has to reach a new understanding of the world. We could be offered the perspective on modernity of a protagonist who belongs to the magical domain themselves, such as Patricia Briggs's Mercy Thompson (2006–present) or Kevin Hearne's Atticus O'Sullivan (Iron Druid Chronicles, 2011–19). Parallel or future versions of our world could be used to provide alternative views on modern society, as in Liz Williams's Detective Inspector Chen series (2005–15) and Kim Harrison's Hollows series (2004–present). Even secondary worlds and faerie realms can be modernized and thus display modernity from a (sometimes very) different perspective, with examples such as *The Iron Dragon's Daughter* (1993) by Michael Swanwick and *The War of the Flowers* (2003) by Tad Williams.

The following three chapters examine how modern society is portrayed depending on whose perspective on the combination of modernity and the supernatural the text presents. Each chapter investigates a particular way to portray modernity, by characters from the mundane domain or from the supernatural one, or by characters who live in a secondary world with its own modernity. I have chosen to use the narratological concept of focalization to express which character's perspective is in focus, in particular in chapters 6 (a mundane character encounters the supernatural domain) and 7 (a supernatural character in a mundane, modern society). In chapter 8, all characters are native to and familiar with the supernatural, modern world and thus differ less in their perspectives on what characterizes modernity than in their views on whether modernity is something positive.

The perspective in a text is determined by whose emotions, opinions, and knowledge decide what a narrator describes and how it is described—in this particular case the character whose view of modernity dominates the narrative. Gérard Genette introduces the term *focalization* in *Narrative Discourse* (1980) to distinguish between the voice that tells the story (the narrator) and whose point of view guides the narrative (the focalizer) in a text.[2] Exactly how focalization works in a text has been (and still is) the subject of narratological discussion, but for the purpose of the following chapters, there is no need to elaborate on its different positions and finer points.[3] Karin Kukkonen succinctly captures my own understanding by explaining that "the focalizer provides the horizon of knowledge and the experience through which the narrative is filtered" but also includes "emotional involvement" in focalization.[4] Focalization is not only about a visual perspective; it covers the many ways that determine how we perceive and think about the world. Shlomith Rimmon-Kenan suggests that the totality of focalization can be divided into three facets: the psychological (both cognitive and emotive), the perceptual, and the ideological.[5] In my readings, the ideological facet, the norm or norms that the text conveys, are of particular importance as I look at how modernity is portrayed.

Focalization, like narration, is not necessarily consistent and unchanging in a text. The two main cases for chapters 6, Ben Aaronovitch's Rivers of London series (2011–present), and 7, Hearne's Iron Druid Chronicles, have single, first-person narrators. They are told in the past tense, but there seems to be no separation between the characters-as-narrators and the characters-as-protagonists.[6] Nevertheless, as Petter Aaslestad points out, even texts that appear to be conveyed through a central consciousness can include large variations of perspective on the microlevel,[7] and in the case of Aaronovitch, I have also included some of the graphic novels that are part of the series, which shift between several focalizers (interested readers are referred to Kai Mikkonen's excellent chapter on focalization in comics in *The Narratology of Comic Art*, 2017). For lack of space, the following readings focus on the main perspectives promoted by the focalizing characters, even when other perspectives are introduced. (Each of the main examples in the following three chapters deserves book-length studies of their own; regrettably, this book is not one of those studies.)

This has been a very short introduction to focalization. The following three chapters analyze how urban fantasy can present various views of—and opinions about—our modern world, and such views and opinions depend on whose perspective of the world is served up to the reader. There is much more to say about focalization, especially if you are interested in *how* these perspectives are communicated. The brief paragraphs here have to suffice for now, however.

CHAPTER SIX

FINDING THE FANTASTIC

When something strange and impossible intrudes upon the familiar and everyday, everything we held as true is suddenly under threat; we need to revise our view of what the world includes. In urban fantasy, characters are constantly confronted with the supernatural and have to find a way to incorporate the magical into their view of the world. In doing so, they also convey a stance on modernity and on the supernatural.[1] Modernity can, for instance, be portrayed as fragile and imperiled by magical forces, or it can be constructed as a set of social principles equally applicable to the supernatural and the mundane. It can even be depicted as brutally suppressing a feeble, unseen supernatural domain. In this chapter I examine how modernity is portrayed from a mundane and modern perspective, using Ben Aaronovitch's Rivers of London books (2011–present) and graphic novels (2016–present) as my main example.[2]

Stories about protagonists who unexpectedly meet the supernatural have been a mainstay of literature for millennia, but not all such stories cause protagonists to reconsider the nature of their world. Tales of encounters with fairies, ghosts, spirits, and divine beings have been told and retold and provide a significant portion of what is bubbling in J. R. R. Tolkien's Cauldron of Story.[3] These stories include folktales, myths, and wonder tales but also plays, narrative poems, and novels, and they can be divided up in a number of different ways depending on what particular aspect of them one would like to discuss. This chapter looks at the urban fantasy scions of those encounters with the supernatural where the mundane protagonist's view of the world changes. A large part of the tales referred to above are set in worlds in which the supernatural might be separated from the mundane but where the protagonist nevertheless accepts its existence. Gods, fairies, ghosts, and spirits are accepted parts of the world, and running into one might come as a surprise but does not change one's entire worldview. But there are stories in which the supernatural is more than surprising and causes the protagonist to reevaluate completely what they thought they knew about the world. Suddenly everything they have believed so far is challenged, open for reevaluation.

Stories with such encounters have to be set in a secular, mundane world where the supernatural is not really something that society believes in. These are modern societies and modern characters confronted with incontrovertible evidence that the mythical and magical exists. In the face of such evidence, they must adjust their view of modernity, in order to somehow account for the supernatural. How they do this differs, and this is the subject of this chapter: How does someone in urban fantasy view modernity when forced to incorporate the supernatural (and often inexplicable) into their conception of the world?

Stories of characters who come to some insight about their world and have to revise their worldview are common. Arguably, such stories can be found in all genres, covering all kinds of insights: about a close friend or relative, an ideology or belief, or who actually runs the country, to name some. Discovering that magic actually works, that the dead can actually return from the grave, that fairies are actually real . . . such insights can undermine the very foundations of secular modernity. In urban fantasy, protagonists frequently have to face this other truth and somehow relate to it, because they have no choice. The supernatural not only appears; it requires something from them and it cannot be denied.

The large majority of urban fantasy stories about mundane protagonists who come into contact with the supernatural tell of more than a single encounter. Instead, the protagonists are made aware of the existence of the entire supernatural domain, although this domain can take various forms. Aaronovitch's supernatural domain, for instance, is a "wainscot society,"[4] whose denizens are not invisible, as such, but stay out of sight in the hidden spaces of modern society.[5] It is called the "demi-monde"—a term that can also mean "courtesan"[6]—and includes beings who are utterly different from humans (e.g., river deities, fairies, vampires, ghosts, and talking foxes) as well as humans who just keep a low profile when it comes to their use of magic. The series also includes a fairy realm that both is and is not located in the same landscape as the mundane realm and that requires supernatural power to access. This realm is not so much a wainscot society as a parallel world.

The supernatural domains that mundane urban fantasy focalizers[7] encounter range across a spectrum that stretches a bit beyond John Clute's wainscots, but the encounters fall into two main categories. The supernatural could suddenly become part of the focalizer's previously mundane and modern life, irrupting into it and introducing a measure of the supernatural into the modern, such as in Emma Bull's *War for the Oaks* (1987), Tanya Huff's Blood Books (1991–97; 2006), or Paul Cornell's Shadow Police novels (2012–16). These texts have a trajectory similar to what Farah Mendlesohn refers to as "intrusion fantasy": "the world is ruptured by the intrusion, which disrupts normality and has to be negotiated with or defeated, sent back whence it came, or controlled."[8] In urban fantasy, the intrusion can offer both a supernatural threat to be dealt with and a realization that the supernatural exists.

This realization often translates into an ability to understand and even become part of the supernatural domain; in urban fantasy, unlike in Mendlesohn's intrusion fantasy trajectory, normality is not completely restored. Alternatively, the focalizer could find themselves transported into a separate, supernatural domain. The extent to which this domain is separated from the mundane domain varies: It could be considered its very own world, such as the UnLondon in which the main characters of China Miéville's *Un Lun Dun* (2007) end up; it could be separate but only just, such as the *other* Manhattan in Mike Resnick's Fables of Tonight (1987–12); or there could be separate domains existing largely in the same space, as the London Below of Neil Gaiman's *Neverwhere* (1996). These stories are more similar to Mendlesohn's portal-quest fantasies, using a basic structure based on "entry, transition, and exploration."[9] But although these two poles of the spectrum appear to be different when examined from Mendlesohn's perspective of how the fantastic enters the text,[10] they are similar in terms of how the focalizer's portrayal of modernity emerges in the confrontation with the supernatural.

Common to the urban fantasy in which mundane and modern characters encounter the supernatural is that they learn to handle the supernatural domain. Mendlesohn refers to this as intrusion fantasy's trajectory from *denial* to *acceptance*,[11] to which I would also add *proficiency*. This trajectory is particularly noticeable in book series, in which the story shifts from the focalizer coming to grips with the supernatural, early in the series, to their using an increasing understanding of the supernatural domain to engage with supernatural threats. Aaronovitch's books are an example of this: the focalizer has to learn more and more about the supernatural domain, and during the first seven novels (the "Faceless Man" story arc), the scope and scale of the antagonist's magical skills are revealed a little at a time. Eventually, the rhetoric of the novels shifts as the fictive world departs ever further from the actual one, and what Mendlesohn observes regarding Laurell K. Hamilton's

Anita Blake, Vampire Hunter novels (1993–present) also happens with Aaronovitch's Rivers of London: the crime rather than the fantastic elements becomes the intrusion.[12] Regardless of whether the city is called London, Toronto, New York, or something else, it gains increasingly more degrees of "secondariness" as it deviates ever more from the actual world.[13] This focal shift toward the supernatural domain is common also in stand-alone urban fantasies and short series, where the protagonist, rather than returning home, remains in the supernatural domain.

This chapter examines how modern society is portrayed in texts that are focalized mainly by mundane characters who encounter the supernatural. Urban fantasy offers various kinds of such encounters, but they all share the need for the mundane focalizer to revise their worldview to include both modern society and the supernatural, and the way they do that provides a perspective on modernity. The main case discussed in this chapter, Aaronovitch's Rivers of London series, is almost entirely focalized through the police officer Peter Grant, through his first-person narrative. His view of the meeting between modernity and the supernatural therefore dominates the way the world is conveyed to the reader, and the novels provide a distinct example of how mundane modernity can be constructed in relation to magic and supernatural creatures. Through Peter, modernity comes across as a robust approach to the world, capable of including the supernatural within it. The discussion is followed by a brief overview of how other urban fantasy texts deal with the relation between the modern and the supernatural.

MAGIC AND RADICALIZED MODERNITY: BEN AARONOVITCH'S RIVERS OF LONDON SERIES

Peter Grant is the son of a British jazz musician and a Fula woman from Sierra Leone, born and raised in London. He is in his mid-twenties to early thirties during the series, and in the first novel, *Rivers of London* (2011), he has just finished his probationary period as Police Constable in the Metropolitan Police ("the Met") in London. An encounter with a ghost propels him into the "Special Assessment Unit," the branch of the Met that deals with magic and supernatural creatures. He becomes apprenticed to Detective Chief Inspector Thomas Nightingale, the only wizard on the police force. Through the series, Peter relates a tale of paranormal law enforcement, magical training, and adaptation to the supernatural community in a world where magical activity is slowly on the rise.

The Rivers of London series begins as an intrusion fantasy in a world divided into two domains but without a sharp boundary between the mundane and the supernatural. Although members of the mundane society are not familiar with the existence of magic and magical creatures, nothing prohibits the dissemination of information about the supernatural except that it makes most people uncomfortable and the population at large simply do not believe in magic. There is also a vague, unwritten "Agreement" that the existence of the supernatural domain is not widely advertised. The Special Assessment Unit, with the official call sign "Falcon" (*Foxglove* 33) but generally referred to as "the Folly" after their headquarters at Russell Square, is not a secret as such within the police force but is generally not talked about. The various cases Peter is involved in result in raising the Folly's profile as the series progresses, however.

Apart from Peter and Nightingale, the supernatural domain contains a range of supernatural beings. Foremost among these are the goddesses and gods of the river Thames and its tributaries, powerful *genii locorum* that might even be divine. Mama Thames and her daughters rule the lower part of the river and its estuary, while the upper course is presided over by the far older Father Thames and his sons. There are also various unspecified fairy creatures, trolls, vampires, ghosts, spirits, and talking foxes, and, among the criminal elements, "ethically challenged magical practitioners"—as a person of color, Peter resists the term "black magician" (*Moon* 88). Peter is also once transported into a magical fairy realm that is almost, but not entirely, separated from the primary world (*Foxglove* 364–73), and he experiences several dreamlike visits to London of the past (*Rivers* 363–72; *Whispers* 307–12; *Lies* 190–99, 379–91).

Aaronovitch's series has received some critical attention. Helen Young addresses how race is related to *genii locurum* of the rivers,[14] and Sylwia Borowska-Szerszun reads the series as challenging the white-centric paradigm of much fantasy literature by focusing on diversity issues and approaches to social and racial difference.[15] Aleksandra Łozińska examines how London's topographical, social, and magical spaces are (re)constructed through Peter's gaze,[16] and Yulia Georgievna Remaeva explores the spatiotemporal construction the *dvoyemiriya* (bi-worldness)[17] of the mundane and supernatural domains. Hadas Elber-Aviram sees the series as part of a tradition of progressive, urban tales of the fantastic that stretch back to Charles Dickens and points to how the central conflict between the Folly and the Faceless Man symbolizes a clash between rural and urban varieties of fantasy.[18]

The portrayal of modernity in the series of novels is predominantly communicated through Peter's narrative and colored by his views as he is confronted by an increasingly complex supernatural domain. The novels maintain Peter's first-person narrative throughout, with little or no distinction between Peter-the-character and Peter-the-narrator (despite their use of the past tense). Others' perspectives (for example those of his Met colleagues) are filtered to the reader through Peter's narration. Occasional short stories and the novella *What Abigail Did That Summer* (2021) apply other perspectives, and the graphic novels, due to the nature of the medium, provide more ambiguous focalization. Because the "visual representation of a fictional mind in comics is difficult to sustain,"[19] focalization is necessarily local, understood as a combination of visual framing and verbal information, such as speech bubbles and captions.[20] In *Rivers of London*, Peter enters the story with a worldview grounded in the mundane and the modern, a nonmagical world that might not be ordered but which *can* be ordered. He is characterized by intense curiosity, a strong belief in empiricism, a scientific approach to problems, and commitment to the systematic and eliminatory processes that he describes as the core of modern policing. Throughout the stories, his growing skills as a wizard and increasing understanding of the supernatural domain are coupled with constant questioning of and reflecting on the nature and function of magic and magical beings.

A number of perspectives are combined in Peter's narrative. The Rivers of London books are predominantly police novels, and his role as police officer centers Peter's narration. The plots are constructed mainly around finding explanations to crimes and apprehending perpetrators, and Peter provides a wealth of details regarding the procedures, structures, and activities of a modern police force. Another distinctive narrative perspective is his background as a young, mixed-race man from London. His mother's profession as a cleaner gives him useful experience and knowledge to draw from, as does his father's musical career, and Peter's cultural awareness is based in West African as well as in immigrant cultures. A third perspective that influences Peter's narration is his interest in modern popular culture and technology, in terms of allusions as well as direct references and parallels; and finally, his past as a student of architecture adds a particular level of detail and commentary to the way in which the urban setting is described (Łozińska examines how this contributes to a class perspective on the novel's social environment[21]).

Peter is a distinctly late-modern character, which shapes his core portrayal of modernity. His viewpoint is formed by his immigrant, ethnically aware background as well as by the carefully regulated nature of modern policing.[22] Added to this is his scientific orientation. In school he took sciences, and during Peter's first day, Nightingale asks him whether he understands the scientific method. Peter replies in the affirmative, thinking "Bacon, Descartes and Newton—check. Observation, hypothesis, experiment and something else that I could look up when I got back to my laptop" (*Rivers* 35–36). Peter is thus presented as a modern person but in a very particular sense of modernity, which also underpins the view of modernity that emerges as he narrates his encounters with the supernatural domain. It is a portrayal of modernity not as *opposing* the supernatural and the traditions that it espouses but as able to *integrate* them.

My reading of the Rivers of London series focuses on how modernity is portrayed as adaptive, resilient, and reflexive. It is a way of understanding and dealing with the world that is not in opposition to the supernatural but that is able to accommodate the supernatural within it. Through his trust in professional systems, an inclination to question received knowledge, and a scientific worldview, Peter integrates the supernatural in a modern paradigm. Some cracks remain in Peter's portrait of modernity, however, details that paint the supernatural as a challenge to modernity.

A New World of Orderly, Rational Magic

"I don't think the old world's coming back any time soon [. . .] In fact, I think the new world might be arriving" (*Moon* 88). Peter's words capture the underlying theme of the Rivers of London series. It is a world of change, and the young police officer/wizard is its harbinger (this is later stated explicitly in the ninth Rivers of London novel, *Amongst Our Weapons*, 2022[23]). While Nightingale interprets the return of magic as a return to what things used to be like before World War II, Peter sees how magic and the inhabitants of the demi-monde are entering a new stage. This is a world in which the old truths are not valid anymore, and new questions are required to understand it. It is a world that requires both police officers and wizards to be prepared to adapt to the changes that are coming, and as Peter can negotiate both the mundane and supernatural domains, he is well suited for the job.

The portrayal of modernity that dominates Aaronovitch's series has much in common with the radicalized form of late modernity theorized by Anthony Giddens, with particular focus on a reflexive approach to knowledge. In *Consequences of Modernity* (1990), Giddens argues that there are three distinct but interconnected sources that underlie the dynamism of modernity:

- the reflexive ordering and reordering of social relations (changing society based on new knowledge about society)
- disembedding of social relations (basing social actions on other than local or personal knowledge, such as trusting in experts or money), and
- the separation of time and space (ways of dealing with times other than now and places other than here, such as instant communication over vast distances).

These features of modern society and its institutions combine to drive the modern world forward[24] and are foregrounded in the portrayal of modernity that emerges from Peter's focalization in Aaronovitch's series. A great deal can be said about them regarding the actual world, but I limit my explanation to that which is of relevance in Aaronovitch's texts.

Peter's approach to knowledge is distinctly modern in its nature. One of the three sources that Giddens argues underlie modernity's dynamism is "*the reflexive ordering and reordering* of social relations in the light of continual inputs of knowledge affecting the actions of individuals and groups."[25] In the Rivers of London, this is mainly expressed through Peter's curiosity, scientific mindset, and tendency not to accept knowledge unquestioningly. Giddens discusses reflexivity largely in terms of how "social practices are constantly examined and reformed in the light of incoming information about those very practices, thus constitutively altering their character."[26] Peter's perspective concerns itself mainly with a particular type of social practices, namely of finding solutions to unanswered questions, in terms of how magic works and in terms of police investigations. But the reflexive application of new information to revise previous practices ultimately permeates his entire worldview.

Giddens's concept of reflexivity is central to much of his discussion on modernity. He has developed it over time and in collaboration with, for instance, Ulrich Beck and Scott Lash in *Reflexive Modernization* (1994), in which they "define reflexive modernization as the increasing capacity of self-conscious individuals and groups to critically apply knowledge to themselves and their societies."[27] It is much too wide a concept to cover exhaustively from a sociological perspective, and the discussion below illustrates only how parallels can be drawn between Giddens's view of modernity and "reflexivity" in particular, and the portrayals of modernity in Aaronovitch's series.

Wizard and Modern Officer of the Law

Rivers of London is a series of police novels in a supernatural setting, something that contributes greatly to the portrayal of modernity that emerges through Peter's focalization. Already during the very first pages of the first novel, Peter foregrounds policework before introducing himself and the ghost that propels him into a magical police unit. For him, modernity is epitomized by rational science and modern policing (both relying on disembedded expert systems), and the latter is reflected in his view of the Folly as a part of the Metropolitan police. Parallel to the main story arc of the first seven novels (the "Faceless Man" arc) runs the story of how Peter strives to make the Folly a part of the Met's modern organization. When the Folly is accused of lacking resources trained in the use of magic, Nightingale responds like a wizard: "It takes time to train new apprentices [. . .] It's not a process that can be rushed" (*Hanging* 201). Peter replies like a police officer rather than a wizard, however:

> "The Special Assessment Unit has recently instituted a programme of capacity expansion in order to build greater operational robustness and provide a more efficient service to our partner OCUs [Operational Command Units] when dealing with both Falcon and pseudo-Falcon incidents. The first phase of which is already underway." (*Hanging* 201)

The Folly is defended from bureaucratic attacks by Peter's adroit use of bureaucratic language and by his keen awareness of how the modern police force functions even in relation to the supernatural. He demonstrates his grasp of translating the resources that the Folly can bring to bear against supernatural threats into "that strangled mixture of cop-speak and management-ese that has proved the modern police officer's friend" (*Foxglove* 77), while at the same time avoiding an admission that training new Falcon (i.e., magic-capable) officers takes time. Instead, he lists specialist medical and forensics support, a best-practice guide for supernatural incidents, and a "consultation document" for circulation among "priority Falcon stakeholders"—all implemented under current "Home Office guidelines" and "financed entirely from within the current SAU budget" (*Hanging* 201). Although doubly junior—as wizard and police officer—Peter still manages to describe one sphere in the language of the other.

Peter would like the Folly to fit within the structures of modern policing but is aware of how the unit has failed to keep up with late modernity. He admits that the Folly's operational structure needs updating (*Hanging* 202) and does his utmost to modernize both Nightingale and the Folly's organization. This modernization process is referred to and progresses throughout the series but takes on a near-Sisyphean quality. The "best-practice guide" for Falcon procedures (*Hanging* 177, 201) seems to shift and expand, into a consultation document with new additions (*Hanging* 223), a Falcon Operations Manual (*Hanging* 282), and, by the end of the story arc, an "ever-expanding Folly Expansion document" (*Lies* 403). Additions are also made in terms of IT resources and staff, but more important are the attempts to update the Folly's (that is, mainly Nightingale's) views on things. For instance, Peter has to argue against his senior officer that vampires, chimeras, and other supernatural creatures have rights under the Human Rights Act and that it cannot be up to the individual police officer to act as judge, jury, and executioner (*Moon* 278–80). For all that these creatures are supernatural killers, the rule of law still applies, especially for the police, he maintains; Nightingale and the Folly's group of clandestine paratroopers cannot simply sweep in and put the creatures to death. Peter attempts to treat members of the supernatural domain in the same way as those in the mundane domain. He strives "to actively promote police/magic community stakeholder engagement in order to facilitate intelligence gathering" (*Broken* 209) and fosters close relationships with the families of both Mama Thames and Father Thames. As a result of his efforts, the Folly eventually takes on another "cryptopathologist" for autopsies (in *The Hanging Tree*), makes use of talking foxes as informants (in *Lies Sleeping*), builds "magic-proof" holding cells, and cooperates more closely with other police units.

The police investigation as a form of knowledge creation demonstrates Peter's dedication to late modernity. He repeatedly, albeit occasionally facetiously, iterates his commitment to "intelligence-led policing" (*Moon* 69) and gives detailed explanations of how police investigations work. Focus is on collection and collation of information: according to Peter, careful elimination of all possible leads is key to a police investigation. Successful police work is not the result of one person's "brilliant deductive reasoning" (*Rivers* 64) but of masses of information collected, collated, and analyzed by masses of officers. Peter repeatedly emphasizes how the police are a modern, *disembedded* organization for gathering and examination of information. Disembedding of social relations is another source for modernity's dynamism, according to Giddens, and permits the interaction across time and space with unknown people, for instance through expert systems. These are the "systems of technical accomplishment or professional expertise"[28] that we can place our trust in, rather than personally knowing the people involved and trusting them. The police constitute such an expert system, with a host of unknown colleagues who eliminate or analyze the plenitude of minute clues within the frame of an investigation, each trusting to the system rather than to known individuals. It is one of many instances where the police are portrayed as a force of modernity through the emphasis on one of Giddens's four institutional dimensions of modernity: the nation-state's control of information and social supervision. This dimension, which Giddens calls *surveillance*, includes but also goes beyond the concrete surveillance of prisons, schools, or the use of cameras in the public space. It includes the administrative capacity for collecting information and supervising the population, including ways of sorting, structuring, searching in, and analyzing information about the population.[29] The routinization of controlling everyday life that police carry out hinges largely on "expanding surveillance capacities."[30] Such surveillance provides the basis for police work, according to Peter, whether in the form of a HOLMES II database in which all information about a particular case is entered or as an IIP (Integrated Intelligence Platform) check, which brings up information about a person from several different information systems. Results from IIP checks are frequently referenced (e.g., *Lies* 5, 23–24) and are described in visual and verbal detail in *Body Work*.[31] Knowledge creation in modern police work is thus portrayed as an expression of modernity, through a systematic organization and a surveillance bureaucracy.

One aspect of policing that Peter accentuates is how the police organization is a system and that this system is the basis for solving crimes. He explains that "[p]olice work is all about systems and procedures and planning—even when you're hunting supernatural entities" (*Rivers* 261; cf. *Moon* 37–38) and points out that the police are a system for generating information and moving that information forward—it is not one person who collects and analyzes the information (*Lies* 83–84, 70). This is a late-modern way of describing the police and, on the whole, makes the organization come across as an "expert system," to use Giddens's term. These systems, according to Giddens, "routinize everyday life by institutionally confining madness, sickness, criminality, and death, and separating the moral issues surrounding them from daily activities."[32] The routines and regulations that Peter strives to apply also to police activity in the supernatural domain spring from the routinization of an expert system. Criminality, whether mundane or supernatural, should be dealt with by the expert system that is the police, according to the routines that exist within that system. That is Peter's view of the modern world.

Relying on modern police procedures is another way in which Peter makes use of modern tools to manage in the supernatural domain. Not only does he apply modern criminal investigation techniques to magical crimes, Peter also assumes that the procedures he has been taught in the mundane police force are equally valid in dealing with the supernatural domain. Already in his very first encounter with the ghost that claims to be a witness, he tells himself that "just because you've gone mad doesn't mean you should stop acting like a policeman" (*Rivers* 7). The procedures of the Metropolitan Police, which he learned during his training and which he keeps studying in order to advance within the force, aid him in his various encounters with supernatural culprits as well as in his relations with the magic community in general. Occasionally, procedures are not enough, and he falls back on his oath as a police officer to "prevent all offences." He risks his own life in order to save tenants from a building rigged with explosives, in contravention to regulation (*Broken* 330–31), and offers himself up as hostage to rescue children kidnapped by fairies (*Foxglove* 356–63). Keeping members of the public safe comes first.

Nightingale does not follow modern procedures, and it falls on Peter to introduce them in the Folly and apply them to supernatural situations. His rank notwithstanding, the senior officer pays little attention to modern routines. Peter relates how Nightingale cannot recall the full modern caution when he arrests a suspect (*Broken* 301) and dryly remarks that "in his day such things as assessments and case reviews hadn't been invented. At least, not at the Folly they hadn't" (*Foxglove* 81). A reason for this is that for decades, Nightingale was the only officer of the Folly, which was mainly ignored in the police bureaucracy,

> partly because we do stuff nobody likes to talk about, but mostly because we have no discernible budget. No budget means no bureaucratic scrutiny and therefore no paper trail. [. . .] Despite doubling the staffing levels when I joined and catching up on a good ten years of unprocessed paperwork, we maintain a stealthy presence within the bureaucratic hierarchy of the Metropolitan Police. (*Moon* 19)

This passage, from book two in the series, implies that the unprocessed paperwork was dealt with by Peter. Over the course of the "Faceless Man" story arc, the Folly's presence in the "bureaucratic hierarchy" becomes significantly less stealthy. The machinations of the Faceless Man requires the police to begin talking about the supernatural and to expand the Folly's budget. Ultimately, Peter is responsible for a modernization of the Folly and of Nightingale.

Peter not only processes a decade's worth of paperwork; he updates the Folly as best he can to allow the application of professional best practice to supernatural cases. At one point, he remarks that at the Folly, "we make most of our procedures up as we go along" (*Whispers* 29), but he is enthusiastically trying to address that problem. In order to make the procedures available to anyone working with the Folly, he starts writing a procedural manual. The manual may concern the supernatural, but it also offers a succinct example of Giddens's three sources of modernity's dynamism: Peter reflexively reevaluates its contents (e.g., *Hanging* 177), it is disembedded from its original social context, that is, Nightingale and Peter at the Folly, and it communicates information independently of time and space[33]—people who are spatially or temporally separated, for instance, in a large organization, can use the manual to interact effectively. Peter's manual also provides an illustration of his development over the series. In the first novel Peter peruses *Legends of the Thames Valley* from 1897 while his colleague reads the latest *Blackstone's Police Investigator's Manual* (*Rivers* 120). Peter's reading matter, which calls back to premodern times and the supernatural domain, is contrasted with modern, mundane police procedures. Five novels later, his own "dog-eared" (suggesting much-read) copy of *Blackstone's Police Operational Handbook* is juxtaposed with Peter's manual for dealing with supernatural incidents (*Hanging* 176). This time, Blackstone's comes across as outdated compared to the new manual that introduces police regulations for the supernatural domain. It is a result of Peter's double career as police officer and wizard and his success in combining the modernity of the former with the traditions of the latter.

The culmination of bringing the Folly into the modern organization of the Metropolitan Police comes at the very beginning of the seventh novel, *Lies Sleeping*. It opens with a three-page prologue (1–3) with what looks like an official proposal to the police commissioner to amalgamate a number of existing operations (from previous novels) into "Operation Jennifer," to be run by the Special Assessment Unit. The prologue breaks a pattern. Instead of opening in Peter's voice, the text confronts the reader with a table of administrative-looking items, bureaucratic language, and references to formal names and appendices. While on the one hand providing a summary of the operations of the first six novels, on the other, it indicates how the hunt for a supernatural criminal can be managed within the structure of a modern police organization. Ultimately, the prologue emphasizes how much the Folly has changed during Peter's three years there.

Lies Sleeping does not mark the final point in modernizing the supernatural unit of the police, but it shows a supernatural domain clearly dealt with in a modern fashion. With Operation Jennifer under way, the Folly is "treated as a genuine nick [police station]," and a full complement of police personnel are now working there (36–37), not just Nightingale and Peter. But more work remains in order to fully modernize the Special Assessment Unit, and when the Faceless Man is finally dealt with at the end of the novel, Peter is still not ready to quit, because he is not done with "[t]he magic, the policing, the reorganization" (404)—the modernizing of supernatural crime-fighting.

Magic, the Scientific Principle, and Curiosity

Next to the meeting of magic and the modern police organization, the meeting of magic and science is the most visible theme that contributes to how modernity is featured in the series. Two powerful drivers behind Peter's desire to modernize the Folly and supernatural police work are his deep-seated curiosity and his highly reflexive view of knowledge. Just a few pages into *Rivers of London*, an exasperated colleague explains to Peter that she does not want to know what is written on a lion statue in Trafalgar Square, how siphoning works, or why one side of a particular street is a century older than the other (17). Peter is too curious, without proper focus on the police work in front of him, she tells him. Her opinion is echoed by other characters throughout the series. Nightingale thinks Peter's "inquiring mind" distracts him from learning (*Rivers* 164; cf. *Broken* 26–27), and the goddess of the river Tyburn observes that he "think[s] too much for a policeman" (*Lies* 190). To Peter, curiosity and inquisitiveness are positive traits, however. He deals with difficulties by asking questions (*Hanging* 40), and although modern science may not have all the answers, it certainly has the best questions (*Moon* 35). Curiosity and inquisitiveness are not just positive traits; they are virtues and expressions of science and reason.

Peter is presented throughout the series as a person of reason and someone who believes firmly in empirical evidence. He expresses this not just in his remarks to the reader but in discussions with other characters:

> "You find out that magic and spirits and ghosts are all real," she said. "And you're just fine with that? You just accept it?"
>
> "It helps that I've got a scientific brain," I said.
>
> "How can that possibly help?"
>
> "I met a ghost face to face," I said, with more calmness than I'd felt at the time. "It would have been stupid to pretend it didn't exist." (*Whispers* 410)

This brief exchange with a colleague from the United States illustrates a basic tenet of the series: if you are presented with incontrovertible proof of the supernatural, the rational reaction is not to insist that it *cannot* be but to ask how it *can* be. Denying the reality of something is not rational or scientific if there is evidence to the contrary. There is an echo of Sherlock Holmes's famous maxim: "when you have eliminated the impossible, whatever remains, *however improbable*, must be the truth."[34] Peter does not feel the need to go so far as to eliminate every explanation (which would require omniscience); he is happy to apply a range of logical tools in his thinking about magic and the supernatural. He observes that absence of evidence is not evidence of absence (*Foxglove* 66), for example, and appeals to a particular application of Occam's Razor: there is usually a rational explanation for the weirdness he encounters: a wizard did it (*Foxglove* 35, 188; cf. *Rivers* 92). Rationality and logic thus become Peter's signature approach to the supernatural, as a means of understanding it and defending himself against it.

Aaronovitch establishes a magic system that is not only scientific but ineluctably modern. One of the five narrative strategies that Agnieszka Anna Jędrzejczyk-Drenda explores in her "*magi-focal*" reading of fantasy texts is "the strategy of knowledge," in which the magician calls to mind a scholar, scientist, or academic; magic is "presented in a framework that readers recognize as 'scientific' or at least 'academic.'"[35] Jędrzejczyk-Drenda concludes that treating magic as an academic discipline affects the structure of the fantasy world.[36] This is true for the Rivers of London series, but Aaronovitch takes his magic system beyond just "academic." The underlying principles behind the magic that Peter learns were originally developed by Sir Isaac Newton, renowned for his major contributions to science and mathematics in the late seventeenth and early eighteenth century—that is, in the early modern era (*Hanging* 79–80). Newton's role in establishing modern magic is repeatedly addressed in the narrative (e.g., *Rivers* 79; *Whispers* 93, 255; *Lies* 131), and some members of the demi-monde refer to the wizards of the Folly as "the Isaacs" (*Whispers* 141). Thus, magic is constructed as a modern and "academic" (if not scientific) phenomenon rather than as the antithesis of modernity.

This construction of magic as something modern is emphasized by the fact that anyone can learn how to cast spells; a wizard does not have to been born with a particular "gift" (e.g., *Hanging* 41–42)—it is an expert skill available to anyone who practices. "The rise of expertise is a key part of modernity," Giddens explains and continues:

> [t]here is a difference between expertise and the traditional claims to knowledge of religious officials, witch doctors, spiritual leaders or whatever, because expertise depends upon knowledge which, in principle, anyone could acquire, and without having to perform specialized, arcane rituals to do so.[37]

The typical fantasy magician who is born to their powers or has gained them through mystical means falls into the group of "religious officials, witch doctors, and spiritual leaders" that Giddens suggests are the *traditional*, that is, premodern, bearers of knowledge. Aaronovitch's magical practitioners are not part of this group. Etymologically, the word "wizard" derives from "wise"; a wizard, in other words, is a person of knowledge. The Folly upholds this equivalence between knowledge and magic: above its front door is carved the motto "Scientia Potestas Est" (knowledge is power) to underscore how the source of power for Aaronovitch's wizards is knowledge rather than some innate force. Magical knowledge is acquired through training and learning like many other modern skills, and wizards are experts on magic, not mystical holders of arcane powers.

The combination of science and magic is connected to modernity from the very start of the series. The meeting at which Peter is asked to join the Special Assessment Unit describes a trajectory from reason to magic. He is asked to explain his questioning attitude and belief in empiricism, has to affirm his understanding of the scientific process, and is finally confronted with the traces of magic called *vestigia* (*Rivers* 33–38). The mysterious and inexplicable about the experience is made undeniable through an appeal to scientific rationality. The encounter proves typical for the relation between magic and science: denial of the existence of magic (from a scientific standpoint) is presented as irrational, unscientific. The question shifts from whether magic exists to how it functions, a perspectival shift underscored by the Folly's "cryptopathologist," Dr. Walid (*Rivers* 67). Throughout the series, Dr. Walid and, eventually, his colleague provide a medical/physiological, empirical perspective on the supernatural. To emphasize the danger of using magic without training, they show Peter and his colleagues MRI scans of what a brain looks like when you have used magic irresponsibly (e.g., *Rivers* 69; *Whispers* 18, 281–82; *Foxglove* 101; *Hanging* 39–42). Their understanding of the supernatural and how magic interacts with the body is based on various types of data (e.g., *Hanging* 39–42; *Lies* 68, 112). Unlike Nightingale,

Dr. Walid appreciates Peter's empirical approach to understanding magic (*Broken* 25–26) and encourages the application of a scientific paradigm to magic.

The modern, academic magic is treated, by Peter, in a rational, scientific way, and reflexivity provides the basis for his approach. Peter turns to science whenever he fails to find satisfactory answers to his questions about the supernatural domain, and through methods of scientific inquiry he manages to develop new, or improve upon existing, technology. He reflexively questions received wisdom and traditional answers. Not least the work of his wizardly predecessors is contested in the light of new knowledge and criticized for shortcomings and illogical organization (*Foxglove* 234)[38]—indeed, he describes them as "often thicker than a bag full of custard" (*Hanging* 305). Although he never mentions Karl Popper, Peter clearly feels that theories should be passed on along with a critical attitude, a "challenge to discuss them and improve upon them," in Popper's words.[39] "In science *nothing* is certain [. . .] even if scientific endeavour provides us with the most dependable information about the world to which we can aspire,"[40] and why, according to Peter, should the "science of the supernatural" be any different? Earlier magical research should be reexamined, because research never provides the truth, only better hypotheses.

From his very first magic lesson, Peter begins to inquire about the nature of magic, prompted by a scientific understanding of the world. Magic raises so many questions: is the so-called werelight a product of oxidization? At what distance does a spell destroy silicon chips? From where does the power come when you levitate an apple? Does a spell draw magic out of an object or put magic into it? (*Rivers* 93, 173, 174, 200). These questions are not just idle curiosity but are framed in a scientific discourse:

> What worried me was where the power was coming from. [. . .] [L]evitating one small apple against the earth's gravity—that was essentially the standard definition of one newton of force, and it

> should be using one theoretical joule of energy every second. The laws of thermodynamics are pretty strict about this sort of thing, and they say that you never get something for nothing. Which meant that that joule was coming from somewhere—but from where? (*Rivers* 174)

A modern approach to the workings of magic with regards to the physical universe is not unique to Aaronovitch, but rarely do fantasy or urban fantasy authors couch the gnarly nature of magic and supernatural phenomena in such explicitly scientific language and perspectives. Peter does not only think about magic in scientific terms; he is "worried" about how it relates to a scientific universe. He tries to think about magic in terms of power output (in watt) (*Foxglove* 65; *Lies* 178) but also in terms of radioactive decay and a field (*Whispers* 239, 313). Eventually he has to admit that he has no idea about what magic is: Is it a "field? Subspace dimensional manifold? Banana flavoured milkshake?" (*Broken* 235). Despite his attempts to find scientific answers, Peter eventually has to just accept that it exists and it works.

Magic, though unexplained, largely fits within a scientific paradigm, especially through Peter's approach to the supernatural domain. The Newtonian origin of magic in combination with a widespread portrayal of magic as a scientific discipline provides a basis for this scientific form of magic. The impression is reinforced by the teaching and research laboratories in the Folly, which clearly emphasize the link between magic and science with their close similarities to chemistry labs (e.g., *Rivers* 91). Nightingale disapproves of Peter's experiments, noting that others have experimented before him (e.g., *Rivers* 164; *Moon* 240; *Broken* 26, 261; *Lies* 324, 397), but their approach is dismissed as unscientific (*Lies* 131, 183). Unlike his predecessors, Peter carries out his experiments in controlled settings, following established protocols. His first findings concern the effect of magic on microprocessors. Having observed two separate instances when magic had reduced silicon chips to sand, he formulates a hypothesis and sets up some simple experiments (*Rivers* 172–73, 197–98). His findings are of fundamental importance throughout the series, resulting in both technological tools and theories regarding the nature of magic. Inventing a way to measure the strength of magic reliably is another important project that Peter returns to over the course of the series. In *Moon over Soho*, he explains how the history of science is the history of how we measure the universe, which prompts him to develop a way to measure the strength of *vestigia*. He observes how the barks of his dog correlate to the strength of *vestigia* (*Moon* 25–26), devises a protocol to determine how to measure that strength (*Broken* 25–26), and ends up with the "ultramodern Yap scale of magical influence" (*Foxglove* 245). The facetious name notwithstanding, Peter can then use the dog to determine how long different materials retain *vestigia*, thus creating a forensic basis for magic (similar to techniques used to determine a corpse's time of death, for instance).

A key part of integrating magic into a modern, scientific paradigm is using a strict nomenclature to allow for precision in descriptions and experiments. During the early modern era (seventeenth and eighteenth centuries), the wizards of the Folly suffered from "a predictable mania for classification" (*Hanging* 62). Peter notes the particular problems with the class of beings called "fae" and hopes for a taxonomy for magical creatures based in medical science (*Whispers* 344–45; *Foxglove* 21; *Lies* 66–68). To facilitate his theoretical thinking around the supernatural, he tries to come up with new terminology, for instance for ghost types and magic particles (*Whispers* 311; *Lies* 298). However, the text cautions against believing that labeling is analyzing. Peter mentions that he has been warned by Dr. Walid not to use terms he does not know the meaning of. Both Nightingale and the cryptopathologist have also emphasized that labeling things you do not understand can lead to reductionism (*Whispers* 345; *Broken* 208). By relating the admonitions of the scientist Dr. Walid and the magician Nightingale,

Peter conveys the view that there is a common principle underlying both science and magic, that naming something is not the same as understanding it. Science and magic are ultimately contained within the same modern paradigm of rational thought and exploration.

Modernity's ability to contain magic is demonstrated by how science is applied to magic. From the beginning of the series, Dr. Walid serves as a source of inspiration to Peter when it comes to applying not only the scientific method but science itself to the supernatural. For a magical tradition founded by Newton, this should be the obvious way to go, but according to Dr. Walid, "for most of the early wizards the Baconian method was something that happened to other people" (*Foxglove* 281). Together with Dr. Walid, Peter uses DNA sequencing in an attempt to identify supernatural creatures, such as a chimera and a changeling (*Broken* 24; *Foxglove* 308–10, 332–33), and he masks his magical plan in *Foxglove Summer* by pretending that it is a science experiment (181). Peter's expertise in applying science to the supernatural is highlighted in *Black Mould*. He declares himself an expert in both science and magic, who should be trusted "with anything *outside* the realm of scientific understanding and rational thinking" as well as "with anything *within* the realm of scientific understanding and rational thinking."[41] His narrative comments offer a "little science lesson," explaining how wine is turned into vinegar by aerial bacteria, and he points out that mold can only exist within a narrow band of pH, which is why vinegar kills it.[42] When Nightingale is unable to use magic against a mold monster, he sends Peter to the laboratory for some kind of weapon, leaving it to Peter to figure out what. The implication is clear: Peter's scientific knowledge is required to fight the magical mold.[43]

His ability to apply science to magic also allows Peter to combine magic and modern technology. Giddens describes how "only in the era of modernity is the revision of convention radicalized to apply (in principle) to all aspects of human life, *including technological intervention into the material world.*"[44] To Peter, the material world includes the supernatural domain, and he translates his findings about the nature of magic into technological advances. In particular *Broken Homes* includes a number of magico-technical inventions, based on the magical, premodern explosive devices called "demon traps" (e.g., 263, 285–86, 340–41), but it is in *Rivers of London* that Peter makes the most important discovery about late-modern technology and magic: that magic destroys silicon chips if they are connected to a power source (172–73, 198). This finding provides the foundation for several technical solutions, such as the switch that disconnects his phone battery to protect the phone from magical destruction, the magic detectors that are used to search for unicorns, and the "screamers" that automatically phone for help (*Moon* 6; *Foxglove* 265; *Hanging* 288). He conducts experiments on other technical components as well, and updates magical rituals from requiring animal sacrifice to using electronic calculators (*Rivers* 214–15; *Hanging* 142). Finally, he also adapts magical spells, not only to create new effects (like many wizards before him, he experiments with that) but to develop spells specifically for use against technology (*Foxglove* 91–92). Through his technical inventions, the mundane and the supernatural are combined, concrete examples of modernity as a paradigm that does not break when it comes into contact with a supernatural domain.

Reason, science, and technology are valorized by Peter's portrayal of modernity. One way to conceptualize modernity is to see it as a

> struggle of Reason against emotions or animal instincts, science against religion and magic, truth against prejudice, correct knowledge against superstition, reflection against uncritical existence, rationality against affectivity and the rule of custom.[45]

Zygmunt Bauman's description captures much of how Peter portrays modernity: he illustrates the values of science, truth, correct knowledge, reflection, and rationality. He particularly shuns uncritical thought and the rule of custom and is prepared to constantly test received knowledge to achieve a better understanding of a world in which magic is a demonstrable truth. Through his perspective, we see a modernity that can integrate the supernatural through a reflexive view of knowledge and modern bureaucracy. As a person of late modernity, who can combine the modern and the magical, Peter fights supernatural crimes with whatever tools are best suited for the job.

That combination of tools is necessary, because many of his opponents similarly combine magic and modernity. The Faceless Man, the main antagonist in the first story arc, also develops new magic and magical technology, even though he ultimately strives to completely unmake the modern world. Lesser antagonists also combine the supernatural and the modern, particularly in the graphic novels. In *Body Work*, an ancient, malevolent force possesses cars with murderous intent, and in *Black Mould*, a vengeful, fungal assassin is created by combining scientific knowledge with age-old, magical powers. To solve these cases, Peter needs to use the best tools at his disposal, which means combining modernity and magic.

In Aaronovitch's urban fantasy, Peter portrays a modern society dominated by a sense that modernity's methods are robust enough to integrate the supernatural domain, yet there is also a counter-portrayal. Borowska-Szerszun argues that from a perspective of diversity and multiculturalism, Aaronovitch's world is "a zone of cultural tension and friction, which creates both opportunities and threats."[46] The same pattern can be seen in how modernity relates to the supernatural, where modernity's robustness is challenged even in Peter's narrative. The resistance from much of the Metropolitan Police to the magical forces that they are expected to use in their policing of the supernatural domain is established from the start. Detective Chief Inspector Seawoll from Serious Crimes makes no secret of his strong dislike of the supernatural

(*Rivers* 47), and although Seawoll and his second-in-command, Detective Inspector Stephanopoulos, come to accept the supernatural over the course of the series, they disapprove of the use of the "M-word" ("magic") and do not consider Peter's work for the Folly as "proper policing" (e.g., *Foxglove* 156).[47] However, Peter's proficiency in "proper policing," and the obvious need for supernatural law enforcement, wins some grudging acceptance from his colleagues, which suggests a desire to believe in magic while maintaining a certain skepticism. Empirical evidence tends to win the day, even changing Stephanopoulos's opinion somewhat; when she sees Peter conjuring up a werelight, her face "broke into [. . .] a wide smile of unalloyed delight" (*Rivers* 271). The "M-word" might be banned, but magic as a phenomenon can delight—as well as traumatize—modern police officers. The resistance to the supernatural in the force is an obstacle slowly overcome, not least by Peter's willingness to submit magical policing to modern operational standards.

Another counter-portrayal is the many supernatural issues that remain mysterious, despite attempts from Peter and his allies to find answers. Peter quickly realizes that the rational attitude to magic is that it works—the question is *how* it works (*Rivers* 92). For all that magic is described in technical and scientific terms, and supernatural beings such as ghosts and vampires are rationalized within a magical paradigm, it is only the effect of magic that becomes known, never its function. Other aspects of the supernatural remain similarly unknowable: Are the Rivers really gods and how do their powers function? What kind of creature is the Folly's uncanny housekeeper? What and where is Faerie? Ultimately, Peter has to accept that even though the supernatural can be treated scientifically, it cannot necessarily be explained through existing knowledge (demonstrated by the need for such an inexact scale as the "yap," the intensity and frequency of a dog's barking near magic). Magic can be subject to scientific inquiry, but it has a rationality of its own and remains beyond human knowledge.

The "typically modern view of the world" may be that "adequate knowledge [of the 'natural' order] is, in principle, attainable,"[48] but in the world of the Rivers of London, such knowledge might not, in fact, be attainable in the realm of the supernatural.

In the meeting between the supernatural and the modern, modernity—in particular radicalized modernity—comes across as a way of viewing and arranging the world and society that is robust enough to integrate even completely new knowledge and states of being. This portrayal of modernity is not the only possible one in urban fantasies with mundane focalizers that encounter the supernatural domain for the first time. The counter-portrayals lodged within Peter's narration remind the reader that his is only one view, and his police colleagues, Nightingale, the Rivers, and other members of the supernatural domain all have their own ideas of how modernity relates to the supernatural. Peter's portrayal may dominate the narrative, but it is neither totalizing nor unchallenged. Instead, the many alternative portrayals of modernity offered, though present mostly in the margin, serve to demonstrate how urban fantasy stories in which a mundane, modern focalizer meets the supernatural domain must ultimately deal with the question of whether, and how, the modern can integrate the supernatural.

A MEETING BETWEEN MODERNITY AND THE SUPERNATURAL

From Peter Grant's perspective, modernity is both robust enough to integrate a supernatural domain and useful enough to combine with it. When the two domains meet, he has no problem allowing them to mix, reflexively adapting his worldview to the evidence in front of him. Not all urban fantasy focalizers from the mundane domain react in the same way, however. While many convey a view of modernity as a versatile paradigm that can integrate with or even dominate the supernatural, others present the opposite perspective, portraying modernity as weaker than magic and monsters and of little use against supernatural threats.

Modernity can be mixed with a supernatural domain in a variety of ways. In Resnick's *Stalking the Unicorn* (1987), the focalizer, John Justin Mallory, is a private detective engaged by an elf to find a stolen unicorn in a parallel version of New York. Like Peter, Mallory quickly accepts that a different logic governs this supernatural domain and sets about learning it in order to find the lost unicorn. Whereas Peter is forced to do much of the work combining the two domains himself, Mallory encounters an already established mix, a domain that is mostly modern for all that it is also mostly supernatural. Other forms of mixing can be found in several of Charles de Lint's Newford stories, but in those stories, the line between the supernatural and mundane domains is more blurred. For instance, in "Bird Bones and Wood Ash" (1995), a woman gifted with powers from animal spirits collaborates with a social worker to find and "neutralize" child molesters. In this bitter comment on superhero stories, de Lint shows how supernatural powers can be used to save us from some of the darkest aspects of our modern society. The powers of animal spirits and the powers of modern surveillance combine to save children from monsters that neither can fight on their own. Another version of combining the modern and the supernatural in order to save modern society from a dangerous threat can be found in N. K. Jemisin's Great Cities duology (2020–22).[49] Here, the threat is existential, an entity seeking to destroy the very soul or spirit of New York, along with the people who have turned into paragons of the city. The supernatural springs out of modernity, however, and out of the modern city itself. Where de Lint's story exemplifies the "fundamental strain" of urban fantasy that Alexander C. Irvine describes as insertion of a folkloric tradition into the city, Jemisin writes more toward Irvine's other pole, emphasizing the nature of urban existence.[50] Rather than combining the modern and the mythical, her supernatural domain is by its very nature an expression of modernity. Where the supernatural domain in Aaronovitch's novels remains at least partially tied to premodern tradition, Jemisin creates a supernatural modernity. Where Resnick's supernatural modernity mainly provides an exotic setting for Mallory to solve puzzles, Jemisin uses hers to engage fully with the many problems of modern cities.

Occasionally, modernity is portrayed as stronger than the supernatural domain. Mendlesohn observes that "many [nonhorror] intrusion fantasies" have protagonists that succeed in managing the supernatural problem "by challenging the rules [of the supernatural domain] or changing them—usually in the face of the pessimism of their colleagues from the fantastical lands."[51] This manipulation of the rules can be related to the questioning of received knowledge that Peter exemplifies, the refusal of accepting dogma. To Mendlesohn, it also captures an aspect of "the colonialist fantasy of rescuing the natives from themselves."[52] In her reading of Bull's *War for the Oaks*, Mendlesohn explains how the protagonist, Eddie, "functions as a guide to her world for the [fairy] intruders."[53] But I would argue that Eddie does more than that: she teaches the fairies ways to use modern society to their advantage, and her own modern ways eventually help the Seelie Court to win. Eddie is one of several protagonists from the mundane domain who are lured into ultimately becoming the champion that saves the supernatural day. This does not necessarily mean that modernity in itself is portrayed as stronger, however. In Bull's novel, the way in which modern society develops ultimately depends on which fairy court wins the conflict: under the Unseelie Court, cities do not thrive but suffer urban and social decay.[54] The domains have different powers, set against each other.

A somewhat different kind of opposing forces shows modernity as a power that threatens the supernatural domain while being ineffective within it. In the Finnish author Maria Turtschaninoff's *Underfors* (2010), most folkloric beings have been driven underground by humanity, in particular because of industrialization.[55] Most of them are forced to live in a dark realm deep under the streets of Helsinki, far from their forests, lakes, and mountains. Those who have stayed behind have learned to understand the value of money, accepting euros instead of cherished memories or a first-born child.[56] Still, the two teenage protagonists that get embroiled in releasing and then defeating an ancient demon have very little use for their modern abilities or knowledge. They are forced to understand how the supernatural domain works, and although parkour skills are useful in extracting venom from a lindworm, these skills are not what prevents the demon from laying waste to the mundane and supernatural domains alike. This doubleness, in which modernity is described as dominant but ultimately ineffective, is also found in the Swedish novel *Udda verklighet* (2010), by Nene Ormes. For all that the novel's community of "strange" people has strict rules against revealing their existence to the "ordinaries" in fear of what modern society would do to them, modernity has little value in the supernatural domain.[57] Unlike in Aaronovitch's London, police and public authorities hold no sway over the supernatural domain,[58] and although "the Council" appears to be a force of power and surveillance that comes across as (almost) modern, it is feared by the strange rather than recognized as their legitimate ruler. Ultimately, the protagonist's attempts to frame the supernatural domain of the strange within the paradigm of modernity fail. In both Ormes's and Turtschaninoff's novels, the portrayals of modernity as an existential threat to the supernatural is only used to keep the domains apart. This motif—of human modernity, industrialism, colonialism, or religion driving magical beings away—is widespread in modern fantasy, and Saga Bokne observes its presence as early as in Geoffrey Chaucer's *Canterbury Tales* (c. 1400) and discusses the motif in a number of texts, including the stories set in Bordertown (1986–2011) and Kim Harrison's Hollows series (2004–present).[59] Both *Underfors* and *Udda verklighet* also demonstrate how modernity can be only marginally useful within the supernatural domain.

Many focalizers that superficially appear to come from the mundane domain in fact belong to the supernatural domain without knowing it. The marginal usefulness of the modern at least in part emerges from the fact that Turtschaninoff and Ormes use focalizers who discover that they are part of the supernatural domain. They want to understand the new environment to which they find themselves belonging. Clary, the focalizer of Cassandra Clare's Mortal Instruments series (2007–14), also grew up without knowing that she belonged in the supernatural domain. When she is introduced to it in *City of Bones* (2007), Clary unquestioningly accepts the supernatural domain in which modernity holds little sway. While abilities can be trained, mysterious, innate "gifts" are of primary importance, and "[y]ou cannot call the police and tell them your problem is vampires."[60] For Clary, adapting to the supernatural domain is a matter of letting go of how modernity works, not of combining the supernatural and the modern.

Some texts very clearly come out in favor of the supernatural being the dominant domain. An early example is Fritz Leiber's *Conjure Wife* (1943), in which the mundane and supernatural domains clash in the life of the focalizer, and the supernatural prevails. The story is focalized through Norman, a professor of sociology, whose wife, Tansy, has the ability to use magic. Norman's narrative voice conveys his disbelief in the supernatural while events clearly indicate to the reader that he is wrong (and pigheaded about it) and that supernatural events occur around him. Modernity is portrayed by Norman as excluding the supernatural, but his view is ironically undercut, and he is eventually forced to accept the existence of rules-bound magic. When the antagonist is defeated and Tansy is saved from a magical attack, his wife asks Norman whether he honestly believes in the supernatural or whether he is just pretending for her sake. The novel ends with his honest admittance of uncertainty: "I don't really know."[61] Norman's scientific mindset fails to incorporate the supernatural in his modern outlook, revealing the weakness of his dogma in comparison to Peter's reflexivity.

While Leiber's proto-urban fantasy uses an ironic narrative stance to demonstrate the weakness of dogmatic modernity, Gaiman's seminal *Neverwhere* employs a reversal of values instead. The result is the same: modernity and the mundane domain come across as weak in comparison to the supernatural domain. *Neverwhere* includes a number of focalizers, but it is Richard Mayhew's perspective that offers a view of modernity in its encounter with the supernatural. He witnesses firsthand how his ability to interact with the mundane domain decreases even while he physically remains in it: he cannot interact with ATMs or underground ticket machines, he loses his flat and possessions. Once in the supernatural domain, called London Below, machines yield up soft drinks and chocolate to the feudal Earl's Court, and the fashionable Harrod's provides the setting for a London Below "Floating Market." As I have pointed out elsewhere,[62] it is at this market that Richard experiences how even values are inverted in the supernatural domain, as stalls proudly sell "Rubbish! [. . .] Junk! [. . .] Garbage! Trash! Offal! Debris! [. . .] Nothing whole or undamaged!" and "Lost property. None of your found things here."[63] Elber-Aviram discusses the market and its spatial practices and values as "an alternative to the rigid structures of global capitalism."[64] At the Ordeal for the Key, reasonable explanations for Richard's experiences are depicted as deceitful attempts to make him doubt his sanity, and his attempt to be helpful by doing the logical thing and employ an expert, a guide, results in him being deceived by the vampiric Lamia. Finally, when he has successfully completed his quest and is offered the reward of a perfect life in the mundane domain—also within the power of the supernatural to provide—he still decides to return to London Below, turning his back on modern society. Irvine sees in Richard's return some of the genre's "constituent qualities": "[a] sense of alienation from city life" that finds relief through "the encounter with the uncanny" and "the flight from the city in the end."[65] According to Elber-Aviram, it even "redoubles" the "allure of London Below," which, she claims, "is so great that it leaves the reader with the indelible impression" that the life lead in London Below as "homeless and dispossessed" is preferable to life in the normal domain.[66] I will refrain from making proclamations about what impressions readers might be left with but agree that urbanity—and I would say modernity—comes off as decidedly unsatisfactory in Gaiman's novel.

• • •

When someone from the mundane domain encounters the supernatural, they invariably relate it to their previous, modern, life. There is no consensus among urban fantasists about how modernity should be portrayed through these encounters. Instead, writers adapt their portrayals depending on their characters and the focus of their stories. They cannot escape conveying some form of view of modern society, however, whether as robust enough to incorporate the supernatural, as flexible enough to combine with it (resulting in something more powerful), as weak and useless in the face of magical threats and challenges—or possibly as something utterly dominated by the supernatural domain. Regardless of which portrayal the focalizers offer, this portrayal is part of the genre's prevalent commentary on our society.

CHAPTER SEVEN

MEETING THE MODERN

Looking at our world through the eyes of someone else allows us to see something familiar as alien and to question what we have hitherto taken for granted. Through the experiences of others, fictional or real, we can discover injustices, peculiarities, and wonders that we did not spare a second glance before. Urban fantasy offers the possibility to take a step not only outside of our own culture, social group, or gender but also outside of modern civilization itself.[1] But that is not necessarily what happens when the reader is invited to share the perspective of a focalizer from the supernatural domain.[2] Rather than portraying modernity in strange terms, the supernatural focalizer can reduce modernity to a simple background, uninteresting, harmless, or, at best, convenient. Using Kevin Hearne's Iron Druid Chronicles (2011–19)[3] as a test case, this chapter explores how modernity is portrayed from a supernatural perspective.

By relating the story at least partly from outside of the mundane domain, it is possible to present modernity as dangerous or comical, incomprehensible or irrelevant. The stranger in our midst can misunderstand almost anything: frozen metaphors, cultural norms, technological creations, or anything else that is obvious to us. To describe modern society from a supernatural perspective is in no way uncommon in fantasy fiction. The number of stories dealing with medieval or fantasy knights who end up fighting cars are too many to list, although Esther M. Friesner might be alone in writing about a dragon who wants a baseball diamond for its hoard ("Take Me Out to the Ball Game," 1992). J. K. Rowling makes the magical commonplace and the technical wonderful in the Harry Potter books (1997–2007), for example, through Mr. Weasley's fascination with Muggle inventions. In the television series *The Good Place* (created by Michael Schur, 2016–20), on the other hand, the demon Michael's fascination with all things human draws attention to the ridiculous and incomprehensible of familiar phenomena, like stress balls, paper clips, and various parts of the human anatomy. And through the eyes of the protagonists of Alan Aldridge and Steven R. Boyett's *The Gnole* (1991), much of human society and technology comes across as confusing or terrifying (with the exception of the sweet, cold marvel that is ice cream). Martin Millar's two fairies offer a New York City estranged by the fairies' tiny scale as well as by their supernatural perspective (*The Good Fairies of New York*, 1992). This perspective allows the reader to examine their own culture, to look behind the veil that is familiarity and learn something that was previously hidden from them.

The outsider's perspective on modern society is not unique to the urban fantasy genre. Viktor Shklovsky uses Leo Tolstoy's "Kholstomer: The Story of a Horse" (1886) as an example of estrangement, a story in which a gelding horse is one of the focalizers, and which describes how the horse views human society.[4] But the outside perspective is much older than that. In Homer's *Iliad* (c. eighth century BCE), the gods meddle in human affairs and comment on what the humans are doing from their own divine point of view. To the extent that it depicts modernity, fantastic literature has long used outsiders as focalizers to estrange modern society. The science fiction genre in particular has a rich tradition of turning an outsider's or stranger's gaze upon our world. H. G. Wells's "The Star" (1897) ends its account of a calamitous event on Earth by shifting to the perspective of watching Martian astronomers, and since then, science fiction has presented human society through focalizers who are extraterrestrials, animals, artificial intelligences, and visitors from the future, to name but a few. By estranging modern human behavior, their perspectives warn, amuse, or engage; the reader is allowed to regard modern civilization from a distance.

Nonfantastic literature has also told stories focalized through the Other. Migrant literature offers numerous alternative perspectives on Western societies, detailing the migrant experience of relating to a new place and culture and the attempt to establish a new sense of self. Unlike those in much of science fiction, the outsider perspectives in migrant literature are largely distinguished by a "cultural 'hybridity,'"[5] where the protagonist is positioned, or positions themselves, between two cultures. It is a perspective particularly striking when the migrants come from places that are, as postcolonial theorist Homi K. Bhabha puts it, "constituted [. . .] 'otherwise than modernity.'"[6] These stories are not just recountings of the writer's experiences in moving from one country to another; they are accounts in which hybridity and in-betweenness as well as mobility and transnationalism are important.[7] As such, they can provide a double vision of modern Western society that is similar to much supernaturally focalized urban fantasy.

Urban fantasy stories that focus on or deal with migrant stories are uncommon but not nonexistent. Charles de Lint's Newford stories (1987–present) include fairy creatures who have emigrated from Europe together with the humans who believed in them, and the stories occasionally detail conflicts between the immigrant fairies and the original magical beings of North America (e.g., *Widdershins*, 2006). Millar's New York fairies are similarly immigrants, as is Tanya Huff's Toronto vampire in the Blood

Books (1991–97; 2006). Ben Aaronovitch's Rivers of London series (2011–present) includes numerous immigrant members of the supernatural domain, such as the river goddess Mama Thames. The Indian tiger demon Jhai Tserai moves to Singapore Three in Liz Williams's near-future Detective Inspector Chen series (2005–15). Less obvious migrants are the many long-lived magical beings of urban fantasy. Vampires, werewolves, and humans who enjoy magically extended lives are forced to migrate from place to place in order not to be revealed as the ancient and ageless creatures that they are. For all that they grow up with the culture that surrounds them, they are also new to it, immigrants who always have to settle down and adapt anew. The longevity that makes them familiar with mundane modernity also forces them to constantly wander within it. Only rarely, however, are these immigrants portrayed as dealing with the cultural hybridity and in-betweenness found in nonfantastic migration literature.

Through the use of variable or multiple focalization, a narrative can complement two or more points of view to provide a broader, more complex portrayal or to emphasize particular aspects of the world. Focalizers from different domains can provide different perspectives on modernity. The many focalizers in Huff's novels include beings from the supernatural domain, most notably Vicky Nelson's vampire partner. De Lint's Newford stories, in which both mundane and supernatural characters are focalizers, contain a harsh critique of how modern society treats those in its periphery. The Skyscraper Throne trilogy (2012–14) by Tom Pollock presents London's supernatural domain through the perspectives of two girls from the mundane domain and that of Urchin, son of the Goddess of London. The different views can complement each other in how modernity is viewed, or they can provide counterpoints to the portrayal of both domains.

This chapter examines how modern society is portrayed in texts that are entirely or predominantly focalized by characters from the supernatural domain. In urban fantasy, wizards, vampires, werewolves, fairy creatures, even angelic and divine beings can provide estranged views of modernity through their perspectives, whether they are cast as marginalized outsiders or as power-players at the heart of society. The text that I discuss in more detail in this chapter, the Iron Druid Chronicle, is narrated by an ancient druid. Its consistent first-person narrative and fixed, internal focalization provide a distinct example of an Other perspective on mundane modernity. Like a majority of urban fantasies with focalizers from the supernatural domain, it centers on conflicts in the supernatural domain and uses the mundane domain as backdrop.

KEEPING MODERN PROBLEMS AT ARM'S LENGTH: KEVIN HEARNE'S IRON DRUID CHRONICLES

Atticus O'Sullivan, born more than two millennia ago as Siodhachan O'Suileabháin, is the first-person narrator of Hearne's Iron Druid Chronicles. Atticus looks like he is twenty-one but was already more than halfway through his second millennium when modernity arrived in the late fifteenth or early sixteenth century, making him more premodern than modern.[8] His narration gives the reader a view of modern civilization through the eyes of an ancient, supernatural person who uses magic, can travel to the various mythical planes, and associates with supernatural creatures such as gods, werewolves, and elementals. His world closely imitates the reader's, but the druid's perspective on modernity provides a biased impression of that world, in which the supernatural domain is valued over the mundane, and modernity is mainly a lifestyle.

Atticus has stayed alive throughout the centuries partly because of the "Immortali-Tea" that keeps him from aging, partly because of a deal he has made with the Morrigan, the Celtic goddess of war and Chooser of the Slain (*Hounded* 9). She has promised him that he will not die in battle, which has allowed him to stay alive despite the fact that he has made a mortal enemy of Aenghus Óg, a Celtic love god with a truly dark side. Atticus is hiding from the love god's Fae flunkies in Tempe, in the Phoenix Metropolitan Area in Arizona, a place that is difficult to reach from Tír na nÓg. The story in *Hounded* centers on Atticus finally being found and confronted by Aenghus Óg's pawns and allies and, eventually, the love god himself. In the subsequent three books, the druid takes on fallen angels, bacchants, and evil witches (in *Hexed*); Thor and other Norse gods and mythical beings (in *Hammered*); and Native American skinwalkers (shape-shifters) (in *Tricked*). Each time Atticus prevails by wit, magic, and fighting skills, and with the assistance of various companions and allies.

As in most if not all urban fantasies set in the primary world, the world in the Iron Druid Chronicles is divided into two domains. There is a mundane domain of modern society, dominated by modernity, and a supernatural domain of myth and magic. The supernatural domain is inhabited by a range of beings who often enjoy immortality or extreme longevity, such as gods from different religions, fairy creatures, various users of magic, vampires, and werewolves. The domain also encompasses other worlds (called "planes") from various myths, such as Tír na nÓg (Celtic), Yggdrasil (Norse), and the First, Second, and Third Worlds (Navajo). The events take place in the supernatural domain, with only minor effects on the mundane—modern—one.

Hearne's texts are crafted to encourage the reader to consider the fictional world as a copy of the actual world. Brian Attebery argues that once the reader has identified a narrative as fantasy, it is no longer certain that they can assume that the narrated world can be extended even if it appears familiar: "No longer can we be sure that the fictional London is situated across the Channel from a fictional Paris or that its history matches any part of the history we know," not until the narrator tells us so.[9] Although we cannot be certain that the fictional world possesses a particular property, I would suggest that readers are still willing to assume that such extension of the world is possible until they are informed otherwise, in accordance with what Marie-Laure Ryan calls "the principle of minimal departure."[10] This applies even more if the text signals that the setting is, in fact, *almost* the actual world, as is the case in much urban fantasy, including the Iron Druid Chronicles. Not only does Hearne point out in his acknowledgments that he uses real locations in our world "albeit in a fictional way" (*Hammered* 312; see also *Hounded* 292; *Tricked* 340); his fidelity to the actual-world settings are clear from, for instance, the detailed descriptions of places and travel routes provided in the narrative. Already in the third chapter in *Hounded*, a likely actual-world candidate for the druid's house in Tempe can be identified, either from familiarity with the area or by using a map application with satellite view (see *Hounded* 25–26). The narrative's great attention to geographical detail and the wealth of cultural and, not least, popular-culture references encourages the reader to read the fictional world as a near-copy of the actual one.

Because of the textual insistence that its world be treated as the actual world, I begin my reading of Hearne's series against an actual-world description of the area in which the novels are set. Atticus is the last druid and a champion of Gaia, the earth's spirit; he gains his powers from the earth, and he is pledged to protect her (*Hammered* 60–61). As such, he can be expected to embrace sustainability issues. My choice of parallel text is therefore *Bird of Fire: Lessons from the World's Least Sustainable City* (2011) by Andrew Ross. Published in the same year as the first three novels in the series, Ross's book addresses a range of environmental and sustainability issues in the Phoenix Metropolitan Area.[11] Reading the druid's portrayal of his environment against Ross's presentation of the same area reveals how Atticus's focalization constructs a pattern of modernity as less worthy of attention than the supernatural domain. From that position, it is possible to see how the narrative constructs the combination of modern and supernatural as superior to either domain on its own. Finally, I address the focus on modernity as primarily an era of entertainment, convenience, and comfort.

"Vulnerable to Human Stupidity"

The most visible part of the pattern of magic as more important than modernity is seen in the clash between Atticus's role as protector of Gaia and the portrayal of his surroundings that makes him come across as unconcerned with sustainability. The druid's magic is given to him through so-called elementals, the spirits of "regional ecosystems" that require his protection because they are "vulnerable to human stupidity" (*Hammered* 106). In the first three novels, Atticus lives in Tempe, but although his narration describes various locales in that area, he pays little or no attention to any "human stupidity" that threatens the regional ecosystems there. This becomes visible from reading the druid's actions and nonactions against Ross's book about the actual Phoenix Metropolitan Area.

If the reader expects a druid who draws his power from the earth to express concern about the state of his environment, they will be baffled by how Tempe comes across through Atticus's narration. For three novels, Atticus describes Tempe and the Phoenix Metropolitan Area as a pleasant place to live, with few problems arising from the mundane domain. Only rarely does he suggest that there are any environmental problems worth mentioning. To the reader who expects the setting to be mostly like the actual-world Phoenix, the druid's portrayal might seem somewhat too Edenic. Read against Ross's *Bird of Fire*, Atticus seems to blatantly ignore many of the environmental challenges of his hometown. *Bird of Fire* is meant to "offer a composite picture of Phoenix's potential for a greener future along with the many obstacles that lie in its path,"[12] and it is difficult to avoid the impression that the picture is bleak, the potential slim, and the obstacles many. Although *Bird of Fire* includes a thorough investigation into a multitude of Phoenix's main problem areas, the twin scourges of water shortage and temperature increase emerge as the two most ominous horsemen of climate crisis apocalypse. In the fictional Phoenix Area painted by Atticus in *Hounded*, *Hexed*, and *Hammered*, on the other hand, they apparently pose no problem whatsoever.

Bird of Fire details the many sustainability problems that the actual Phoenix Metropolitan Area faces. Ross repeatedly returns to the problem of water management in an urban area of more than four million people, situated in the middle of a desert. By 2011, Phoenix Metropolitan Area had entered its second decade of possibly the worst drought in five hundred years.[13] The Colorado River, which provides the majority of the Metropolitan Area's water, was running at 66 percent of normal levels, and the big canal that delivered the water risked running short for the first time.[14] At the same time, the residents enjoyed one of the lowest consumer water rates in the United States. With temperatures reaching almost forty degrees Celsius—one hundred degrees Fahrenheit—on average two days out of every five, rate of evaporation is high and water supply critical. Aquifers are becoming depleted, and water has to be pumped three hundred miles uphill from the Colorado River.[15] In the actual-world version of Atticus's hometown Tempe, the artificial Town Lake loses five hundred million gallons of water—half its volume—to evaporation each year. The lake is constantly topped up by Colorado River water.[16] Urban heat islands are common, with a high number of deaths from heatstroke in the summer months.[17]

In the first three novels, these sustainability problems are all but ignored by Atticus. The high temperatures of Arizona are mentioned parenthetically and not as a problem (*Hounded* 26; *Hexed* 63; *Hammered* 93); neither heat islands nor heatstroke are mentioned. He describes private gardens with fruit trees and a public park with old oaks and verdant lawns. These are simply sources of magical earth power for the druid, not any indications of how scarce water resources are mismanaged in a desert area. Groundwater in the Sonoran Desert is a problem only insofar as it can damage his buried books of druidic secrets (*Hammered* 99); there is no mention made of how the Indian Bend Wash aquifer under Scottsdale and Tempe has been contaminated by toxic chemicals in what was "one of the nation's worst recorded cases of groundwater pollution."[18] Atticus briefly considers whether a prophecy that tells of how the world will burn might refer to global warming (*Hammered* 199) and observes how a frost giant provides an almost carbon-neutral method of transportation (*Hammered* 257) but gives no thought to climate effects on the regional ecosystems near his hometown.

One ecosystem *is* severely damaged in the novels, but the damage is not connected to human intervention. Instead, it originates solely in the supernatural domain. In the final confrontation between Aenghus Óg and Atticus in *Hounded*, the Celtic god commits what to the druid is a terrible crime. In his attempt to defeat Atticus, Aenghus Óg draws too much power from the earth, depleting and killing it for miles around (256). The result is a blighted zone, eight miles in diameter, in which

> [t]he trees were little more than standing dead wood, and the cacti were lumps of desiccated tissue stretched over dry wooden ribs. The brush was all kindling now, lifeless and essentially petrified: There were no ants, no beetles, no bacteria or fungi to break down the plants and nourish new growth in the spring. (*Hexed* 292)

This image of dead land taps into a tradition of landscapes of evil from fantasy as well as earlier texts, a tradition that can be traced back through Robert Browning and John Milton to *Beowulf*.[19] It combines the magical destruction with a modern, scientific view on what a lifeless land means: no plant or animal life, no bacteria or fungi. This place is worse than even the inimical plains of Tolkien's Mordor; it is the dry land of death in Ursula K. Le Guin's Earthsea books (1968–2001), but made all the more terrible for being set in the primary world. This magical desolation becomes the motivation for Atticus to remain in the area in the following books, in order for him and his apprentice Granuaile to heal it, one slow step at a time. To the druid, this misuse of the earth's power "bespoke of an evil [he] could not countenance" (*Hounded* 256). Killing the earth in this way is far worse than betraying and murdering—if it is done by magical means. What humans do with all the destructive tools of modernity at their disposal appears to make no difference to Gaia; whatever they do can never be as utterly destructive as this. This position is emphasized after Atticus's victory over the love god. The druid needs water to heal a companion and asks his wolfhound Oberon for help:

> "Oberon, do you smell water anywhere nearby?"
>
> He raised his snout to the air and took a few good, long snuffles [. . .] but he sounded sorry when he replied, <I can't smell anything over the blood and demon stench. Why don't you just bring some up from the earth? I've seen you do it before.>
>
> "Aenghus Óg killed the land here. It won't obey me now." (*Hounded* 276)

This is an example of how the supernatural and mundane domains are treated quite differently, with the latter accorded less importance. In the actual world, this area has suffered from more than a decade of severe drought,[20] so the absence of water and Atticus's inability to "just bring some up from the earth" are quite understandable. Yet none of the region's many mundane, water-related problems are addressed by the druid. His ability to draw water from the land is not hampered by drought but by Aenghus Óg's overuse of magical earth power, and Oberon cannot smell any water because of the stench of blood and demons, not because there is no water due to human overuse.

Other situations also demonstrate how protecting the regional environment from human stupidity is of little concern to the druid. In return for a favor from the Sonoran Desert elemental, Granuaile takes on the work of removing crayfish from a river, because they are "a nonnative invasive species that [are] slowly killing off the native fish and frogs in the river by eating their eggs and competing for food" (*Hammered* 105). Her task is the first case of protecting a regional ecosystem from harm caused by humans, who presumably introduced the crayfish, and she is keen to do it. The initiative does not come from the druid or his apprentice, however, but from the elemental that represents the ecosystem in question. Granuaile is just enthusiastic about taking on the task, but Atticus see some clear benefits to it. It helps build a relationship between Granuaile and the elemental, and it takes her out of town at a time when the situation there is dangerous (*Hammered* 106). From his perspective, the apprentice's excitement springs from the wonder at a first interaction with an elemental, not from the chance to do something concrete for the environment (*Hammered* 107). Magic is more interesting than ecosystems.

The fourth novel in the series explicitly addresses the druid's lack of concern for mundane environmental problems: whatever mundane humans do will not harm Gaia because her lifespan is so incredibly vast. In *Tricked*, Atticus is asked to close down a coal mine, in return for a favor from another elemental. This task triggers both discussions about and reflections on a druid's role in relation to environmental damage caused by humans. Although Atticus considers "clean coal" to be "an Orwellian oxymoron" (114) and explains that, as far as he is concerned, "there isn't a vampire in the world who's worse than an oil executive" (200), he also sees the futility in becoming a magical ecoterrorist:

> I could spend my entire life doing it, shifting from place to place, and I still wouldn't stop them. I can do one big mine, maybe two, a day. So that's 730 mines a year if I don't take a day off and never spend two nights in the same place. Do you know how many mines there are in this country alone? Tens of thousands. And for every mine I shut down, another one will start somewhere else. Even the

> ones I shut down will reopen after a while. And that's doing nothing about developing and dams and overfishing and oil spills and clear-cutting virgin rain forest for cow pasture so some fat man in Rio can have a steak. There's no way I can keep up. (116)

For all his magic and immortality, the druid is only one person. His resources are not sufficient to do something even about all the human threats to Arizona's various ecosystems, let alone the entire world's. His argument is rational and, on the surface, irrefutable. Unlike in the first three novels, he comes across as aware of and concerned about the environmental destruction caused by modernity. The argument is tinged with resignation and is hauntingly familiar from that ubiquitous defense against addressing any major problem: a single person's vote, one customer's boycott of a company, or a small country's carbon emissions, are just tiny drops in their respective buckets and will not affect the big picture. Even in the light of the satisfaction it gives him to sabotage the operations of the mine and thus do something concrete to protect the regional ecosystem (119), Atticus does not see himself as a solution to modern, environmental problems. Those problems belong to the mundane domain and are not his main concerns.

Ultimately, *Tricked* ends up defending the position of the previous three novels: magical damage to the earth is what counts, and what human society does is irrelevant and uninteresting. "[P]reventing ecological disaster isn't a Druid's primary function" (243), Atticus explains when Granuaile confesses that her motivation for taking on the twelve years of study required of an apprentice druid is her desire to become the opposite and nemesis of her oil-executive step-father. Gaia can survive whatever humans do given her geological timescales; druids were created to protect the earth's magic. When the trickster god Coyote tries to gain Atticus's assistance by pretending that the aim is to establish a solar power project, the possibility of clean energy is only a step in the right direction to the druid. The main attraction of the trickster god's project lies in how it will help persuade the local elemental, which wants to replace the coal mine with a clean alternative. To the extent that the fictional world copies the actual Arizona, the solar power project makes Coyote come across as either duplicitous or naive. Although the state has 334 days of sunshine annually, it also has one of the largest nuclear power plants in the United States, and solar power has so far failed to succeed there.[21] Nothing in the novel suggests that Coyote's project would fare any better. Whether Atticus is aware of this or not, the clean energy source is not his priority, only a means to an end.

For all that druids in the Iron Druid Chronicles are meant to protect regional ecosystems from human stupidity, the first four novels of the series present a narrative position that places magical threats to the environment above the human damage caused by modern society. Even the fourth novel, which explicitly addresses the druid's concern for the environment, only reinforces that position. Protecting the earth from magical damage is paramount. What is done to Gaia by people in the mundane domain is regrettable but ultimately irrelevant. Atticus's view is that of an immortal being: in the long run, what humans do to the world will heal. To paraphrase Andrew Marvell's "To His Coy Mistress" (1681), there *is* world enough, and time. And this position, of magic above modernity, is part of a wider pattern in the novels.

Either Is Good, Both Must Be Better

That the protagonist draws his power from the earth but has little concern for the looming ecological disaster around him fits into a larger pattern of how he portrays modern society as a whole. The relation between the domains is not symmetrical. Deities in particular belong to the supernatural domain and often fail to adapt fully to the rules of the mundane domain when called to visit it, but they are aware that it exists. In fact, many of the supernatural beings only occasionally visit the mundane domain or even the earth. The existence of the supernatural domain is largely kept hidden from the mundane domain (*Hexed* 135). The human characters in the story, such as Atticus's neighbors, the customers of his shop and the staff who work there, the police officers that investigate him, and staff in various restaurants are people of late, rational modernity and reside in the mundane domain. These characters do not consider, and even refuse to acknowledge, the existence of the supernatural and mostly fail to understand it when they come into contact with it.

There are some characters who straddle the two domains, making themselves at home as much as possible in both. Like migrants, they have not settled for either domain but inhabit a "hybrid in-betweenness,"[22] and their ability to negotiate both domains is valorized in the text. Atticus is the most prominent example of this domain hybridity. His magical abilities and longevity not only combine with but are constructed in terms of modern characteristics. Druidic training, as Atticus's training of Granuaile demonstrates, is described more as modern expertise than traditional (esoteric) knowledge. It "depends upon knowledge which, in principle, anyone could acquire, and without having to perform specialized, arcane rituals to do so"[23] and is at least in part tied to an understanding of the natural world in scientific terms. Through the migrant lifestyle required of him because of his long life, Atticus also typifies a form of that "banal cosmopolitanism" that Ulrich Beck associates with what he calls "second modernity."[24] During his long life, the druid has lived on at least four continents and speaks multiple languages, a global citizen who predates the modern nation-state but also transcends it, his citizenship determined only by his latest set of forged papers. Modernity and supernatural characteristics are intertwined for him, just as it is for a range of other supernatural beings that live in both domains, such as the witches in the local coven and the vampire and werewolves that serve as Atticus's lawyers.

Characters who are confined to, or confine themselves to, only one of the domains are often presented as naive and ridiculous—occasionally fatally so. The goddesses Flidais and the Morrigan both fail to keep up with the times, are unfamiliar with the Internet, and do not understand how electrical appliances work. Aenghus Óg's reliance on old Irish fencing patterns becomes his undoing when Atticus attacks with styles he has learned during centuries in Asia and a decade of sparring with an Icelandic vampire. Even the vampire, who is one of Atticus's lawyers, is made fun of for his inability to adapt to present day language, dress, and popular culture. Although the druid never says as much, it is clear that failure to keep up with the changes in the mundane domain and its cultural codes makes you deserving of mockery from those who do.

Humans who are aware of only the mundane domain are similarly ridiculed. The neighbor across the street is repeatedly humiliated: he is infuriated by the incomprehensibility of an invisible Oberon pooping on his lawn; when he reports a fight between Atticus and some giants to the police, the druid makes him appear *non compos mentis* by magically camouflaging the giants' bodies; and he faints when witnessing a demon being defeated by a giant cactus (*Hounded* 132, 121; *Hexed* 23–25). The police officers who investigate Atticus and his hound for various crimes are frustrated by camouflage magic, werewolf lawyers, and the magical regeneration of a ruined ear (*Hounded* 165–71; *Hexed* 181–83, 234–35). Atticus even sees magic as a way to play deliberate tricks on humans. He contemplates learning how to make his eyes flash green to freak out baristas who get his order wrong, compels two policemen to have a slap fight, and gives a magical wedgie to a paramedic (*Hexed* 163, 125–26; *Hounded* 183). Even present-day, mundane (United States) society more broadly is set up for mockery, for instance of its sexual mores, attitude to body hair, and appreciation for meaningless gadgets (*Tricked* 191; *Hammered* 303, 54).

Knowing that both domains exist is not enough for a character to count as cool in the Iron Druid Chronicle. Domain hybridity is required: those who have the ability to understand and play by the rules of both domains are represented as being better than others. Atticus is impressed by how some ghouls combine the supernatural and the modern by having a refrigerated van (for storing corpses they cannot immediately eat) (*Hounded* 122–23). The shape-shifting ability and ferocity of the werewolves are described just as favorably as are their professional skills as lawyers and surgeons. And most of all, the druid is smugly satisfied about how he combines his own magical abilities and longevity with an understanding of the mundane domain. He can mix contemporary slang and old-fashioned phrases freely (e.g., *Hounded* 74–77) and understands his magic and herbal lore in terms of natural science (e.g., *Hounded* 77–78; *Hammered* 250–51), and even though he mentions in passing that there are difficulties involved with being a magic user and pagan in the modern world (*Hexed* 103), that is apparently a shortcoming of the mundane domain, not of the supernatural—or of himself. The domain hybridity also largely coincides with being migrants. Atticus and his vampire, werewolf, and witch allies are all old enough to be immigrants in the United States, all of them having been born in Europe centuries ago. They are cultural as well as domain hybrids, and Atticus celebrates this, his tone conveying a sense of superiority over mundane humans and supernatural Fae alike, stuck as they are in their domains as well as their native cultures.

Modern society provides a setting for the story, but it is generally relegated to the periphery, treated as little more than a source of convenience, creature comforts, and entertainment. The sense of superiority that accompanies being in command of both domains does not translate into a portrayal of the domains as being equal. As is indicated by the druid's concern with supernatural threats to the environment, it is the supernatural domain that is in focus. The events in the novels are driven by what happens in the supernatural domain and what has happened, mostly in the distant—premodern—past. Yet, some aspects of late modernity have influenced the druid, for instance, a modern lifestyle.

"Lifestyle issues become dominant in the late modern era, as they [. . .] 'give material form to a particular narrative of self-identity.'"[25] The "self-identity" that Atticus conveys quickly resolves itself into a narrative of convenience. When he introduces the reader to his life as a 2,100-year-old druid in modern Arizona, he explains that to most "old souls" that he knows, "the attraction of modernity rests on clever ideas like indoor plumbing and sunglasses" (*Hounded* 2). To him, the relative absence of gods and the fact that people can be different without being killed are the main advantages of the modern United States (*Hounded* 2–3), but he is also very fond of bicycles and extols the usefulness of the Internet (*Hounded* 4). He stresses the convenience of the ghouls' refrigerated van, of his own combination of scientific understanding with herbal lore, and of modern weapons in fighting witches (*Hexed* 262–63).

Another characteristic of modernity that is prominent in Atticus's focalization is the abundant opportunities for modern indulgences, not least in terms of food. Through Atticus's narration, Oberon the wolfhound comes across as the most food-fixated character in the novels, his main desire being sausages of various kinds. He insists that there is a "bacon latte" and that the Holy Grail of coffee products is the "liquid paradox" called "Triple Nonfat Double Bacon Five-Cheese Mocha," currently (Oberon claims) under development by Starbucks (*Hammered* 102). This surreal example of canine culinary inventiveness succinctly captures a late modernity where food is the result of industrial creations set to capitalize on customers' contradictory desires in which recipes are only limited by imagination—and chemistry. Atticus himself is not as culinarily imaginative as his dog, but he still expresses great enjoyment of modern food. Food as an experience rather than as sustenance is a recurrent theme, from a restaurant specializing in highly unusual foodstuff (*Tricked* 184) to a vivid description of Atticus's favorite breakfast (*Hammered* 92). His preferred bars and restaurants are regularly mentioned or visited, and the druid frequently waxes lyrical about the fish and chips served at a particular pub (e.g., *Hounded* 83–84). But characters who only keep to the supernatural domain, it is suggested, have no business picking favorite food from the mundane domain. When Flidais and the Morrigan reveal their weaknesses for certain modern foodstuff—smoothies and ice cream, respectively—Atticus's narrative is tinged with light derision. Goddesses apparently do not deserve comfort food. A similarly facetious tone suffuses the description of how Jesus Christ enjoys Atticus's favorite fish and chips so much that he makes the dish miraculously appear in front of all the other patrons (*Hammered* 113).

Most of all, however, modernity is portrayed as a source of entertainment. Atticus has been around for a long time and makes numerous cultural references that paint him as a well-read and cultured person. His references include paraphrases of William Carlos Williams (*Hammered* 32–33), throw-away references to Dante Alighieri, Victor Hugo, and William Blake (*Tricked* 4, 80, 95), parallels between Caravaggio, Titian, Guido Reni, and Nicolas Poussin (*Hammered* 144), and reflections on music from Richard Wagner's Ring Cycle (*Hammered* 38). All four books also include numerous references to the works of William Shakespeare, including a quoting duel between Atticus and his vampire lawyer (*Hammered* 145–47). Atticus is a great fan of the Bard's work, to the point where Flidais remarks on his anachronistic use of the expression "vent their spleen," asking whether it is an attempt to quote Shakespeare. The druid explains that he occasionally confuses his idioms and that the contemporary expression would be "go apeshit on my ass" (*Hounded* 250). While Flidais can identify the inappropriate usage, she does not know enough about the modern idiom to determine what would be more appropriate and adopts Atticus's suggestion. The highly colloquial expression is established as contrast to the old-fashioned form for comedic purposes and turns into a running joke for the chapter, but it also demonstrates the ease with which Atticus slips from Shakespeare to popular culture. The Shakespeare duel with the vampire offers a similar example, where the druid goes from quoting Shakespeare to using "Lolcat" language (*Hammered* 148), to the vampire's exasperation. The juxtaposition of Shakespearian or Elizabethan language and modern idioms draws attention to the various registers available to the druid and to his command of the very contemporary as well as the long-gone past. It also demonstrates how Atticus connects the Bard of Avon to popular rather than "high" culture. His view of Shakespeare remains, in a sense, Elizabethan: as a playwright who wrote for all kinds of audiences and not just for a cultural elite. Elizabethan theatre appealed to all classes of society,[26] and Shakespeare remains its foremost representative. Through Atticus's voice, Shakespeare comes across as an enduring symbol of popular entertainment, a symbol that arose during early modernity. The druid's constant references to Shakespeare thus reinforce the centrality of popular culture to modern life in the Iron Druid Chronicles.

Through his multitude of references to popular culture, the ancient druid firmly establishes himself as modern. The variety and quantity of popular-culture allusions, mentions, and examples constitute one of the novel's most prominent stylistic characteristics. Atticus peppers his narration and conversations with references to a wide range of popular-culture phenomena, and he appreciates others' allusions to popular culture as well. Not least his communication with Oberon shows the two of them sharing a deep interest in movies and television shows, but references to literature, music, sports, and other forms of cultural expressions also abound. A large part of the references relate to genre fiction in various media as well as to fan culture, establishing Atticus, Oberon, and to some extent Granuaile as, in particular, science fiction and fantasy afficionados. Well-known science fiction films, television shows, and franchises, including *Star Wars*, *Star Trek*, *Battlestar Galactica*, *Avatar*, *Terminator 2*, and *Stargate*, are mentioned or alluded to alongside more mainstream fare, such as *Field of Dreams*, *Kill Bill*, *Smokey and the Bandit*, *Die Hard*, *Bull Durham*, and *The Colbert Report*. Literary allusions include Tolkien's works as well as Stephenie Meyers's Twilight series and Douglas Adams's *The Hitchhiker's Guide to the Galaxy*. Atticus demonstrates familiarity with music by, for example, Danny Elfman and John Williams, INXS and Robert Johnson, as well as with popular-culture phenomena such as Jell-O shots, zombie attacks, the game Twister, and San Diego Comic-Con. He mentions the Oscars and Netflix, and even resorts to gamer jargon to one-up a witch: "If we fought the Tuatha Dé Danann, we'd get so *pwned*" (*Hounded* 147), *pwn* being gamer jargon that indicates the defeat or domination of an opponent. By constantly employing popular-culture references, Atticus projects an image of himself as a person of modern culture.

Atticus's cultural frame of reference comes across as that of someone who is born in the 1960s and enjoys popular entertainment, and that frame of reference also signals what is important about modern life and the mundane domain in Atticus's narrative. Modernity mainly provides entertainment, good food, and some practical inventions. It is rarely a source of threat or danger, unless there is a supernatural root cause. The police officer who is dead set on finding Oberon and ends up shooting Atticus is controlled by Aenghus Óg. High rates of crime, poverty, and car accidents are explicitly not caused by "[s]ocioeconomic status and poor civil engineering" (*Hexed* 47) but by evil supernatural actors. Tempe is about to "pass through the Valley of the Shadow of Deep Shit" because of an invasion of vampires, angry gods, and fanatic Kabbalists, not for any mundane reason (*Hammered* 74). It is also demonstrated how people in the mundane domain try to explain events in the supernatural domain. Sixty-three vampires killed at a sports event are, for instance, explained by gang warfare, terrorism, illegal immigration, or human trafficking (*Hammered* 93). Only in *Tricked* are social and environmental problems addressed as arising in the mundane domain, and they are introduced in the conversation by the trickster Coyote (22–23) and the apprentice Granuaile. The importance of such problems is ignored or undermined by the druid, implying that they fall outside of his interest in modernity.

As modernity is just a source of practical inventions, a comfortable life, and amusement, it is hardly surprising that the druid makes nothing of his living in "the World's Least Sustainable City." For all that he congratulates himself on being more than two millennia old and still able to pass as a man in his twenties, and despite his powers coming from contact with the natural world, Atticus refrains from addressing problems of mundane, modern society. The man-made drought and water-wasteful society that surrounds him is not nearly as problematic as the blighted area created by his ancient, divine enemy. The waste of water, the pollution, the lethal, urban heat islands, even the danger inherent in a nuclear power plant without access to a large body of water for cooling—they are not what druids are set to worry about. Atticus's somewhat smug remark about other immortals could refer to his own blinkered view as well: "Immortals don't always pay much attention to current events" (*Hounded* 14).

Drawing or Withdrawing Attention

"Estrangement" refers to the way in which a literary device, intentionally or unintentionally, changes the way in which the reader views a familiar phenomenon. Using a magic-using druid from the Iron Age as first-person narrator could be expected to have great potential for estranging the modern society. However, because the narrator and the narrative maintain a steady focus on the supernatural domain and establish a value system in which the supernatural domain provides the important issues and the mundane domain furnishes entertainment and indulgences, the potential for estranging modernity is drastically reduced. The offer to consider the world in a different light is countered by an offer not to consider the world at all.

To accept the Iron Druid Chronicle's offer of estrangement requires the reader to perform a sort of mental contortion: they need to maintain their established view of the world in order to see it differently. The values promoted by the narrative are seductive: it offers escape from the challenges of modernity into a world governed by myths and magic. The world might still be the same, but its problems are reduced by comparison to magical threats and mythical powers. The text contains the counter to Atticus's voice, however. If the reader remains aware of the many problems of modernity, the druid's position jars. And when finally juxtaposed with descriptions of those problems, it is possible to decide that all the entertainment of the modern world cannot hide the fact that dire threats abound: existential threats to our climate, to our natural environment, to ourselves. The social commentary is present, but as readers, we are offered a chance to ignore it.

MARGINAL MODERNITY AND FOCUS ON THE SUPERNATURAL

Hearne's books are typical for urban fantasy with supernatural focalizers in a modern setting. Unlike the modern character who strays from the mundane domain into the supernatural, the supernatural focalizer is often familiar with both domains or is at least aware of the existence of the mundane. Like all urban fantasy, however, their stories are constructed around and focused on characters and events in the supernatural domain. All the excitement takes place in a domain that they are familiar with, and the mundane domain recedes from view, into the background or toward the margin. Unlike with mundane focalization, there is nothing alien to fear, marvel at, or ponder—nothing strange to describe. Supernatural focalization offers an insider's view of the mysteries of the supernatural without much need to draw attention to the familiarity of the modern and mundane.

Marginalizing the mundane does not mean that modernity is ignored or cast in a neutral light. Through Atticus's focalization, modernity comes across as comfortable, practical, and entertaining.

As a character, he is defined by his enthusiasm for popular culture and his appreciation for modern conveniences. His long life, most of it spent in premodern times, creates a dissonance in itself by setting youthfulness and modern interests against his being an ancient druid. In other urban fantasies, the focalization through supernatural beings produces different views of modernity, positive or negative, or, occasionally, balanced between the two. What follows are examples of how some urban fantasy stories portray modernity differently through the supernatural focalizers.

Hearne's druid belongs to a group of urban fantasy focalizers through whom modern civilization comes across in a positive light. He has lived mostly in traditional, premodern societies, to which the current comforts and plenty (not least his own apparently unlimited wealth) contrasts sharply and positively, but he has lived through modernity from its very beginning. Like many other long-lived supernatural focalizers, he is more familiar with modern society than are the people of the mundane domain. Vampire and werewolf protagonists in particular generally enjoy long lives and may have lived through the development of modern civilization. The vampire Henry Fitzroy, in Huff's Blood Books, is the bastard son of Henry VIII and thus born right at the beginning of modernity. Henry hides his vampiric nature behind a façade of gentility and a writer's eccentricities. In *Blood Price* (1991), he repeatedly parallels contemporary life with premodern times and, like Atticus, makes it personal: modernity is comfortable and convenient. The night life of clubs and bars in a big city and the sexual freedom of the early 1990s make his feeding and nocturnal habits simple. His condominium in central Toronto gives him access to late-night revelers to feed on.[27] The threats to his existence are supernatural; the mundane domain is safe, a source of sustenance and comforts. Jake Marlow, Glen Duncan's two-hundred-year-old werewolf (*The Last Werewolf*, 2011), is a spring chicken compared to Henry and Atticus but is old enough to wrestle with the ennui of having seen everything countless times.[28] Jake's perspective on modern life is one of world-weary cynicism. In his attempts to make up for his own monstrosity, the werewolf tries to combat human evil by helping the sick, poor, and oppressed and turning his inner monster on "scumbags" who deserve it.[29] His actions and the justifications of those actions paint a dark picture of modernity, where prostitutes are compared to mercenaries and therapists,[30] and a hedge-fund specialist is a person no one wants.[31] Like Atticus, Jake's and Henry's long lives have made them wealthy and they have all the mundane comforts that they desire. Like the druid, neither the werewolf nor the vampire experience mundane modernity as strange; it is only occasionally estranged by the focalizer's comparing it with historical (even premodern) times. When the modern obsession with news cycles and breaking news and the habit of contemporary people always to travel with identification are addressed from perspectives that span centuries, modern life is briefly regarded from afar and outside.[32] For a moment, the reader can step back and question the familiar through the supernatural focalizer's historical perspective.

Other texts use supernatural focalization to reflect modernity negatively. In my reading of de Lint's novels and short stories about the imaginary city of Newford, I found that the domains of nature, magic, and nonhegemonic culture overlap.[33] The stories' focalizers are either people who find themselves confronted with the supernatural domain, or they are fairy creatures and animal people who belong to that domain. De Lint's focus is consistently on the darker and colder aspects of modern society, often contrasted with the supernatural domain as a positive force, whether as a source of wonder (e.g., "A Tempest in Her Eyes," 1994), comfort (e.g., "Waifs and Strays," 1993), or retribution (e.g., "Bird Bones and Wood Ash," 1995). Regardless of what focalizing position or positions they employ, the Newford stories hold up a modern society dominated by the many social failures in Western urbanism, such as child abuse, prostitution, homelessness, and substance abuse[34]—and a lack of acceptance for magic and wonder.

A negative portrayal of modernity does not have to arise from a supernatural domain that coincides with the social periphery. In Jim Butcher's Dresden Files (2000–present), the first-person narrator is a wizard-for-hire. Harry Dresden, like many of urban fantasy's supernatural characters, relies on people in the mundane domain to disbelieve the supernatural. That disbelief allows him to advertise as, and have a sign on his door that says, "Wizard," safe in the assumption that only those who know that magic exists will believe him.[35] The view of modernity that is focalized through Harry is largely defined by his collaboration with Chicago's police department. He comes across as a typical investigator figure, and as such he moves between different groups of society as part of investigations, revealing the flip side of both mundane and supernatural society.[36] The modern, mundane domain is a place in which he does not quite fit: "I don't trust electronics. Anything manufactured after the forties is suspect—and doesn't seem to have much liking for me. You name it: cars, radios, telephones, TVs, VCRs—none of them seem to behave well for me. I don't even like to use automatic pencils."[37] This idea of magicians belonging, somehow, to a past era is not uncommon—magic as an old-fashioned or preindustrial activity is well-established fantasy fare that gained broad popularity not least through Rowling's Harry Potter books about a contemporary wizarding community in which they still write with quills, send mail by owl, and travel by steam train—but Butcher's spell-wielding freelancer is still clearly a resident of modernity. Anthony Giddens points out that "[t]he rise of expertise is a key part of modernity,"[38] and Harry Dresden paints himself very much as an expert and a magical professional in his roles as freelance wizard and consultant to the police's Special Investigations. In line with Giddens's view of modern expertise, magical power in Harry's world is dependent on hard work more than on any innate ability or special rituals. Much like Atticus, Harry resides in both the supernatural and the mundane domain and can negotiate both, but the two domains are more intertwined in Butcher's books. For all that Harry does not get along with modern technology, modernity is something that dominates the supernatural as well as the mundane domain, and through Harry's focalization modern civilization does not come across in a particularly positive light.

Another negatively slanted portrayal of modernity is presented in Pollock's Skyscraper Throne trilogy.[39] The London of the trilogy is a complex world in which the mundane and supernatural domains become fused together over the course of the story. Just as in Kate Griffin's Matthew Smith books (2009–12), urban modernity provides the source of the supernatural, but Pollock's work is uncommon for urban fantasies set in the primary world. The conflict in the supernatural domain eventually comes to influence the mundane domain to the point where supernatural effects change the physical nature and topography of London, drive much of the population out of the city, and are broadcast on television. This process of change is portrayed by variable focalization through a number of major and minor characters from either domain. The view of modernity remains consistently negative, however, with the main antagonists and threats closely connected to the modern urban environment, including the vain Crane King who replaces old architecture with glass towers, the Chemical Synod who charge terrible prices for their modern alchemical services, and a Father Thames set on destroying the British capital as retribution for having been shackled for centuries. Enemies and allies alike provide estranged examples of modern urbanity: asphalt and rubbish sustain and heal, scaffolding and barbed wire birth monsters, and glass façades are portals to perilous otherworlds. With focalization through characters from the supernatural domain, the modern city becomes a realm in which values are inverted: construction work is a threat, gasoline in your blood an ambition. Rather than offering a purely negative portrayal of modernity, Pollock's series combines the mythical, magical, and modern into a nuanced critique of urbanity and modernity.

Nuanced portrayals of modernity are rare in the urban fantasy focalized through supernatural characters, but there are works that offer a fairly neutral or balanced view of modernity. In the graphic novels in Aaronovitch's Rivers of London series, focalization is more varied than in the novels, also bringing out, for instance, the perspective of the river goddess Beverly Brook. She combines her immense supernatural powers with modern conveniences such as a mobile phone and a wet suit, as well as with modern science—she is portrayed as studying a textbook on the atmospheric sciences.[40] The modern details are presented as useful to her in her life as *genius loci*, but never as indispensable. In Trent Jamieson's Death Works trilogy (2010–11), the focalizer and protagonist, Steven de Selby, begins as psychopomp at Mortmax Industries: he is in the business of professionally channeling dead souls to the Underworld.[41] For all that his work is supernatural, he belongs just as much to the mundane domain, born and raised in contemporary Brisbane. His job as a "Pomp" is like any other modern profession, even though it takes place in the supernatural domain. His focalization does not estrange modernity; its focus is firmly on the strangeness of the supernatural-turned-modern. The "pomping" that Steven and his family do, and the results of the "hostile take-over" to which his family firm is subjected, is rendered eerily familiar—the alien made ordinary by the modern perspective. The television series *Lucifer*, created by Tom Kapinos (2016–21), focalizes much of the events through Lucifer Morningstar, runaway ruler of Hell. Lucifer's engagement with modernity is more varied than that of many focalizers from the supernatural domain in other works. His hedonistic perspective emphasizes entertainment, (sexual) freedom, and capitalism by estranging those aspects of modernity and calling them into question. But that perspective on modernity is countered by the chances offered by modern civilization for self-realization, a respect for expertise (Lucifer's blatant disrespect for experts is frequently employed as a comedic device at his expense), and personal freedom within a system of social responsibility. Through Lucifer's perspective and demeanor, both negative and positive aspects of modernity are brought to the fore and offered up for the viewer's consideration.

Another way of presenting a balanced view of modernity is by keeping the story so much in the supernatural domain that the focalizers barely reflect on modern life. Benedict Jacka's Alex Verus series (2012–21) is set in a contemporary London, ostensibly in the same world as Butcher's Dresden Files—the narrator has "heard of one guy in Chicago who advertises in the phone book under 'Wizard.'"[42] Very little of the mundane city is portrayed through Alex's eyes: in the first novel, *Fated* (2012), the story is driven by events in the supernatural domain from almost two millennia ago, and modernity is reduced to a mise-en-scène, providing a few physical milieus but little else. The magical community in Kat Howard's *An Unkindness of Magicians* (2017) has a similar portrayal of modernity. Contemporary New York functions as a backdrop to the powerful magical houses and their Unseen World.[43] Like Alex Verus, Howard's magicians are both modern and magical but interact very little with the mundane domain. They lead lives so separated from the mundane domain that the settings could be considered as worlds separate from what we, the readers, know, only a short step away from the secondary modern worlds that provide the topic of the next chapter.

• • •

Urban fantasy focalizers who belong in the supernatural domain are still aware of the mundane domain, regardless of whether they are fairy creatures, magicians, or other beings of extended lifespan. Occasionally, they have strayed into modern society and are taken by surprise by it, but more often, they live in both domains, part of a modern–supernatural cultural hybridity. In either case, they tend to express comparisons between modernity and its supernatural Other in terms of a magical community or a long-gone past. Such comparisons address particular aspects of modernity, calling them into question, criticizing them, or celebrating them.

These explicit comparisons are not the only way in which supernatural focalization contributes to the genre's social commentary. Focalizers of this type always stand at least partly outside of modern society, and their focalization cannot but convey their views from an outsider's perspective. Their values are woven into their way of seeing and relating to both domains, constructing a less direct commentary on the modern world. Such values can be expressed through, for instance, habits, preferences, and priorities, suffusing the text with a particular perception of modernity. Modernity is not so much commented on as presented in a certain light. As such, supernatural focalization can provide both the subtlest and the most direct estrangement and critique of modern society.

CHAPTER EIGHT

MODERNIZING THE FANTASTIC

Every fictional modern world tells a story about modernity.[1] Such a world can include any number of narratives, something that is an almost banal statement about a primary world but that remains true about secondary worlds. The key difference is that the more a primary world resembles the actual world, the less the world can be adapted to the requirements of its stories. A secondary urban fantasy world can be constructed in any number of ways to tell different stories, not just about characters, events, and spaces but also about modernity. The story could address the injustices and inequalities of modern society, its benefits and values, or its possible future developments. It might be a portrayal of modernity in contrast to the supernatural, but more likely it is a modernity of the magical and mythical, revealing what our own modern society is like by building a very different—and yet similar—one. The main example in this chapter, Max Gladstone's Craft Sequence (2012–17),[2] builds a modernity that is both strikingly different and eerily familiar, and that shows us the problems of modern society and hints at a possible solution.

Though the category is not particularly large, urban fantasy stories set in modern, secondary worlds are not uncommon. In these worlds the meeting between the fantastic and modernity is not the central issue. Unlike the texts discussed in chapters 6 and 7, secondary-world urban fantasies portray worlds in which the modern has developed together with, within, or as a result of the fantastic. They are not dyadic, divided into mundane and supernatural domains. The supernatural *is* natural. Urban fantasy stories set in secondary worlds combine magic and a rational worldview, dragons and mass production, fairy creatures and capitalism into a single domain rather than keeping them separate.

The combination of modern and magical is not uncommon in fantasy literature, whether the result of authorial oversight or intentional application. A modern mindset, in particular, can easily make its way into an otherwise pseudomedieval world. Examples include the dark shadow of industrialism that threatens the Shire in J. R. R. Tolkien's *The Lord of the Rings* (1954–55) and the modern, United States-style democracy Andy Duncan introduces to the Shire hobbits in his reckoning with Middle-earth's implied racism ("Senator Bilbo," 2001). In Hugh Cook's *The Wizards and the Warriors* (1986), a post-Semmelweis understanding of bacterial infections is indicated by the suggestion that gangrene and septicemia can be avoided if soldiers sterilize their weapons before combat. The hero in *Nobody's Son* (Sean Stewart, 1993) wins the princess's hand in marriage, but she argues in modern, almost feminist terms against having sex because she wants to avoid pregnancy. Modern technology can also sneak into secondary fantasy worlds, with examples ranging from Mrs. Beaver's inexplicable sewing machine in *The Lion, the Witch, and the Wardrobe* (C. S. Lewis, 1950) to the jeans and newspapers that are part of the idiosyncratic world in Steph Swainston's *The Year of Our War* (2004). Contrasting fantasy and modern technology can be used for satirical purposes, such as in Mary Gentle's *Grunts!* (1992), in which a band of orcs comes across a cache of modern military equipment and proceeds to change their entire world—themselves included. Indeed, many fantasy stories introduce modern features in order to estrange, satirize, or amuse—or simply by mistake. Modernity is not necessarily consistently included in the examples above, nor are they urban fantasies, however.

The topic for this chapter is secondary worlds that are consistently portrayed as modern, and two fundamental dimensions need to be borne in mind when discussing urban fantasy set in such worlds. In chapter 1, I explained how urban fantasy settings differ from the actual cities to varying extents. At one extreme are settings that closely imitate existing cities like London, New York, or Toronto, or that are slightly different versions of existing places. At the other extreme we find the secondary worlds of this chapter. Their connection to a primary word is unimportant or nonexistent. Examples of cities with no such connection include Michael Swanwick's Babel, Terry Pratchett's Ankh-Morpork, China Miéville's New Crobuzon, Gladstone's Alt Coulumb, and Jeff VanderMeer's Ambergris. Cities to which magical travel is possible include Tad Williams's modernized Fairy, Catherynne M. Valente's Palimpsest, and Simon R. Green's Nightside, as well as versions of primary-word cities, such as Miéville's Un Lun Dun, Tom Pollock's London-Under-Glass, and Mike Resnick's otherworldly version of Manhattan.

The extent of modernity in a fictional world correlates with its divergence from the actual world. Mark J. P. Wolf suggests that fictional worlds differ in their "secondariness,"[3] the extent to which they diverge from the actual world. Worlds that are highly secondary are less determined in their modernity; they can be as modern as our actual world is, or even more, but they can also be classically modern or early modern—or premodern, such as Fritz Leiber's Lankhmar. Creating a secondary world grants writers considerable freedom, enabling them to include, exclude, and modify world elements as required by the story. That freedom of choice means that it is possible to analyze the world as an aesthetic whole.[4] Regardless of what aspects of modernity are included in the world and how they are portrayed, they are part of a whole and have meaning and function in the world. I have previously argued that a fantasy setting can be fruitfully analyzed by giving it the same attention that is commonly accorded to character or plot[5] and now suggest that the same can be done with modernity in a secondary-world urban fantasy. Modernity is portrayed and conveyed in a way that tells a story about it—the question is what story that is. And in its story, is modernity cast as hero or villain? A help or hindrance? An exciting environment or monotonous milieu?

To fully grasp modernity in a secondary world, one must consider every indicator of modernity. In Interlude I, modernity is briefly outlined in terms of some characteristic attitudes, institutions, and systems that underlie it. As macrolevel world-building features, they explain what modernity is in a particular fictional world and how it developed (or develops) in that world. They help us understand how a fictional modern society can be analyzed. However, there are also features that make us interpret a setting or character as modern without directly relating to the macrolevel. Examples of such features are cars, dog parks, iPads, shops for scented soaps, swiftly changing fashion trends, popular music, best-selling cook books, universal human rights, cooperative board games . . . The inclusion of such meso- and microlevel details signifies a modern world (for most of my examples, late modern) by requiring, and thus implying that there are, macrolevel modern features in the world. When analyzing secondary-world modernity, it is crucial to consider all levels and their integration with the world as they collectively form the story told about modernity.

This chapter focuses on how the story told about modernity can be explored in urban fantasy set in a secondary world. Each such story is its own, offering a certain perspective on modernity and how we can or should relate to it. The central case, the Craft Sequence, is a world that is both very different from the actual world and very similar to it. Gladstone's narratives shift between focalizers[6]—protagonists, antagonists, and supporting characters—but together, their perspectives on the modern world that they inhabit tell a story of how modernization has failed to help humanity and how postmodernity may offer some hope for a better tomorrow.

THE MODERN WORLD OF MAX GLADSTONE'S CRAFT SEQUENCE

The secondary world of the Craft Sequence is, in many ways, a typical fantasy world. It contains powerful magic known as the Craft, divine presence, a host of fantastic beings, such as demons, dragons, soul-sucking insects, and a cast including gargoyles, vampires, and zombies. It is also a modern world of bookkeeping, insurance companies, business concerns, luxury hotels, single malt whisky, and an avant-garde art scene. It is a world in which the fantastic and modernity are closely intertwined. The Craft is a magic of contracts and arguments, and the "soulstuff" that powers it also functions as legal tender; dragons are used for long-distance air travel; and gods are enslaved power stations or soulstuff producers for their churches. The familiar and the alien combine to provide vivid new perspectives on modern society.

The six novels of the Craft Sequence form an overarching narrative, and several characters appear in two or more novels. The stories are mainly set in and around the city-states of Dresediel Lex, Alt Coulumb, Agdel Lex, and in the small island nation Kavekana, some four decades after the God Wars, when human Craftspeople (magicians) defeated the gods. Like much urban fantasy, it contains numerous supernatural creatures drawn from the fantasy and Gothic traditions, and magic is common. The Craft world is not dyadic; the supernatural is everywhere and mostly understood in rational terms. The main feature that sets the world apart, and why I selected it for my main case, is the extent to which it concentrates on issues of fantastic modernity.

The social relation to modernity is not just a conspicuous theme in Gladstone's world; it is a major thrust behind the overarching plotline of the six novels. The backstory to the Sequence is the rapid modernization that took place after the God Wars. The stories interrogate the various actors and forces of modernity, including the damage they cause the world and its people, and they also propose a possible route forward to a sustainable society. By tracing the development of modernity in the Craft world and examining some of its more striking modern features, I discuss how the image of modernity encourages the reader to consider their own modern society. Zygmunt Bauman's "legislator" and "interpreter" roles of what he calls the "modern" and "post-modern" intellectuals (related to modernity, not to [post]modernism) are used to understand the alternative models of modernity provided in the texts.[7] The Craft societies in Gladstone's stories are shown to suffer from a modernity dominated by "legislator" Craftspeople. The hope for a better future rests in "interpreters" who can translate between the modernity of the Craft and the traditions of the gods.

Rushing into Modernity

The modern civilization in the Craft world mirrors and estranges that of the actual world, inviting comparisons between them. The secondary world foregrounds its modernity not least through vivid descriptions of urban-capitalist-industrial milieus and situations. Often, such passages have nothing or little fantastic about them to attract attention. Instead, they do so stylistically, portraying the life in a modern city through a vibrant and elaborate style, imbuing the city with life and symbolic meaning. (See for example the opening paragraph to chapter 18 of *Three Parts Dead*.) The world feels close enough to the actual to tempt the reader into looking for parallels and analogues. At the same time, it maintains its alienness through distinct differences, the most striking of which is the absence of electric technology. The use of electricity is generally replaced by magic, such as Craftwork, "applied theology" (the channeling of divine power), and the use of demons. Reader engagement is rewarded by the modern nature of the Craft societies and their fusion of familiar and unfamiliar.

Modern technology is mostly recognizable in form and function but with magical components that help estrange it. A typical example is the hospital setting. Scenes set in hospitals occur in each of the six novels and in the two interactive texts, and the impression is consistently of a modern hospital, with objects, behaviors, and situations that are familiar to—and expected by—a modern reader. These objects, behaviors, and situations are adapted to a world in which magic is also used in treating people, however, and fantastical diseases and wounds afflict the patients. A dislocated shoulder is set by a doctor reaching *into* the patient (*Two* 62–63), and a child with bleeding religious symbols is treated with "chemicals and talismans" in a trauma ward (*Last* 293). Modern vocabulary (such as *operating theatre*, *recovery room*, *disinfectant*, *trauma*) is contrasted with the use of Craft: "a metronome ticked the beat of [a patient's] heart," "[a] neutral odor of bad smells scrubbed away by Craft" (*Last* 293). The hospitals are blended spaces in which the modern is estranged and the fantastic is familiarized, prompting the reader to ponder both. Alternatively, descriptions of modern features can be used to make familiar things seem strange. The more unfamiliar the terms, the greater the estrangement, even to the point of lack of recognition. Plastic containers, for instance, are described as "airtight vessels made from the processed bones of eons-dead monsters," having a "flat nothing-scent" (*Four* 67). Processing the remains of eons-dead monsters (read: dinosaurs) could be decoded as refining oil; airtight, odorless vessels could be decoded as plastic containers. There is nothing that guarantees that decoding, though, and the reader might take it for some alien magical artefact instead.

The world and narratives span a period of time transitioning from traditional, religious societies, through a rapid transformation into a late modernity. Central to setting the stage for the Craft Sequence is the God Wars, the conflict that began a century and a half before the narrative present, resulted in the defeat of most of the world's deities, and enabled the transition into modernity. A diversity of voices are allowed to give their views on the Wars, creating a balanced but varied perspective, although the conflict is consistently explained by humans discovering how to use the Craft rather than relying on the power of the gods. During the Wars, both sides committed atrocities, destroyed society, and killed innocent bystanders, in particular people of science and learning. There were "[r]iots, pogroms, lynch mobs. Many of the victims had not been Craftsmen at all but mathematicians and philosophers, anatomists and chemists and scholars of ancient languages. Universities around the world were razed," according to the Craftswoman Tara (*Three* 152). Her description of a backlash against secular learning calls to mind similar events in the actual world, from the Spanish Inquisition and the witch trials to the Chinese Cultural Revolution and the Khmer Rouge purges. When the gods had been defeated, the victorious Craftspeople created new, secular societies based on what they saw as the sensible application of Craft, to replace the theocracies that had existed previously. Modernity took the place of traditional society.

The God Wars illustrate an abrupt transition from traditional, religious societies to rational, secular ones. The transition from theocratic to secular rule is one of the clearest signs of how the God Wars ushered in modernity. The social transformation corresponds to what happened when Western Europe shifted from an "eschatological Christian world-view" to a world in which there is "no purpose beyond natural man [. . .], which determines social, personal, or political order."[8] The "divinely ordained world" of premodernity[9] is replaced by a world run by Craftspeople. The sharp contrast between before and after recalls Anthony Giddens's view that "[i]nherent in the idea of modernity is a contrast with tradition."[10] Giddens observes that this contrast does not preclude combinations of the modern and the traditional in specific social settings, however, and the modern societies of the Craft world have found ways to incorporate the divine in their workings. Examples include gods that willingly or under duress work as power sources, divinity refashioned into a manifestation of Justice, and artificial but semidivine idols that provide returns on invested faith. Each of these examples can also be read as symbols of modern, secular worship—of the industrial, legal, and financial systems. Various religious traditions still remain in the everyday lives of people, as modernity is only a few decades old—divinity is accepted if it makes no claim to run society.

The speed with which Craftspeople accumulate power, and the fast development of how to use that power, resulted in a very swift modernization process in the Craft world. The transition from a traditional, theocratic society to the late modernity of the narrative present has been accomplished in only a hundred and fifty years, with more than half of that being taken up by the God Wars. What took the actual world half a millennium to accomplish in terms of modernization, the Craft world achieved in half a century. One idea associated with modernity, according to Giddens, is "of the world as open to transformation by human intervention," and he considers modernity to be "vastly more dynamic than any previous type of social order."[11] The Craft world echoes this. Driven by a vision to improve society for their fellow humans, the Craftsmen and Craftswomen rapidly transformed the social and physical world around them (e.g., *Three* 261). The voices in favor of modernity repeatedly argue that although the result may not be perfect, it is an improvement. In Dresediel Lex, for instance, modernity's foremost accomplishment is its abolishing of human sacrifices. In that city, the recurring debate for and against modernity always boils down to that; the technical and economic development might be unequally distributed, and there might be social unrest, but there is no more killing of innocents to appease the gods—and that makes all the difference. In the words of Caleb, protagonist of *Two Serpents Rise*, "[o]ur city is cruel. It exploits its children. But it does not corral those it fears and hates, does not kill them to appease bogeymen" (198). Modern society is imperfect, but it is better than its predecessor.

The rapid modernization process has resulted in undeniable improvements but also massive social and demographic upheaval within a few generations. When Marshall Berman describes a "modern public [which] can remember what it is like to live, materially and spiritually, in worlds that are not modern at all,"[12] his words could apply to Gladstone's Craft world. In fact, Berman refers to what he calls modernity's second phase (1789–1900), during which premodernity had not yet been forgotten everywhere. This changed in the third phase (late modernity). Now, people "live in an age which has lost touch with the roots of its own modernity."[13] In the Craft world, these phases are combined. People live with an acute awareness of being modern while also remembering their premodern past. In a sense, the Craft world has been modernized so rapidly that it can be said to meld all three of Berman's phases of modernity into one, and it is teetering on the edge of a new phase, a phase that Ulrich Beck calls a "second modernity" and Bauman refers to as "post-modernity."[14]

After sixty years or more of intense modernization, the process still goes on. Modernity has reached only parts of the Craft world, leaving others behind, and optimistic proponents of modernity envision a world where everyone can win. "[T]hose parts of the world still reeling from the God Wars, or the resource conflicts, proxy battles, and zombie plagues that rippled from the wars themselves, would recover to join Dresediel Lex and Agdel and Alt Coulumb and Iskar and the Shining Empire and Camlaan in the light of modernity" (*Ruin* 37). Even after the God Wars, modernity is not for everyone, and the phrase "would recover" reveals the speaker's doubt: the current system might not be able to support a world where everyone comes out on top. For some states to enjoy modernity, others might have to lead a life of hardship and poverty in modernity's shadow. In the actual world, modernity started in Western Europe and reached other parts of the world slowly and over time, maintaining a periphery of countries which even today mainly provide (cheap) unskilled labor and (cheap) natural resources for the modern core. Even though the Craftspeople are held to be the winners of the God Wars and the bringers of modernity, and despite the speed with which modernization took place, their world only exhibits a modern surface, underneath which the premodern lurks.

The Craft: Money, Power, and the Force behind Modernity

The modern Craft world is portrayed as a world of intellect and reason, based on the use of the Craft. The typical Craftsperson considers the Craft a better way to manage the world than was divinity, as it represents intellectual freedom, unlimited potential, subtlety, and flexibility. "Anyone with will could learn. Smart people could run the world better than Gods" (*Ruin* 424). Tara's words hide her doubt because she has begun to notice the imperfection of modern society, but she nevertheless repeats the Craftpeople's mantra of enlightenment, reason, and science. It is a worldview that rings of modernity's concern with order, rationalization, and production of knowledge by reflection and revision.[15] At the heart lies the Craft and its way to extract, transfer, and use soulstuff in a network of magical contracts that controls the world. Craftspeople rule the world in the role of Bauman's "legislators," the authorities and arbiters of what is correct and true.[16]

On the face of it, the Craft is magic, but it actually takes on several functions that are central to modernity. According to a Craftswoman, the Craft "is the art and science of using power as the gods do. [. . .] Craftsmen draw power from the stars and the earth, and are shaped by them in turn. We can also use human soulstuff [. . .], but the stars are more reliable than men" (*Three

181). The word "science" reveals the Craft to be a rational rather than mystical endeavor, a modern force. Although it can be used for some typical fantasy effects, the Craft can also be read in terms of what Giddens calls "disembedding," mechanisms that allow social relations to be separated from a local context and extended over time and space. To Giddens, disembedding is of basic importance to the nature of modernity. For example, disembedding in the form of "symbolic tokens" makes it possible, for instance, to purchase a foreign watch with the surplus from last year's potato harvest. Money is a kind of symbolic token, a universal medium of exchange that can be used without regard to the characteristics of the person or group currently using it.[17] The distance in time and space between harvest and watch production is bridged by the use of money, a symbolic carrier of value. The Craft turns soulstuff into such symbolic tokens, but, unlike the money we know, soulstuff has intrinsic (rather than symbolic) value, and the economic dimension of the Craft modernity rests on the disembedding made possible through soulstuff-as-money.

Through the intrinsic value of money, wealth and power are quite literally equated, and poverty in modern society becomes an explicitly existential threat. Power is the currency used for small, everyday purchases as well as large international transactions. The creation of money takes place not only within the banking system (as in the actual world) but within humans and gods themselves, at differing rates. The soulstuff can be used as money. It is used as payment by placing a small amount in a metal "coin" or by contractual transfer; it can be borrowed, earned, stolen, or saved; and it provides the basis for any number of financial instruments. This makes poverty risky. Running low on cash means running out of soul, literally. A street kid has "to stop herself from swaying as the shop gray[s] out," when she spends her last few "thaums" (*Full* 18), and a desperate mother overspends in an attempt to save her wounded son. Almost out of soulstuff, she loses the ability to see in colors, to think clearly, to even remember how to walk.

Fortunately, she makes it to the Craft version of an ATM, a booth where she can receive a transfer of soulstuff from her account (*Last* 266–67). In a world where wealth is power and power is soul, no money means no life.

In a sense, having no money is still better than having less than no money, of being in debt, and the mortgaging of power and souls is a recurrent motif in the stories. Borrowing from someone's surplus and repaying with interest was central to modern capitalism and a vital mechanism behind the development of modern society in the actual world. In *Choice of the Deathless*, "Debt" is one of the stats, or values, which are affected by player/reader decisions and which in turn affect the story. If the player/reader manages to repay the debt within the game, a brief scene describes the sense of well-being that follows, combining the relief of being free from a financial obligation with the equation of money and soul. In *Four Roads Cross*, it is explained how Tara's student loans could save her from dying, but the creditor would have enormous leverage over her, and they might keep only those parts of her alive that are required to repay the debt (205–206). The mortgaging of divine power drives the plots in three of the books. Such mortgaging is explained in terms of interest on borrowed capital:

> One god gave of his power to another, or to a group of worshippers, on a promise of repayment in kind, and of more soulstuff than had been initially lent. Gods grew knit to gods, pantheons to pantheons, expecting, and indeed requiring, their services to be returned. Power flowed, and divine might increased beyond measure. (*Three* 66–67)

The divine economy is a basic investment economy, where capital (grace) moves to where it yields the best returns on investment. But investments come with risk, and in the modern Craft world, divine investment and the concomitant risk are safeguarded by contracts that are enforced by Craftspeople. When the sun god

Kos is killed in *Three Parts Dead*, his creditors insist on resurrecting the god as a divine "zombie," mindless but still able to honor his contractual obligations, and when, in *Four Roads Cross*, Kos is suspected of an unlimited and "off-the-books" obligation to his moon goddess consort, he is taken to court for harboring an undisclosed risk. In *Full Fathom Five*, the Kavekana priesthood creates "idols," artificial godlets with just enough divinity to provide a return on investment by connecting them to other gods and business concerns. In modern society, gods do not primarily dispense grace but wealth, parts of a global system of complex flows of soulstuff. They profit from it but are primarily bound by it, chained by contractual obligations, and thus providers of the wealth and power required to drive modernization.

Debts and mortgaging are contractual obligations, one of the most prominent features of modernity in the Craft world. To have power is to have obligations placed on oneself, in an intricate system of contracts and requirements that provide key plot points in several of the texts. The Craftswoman Elayne exploits the obligations of an insurance contract to access the soulstuff that she needs to protect a city district from going up in flames (*Last* ch. 61). The owner of Dresediel Lex's water company has literally millions of obligations to his citizens to provide them with water, and when his major energy source, a captured sea god, is killed, he is incapacitated by the debilitating effect of these obligations in combination with a duplicitous merger deal (*Two* 261–62). Tara and Elayne must find out why Kos died before the dead god defaults on his Church's numerous contracts (*Three* 66–68), and Tara must defend him from his investors' accusations of hiding an unlimited obligation to his consort (*Four* 59–61). Investment broker Kai discovers how bad investments are used to destroy idols as they achieve godhood (*Full* 304–6). Each of the five first novels has a central theme or pivotal plot point that constructs the Craft as a science of financial investments, contracts, and wealth as much as an art of divine grace and the human soul. Through the disembedding function of the Craft, modernity is portrayed as a rational, rule-bound system.

The Craft is largely a magic of modernity, built on concepts such as finance, contracts, and arguments. The Craftspeople are presented as members of a modern, legal profession. Although Craftspeople are portrayed as a range of modern intellectual callings, from investment managers to scientists, their foremost depiction is as lawyers. When Elayne uses the insurance contract to protect a city district from burning down, she does so by constructing the argument that although parts of buildings were on fire, "each piece was part of a building, and the building as a whole did not burn merely because one piece burned. And yet how could a part be burning if the whole was not on fire? [. . .] Sophistry, but you didn't need to work hard to outfox flame" (*Last* 346). In Gladstone's texts, Craftspeople take on roles of counseling, defending, investigating, and negotiating for their clients. The Craft is a ruthlessly logical, rational form of magic, ultimately adjudicated by the Courts of Craft and their impartial judges, and the modern society is similarly based on logic and reason.

The parallel between Craftspeople and lawyers might suggest that the modern society of the Craft world is governed by the rule of law, but stronger emphasis is placed on a society ruled by lawyers. Tom Bingham, in *The Rule of Law* (2010), argues that the core principle of the rule of law is "that all persons and authorities within the state, whether public or private, should be bound by and entitled to the benefit of laws *publicly made*, taking effect (generally) in the future and *publicly administered in the courts*."[18] Law *enforcement*, in various forms, is a significant part of the plots in the six novels. The semidivine Justice in Alt Coulumb most clearly symbolizes the impartial courts. Justice's statue is recognizable from Justitia of the actual world, blind and holding a sword and scales (*Three* 280), but although there are witnesses and evidence

(*Three* 163), it is never specified whether the law in Justice's courts is publicly administered. The police force in Alt Coulumb, as well as Dresediel Lex's Wardens and Agdel Lex's Rectification Authority agents, are masked and anonymous, recalling authoritarian states rather than democratic rule of law. These are the institutions that capture, convict, and punish lawbreakers, but little is said about law-*making*. Laws are not made, publicly or otherwise; they just exist, as immutable as other natural laws. The Craft has to do with knowing and being able to negotiate those immutable laws, often publicly, even though general members of the public cannot perceive the administration of the law. In other words, the modern society of the Craft is governed by what Niall Ferguson calls "the Rule of Lawyers," not the rule of law.[19] He refers in particular to the large proportion of lawyers in the legislatures of the United States and Great Britain, but the expression aptly captures the modernity of Gladstone's world as well. States are ruled by Deathless Kings, powerful Craftspeople who have transcended life itself, and conflicts are adjudicated by the godlike Judges of the Courts of Craft, who are the interfaces between the human realm and the Craft of the Court. Below them are the multitudes of Craftspeople whose powers widely surpass those of normal people, through their amassed wealth of soulstuff and their ability to manipulate the social and physical world.

Gladstone's Craftspeople rule modern society but they also dominate it intellectually. Bauman uses the metaphor of the "legislator" to characterize the modern (as opposed to "post-modern") intellectual. The legislator role consists of "making authoritative statements which arbitrate in controversies of opinions and which select those opinions that, having been selected, become correct and binding."[20] Legislators have, Bauman argues, access to universally valid, procedural rules that can determine what is true, morally correct, and artistically proper. Neither they nor the knowledge they produce are bound by traditions that are localized or communal.[21] The Craftspeople concretize Bauman's role: they are trained in the Hidden Schools, an academy without a fixed geographical location, where they are trained in the Craft, the underlying, universal rules of the world. Their approach to knowledge-production follows the "procedural rules" of Bauman, and they are both motor and rudder of the rapid modernization of the world. They constitute a cosmopolitan elite that travels the world, a global constant among local systems, modernity's intellectual arbiters.

Craftspeople are most evident as legislators when they act as lawyers, but they are also cast in other legislator roles. In Gladstone's stories, the representation of modernity is chiefly characterized by these legislator intellectuals, and their Craft underpins a significant portion of the modern world's scientific and technological advances as well as its financial system. Craftspeople saved scientists and philosophers who faced pogroms and lynch mobs during the God Wars (*Three* 152), and modern science is portrayed as closely linked to the Craft. There are laboratories and research facilities for Craftwork, and Craftspeople have developed theoretical concepts recognizable from a range of scholarly fields, from economics—the "invisible fingers" that sort out supply and demand (*Ruin* 295) recall Adam Smith's "invisible hand"—to philosophy—gods are described as "*n*-dimensional noosphere entities" (*Four* 168). Craftwork research has led to the invention of psychoactive drugs and anesthesia, high-capacity calculation technology, robot-like golems, and space suits (*Last* 120; *Two* 280; *Four* 168; *Full* 144–46; *Ruin* 513). The Craftspeople's legislator role has also resulted in the development of many of modernity's many isms, along with most of their drawbacks, identifiable from the actual world.

Modernity and Its Complications

Late modernity, as it is portrayed in the Craft Sequence, is dominated by a number of areas of social life and the world in general that, taken together, convey a view on modernity in general and late modernity in particular. Capitalism and industrialism are the main components of the institutional framework, colonialism is the most prominent theme of *Ruin of Angels*, and globalization, in a variety of forms, is a theme that defines the entire Craft Sequence. These areas are all presented as interconnected and problematic.

Capitalism & Industrialism

At the core, the economies of the Craft world are characterized by capitalism and industrialism, two of modernity's four institutional dimensions according to Giddens. *Capitalism* is a system in which ownership of the means of production is separated from the paid labor. In *industrialism*, production relies on the use of machines and "inanimate sources of material power."[22] Capitalist businesses, called "Concerns," abound in the stories, ranging from huge, multinational companies and international investment banks and brokers to small businesses, such as coffee house franchises and small start-ups. The plots of the novels are constructed around various forms of business ventures: a merchant collective's attempt to gentrify an urban slum (*Last First Snow*), the merging of two major water companies (*Two Serpents Rise*), a church's fight against their god's creditors (*Three Parts Dead, Four Roads Cross*), the shady dealings of an investment broker (*Full Fathom Five*), and an attempt to connect investors and companies in need of venture capital (*Ruin of Angels*). Industrial complexes are not as prominent in the Craft world, and industrialism is partly undercut by the fact that slaves and demons are used in production instead of machines and "inanimate sources" of power. However, the settings are clearly industrial or postindustrial, and occasional industries are mentioned, for example Dresediel Lex's minor Concerns and its industrial-size abattoir (*Last* 115; *Two* 69). Even the god Kos is repeatedly described in industrial terms, his grace providing the material power, to the point where his servants are called "technicians" (e.g., *Three* 7). The industrial past and present is evident from descriptions such as that of a city's "forsaken places [. . .] where real estate's cheap and factories sprawl like bachelors in ill-tended houses, secure in the knowledge their smoke won't trouble the delicate nostrils of the great and the good" (*Four* 27). This passage stresses the connection between the capitalist owners and their industries by dividing them: the real estate has the double advantage of saving the owners money and keeping down production costs and of being located far away from the "great and the good" who live and work elsewhere. The "forsaken places" are not abandoned; they are actually useful places for modern production facilities, intentionally unseen (and unsmelt) but suited to their purpose. Late modernity is an explicitly capitalist economy with industrial underpinnings.

Colonialism

Modernity as a colonizing project is particularly prominent in *Ruin of Angels*, where colonialism is depicted as inherently oppressive and ultimately unfit for modern society. The novel is set in Agdel Lex, formerly a Talbeg city called Alikand but now colonized by the Iskari Demesne, and the plot centers on the process by which the city frees itself from its colonial masters. Colonial rule is portrayed as literal control over reality: the havoc wrought upon the Talbeg city during the God Wars has created a rift that threatens to break the world. The Iskari use the power of their squid godlets to prevent this by imposing a stable reality instead, but it is a reality which is more Iskari than Talbeg.

The relation between the Iskari and the Talbeg embodies a Craft world version of a discourse widely termed "the West and the Rest." Stuart Hall describes the concept of the West as functioning in a cluster of ways that allow the discussion of a type of society as "developed, industrialized, urbanized, capitalist, secular, and modern."[23] This is the role that the Iskari Demesne assigns to itself, but throughout the novel external and critical perspectives consistently challenge this portrayal. Despite the Iskari viewing themselves as saviors of both the world and the perceived primitive, underdeveloped Talbeg, they are portrayed as colonial masters determined to exploit a land and its deemed-inferior inhabitants. The Talbeg are the Other that must be changed and controlled.

This desire to change and control parallels that of European (Western) colonial relations over the five centuries of modernity. During that time, Western colonial powers "went from 'convert to Christianity or I'll kill you' in the 16th century, to 'civilize or I'll kill you' in the 18th and 19th centuries, to 'develop or I'll kill you' in the 20th century."[24] The Iskari merge these three threats, trying to convert the Talbeg into worship of the squid godlets as part of their civilizing and developmental agenda. Iskari people are placed in positions of control and the Iskari language must be used by the Talbeg inhabitants. Streets get renamed, drawing from either Iskari cultural references or their approximations of old Talbeg names (*Ruin* 60). Agdel Lex's schools teach the official history about the colony being "revitalized" by rational administration and trade based on raw material exports (the Iskari Demesne advocates competition and free trade), and it is suggested that the city will eventually transition from resource to knowledge and service industries (*Ruin* 100–101). These attempts to "modernize" the Talbeg society do not make the colonial masters universally liked by their colonized subjects. When a Talbeg woman who has just illegally accessed the old Talbeg city encounters a group of guards, she expresses her dislike of the Iskari and those Talbeg who work with them. To get away from the guards, she fakes "the thick accent and verb-free grammar Iskari mystery play actors used when they impersonated Talbeg people" even though "[t]he apology and accent tasted like wadded socks" (*Ruin* 46). The stereotypical accent and apology signal submissiveness as well as stupidity to the guards, but to the reader, the situation shows a conceited, colonial West constructing themselves as superior to the Rest.

The Iskari colonial rule is portrayed as centering around a cultural repression aimed to control reality at a most concrete level.

Repressing the culture and modes of knowledge production in colonies is recognizable from actual world history. Aníbal Quijano describes how a similar form of repression, along with massive genocide, "turned the previous high cultures of America into illiterate, peasant subcultures condemned to orality."[25] In Agdel Lex, cultural repression manifests as restricted access to Talbeg history and geography. Because of the magical nature of the Craft world, the restriction is also literal: it is not just about controlling knowledge and naming conventions but also about prohibiting travel in Alikand's streets or to its dead past. Two realities literally stand against each other, and the colonial rulers determine which of the conflicting realities applies by forcing their version of the city to be the real one, both temporally and topographically.

The control strategies employed by the Iskari are justified by their endeavor to uphold the "safer" reality. The Iskari city Agdel Lex exists, in some sense, simultaneously and in the same place as the dead city of Alikand, a place perpetually battle-scarred and locked in time. Crossing over into it weakens the reality of Agdel Lex and is prohibited by Iskari law. Symbolically, it is the Talbeg's precolonial and inaccessible past, a forbidden reality suppressed by the colonial power. It is the modern Agdel Lex's Other, a dangerous premodern threat controlled by the power—magical and social—of the Iskari. The character Zeddig is one of the intrepid or desperate people who enter Alikand to reclaim treasures and knowledge from their past. She searches the dead city for books to give to the secret archivists that seek to preserve the Talbeg heritage. The archivists are key in keeping the Talbeg reality alive. They maintain a third city, subversively hidden "between" the realities of Agdel Lex and Alikand, "around the world of iron words the Iskari forged" (*Ruin* 213). In this third reality, Talbeg traditions and culture as well as the old topography and street plans of Alikand are not a dead past but are surreptitiously kept alive. Modernity cannot be imposed from above; there will always be resistance.

Ruin of Angels presents a place under colonial administration, but a colonial matrix of control and power can be seen as part of modernity through other cities in Gladstone's novels as well. Using Quijano's concept "coloniality," the underlying logic or power structure that led to the colonialism of Western countries and remained even when the colonies became independent,[26] Walter D. Mignolo suggests that there is no modernity without coloniality. Coloniality is, according to Mignolo, the darker side of modernity.[27] Where Agdel Lex presents a colony directly ruled by a colonial power, other city-states show other ways in which coloniality can be expressed in a modern world. Dresediel Lex is run by the Deathless King who defeated its gods and conquered it, its ruler the very embodiment of modernity. In Alt Coulumb, the church and its divinities have been forced to yield to the Craftspeople representing the forces of modernity. The island-nation Kavekana, whose gods deserted it, has been forced to serve the needs of a modern economy. The logic that underlies the Craft as a modernizing force also dominates the different settings in the novels, demonstrating how the Craft could be considered as an expression of Mignolo's observation that modernity and coloniality are inextricably linked.

Ruin of Angels ends with the defeat of Iskari colonial rule and with the message that regardless of how modern the colonizers, colonialism is not the way into the future. The Iskari are portrayed as a modern nation but are made suspect by their insistence on clinging to their tentacled deities. Agdel Lex and Alikand are eventually separated from each other. Released from colonial control, Alikand and its people are free to make their own future while retaining their historical and cultural heritage. The two cities will have to compete and trade—bywords of capitalist, globalist modernity—even though Kai admits that Alikand likely offers superior investment opportunities (*Ruin* 560–61). Repressive colonialism is not fitting for late modernity; global trade and competition of free agents is the way to move forward.

Globalization

Modernity's globalized world, with its problems and their possible solutions, sits at the core of the Craft Sequence. An in-depth presentation of everything Gladstone's texts have to say about globalization is beyond the scope of this chapter. Here, I give a broad outline of Gladstone's Craft version of globalization with focus on its basic requirements, the disembedding that is caused by separation of time and space. Disembedding through long-distance travel and communication, and the international trade, investments, and tourism that result from it, are examined. Finally, globalization's effects on the local communities and ecosystems are addressed.

Modernity in the Craft Sequence is characterized by inequal access to the world and by the tension between local and global. When Kai meets with the venture capitalists of Agdel Lex, her eyes open to the complexity and interconnectedness of the world and its problems, and the simple explanation is that "[t]he world [. . .] is becoming increasingly global" (*Ruin* 198–99). This platitude summarizes a key theme in the series as well as a prominent feature of how modernity is portrayed in the Craft world. Trade of soulstuff, raw material, manufactured goods, and services is a vital part of the global economy. Travel over long and short distances is made possible, for business and pleasure. The resources required to trade, communicate, and travel are not equally distributed, however. To those who already have wealth and power, modernity provides means to increase that wealth and that power, by trade and investments on an international scale and in global business concerns. These global concerns have (often deleterious) effects on local communities and ecosystems, resulting in conflicts or migration.

Globalization in Gladstone's world is mainly an economic and political process, but it also has resulted in global spread of culture. One way (of many) to define globalization is as a "social process in which the constraints of geography on economic, political, social and cultural arrangements recede, in which people become increasingly aware that they are receding and in which people act accordingly."[28] Regardless of whether this process has been around throughout history, coincides with modernity, or arose in late modernity, it accelerated during the late-modern era.[29] In the Craft world, globalization is portrayed as a process that has accelerated because of Craft-driven (late) modernity. It is predominantly an intimate combination of economic and political arrangements, although the texts also include scattered references to a global spread of culture in terms of fashion, sports, and literature (e.g., *Four* 219–20; *Ruin* 101, 292).

Travel, communication, and mass media are conspicuous facets of modernity in the Craft world. Bauman and Giddens point out how time and space are separated in the modern era, something Giddens sees as part of the concept of disembedding, that is, separating something from its local context. I discussed disembedding above in terms of money, but modernity also separates time and space through modern ways of transport and communication. Such disembedding leads to a world that is, in a sense, smaller and more knowable and relatable to its inhabitants. When the distance traveled in a unit of time depends on the means of travel rather than on natural tools of mobility, what is available locally suddenly has less meaning. We can have fresh fruit in the winter and have a brief meeting with people from different countries. We send instantaneous messages or even talk to people almost anywhere on the planet.[30] In Gladstone's texts, disembedding through travel, communication, and mass media are portrayed as distinct parts of modernity, through solutions based in the magical reality of the secondary world.

The disembedding caused by time-and-space separation brings the brutal inequality and cruelty of the "legislator" modernity of the Craft world to the fore. The various methods of travel available to the inhabitants display a range of modern and premodern possibilities. Goods are carried by sailing ships and golem-drawn carts; dragons take paying passengers quickly between continents, and insectile "optera" and saurian "Couatl" serve as flying taxis or steeds; enormous freight trains cross dangerous landscapes while air buses and elevated trains transport urban workers; and Craftspeople move through the air by Craft. The more you can pay—the greater your access to soulstuff—the greater time-and-space separation you can afford. Modernity is an era of the wealthy, while the poor in the cities and the countryside remain embedded in their local contexts. This modernity of wealth is further emphasized by the disembedding created by the separation of time and space facilitated by long-distance communication. In lieu of electricity, communication infrastructure is based on other forces. In *Ruin of Angels*, Kai can use prayer for brief communication, and the drug "dreamglass" enables a limited kind of communication, too, but throughout the stories, the dominant technology is the Craft-based "nightmare telegraph." This is a form of communication that emphasizes a modern disregard for whether suffering is created within a capitalist system where labor is bought by capitalists, who then insulate customers from experiencing that suffering. The nightmare telegraph allows customers to meet deep inside the nightmares of two other people. The standard fantasy motif of communications through dreams is transformed into something quotidian: portent is turned into business meeting. The psychological damage to the employees who have incessant nightmares is reduced to a problem of technical sustainability: the use of "deep evolutionary terrors [for the connecting nightmares] burns out *the communicating parties*" in about eighteen months, because the "*human filament* can't bear any more. Even with post-occupational counseling, therapy, and hypnosis, that's a *steep cost*" (*Ruin* 406, my emphasis). Workers are turned into components, "human filaments," with a certain life span and giving rise to costs in the production process. The deep-seated nightmares that unite all people become a technical solution and a technical problem, the human implications of constantly suffering from those nightmares ignored. This aspect of modernity in Gladstone's stories is perhaps the most chilling, the way it so explicitly accepts human suffering as a necessary cost for disembedding.

Mass media constitute a form of communication that provide the members of the modern society with information. Mass media in the Craft society are mostly recognizable as print media—broadsheets, newspapers, and magazines—with the exception of Alt Coulumb. They have a Crier's Guild that sing the news in the streets, once for free and then again if they receive sufficient tips (*Four* 20). This medial model recalls premodern news dissemination, not printed publication, with news dispatches arriving on slow ships rather than by nightmare telegraph (*Three* 103–4). The newsroom of the Guild is described very much in terms of a modern newspaper, though, resulting in a mass medium that mixes modern and premodern (*Four* 20). The issue that is mainly accentuated by the portrayal of mass media is the revelation and dispensation of factual information to a wider audience. The predominant image of mass media is as valuable and trustworthy, although *Last First Snow*, in particular, also presents how it can be used for propaganda and warmongering (e.g., *Last* 120). Journalists chase comments on newsworthy topics (e.g., *Last* 38–39) and two stories have investigative journalists among their central characters—Gabby Jones in *Four Roads Cross* and Caspar Jones in *Deathless: The City's Thirst*. Gabby's rhetoric is familiar from reporters in the actual world. She trusts her own investigations, wants to protect her sources and get quotable comments "on the record," and insists that "the city deserves the truth" (*Four* 24–26). Truth, to Gabby, is more important than social stability, a position which is similar to that of Kos's creditors in their insistence on full disclosure of his obligation to his consort. There is no room for secrets in modern contracts, whether social or financial. Truth and news are just commodities to be traded on a market.

The rise of modernity has come with an increase in international trade, and the enormous volumes of commodities traded over vast distances that mark late modernity in the actual world are mirrored in the Craft world. The ports of Alt Coulumb, Dresediel Lex, Agdel Lex, and Kavekana receive container ships with cargo from all over the world. On land, goods are transported by rail, for instance by the five-story trains of Agdel Lex. All kinds of products are traded, including spices and agricultural produce, metals and manufactured goods, "magisterium wood" and "synthetic dragon scales" (for a detailed description from Alt Coulumb's harbor, see *Four* 67). All this trade drives the economies and generates profits, which are then invested on a global finance market to generate more profits.

Financial investments are used throughout the series to combine a style of familiar and unfamiliar language to offer a bridge between the fictional modernity and the modernity of the actual world. The complexity of global investments in late modernity is highlighted mainly through Kai's perspective in *Full Fathom Five* and *Ruin of Angels* but is also the root cause behind Tara's investigations in *Three Parts Dead* and *Four Roads Cross*. In both cases, capital grows by investing in divinities, for example the return of grace with interest from the god Kos or Kavekana's semidivine idols, created and managed to provide high-yield, offshore portfolios. The language recalls that of Wall Street bankers and investment advisors rather than of a priesthood:

> "You should short Shining Empire bonds," [Kai] said then [. . .]. "Hard and fast. Today. Exchanges don't close in Alt Coulumb until eight. Plenty of time to arrange the trade."
>
> [. . .]
>
> "Alt Coulumb's index funds are up, and the Shining Empire debt market's rebounded. Turns out the rumors of open trade on their soul exchange were wrong after all." (*Full* 41)

Gladstone's style accentuates the modernity of the Craft world, only barely different from the reader's. The text gives the impression of being written specifically for the kind of word-switching game that Ursula K. Le Guin uses to separate Elfland from Poughkeepsie (the primary world at its most recognizable) in her 1973 essay on fantasy stylistics.[31] We could swap the place-names for China and New York and turn "soul exchange" into "stock exchange," and Kai might as well be sitting in Poughkeepsie instead of Kavekana. The texts include several passages like this, where the walls between the secondary and actual worlds become nearly transparent. They serve as reminders that the Craft world is like our world, a mirror of our modernity. The style is a shortcut to amplifying the feeling of modernity and a suggestion that the issues raised and criticism leveled apply equally to our world. It is a style far from the "flat" journalistic prose that Le Guin dislikes in fantasy,[32] however, because although the Craft world is not Elfland, nor is it Poughkeepsie in disguise. It is a modern otherworld, vividly drawn, and the language used to describe its globalized financial system feels so familiar because the language of financial investments—bonds that are shorted hard and fast, index funds that are up, and debt markets that rebounded—is almost as arcane as the language of the Craft. The style of global investment markets is not the only area of globalization that serves to encourage the reader to read beyond the fictionality of the modern society. Another prominent aspect of global modernity mixes familiar and unfamiliar—modern and fantastic—elements for a similar effect: tourism.

The tourism trade constitutes a parallel to the domain of international finance in the Craft world with a similar juxtaposition of modern and fantastic, driving home the modernity of the secondary world with striking and estranging descriptions. International trade and global finance are portrayed with some stylistic restraint compared to tourism. This aspect of globalization is flamboyantly rendered, drawing attention to its bizarreness and inequality. A typical example is the drink that the King in Red has while lounging on the beach. He is a powerful Craftsman who has shed his body and is now an enormous, living, red skeleton. His "skeletal hand held a round glass three-quarters full (or one-quarter empty) of a weapons-grade pink cocktail shaded by four paper umbrellas and sporting a spear of tiny melon cubes interspaced with jadeite giraffes. Ice shifted in the glass" (*Four* 281). The Craft world is rife with familiar drinks (in *Two Serpents Rise* alone, there are gin-and-tonics, single malt, champagne, and tequila), and a pink cocktail with ice and melon cubes is not particularly remarkable, had it not been for the exuberant description and the incongruous image of pink drink and red skeleton. The description slows down the passage and makes the cocktail, and the situation, stand out. The glass is not just "almost full," it is "three-quarters full (or one-quarter empty)," the specificity and parenthetical clarification opening a space for the reader to reflect on the image. Nor is the cocktail just "brightly pink" but "weapons-grade pink," a hyperbole matched by the exaggerated number of paper umbrellas shading it. The melon cubes are "interspaced with jadeite giraffes," emphasizing the luxury a Craftsman of power can indulge in. The description is replete with exaggerations that invite the reader to reflect on the scene and on the implications of a red skeleton in a lounge chair, enjoying a cocktail.

Similar vivid descriptions accompany several tourist scenes, and the luxury hotel on Kavekana is a conspicuous example of tourism as social criticism. "Pilgrims" flock to the island nation in search of investment opportunities, and the rich visit to enjoy the climate. The description of an exclusive resort includes its beach area with pools and cabanas, towels and tanning mirrors, cocktail waiters and a live band. So far it mirrors what can be expected from a similar establishment in the actual world. Like the King in Red, the patrons offer the strongest fantastic element. They are

> the well-heeled of six continents and three thousand cities, of every skin color and creed and species, living and undead, skeletal or carved from stone or pink and flexible, those floppy with excess flesh, these sculpted by surgery and personal trainers into hilariously exaggerated visions of human potential. But their faces all

played small changes on the same bovine physical contentment. (*Full* 84)

Wealth is the great equalizer, disregarding all other identities. The "well-heeled" can enjoy the disembedded luxury far away from home, thanks to modern means of traveling and the inordinate wealth available to them. But this scene is focalized by a girl who lives in the streets of Kavekana, and her perspective brings out the inequality and absurdity of modern luxury tourism. The tourists' obesity, cosmetic surgery, and fitness fixation are disparaged, as is their "bovine physical contentment." And through her focalization, the reader is invited to take a step back and reflect on the contrast between the luxury and bovine contentment enjoyed by the world's "well-heeled" and the situation of the local inhabitants, whether staff or street kid. The portrayal of Craft tourism is a thinly veiled critique of the social injustices and unequal income distribution and, ultimately, of modern, global capitalism.

The adverse effects of global capitalism on local communities is forcefully addressed in the Craft Sequence, in particular in *Last First Snow* and *Full Fathom Five* but present to varying degrees in all eight stories. Globalization leads to what Giddens calls "local transformation," when "what happens in a local neighbourhood is likely to be influenced by factors—such as world money and commodity markets—operating at an indefinite distance away from that neighbourhood itself."[33] The central conflict in *Last First Snow* arises from a clash between the globalization of trade and investment and the local people who want to preserve their homes and their lives from gentrification and inflated rents. The conflict echoes the critique of actual-world globalization, with a heterogeneous group of protesters resisting attempts to force them to accept a future that they do not want. Kavekana, in *Full Fathom Five*, is a small nation with an economy that relies on its usefulness for offshore investments. The price for its independence, in a world where poor migrants "swarm Dresediel Lex and Alt Coulumb in hungry millions" and rich nations deplete the resources of less fortunate countries, is to provide a haven for international investors and resorts for international tourists. Should their value fade, a Kavekana investment manager explains, "the masters of the world will demand something else from us. Build ships. Grow sugarcane. Bow before Iskari squid gods. Host a military base" (*Full* 305). The globalized world is a world globalized *by* certain countries, a modernity of global inequality, of developed and developing (or undeveloped) countries. The modern world is built on access to cheap labor and environmental destruction, to provide goods for a modern mass market in modern northern societies. Global actors only care about the local situation if it is of value to them, and the natural environment has the least value of all.

The powerful Craftspeople, modernity's champions and victors, care no more about the environment than they care about equality. The effects on the natural environment are as little regarded as those on local communities. The Craft itself destroys the natural world, as explained in *Deathless: The City's Thirst* (it is added that "Craftsfolk tend to regard [environmental destruction] as an amusing side effect")[34] and portrayed in *Three Parts Dead*, where Tara "drinks" the life of an oasis, withering the plants around her (11). Craftspeople care little about these destructive effects on a local level, and they fail to see the aggregate effect on the global level. From Kai's finance perspective, "the market has become so complicated nobody understands more than a shade of it, and people optimize local outcomes without concern for global consequences" (*Ruin* 199). Their powers might surpass those of the gods, but they lack the wisdom to understand or the compassion to care for the totality of the world. "Sensible decisions lead to sensible decisions and before long the land lies barren" (*Full* 375), an old god summarizes the danger of the legislator Craftsperson. Modernity is rational, but it is a limited rationality that ignores the destructive effects on anything without economic value—like natural ecosystems or local communities.

Craft-driven modernity causes environmental collapse and destroys the world. The gods kept cities alive with clean energy (*Three* 43),[35] but modern society requires more soulstuff than what is sustainable, poisoning soil and water (*Ruin* 276; *Four* 411). The only faint hope in a world that suffers the consequences of modernity is the Two Serpents Group, a meeting between the modern and the traditional in the form of an uneasy collaboration between some gods and Deathless Kings.

Taking it to the Next Level: A New Modernity

The Two Serpents Group represents the hope that Craft-driven modernity can be transformed into something better. The group works to combine the modern Craft of the Deathless Kings with premodern, divine grace. Tradition and modernity are brought together in order to save the world. The novels tell the story of the group's background, establishment, and development, setting the reconciliation of the traditional and the modern in opposition to the God Wars and their subsequent modernization. Rather than being the legislators of modernity, the characters involved take on the roles of what Bauman calls "interpreters," the intellectuals of postmodernity. The interpreter role "consists of translating statements, made within one communally based tradition, so that they can be understood within the system based on another tradition."[36] The interpreter accepts that there are different traditions, rather than insisting on one universal system of knowledge. The texts promote this shift away from the universalistic ambitions of Craftspeople and their conviction that their modernizing efforts have benefited humanity to a broader view of possible frames within which the world can be interpreted. Saving gods and, by introducing them to the modern framework, addressing the destructive aspects of modern Craftwork is the ultimate victory in the series. A doubleness of perspective and a willingness to accept both modernity and premodernity are offered as the route to salvation in the Craft world.

STORIES TOLD ABOUT MODERNITY

In urban fantasy, every modern secondary world tells its own story about modernity. Gladstone's Craft world tells a story of modernity as humanity's breaking free from divine oppression and entering an era of self-determination only to discover new oppression under a rule of lawyers and the domination of the corporate power of the unconscionably wealthy. The hope for Gladstone's modernity is to bridge the modern and the traditional and find a new balance between them. This is not the story told about modernity in every secondary-world urban fantasy—each world tells its own story.

In Williams's *The War of the Flowers* (2003),[37] modernity is portrayed as a struggle over the control of increasingly scarce resources. Loss of belief as inimical to fantastic beings is a fairly well-established motif in fantasy, with prominent examples including J. M. Barrie's *Peter Pan; or, the Boy Who Wouldn't Grow Up* (1904) and Michael Ende's *Die unendliche Geschichte* (1979; transl. *The Neverending Story*, 1983). The fairyland that Williams's protagonist is brought to has undergone a modernization process as sudden and brutal as in Gladstone's world. The premodern era is depicted as a time of peace, equality, and happiness for all, during which the Queen and King of the fairies guaranteed the prosperity of their realm. When they disappeared, magic began to fade, either due to the usurpation of political power and imprisonment of the royal couple or the dwindling belief in fairies among modern humans. In the modern fairy realm, human lack of belief is used by the new rulers as an excuse to establish a strictly hierarchical society. Those at the social bottom are exploited for their innate magic to provide a better life for those in the middle and at the top.

Modernity is thus portrayed as the basis for conflict in *The War of the Flowers*. Modern society is dominated by brutal forms of capitalism and industrialism, unequal and unjust. The feudal hierarchy is transposed into a class society, with the human-like

Flower Families at the top and goblins at the bottom, and with the main social divide running between winged and wingless fairies. The novel alludes to, and severely critiques, social hierarchies of the actual world in which oppression depends on arbitrary traits such as geographic origin, skin color, or religious beliefs. Although there are many late-modern details (from computers and phones to decadent nightclubs), Williams's world is more akin to a classically modern (nineteenth century) society. It has not undergone any popular-democratic reforms, power resides with a small group of (former) aristocrats, and its laws recall Germany's Nuremberg Laws, South Africa's apartheid system, or the United States' Jim Crow laws. Eventually, a popular uprising overthrows the social order, and the royal couple are freed, but instead of returning to the premodern system, the fairyland has to find a new way forward. Where the Craft Sequence envisages a transformation of modernity into something better, Williams's novel offers a cautionary tale of modernity as a form of oppression that deprived the world forever of a time of plenty and justice. Modernity might be necessary, but it also destroyed something and must itself be replaced or reshaped.

Another text that addresses the shortcomings of a capitalist, industrialist classical modernity is Miéville's *Perdido Street Station* (2000),[38] set in the city of New Crobuzon.[39] Over the course of the novel, New Crobuzon is portrayed largely as a city of classical modernity, clearly based on Gidden's institutional dimensions of modernity: capitalism, industrialism, surveillance, and control of the means of violence.[40] Industries and trade are run by capitalist owners, with steam and clockwork providing the main sources of power. Inventions are driven by discoveries through research, either for consumer markets or to provide the state's military with new weapons to defeat enemies. A secular government rules a society that has recently begun to divide along class lines, and a secret police has the population under surveillance. The rule of law is rudimentary, but there is an elected Parliament as well as courts and a codified penal system. There is also some science and technology similar to or surpassing that of late modernity: computers and a self-aware, artificial intelligence are based on mechanical designs; bombs as destructive and pathogenic as nuclear weapons have been around for centuries; and various sciences have made great advances. In this respect, Miéville's modernity parallels that of Gladstone's; the main difference between the actual, modern world and the fictional civilization is the absence of electricity and reliance on petroleum-based energy and the presence of some form of magic, which is treated within a rational framework of scientific thought.

The story told about modernity in New Crobuzon is one of possibilities and struggles, and modern society is presented as one in which the negative dominates the positive. Industrialism and capitalism combine to destroy the environment—as I have observed elsewhere, in New Crobuzon, "pollution is the most obvious sign of how culture invades and dominates the natural domain."[41] The government oppresses and punishes its citizens, its rule authoritarian rather than democratic. Technology might develop, but society appears to remain unchanging and stagnant. The foil to this negative portrayal is the presence of a university for research and education, an avant-garde art scene, and a political opposition consisting of unions and an underground press. Opposing social forces play tug-of-war, a battle of social stagnation against radical progression, but the negative aspects of modernity outweigh the positive. Miéville does not relate his modernity to a premodern past. Berman proposes that in classical modernity people can still recall what it is like to live in premodern times,[42] but the people of New Crobuzon remember only their modern present. Their modernity is constant, transforming very slowly or not at all over the centuries, the possibility of change only a faint hope always just out of reach. The story Miéville tells of modernity is, ultimately, a dark, terrible, cautionary tale.

Even fantastic worlds that depart from the logic both of the actual world and of traditional fantasy conventions can have modernity woven thoroughly into their fabric. In *Palimpsest* (2009),[43] by Valente, the eponymous city has a dreamlike, surreal quality. Veterans walk around, mute and with parts of animals grafted onto their bodies. One street is paved with layer upon layer of old coats, so deep that you need a gondola to travel along it. The dead are buried standing up and slowly grow toward the stars in immense stands of bamboo. Trains are wild beasts with intricate migratory patterns and mating habits. The children of the overly wealthy are born blank and featureless. Yet, it is clearly a modern city, with horseless carriages and railway lines, factories and museums, and banks and a parliament. Modernity in the city of Palimpsest is fantastic, surreal, and controlling: the wild trains are controlled by building tracks where they roam. Surgeons control the human body by grafting animal parts to people, and the bodies and minds of the featureless children are controlled in a "finishing school" where they are given form.

The plot revolves around the powerful Casimira, herself an embodiment of modernity and of modern control. The book opens with a brief description of her factory, in which a uniformed workforce uses machines to produce the vermin of the city. Mechanical rats, bees, crickets, doves, worms, and cockroaches spread throughout the city and report back to Casimira. Gidden's four institutional dimensions of modernity meet symbolically in her character: she runs a capitalist industry, with a city-wide surveillance operation and, during the civil war, controlled the military forces of one party. She is the picture of a beneficent capitalist; her workers are happy and her products appreciated, she is a patron of the finishing school and the arts, she fights for the rights of immigrants. But above all, she is a person who *controls*. She controls the city (through her power and information-gathering hosts of mechanical creatures), she controls the people around her, she even controls the plot of the novel. The story told about modernity in *Palimpsest*, not least through Casimira, is a story of control.

The story about modernity does not have to be a unified, straightforward whole but can be fractured and contradictory. Swanwick's *The Iron Dragon's Daughter* (1993),[44] set in a modern fairy world, tells the story of the changeling Jane, who was kidnapped from the human world as a young child. The story of modernity told from her perspective is complex and heterogeneous, revealing a society in which premodern traditions have been incorporated in modern social life. Features of late modernity abound, such as television shows, rap music, credit cards, shopping malls, skyscrapers, and cigarette lighters. Dragons are cybernetic, self-aware fighting machines akin to fighter jets, built in factories that provide tangible examples of a "military-industrial complex" in which industrialism and capitalism support the armed forces of the Elven empire. Ancient traditions, such as burning a person alive as a sacrifice to the Goddess, are modernized as media spectacle, with full television coverage, to suit the decadent tastes of the Elves and to entertain the masses. Society is divided by wealth, class, and race, including laws of racial segregation that forbid members from shorter races, such as dwarves and goblins, from mixing with taller fairy creatures. The fairy society might be unmistakably modern, but it is a modernity that has kept the worst of its premodern traditions.

The two themes complicating the negative portrayal of fairy modernity include the theme of learning and that of the relationship to the premodern Goddess. The modern view of learning and science is a consistently positive force. Jane's scientific approach to her life and world is presented as one of her greatest strengths, and learning sustains her through her life. Fairy pedagogy is portrayed as modern, broadly conforming to the ideas of Jean-Jacques Rousseau and John Dewey: the student is expected to come to their own insights and thus own their knowledge. Jane's alchemical training frequently combines terminology and practices from modern chemistry with the principles of conventional fantasy magic, thus demonstrating what science could look like if a modern, reflexive form of knowledge creation existed in a world of magic. The role of the Goddess becomes associated with this scientific magic. For much of the novel, She is described as cruel or, at best, uncaring, in parallel with rather than contrasting the brutal modernity of the decadent Elven capitalists. When Jane eventually meets Her, in what appears as a modern laboratory, it becomes clear that the Goddess has cared for and helped Jane throughout her life; the world's cruelty is caused by people. The negative image of modernity fractures in the light of the possibility of a caring modern (or premodern) society, as Jane returns to the human world, where she is allowed to thrive.

• • •

Not all secondary-world urban fantasies engage in such a broad critique of modern society as does Gladstone, nor does every story suggest a road forward. Although my brief summaries of how modernity is portrayed in these four examples do not do any of them justice (they are all wonderfully complex worlds), they illustrate how the story about modernity can be told very differently. The explicit criticism in Williams's modern Faerie, the possibilities and struggles of Miéville's modernity, the controlling modernity in Valente's dreamlike world, and the fractured and complex relationship between modernity and tradition in Swanwick's fairy world are four ways of telling that story. Other urban fantasies tell other stories, casting modernity as villain or hero, as a complex central character or a flat, innocent bystander. If we look closely, there is always something we can learn—about the fictive world but also, more importantly, about our own.

CODA: THE SHORT ANSWER

I entered this project wondering about two things: Why are there so many disparate opinions about what urban fantasy is? And why does some form of social commentary seem to be inescapable in that which is called, or which looks like it should be called, urban fantasy? The long answer to these questions can be found in the preceding eight chapters. I offer a short answer here.

Urban fantasy is a genre of variety, and it is little wonder that general agreement about what it looks like has not been forthcoming. It developed in stages, without one or a few major works to serve as a nucleus or "seed" around which the genre could crystalize. Instead, the genre formed as a bundle of literary strands, each strand contributing particular traits. Over time, new strands were added to the urban fantasy bundle. Some strands had originally emerged in other genres, others in literature in general, and others yet in a broader social discourse. Regardless of where they came from, they all offered more possibilities to braid together new stories. Because of this growing bundle of possibilities, what we think of as urban fantasy does not depend on a single pattern or collection of features. Rather, the genre is perceived in various ways depending on the strands available at a given time; or it is thought of as a specific collection of similar braids. In this book, I have worked with a cognitive model for urban fantasy that consists of three major concepts: the intermingling of features from several different genres; a dialogue between modernity and the fantastic; and a core concern with the unseen in various forms.

Several of the strands in the urban fantasy bundle of today promote or even require elements of social criticism and bring this with them into urban fantasy. The Gothic strand was one of the early contributors. What I call "proto-urban fantasy" arose as a combination of the Gothic, the story of the modern city, and the tale of the supernatural. In proto-urban fantasy, the Gothic had left ruins and old edifices in the wilderness behind and had entered the cities, replacing dark, labyrinthine tunnels with dark, labyrinthine alleys of poverty-stricken slums. This change of settings would eventually become a major contributor to urban fantasy's critique of modern society, and as supernatural creatures found their home in the Gothic mode, they brought with them alternative perspectives on society. The later addition of crime fiction offered similar critique through the hardboiled detective story's Great Wrong Place, a modern society defined by iniquity, violence, and graft. The police novel provided a more nuanced discussion of society, justice, and power along with its types of investigation plot. Other strands contributed other perspectives on modernity more broadly.

The meeting between modernity and the fantastic constitutes a major portion of the urban fantasy story. When modern life is confronted with the fantastic, modernity has to be portrayed through some sort of reaction to the new information. The world is suddenly different, and a revised view of modernity must be established, whether as resilient enough to withstand or incorporate the supernatural or so fragile that modern society transforms or breaks. Portraying modernity from a fantastic perspective, or transplanting it into a fantastic setting, can also convey alternative values or even revise our views by estranging modern elements that we thought we knew. Each of these three ways of having the fantastic meet modernity draws attention to particular aspects of modern society, encourages the reader to consider social weaknesses and strengths, and even suggests possible alternatives. We are invited to marvel at the fantastic but simultaneously given a chance to contemplate our modern life.

The foremost icon of the modern world is the city. In many urban fantasies, the familiarity of the urban setting necessitates pockets of the unfamiliar—unseen and unknown areas where the supernatural domain can hide. Much like the *science* in *science fiction*, the *urban* in *urban fantasy* has come to be slightly misleading (there does not have to be any science in the former; the setting for the latter does not have to be a city), but cities are still very common settings. Especially in cities that are fictional versions of actual places, there is a need for the story to establish unseen spaces where the supernatural can take place and unseen groups of people who can be involved in the supernatural events. Those unseen people and spaces are often drawn from groups and spaces that we pay little attention to in actual societies and who are portrayed as completely ignored in the fictional world. They could also be the unseen masters of society that we suspect and fear but do not really think exist. These secret masters are brought to life in the supernatural domain of urban fantasy—symbols of society's ills and wrongs. Introducing these unseen elements in a story also imbues the story with the social commentary implied by how those who are unseen, whether marginalized or powerful, are portrayed.

But any attempt to make an actual location into a fictional space can be said to comment on the society that is being fictionalized. The process of turning our world into fiction by necessity includes a selection process. Choosing to describe some things and not others always constitutes a comment, an observation on the original. There is also the kind of commenting that comes from using fantastic elements to change the fictional simulacrum or to replace some of its parts. This might not be the most perspicuous of social commentaries, but it is a kind of commentary that is difficult to avoid in a genre that aims to combine supernatural events with depictions of a world that the reader recognizes.

Perhaps no single urban fantasy story employs all these means to construct its social commentary, and certainly not every reader pays attention to the comments that the story they read makes about society. Some texts criticize the modern world loudly and clearly, while others are more discreet. While texts can encourage readers to reflect on social issues, they cannot force them to do so (even though several texts try very hard). Urban fantasy makes comments on our modern society; it is up to us whether to pay them any heed.

Notes

CHAPTER ONE: URBAN FANTASY TODAY

1 Charlaine Harris, *Dead Until Dark* (2001); K. J. Bishop, *The Etched City* (2003); Suyi Davies Okungbowa, *David Mogo, Godhunter* (2019); Seanan McGuire, *Rosemary and Rue* (2009); Trent Jamieson, *Death Most Definite* (2010).

2 Farah Mendlesohn and Edward James, *A Short History of Fantasy* (London: Middlesex University Press, 2009), 26.

3 Hadas Elber-Aviram, "'The Past Is Below Us': Urban Fantasy, Urban Archaeology, and the Recovery of Suppressed History," *Papers from the Institute of Archaeology* 23, no. 1 (2013): 2; cf. Helen Young, *Race and Popular Fantasy Literature: Habits of Whiteness* (New York: Routledge, 2016), 141–42; Siobhan Carroll, "Imagined Nation: Place and National Identity in Neil Gaiman's *American Gods*," *Extrapolation* 53, no. 3 (2012): 312.

4 Amanda Jo Hobson and U. Melissa Anyiwo, "Introduction: What Is Urban Fantasy?," in *Gender Warriors: Reading Contemporary Urban Fantasy*, ed. U. Melissa Anyiwo and Amanda Jo Hobson (Leiden: Brill, 2019), 3.

5 Alexander C. Irvine, "Urban Fantasy," in *The Cambridge Companion to Fantasy Literature*, ed. Edward James and Farah Mendlesohn (Cambridge: Cambridge University Press, 2012), 200; Young, *Race and Popular Fantasy*, 142.

6 Mendlesohn and James, *Short History*, 26; U. Melissa Anyiwo and Amanda Jo Hobson, "The Urban Fantasy Universe: Or What to Read or Watch Next," in *Gender Warriors: Reading Contemporary Urban Fantasy*, ed. U. Melissa Anyiwo and Amanda Jo Hobson (Leiden: Brill, 2019).

7 Irvine, "Urban Fantasy," 200.

8 Hadas Elber-Aviram, *Fairy Tales of London: British Urban Fantasy, 1840 to the Present* (London: Bloomsbury, 2021), 21.

9 Stefan Ekman, "Urban Fantasy: A Literature of the Unseen," *Journal of the Fantastic in the Arts* 27, no. 3 (2016): 455.

10 Kim Wilkins, "The Process of Genre: Authors, Readers, Institutions," *TEXT* 9, no. 2 (2005): 1.

11 Brian Attebery, *Stories about Stories* (Oxford: Oxford University Press, 2014), 38.

12 Ekman, "Urban Fantasy," 453.

13 This is discussed further in chapter 2. I use the Gothic as a shorthand for the combination of Gothic romance and supernatural and occult fiction that arose in the nineteenth century and developed during the twentieth century. It has brought many nonhuman creatures such as vampires, werewolves, and ghosts into urban fantasy.

14 Brian Attebery, *Strategies of Fantasy* (Bloomington: Indiana University Press, 1992), 9.

15 W. R. Irwin, *The Game of the Impossible: A Rhetoric of Fantasy* (Urbana: University of Illinois Press, 1976), 8.

16 Attebery, *Strategies of Fantasy*, 3; see also Kathryn Hume, *Fantasy and Mimesis: Responses to Reality in Western Literature* (New York: Methuen, 1984), 25; Brian Attebery, *Fantasy: How It Works* (Oxford: Oxford University Press, 2022), 131.

17 John G. Cawelti, *Adventure, Mystery, and Romance: Formula Stories as Art and Popular Culture* (Chicago: University of Chicago Press, 1976), 7.

18 George Lakoff, *Women, Fire, and Dangerous Things: What Categories Reveal about the Mind* (Chicago: University of Chicago Press, 1987), 68.

19 Lawrence W. Barsalou, "The Instability of Graded Structure: Implications for the Nature of Concepts," in *Concepts and Conceptual Development: Ecological and Intellectual Factors in Categorization*, ed. Ulric Neisser (Cambridge: Cambridge University Press, 1987), 102–103.

20 Michael Sinding, "The Mind's Kinds: Cognitive Rhetoric, Literary Genre, and Menippean Satire" (PhD diss., McMaster University, 2003), 42.

21 Sinding, 43.

22 Attebery makes some excellent points in *Stories about Stories* (chapter 6) and *Fantasy* (chapter 3) regarding people's different views on what is "impossible" and thus the difficulty in agreeing on a "consensus reality." In my view, this lack of agreement does not mean that texts cannot deal with the impossible, only that some texts, by some writers, might be interestingly ambiguous for some readers.

23 Mendlesohn and James, *Short History*, 138.

24 Carroll, "Imagined Nation," 312–17.

25 Viviane Bergue, "On the Fringe between Fantasy and Fantastique/Gothic Fiction: The Invention of Urban Fantasy," *Yearbook of Eastern European Studies* 6 (2016): 58; Arno Meteling, "Gothic London: On the Capital of Urban Fantasy in Neil Gaiman, China Miéville and Peter Ackroyd," *Brumal: Revista de Investigación sobre lo Fantástico* 5, no. 2 (2017): 66.

26 Young, *Race and Popular Fantasy*, 141–42.

27 The history of the genre and its label is addressed further in chapter 2.

28 See chapters 6, 7, and 8 for discussions of these examples.

29 Ekman, "Urban Fantasy," 463–66.

30 Something that is addressed in chapters 3 and 4.

31 Emily McAvan, *The Postmodern Sacred: Popular Culture Spirituality in the Science Fiction, Fantasy, and Urban Fantasy Genres* (Jefferson, NC: McFarland, 2012), 2, 13; Leigh M. McLennon, "Defining Urban Fantasy and Paranormal Romance: Crossing Boundaries of Genre, Media, Self and Other in New Supernatural Worlds," *Refractory: A Journal of Entertainment Media* 23 (2014): n.p., https://refractoryjournal.net/uf-mclennon/; Meteling, "Gothic London," 66; Sylwia Borowska-Szerszun, "Ethnic and Cultural Diversity in Ben Aaronovitch's Urban Fantasy Cycle *Rivers of London*," *Nordic Journal of English Studies* 18, no. 1 (2019): 6n5; Hobson and Anyiwo, "Introduction," 2.

32 E.g., Faye Ringel, "Bright Swords, Big Cities: Medievalizing Fantasy in Urban Settings," in *The Year's Work in Medievalism 10* (1995): 176–83; John Clute, "Urban Fantasy," in *The Encyclopedia of Fantasy*, ed. John Clute and John Grant (New York: St Martin's Griffin, 1999).

33 E.g., Martin Boszorád and Simona Klimková, "Never Mind the City Guides: The Topos of a City in Urban Fantasy (with Interpretative Emphasis on Neil Gaiman's Novel *Neverwhere*)," *Ars Aeterna* 13, no. 2 (2021); Yulia Georgievna Remaeva, "Gorodskoye fentezi Bena Aaronovicha: khudozhestvennyye osobennosti izobrazheniya dvoyemiriya Londona (na materiale romanov 'Reki Londona' i 'Luna nad Sokho')," in *V poiskakh granits fantasticheskogo: initsiatsiya, mediatsiya, transformatsiaya*, ed. Evdokia Antonovna Nesterova (Wrocław: Instytutu Profesjonalnego Rozwoju, 2021).

34 Young, *Race and Popular Fantasy*, 142; McLennon, "Urban Fantasy and Paranormal Romance," n.p.; see also Stefan Ekman, "Crime Stories and Urban Fantasy," *Clues: A Journal of Detection* 32, no. 2 (2017).

35 The detective plot and how it influences the social commentary in urban fantasy is addressed in chapter 5, and modernity in Aaronovitch's series is analyzed in chapter 6.

36 In chapter 2, I outline the historical developments that resulted in this genre hybridity.

37 Jeremy Crawford, James Wyatt, and Keith Baker, *Eberron: Rising from the Last War* (Renton, WA: Wizards of the Coast, 2019), 7–8, 10, 12.

38 J. R. R. Tolkien, "On Fairy-Stories," in *The Monsters and the Critics and Other Essays*, ed. Christopher Tolkien (London: HarperCollins, 1997), 132.

39 Gary K. Wolfe, *Critical Terms for Science Fiction and Fantasy: A Glossary and Guide to Scholarship* (Westport, CT: Greenwood Press, 1986), 115.

40 See Stefan Ekman, *Here Be Dragons: Exploring Fantasy Maps and Landscapes* (Middletown, CT: Wesleyan University Press, 2013), 10.

41 Lubomír Doležel, *Heterocosmica: Fiction and Possible Worlds* (Baltimore, MD: Johns Hopkins University Press, 1998), 2.

42 Mark J. P. Wolf, *Building Imaginary Worlds: The Theory and History of Subcreation* (New York: Routledge, 2012), 26.

43 Doležel, *Heterocosmica*, 128.

44 Nancy H. Traill, "Fictional Worlds of the Fantastic," *Style* 25, no. 2 (1991): 198–99; citing Raymond Bradley and Norman Swartz, *Possible Worlds: An Introduction to Logic and Its Philosopy* (Indianapolis: Hackett, 1979), 6.

45 Mendlesohn and James, *Short History*, 26; Kenneth J. Zahorski and Robert H. Boyer, "The Secondary Worlds of High Fantasy," in *The Aesthetics of Fantasy Literature and Art*, ed. Roger C. Schlobin (Notre Dame, IN: University of Notre Dame Press / Brighton, UK: Harvester Press, 1982), 56.

46 Clute, "Urban Fantasy [Clute and Grant]," 975–76.

47 Elber-Aviram, "'Past Is Below Us,'" 2.

48 McLennon, "Urban Fantasy and Paranormal Romance," n.p.

49 Tzvetan Todorov, *The Fantastic: A Structural Approach to a Literary Genre*, trans. Richard Howard (Ithaca, NY: Cornell University Press, 1975), 33.

50 John Clute, "Wainscots," in *The Encyclopedia of Fantasy*, ed. John Clute and John Grant (New York: St Martin's Griffin, 1999), 991.

51 Farah Mendlesohn, *Rhetorics of Fantasy* (Middletown, CT: Wesleyan University Press, 2008), 38.

52 Wolf, *Building Imaginary Worlds*, 28.

53 Gladstone's series is analyzed more closely in chapter 8.

54 Mendlesohn, *Rhetorics of Fantasy*, 148.

INTERLUDE I: AN INTRODUCTION TO MODERNITY

1 Marshall Berman, *All That Is Solid Melts into Air: The Experience of Modernity* (London: Verso, 1983), 15.

2 The relationship between Europe and its colonies is a complex issue; see below. Also see Anthony Giddens, *The Consequences of Modernity* (Cambridge: Polity, 1990), 175; Ulrich Beck and Johannes Willms, *Conversations with Ulrich Beck* (Cambridge: Polity, 2004), 25; Immanuel Wallerstein, *The Uncertainties of Knowledge* (Philadelphia: Temple University Press, 2004), 148.

3 Zygmunt Bauman, *Modernity and Ambivalence* (Cambridge: Polity, 1991), 3n1.

4 Anthony Giddens and Christopher Pierson, *Conversations with Anthony Giddens: Making Sense of Modernity* (Cambridge: Polity, 1998), 98.

5 Jürgen Habermas, *The Philosophical Discourse of Modernity*, trans. Frederick Lawrence (Cambridge: Polity, 1987), 5.

6 E.g., Stephen L. Collins, *From Divine Cosmos to Sovereign State: An Intellectual History of Consciousness and the Idea or Order in Renaissance England* (Oxford: Oxford University Press, 1989), 6–7.

7 Berman, *All That Is Solid*, 16–17.

8 Berman, 17.

9 See e.g., Habermas, *Philosophical Discourse*, 2.

10 Max Weber, *The Protestant Ethic and the Spirit of Capitalism*, trans. Talcott Parsons (London: George Allen & Unwin, 1930), 26.

11 Kenneth H. Tucker Jr., *Anthony Giddens and Modern Social Theory* (London: Sage, 1998), 128.

12 Tucker, 129.

13 Tucker, 128.

14 Bauman, *Modernity and Ambivalence*, 4.

15 Bauman, 4.

16 Collins, *From Divine Cosmos*, 6.

17 Giddens and Pierson, *Conversations*, 110–11.

18 Giddens and Pierson, 110.

19 Giddens, *Consequences of Modernity*, 59.

20 Giddens, 55–59.

21 Giddens, 63.

22 Berman, *All That Is Solid*, 17–36; Margaret S. Archer, "Introduction: 'Stability' or 'Stabilization'—On Which Would Morphogenic Society Depend?," in *Late Modernity: Trajectories towards Morphogenic Society* (Cham: Springer, 2014), 4–6.

23 Walter D. Mignolo, *The Darker Side of Western Modernity: Global Futures, Decolonial Options* (Durham, NC: Duke University Press, 2011), 2; see also Aníbal Quijano, "Coloniality and Modernity/Rationality," *Cultural Studies* 21, no. 2–3 (2007): 172.

24 Simon Susen, *Sociology in the Twenty-First Century: Key Trends, Debates, and Challenges* (Cham: Palgrave Macmillan, 2021), 298.

25 Richard Lachmann, *What is Historical Sociology?* (Cambridge: Polity, 2013), 57.

26 For a discussion about friction as a metaphor to discuss narrative tension, see Attebery, *Fantasy*, 69–72.

27 Giddens, *Consequences of Modernity*, 63.

28 Beck and Willms, *Conversations*, 7–8.

29 Habermas, *Philosophical Discourse*, 2.

30 David Frisby, *Cityscapes of Modernity: Critical Explorations* (Cambridge: Polity, 2001), 4–5.

31 Young, *Race and Popular Fantasy*, 141.

32 Hana Wirth-Nesher, *City Codes: Reading the Modern Urban Novel* (Cambridge: Cambridge University Press, 1996), 17.

33 Carroll, "Imagined Nation," 324.

CHAPTER TWO: A SHORT HISTORY OF URBAN FANTASY

1 What I mean by modernity and modern society is clarified in Interlude I, between chapters 1 and 2.

2 Gary K. Wolfe, *Evaporating Genres: Essays on Fantastic Literature* (Middletown, CT: Wesleyan University Press, 2011), 31.

3 Selma G. Lanes, *Down the Rabbit Hole: Adventures and Misadventures in the Realm of Children's Literature* (New York: Atheneum, 1971), 185.

4 D. D. C. Chambers, "Rechy, John (Francisco)," in *Contemporary Novelists*, ed. James Vinson, (New York: St. Martin's Press, 1972), 1052.

5 Ellen Schwartz, "Paris Letter: January," *Art International* 16, no. 3 (1972): 48.

6 E.g., Carroll, "Imagined Nation," 312; Elber-Aviram, "'Past Is Below Us,'" 2; see also Miéville, cited in Robin Anne Reid, "Urban Fantasy," in *Women in Science Fiction and Fantasy*, ed. Robin Anne Reid (Westport, CT: Greenwood Press, 2009), 308.

7 John Duka, "The Wiz of 'The Wiz,'" *New York Magazine*, October 16, 1978, 92.

8 Duka, 92.

9 Algis Budrys, *Benchmarks Continued: F&SF "Books" Columns 1975–1982* (Reading, UK: Ansible Editions, 2012), 118.

10 E.g., Irvine, "Urban Fantasy," 200; Young, *Race and Popular Fantasy*, 142.

11 Young, *Race and Popular Fantasy*, 141–42.

12 Budrys, *Benchmarks Continued*, 119, ellipsis in the original.

13 Farah Mendlesohn and Edward James speculate that Leiber's novel influenced the television sitcom *Bewitched* (Sol Saks, 1964–72), noting some parallels

between them in *Short History*, 73. The series portrays a witch who is married to a mortal man and who tries to comply with his wish that she behave like a typical (nonmagical) housewife. Regardless of whether there is any actual influence from *Conjure Wife*, *Bewitched* provides an early example of how magic is introduced into modern life, drawing on traditional expressions of the supernatural.

14 E.g., Clute, "Urban Fantasy [Clute and Grant]"; Elber-Aviram, *Fairy Tales of London*.

15 This and other of Dickens's "mysteries" are carefully analyzed in Elber-Aviram, *Fairy Tales of London*, 29–54.

16 Clute, "Urban Fantasy [Clute and Grant]," 975.

17 In *A Geography of Victorian Gothic Fiction*, Robert Mighall discusses the rise of what he refers to as the Urban Gothic, tracing its development through Victor Hugo, *Notre Dame de Paris* (1831) and Dickens, *Oliver Twist* (1837–39) to Reynolds, *The Mysteries of London*. Robert Mighall, *A Geography of Victorian Gothic Fiction: Mapping History's Nightmares* (Oxford: Oxford University Press, 1999), 27–55.

18 Fred Botting, *Gothic* (London: Routledge, 1996), 11.

19 Alistair Fowler, *Kinds of Literature: An Introduction to the Theory of Genres and Modes* (Oxford: Clarendon Press, 1982), 109.

20 Botting, *Gothic*, 12–13.

21 Botting, 13.

22 Mattias Fyhr, *De mörka labyrinterna: Gotiken i litteratur, film, musik och rollspel* (Lund: Ellerströms, 2003), 62.

23 Fyhr, 115.

24 Bergue, "On the Fringe," 56–58.

25 See Mendlesohn and James, *Short History*, 26.

26 Mendlesohn and James, 101.

27 Mendlesohn and James, 93.

28 Irvine, "Urban Fantasy," 201.

29 Sylvia Kelso, "*Loces Genii*: Urban Settings in the Fantasy of Peter Beagle, Martha Wells, and Barbara Hambley," *Journal of the Fantastic in the Arts* 13, no. 1 (2002): 28.

30 Jones's and Lindholm's novels are analyzed in chapter 3.

31 Mendlesohn and James, *Short History*, 183; see also Clute, "Urban Fantasy [Clute and Grant]," 976.

32 Dean-Liathine McDonald, "Urban Fantasy: Conjuring Collapse or a Sense of Place?," *Caliban: French Journal of English Studies* 63 (2020): 238–40.

33 It is unclear which is the first Newford story and when it was published. On his web site, de Lint explains that he came up with the by then still unnamed city

in "Timeskip," written for the 1989 anthology *Post Mortum* (http://charlesdelint.com/faq01.htm#newford). The first Newford collection, *Dreams Underfoot* (1993), contains two stories that predate "Timeskip": "Uncle Dobbin's Parrot Fair" (first published in *Isaac Asimov's Science Fiction Magazine*, November 1987) and "That Explains Poland" (first published in *Pulphouse*, 1988). The former is not set in Newford but introduces a few characters that will be revisited in later Newford stories; the latter builds its setting from places that recur in Newford over the years.

34 E.g., Elber-Aviram, "'Past Is Below Us,'" 1; Borowska-Szerszun, "Ethnic and Cultural Diversity," 5n5; McDonald, "Urban Fantasy," 238.

35 E.g., Mendlesohn and James, *Short History*, 137; Young, *Race and Popular Fantasy*, 141.

36 Charles de Lint, *Dreams Underfoot* (New York: Tor, 1994).

37 Charles de Lint, "A Personal Journey into Mythic Fiction," in *The Urban Fantasy Anthology*, ed. Peter S. Beagle and Joe R. Lansdale (San Francisco: Tachyon, 2011), 17.

38 de Lint, "Personal Journey," 17.

39 de Lint, 17.

40 The investigator and crime fiction are discussed in more detail in chapter 5.

41 Maurizio Ascari, *A Counter-History of Crime Fiction: Supernatural, Gothic, Sensational* (Basingstoke: Palgrave Macmillan, 2007), 79; quoting Michael Cox and R. A. Gilbert, Introduction to *Victorian Ghost Stories: An Oxford Anthology*, ed. Michael Cox and R. A. Gilbert (Oxford: Oxford University Press, 1991), xviii.

42 As demonstrated by Edward James, "The City Watch," in *Terry Pratchett: Guilty of Literature*, ed. Andrew M. Butler, Edward James, and Farah Mendlesohn (Baltimore, MD: Old Earth Books, 2004).

43 Anna Höglund, *Vampyrer: En kulturkritisk studie av den västerländska vampyrberättelsen från 1700-talet till 2000-talet*, ed. Kerstin Brodén, Acta Wexionensia, (Växjö: Växjö University Press, 2009), 299.

44 Höglund, 310–13.

45 Personal reflection: Charnas's novel contains one of the more memorable sentences I have encountered in vampire fiction, one that perfectly illustrates the transformation of human vampires into beings of great personal insight: "I know why I'm a vampire; why are you a therapist?" From *The Vampire Tapestry* (Albuquerque, NM: Living Batch Press, 1980), 159.

46 Michał Wolski, "Krwiopijca kosmopolityczny: Wpływ *Wampira: Maskarady* na współczesną kulturę wampiryczną," in *Gry fabularne: Kultura – praktyki – konteksty*, ed. Roberta Dudzińskiego and Anny Wróblewskiej (Wrocław: Stowarzyszenie Badaczy Popkultury i Edukacji Popkulturowej "Trickster," 2016), 16.

47 Wolski, 22–23.
48 McLennon, "Urban Fantasy and Paranormal Romance," n.p.
49 John Clute and David Langford, "Urban Fantasy," in *The Encyclopedia of Fantasy (online)*, ed. John Clute and John Grant, def. 2. https://sf-encyclopedia.com/fe/urban_fantasy.
50 Laurell K. Hamilton, *The Laughing Corpse* (New York: Jove, 2002), 70.
51 Mendlesohn and James, *Short History*, 154.
52 Examples include Tifa Lockhart in *Final Fantasy VII* (1997) and Sherry Birkin in *Resident Evil 2* (1998).
53 Mendlesohn and James, *Short History*, 155.
54 Mendlesohn and James, 155.
55 Attebery, *Strategies of Fantasy*, 126.
56 Attebery, 126, 129.
57 Mendlesohn and James, *Short History*, 143.
58 Cited in Camilla Del Grazia, "Possible and Impossible Worlds: Reading Contemporary Fantastic City-Novels through the Rhetorics of Fantasy and Social Geography" (PhD diss. Unpublished, Universitá di Pisa, 2022), 37.
59 Ringel, "Bright Swords, Big Cities," 175.
60 Ringel, 176.
61 Clute, "Urban Fantasy [Clute and Grant]," 975.
62 Clute, 975.
63 Cited in Ann VanderMeer and Jeff VanderMeer, eds., *The New Weird* (San Francisco: Tachyon, 2008), 318.
64 David Langford, "New Weird," in *The Encyclopedia of Science Fiction*, ed. John Clute and John Grant, June 7, 2021). https://sf-encyclopedia.com/entry/new_weird.
65 Jeff VanderMeer, "The New Weird: 'It's Alive?,'" in *The New Weird*, ed. Ann VanderMeer and Jeff VanderMeer (San Francisco: Tachyon, 2008), xii.
66 VanderMeer, xvi.
67 VanderMeer, ix–x.
68 John Clute, "Urban Fantasy," in *The Greenwood Encyclopedia of Science Fiction and Fantasy: Themes, Works, and Wonders*, ed. Gary Westfahl (Westport, CT: Greenwood Press, 2005).
69 Reid, "Urban Fantasy."
70 Reid, 307.
71 Kelso, "*Loces Genii*," 13.
72 Kelso, 29–30.
73 Allan Weiss, "Destiny and Identity in Canadian Urban Fantasy," in *Literary Environments: Canada and the Old World*, ed. Britta Olinder (Brussels: Peter Lang, 2006), 109–10.

74 Lazette Gifford, "Whither Wander You? The Long History of Urban Fantasy," *Vision: A Resource for Writers* 9 (2002): n.p., http://visionforwriters.com/vision/index.php/categories/33-fantasy/459-whither-wander-you-the-long-history-of-urban-fantasy.

75 Nanette Wargo Donohue, "The City Fantastic," Collection Development, *Library Journal* (June 1 2008): 64.

76 N. K. Jemisin, "New Urban Fantasy. Same as the Old Urban Fantasy?," Jeff VanderMeer, 2009, https://www.jeffvandermeer.com/2009/12/09/the-new-urban-fantasy-same-as-the-old-urban-fantasy/.

77 Wolfe, *Evaporating Genres*, 24.

78 Wolfe, 24–25.

79 Wolfe, 25.

80 Wolfe, 51.

81 McAvan, *Postmodern Sacred*.

82 Carroll, "Imagined Nation."

83 Clute and Langford, "Urban Fantasy."

84 Irvine, "Urban Fantasy."

85 Irvine, 201.

86 Young, *Race and Popular Fantasy*, 142.

87 Ekman, "Urban Fantasy."

88 Hobson and Anyiwo, "Introduction," 2.

89 Petra Schrackmann, "Wissen als Schwelle: Urban Fantasy für Kinder und Jugendliche," in *Fremde Welten: Wege und Räume der Fantastik im 21. Jahrhundert*, ed. Lars Schmeink and Hans-Harald Müller (Boston: De Gruyter, 2012); Rosalind Krul, "Young Adult Appeal and Thematic Similarity in Urban Fantasy," *New Review of Children's Literature and Librarianship* 22, no. 2 (2016).

90 David Pike, "Commuting to Another World: Spaces of Transport and Transport Maps in Urban Fantasy," in *Popular Fiction and Spatiality: Reading Genre Settings*, ed. Lisa Fletcher (New York: Palgrave Macmillan, 2016); Raphael Zähringer, "'Strange Tricks of Cartography': The Map(s) of *Perdido Street Station*," in *China Miéville: Critical Essays*, ed. Caroline Edwards and Tony Venezia (Cantebury: Gylphi, 2015); Stefan Ekman, "Map and Text: World-Architecture and the Case of Miéville's *Perdido Street Station*," *Literary Geographies* 4, no. 1 (2018).

91 McLennon, "Urban Fantasy and Paranormal Romance."; Kristina Deffenbacher, "Rape Myths, Twilight and Women's Paranormal Revenge in Romantic and Urban Fantasy Fiction," *Journal of Popular Culture* 47, no. 5 (2014); María T. Ramos-García, "Paranormal Romance and Urban Fantasy," in

The Routledge Research Companion to Popular Romance Fiction, ed. Jayashree Kamblé, Eric Murphy Selinger, and Hsu-Ming Teo (London: Routledge, 2020).

92 Jessica Tiffin, "Outside/Inside Fantastic London," *English Academy Review* 25, no. 2 (2008); Meteling, "Gothic London"; Stefan Ekman, "London Urban Fantasy: Places with History," *Journal of the Fantastic in the Arts* 29, no. 3 (2018).

93 Elber-Aviram, *Fairy Tales of London*; Del Grazia, "Possible and Impossible Worlds."

CHAPTER THREE: UNSEEN PEOPLE

1 What I mean by modernity and modern society is clarified in Interlude I, between chapters 1 and 2.

2 Clute, "Wainscots," 991.

3 Michael Levy and Farah Mendlesohn, *Children's Fantasy Literature: An Introduction* (Cambridge: Cambridge University Press, 2016), 130.

4 Clute, "Wainscots," 991.

5 This version of the World of Darkness came to an end with the "Time of Judgement" storyline. Other versions of the game's setting have continued after 2004. Peter Ray Allison, "Shedding Light on World of Darkness, the Gothic-Punk Universe of RPG Vampire: The Masquerade," Dicebreaker, 2020, accessed October 26, 2023, https://www.dicebreaker.com/categories/roleplaying-game/feature/shedding-light-on-world-of-darkness-vampire-rpg.

6 Clute, "Wainscots," 991.

7 Donald Broady, *Sociologi och epistemologi: Om Pierre Bourdieus författarskap och den historiska epistemologin*, 2nd revised ed. (Stockholm: HLS, 1991), 266.

8 Pierre Bourdieu, *The Rules of Art: Genesis and Structure of the Literary Field*, trans. Susan Emanuel (Cambridge: Polity, 1996), 205.

9 Broady, *Sociologi och epistemologi*, 266–67.

10 Attebery, *Strategies of Fantasy*, 133.

11 Pierre Bourdieu and Loïc J. D. Wacquant, *An Invitation to Reflexive Sociology* (Chicago: University of Chicago Press, 1992), 98.

12 References to Megan Lindholm, *Wizard of the Pigeons* (New York: Ace, 1986), are given parenthetically in the text.

13 Attebery, *Strategies of Fantasy*, 135.

14 Pierre Bourdieu, *The Logic of Practice*, trans. Richard Nice (Cambridge: Polity, 1990), 52.

15 David L. Swartz, *Symbolic Power, Politics, and Intellectuals: The Political Sociology of Pierre Bourdieu* (Chicago: University of Chicago Press, 2013), 57.

16 Swartz, 58.

17 Swartz, 58.

18 Swartz, 58.

19 Swartz, 57.

20 Swartz, 35.

21 Swartz, 38.

22 Swartz, 39.

23 Swartz, 98–99.

24 Bourdieu, *Logic of Practice*, 133.

25 Attebery, *Strategies of Fantasy*, 136.

26 Ekman, *Here Be Dragons*, 141.

27 The development of de Lint's treatment of indigenous characters and culture is examined in e.g., Weronika Łaszkiewicz, "From Stereotypes to Sovereignty: Indigenous Peoples in the Works of Charles de Lint," *Studies in Canadian Literature* 43, no. 1 (2018); Weronika Łaszkiewicz, "Decolonizing the Anthropocene: Reading Charles de Lint's *Widdershins*," *Acta Neophilologica* 22, no. 2 (2020).

28 References to Charles de Lint, "But for the Grace Go I," in *Dreams Underfoot* (New York: Tor, 1994); Charles de Lint, "Waifs and Strays," in *The Ivory and the Horn* (New York: Tor, 1995); de Lint, "The Pochade Box," are given parenthetically in the text.

29 Charles de Lint, "The Invisibles," in *Moonlight and Vines* (New York: Tor, 1997), 216.

30 Although it has been claimed that "desperate poverty" is absent from the books, see Cat Ashton, "Sacred Cities: Charles de Lint's Newford Books and the Mythologizing of the North American Urban Landscape," in *The Canadian Fantastic in Focus: New Perspectives*, ed. Alan Weiss (Jefferson, NC: McFarland, 2014), 117.

31 Ekman, *Here Be Dragons*, 141–54.

32 Irvine, "Urban Fantasy," 200; Young, *Race and Popular Fantasy*, 142.

33 Ekman, *Here Be Dragons*, 153–54.

34 References to Lauren Beukes, *Zoo City* (London: Penguin Books, 2018), are given parenthetically in the text.

35 Cheryl Stobie, "Dystopian Dreams from South Africa: Lauren Beukes's *Moxyland* and *Zoo City*," *African Identities* 10, no. 4 (2012).

36 Louise Bethlehem, "Hydrocolonial Johannesburg," *Interventions* 24, no. 3 (2022); Matthew Eatough, "Planning the Future: Scenario Planning, Infrastructural Time, and South African Fiction," *Modern Fiction Studies* 61, no. 4 (2015); Brady Smith, "SF, Infrastructure, and the Anthropocene: Reading

Moxyland and *Zoo City*," *Cambridge Journal of Postcolonial Literary Inquiry* 3, no. 3 (2016).

37 Jocelyn Fryer, "Rewriting Abject Spaces and Subjectivities in Lauren Beukes's *Zoo City*," *English in Africa* 43, no. 2 (2016); Lisa Propst, "Information Glut and Conspicuous Silence in Lauren Beukes's *Zoo City*," *Journal of Postcolonial Writing* 53, no. 4 (2017).

38 Compare for example Fryer, "Rewriting Abject Spaces," 120.

39 Fryer, 118.

40 Fryer, 125.

41 Tatiana Adeline Thieme, "The Hustle Economy: Informality, Uncertainty and the Geographies of Getting By," *Progress in Human Geography* 42, no. 2 (2018): 529–30.

42 Propst, "Information Glut," 420.

43 Andy Sawyer, "*Zoo City* (review)," Review, *Foundation: The International Review of Science Fiction*, no. 111 (2011): 75.

44 Clute, "Wainscots," 991.

45 John Clute, Roz Kaveney, and Gary Westfahl, "Fantasies of History," in *The Encyclopedia of Fantasy*, ed. John Clute and John Grant (New York: St Martin's Griffin, 1999), 334–35.

46 David Langford, "Secret Masters," in *The Encyclopedia of Fantasy*, ed. John Clute and John Grant (New York: St Martin's Griffin, 1999), 848.

47 Brian Stableford, "Immortality," in *The Encyclopedia of Fantasy*, ed. John Clute and John Grant (New York: St Martin's Griffin, 1999), 497.

48 References to N. K. Jemisin, *The City We Became* (London: Orbit, 2020), are given parenthetically in the text.

49 Julian Go, "Decolonizing Bourdieu: Colonial and Postcolonial Theory in Pierre Bourdieu's Early Work," *Sociological Theory* 31, no. 1 (2013): 62; citing Bourdieu, *Logic of Practice*.

50 See e.g., Bedelia Nicola Richards et al., "What's Race Got to Do With It? Disrupting Whiteness in Cultural Capital Research," *Sociology of Race and Ethnicity* 9, no. 3 (2023); Derron Wallace, "Cultural Capital as Whiteness? Examining Logics of Ethno-racial Representation and Resistance," *British Journal of Sociology of Education* 39, no. 4 (2018).

51 Berndt Reiter, "A Theory of Whiteness as Symbolic Racial Capital: Bourdieu 2.0," *International Journal of Humanities and Social Science Research* 6, no. 5 (2020): 114–15.

52 Seung-Wan (Winnie) Lo, "White Capital: Whiteness Meets Bourdieu," in *Unsettling Whiteness*, ed. Lucy Michael and Samantha Schulz (Oxford: Inter-Disciplinary Press, 2014), 165.

53 Reiter, "Theory of Whiteness," 115.

54 Swartz, *Symbolic Power*, 58.

55 Diana Wynne Jones, *Archer's Goon* (New York: Ace, 1987).

56 Farah Mendlesohn, *Diana Wynne Jones: Children's Literature and the Fantastic Tradition* (New York: Routledge, 2005), 148.

57 Mendlesohn, 152. Mendlesohn also refers to other scholars who have addressed this point: C. Butler, *Four British Fantasists: The Children's Fantasy Fiction of Penelope Lively, Alan Garner, Diana Wynne Jones, and Susan Cooper*. (Lanham, MD: Scarecrow Press and Children's Literature Association, 2006); Marilynn S. Olson, "Cats and Aliens in the Unreal City: T. S. Eliot, Diana Wynne Jones, and the Urban Experience," in *Diana Wynne Jones: An Exciting and Exacting Wisdom*, ed. Teya Rosenberg et al. (New York: Peter Lang, 2002), 1–12; Suzanne Rahn, *Rediscoveries in Children's Literature*. (New York: Garland, 1995).

58 Mendlesohn, 152.

59 Kyra Jucovy, "Little Sister Is Watching You: *Archer's Goon* and *1984*," *Journal of the Fantastic in the Arts* 21, no. 2 (2010); see also Mendlesohn, *Diana Wynne Jones*, 155.

60 Levy and Mendlesohn, *Children's Fantasy Literature*, 174.

61 Giddens, *Consequences of Modernity*, 55–63.

62 Olson paraphrased in Mendlesohn, *Diana Wynne Jones*, 151.

63 References to Kat Howard, *An Unkindness of Magicians* (New York: Saga Press, 2017), are given parenthetically in the text.

64 Mendlesohn, *Diana Wynne Jones*, 149–50.

65 Anthony Shorrocks et al., *Global Wealth Report 2023*, Credit Suisse Research Institute (CSRI) (2023), 22.

66 See Wolski, "Krwiopijca kosmopolityczny," 22–23.

67 References to Mark Rein-Hagen, *Vampire: The Masquerade* (Stone Mountain, GA: White Wolf, 1991), are given parenthetically in the text.

68 References to Ronni Radner, ed., *A World of Darkness Second Edition* (Clarkston, GA: White Wolf, 1996), are given parenthetically in the text.

69 Jim Butcher, *Ghost Story* (London: Orbit, 2011), 89.

CHAPTER FOUR: UNSEEN SPACES

1 What I mean by modernity and modern society is clarified in Interlude I, between chapters 1 and 2.

2 In previous publications, I have used Yi-Fu Tuan's concepts of *space* and *place*, in which the former denotes a physical area and the latter refers to a space with (social) meaning. Beware this discrepancy in terminology.

3 Edward W. Soja, *Thirdspace: Journeys to Los Angeles and Other Real-and-Imagined Places* (Cambridge, MA: Blackwell, 1996), 75.

4 Soja, 78–79.

5 Soja, 81–82.

6 Daniela Hodrová, *Místa s tajemstvím? Kapitoly z literární topologie* (Praha: Koniasch Latin Press, 1994).

7 Hodrová, 10, quotation translated by Dagmar Hanzlíková.

8 Michel de Certeau, *The Practice of Everyday Life*, trans. Steven Rendall (Berkeley: University of California Press, 1984), 93.

9 de Certeau, 92.

10 de Certeau, 93.

11 Mighall, *Geography of Victorian Gothic Fiction*, 32.

12 Mighall, 28–33.

13 Mighall, 31.

14 Aliette de Bodard, *The House of Shattered Wings* (London: Gollancz, 2016), 34.

15 de Bodard, 39–40.

16 de Bodard, 2.

17 Aliette de Bodard, *The House of Binding Thorns* (New York: Ace, 2017), 261.

18 Ekman, *Here Be Dragons*, 141–42.

19 Ekman, 152.

20 de Lint, "That Explains Poland," 108.

21 de Lint, 109; de Lint, "Waifs," 16.

22 de Lint, "The Sacred Fire," 139.

23 Ashton, "Sacred Cities," 114.

24 de Lint, "Sacred Fire," 139.

25 de Lint, "Grace," 322–23. Maisie's story is analyzed in chapter 3.

26 de Lint, "That Explains Poland," 108.

27 Charles de Lint, *Widdershins* (New York: Tor, 2006), 199, 254–55.

28 McDonald, "Urban Fantasy," 238–40.

29 China Miéville, *Perdido Street Station* (New York: Del Rey-Ballantine, 2001), 143.

30 Miéville, 144.

31 Miéville, 445–46.

32 Kate Griffin [Catherine Webb], *The Midnight Mayor* (London: Little, Brown Book Group, 2010), 284.

33 Robert Weinberg, *The Ascension Warrior* (Clarkston, GA: White Wolf, 1997), 342.

34 Peter Fitting offers a brief overview of underground worlds in literature: Peter Fitting, "Underground Worlds," in *The Routledge Companion to*

Imaginary Worlds, ed. Mark J. P. Wolf (New York: Routledge, 2018). Rosalind Williams's essay on the underground as an artificial, social environment provides valuable insights on several subterranean settings from (mainly) nineteenth- and early twentieth-century texts: Rosalind Williams, *Notes on the Underground: An Essay on Technology, Society, and the Imagination*, New ed. (Cambridge, MA: MIT Press, 2008).

35 Some settings, while possible to read as urban fantasy, are wholly or largely set underground, such as the industrial, polluted city of Zaun in Riot Game's fictional world for *League of Legends* (2009) and the animated series *Arcane: League of Legends* (Riot Games/Fortiche, 2021). Although Zaun has more lax regulations regarding the use and development of "Hextech" than its sister city, Piltover, it is neither an unseen or particularly fantastic space.

36 References to Neil Gaiman, *Neverwhere* (London: Headline, 2013), are given parenthetically in the text.

37 E.g., Irvine, "Urban Fantasy," 204–5; Elber-Aviram, "'Past Is Below Us,'" 2; Young, *Race and Popular Fantasy*, 142.

38 *Neverwhere* is possibly the one urban fantasy text that has been subjected to the greatest number of critical readings, and a large proportion of them address some aspect of the unseen spaces of London Below. A small selection of examples include Del Grazia's *Possible and Impossible Worlds* (2022); Elber-Aviram's "'The Past Is Below Us'" (2013) and *Fairy Tales of London* (2021); Klapcsik's *Liminality in Fantastic Fiction* (Jefferson, NC: McFarland, 2012); Meteling's "Gothic London" (2017); Pike's "Commuting to Another World" (2016); Pleßke's "The Liminality of Underground London," in *London in Contemporary British Fiction: The City Beyond the City*, edited by Nick Hubble and Philip Tew, 161–76 (London: Bloomsbury Academic, 2016); Tiffin's "Outside/Inside Fantastic London" (2008); and my own "Down, Out and Invisible in London and Seattle," *Foundation: The International Review of Science Fiction* 94 (2005): 64–74; and "London Urban Fantasy" (2018).

39 Elber-Aviram, *Fairy Tales of London*, 176.

40 Irina Rață, "Trials and Tribulations in London Below," *Brumal. Revista de Investigación sobre lo Fantástico/Brumal. Research Journal on the Fantastic* 5, no. 2 (2017): 94.

41 Virgil, *Eclogues, Georgics, Aeneid I–IV* (Cambridge, MA: Harvard University Press, 1999), book 6.

42 Ben Aaronovitch, *Whispers under Ground* (London: Gollancz, 2012), 307–12; Ben Aaronovitch, *Lies Sleeping* (London: Gollancz, 2018), 190–99.

43 Pike, "Commuting to Another World," 141.

44 Pike, 142.

45 Walter Benjamin, *The Arcades Projects*, trans. Howard Eiland and Kevin McLaughlin, ed. Rolf Tiedeman (Cambridge, MA: Belknap Press of Harvard University Press, 1999), 416 [M1,2].
46 Ekman, "London Urban Fantasy," 392–94.
47 Lewis Mumford, *The Culture of Cities* (London: Routledge, 1997), 4.
48 Tom Porter, *Archispeak: An Illustrated Guide to Architectural Terms* (Abingdon, UK: Taylor & Francis, 2005), 105.
49 Elber-Aviram, "'Past Is Below Us,'" 2.
50 Young, *Race and Popular Fantasy*, 142.
51 See, e.g., Meteling, "Gothic London," 80–82.
52 Crawford, Wyatt, and Baker, *Eberron*, 177.
53 Elber-Aviram, *Fairy Tales of London*, 176.
54 Paul Kincaid, "Underground Adventure," in *The Greenwood Encyclopedia of Science Fiction and Fantasy: Themes, Works, and Wonders*, ed. Gary Westfahl (Westport, CT: Greenwood Press, 2005), 844.
55 Ekman, "Down, Out and Invisible," 70.
56 Michel Foucault, "Of Other Spaces," *Diacritics* 16, no. 1 (1986): 24.
57 Foucault, 24.
58 Del Grazia, "Possible and Impossible Worlds," 238; citing as examples Tiffin, "Outside/Inside"; Pleßke, "Liminality"; Elana Gomel, "'Divided Against Itself': Dual Urban Chronotopes," in *Cityscapes of the Future: Urban Spaces in Science Fiction*, ed. Yael Maurer and Meyrav Koren-Kuik (Boston: Brill Rodopi, 2018); Klapcsik, *Liminality*.
59 Elber-Aviram, "'Past Is Below Us,'" 2.
60 I address this in chapter 1.
61 References to Richard Kadrey, *Sandman Slim* (London: Harper Voyager, 2013), are given parenthetically in the text.
62 This novel is discussed in more detail in chapter 3.

CHAPTER FIVE: INVESTIGATING THE UNSEEN

1 What I mean by modernity and modern society is clarified in Interlude I, between chapters 1 and 2.
2 Cawelti, *Adventure, Mystery, and Romance*, 131–36.
3 This chapter is partly based on Ekman, "Crime Stories."
4 Derek Landy, Skulduggery Pleasant series (2007–22); Mike Resnick, Fables of Tonight (1987, 2008–12); Glen Cook, Garrett P. I. series (1987–2013); Simon R. Green, The Nightside (2003–12); Liz Williams, Detective Inspector Chen series (2005–15); Ben Aaronovitch, the Rivers of London series (2011–present);

China Miéville, *Kraken* (2010); P. Djèlí Clark, *A Master of Djinn* (2021); Aneta Jadowska, Heksalogia Dory Wilk [the Dora Wilk Hexalogy] (2012–14); Stephen Carpenter, Jim Kouf, David Greenwalt, *Grimm* (2011–17).

5 I refer to varieties of the investigator plot by different terms, such as the detective story, crime fiction, and police novels, however. They cover slightly different parts of investigation stories, and my reason for this is simply to make it easier to draw on previous scholars while remaining faithful to their particular perspective as much as possible. My focus in this chapter is the criminal investigation, but the investigation plot offers a slightly broader investigative perspective in urban fantasy than just crime.

6 Cawelti, *Adventure, Mystery, and Romance*, 132.

7 Cawelti, 140.

8 Peter Messent, *The Crime Fiction Handbook* (Chichester: Wiley-Blackwell, 2013), 73.

9 Messent, 73.

10 E.g., Harrison, *A Fistful of Charms* (2006); Aaronovitch, *Foxglove Summer* (2014); Harris, *Dead until Dark* (2001).

11 Lucy Andrew and Catherine Phelps, Introduction to *Crime Fiction in the City: Capital Crimes*, ed. Lucy Andrew and Catherine Phelps (Cardiff: University of Wales Press, 2013), 2.

12 Peter Clandfield, "Denise Mina, Ian Rankin, Paul Johnston, and the Architectural Crime Novel," *Clues: A Journal of Detection* 26, no. 2 (2008): 80.

13 Mendlesohn, *Rhetorics of Fantasy*, 115.

14 Mendlesohn, 116.

15 The good fit between detective stories and supernatural mysteries may explain the long tradition of this combination. The historical perspective is addressed in chapter 2.

16 Attebery, *Strategies of Fantasy*, 131; Attebery, *Fantasy*, 2.

17 Marie-Laure Ryan, *Possible Worlds, Artificial Intelligence and Narrative Theory* (Bloomington: Indiana University Press, 1991), 51.

18 Andrew and Phelps, "Crime Fiction," 2.

19 Quoted in Messent, *Crime Fiction Handbook*, 44.

20 P. Djèlí Clark [Dexter Gabriel], *A Master of Djinn* (London: Orbit, 2021).

21 Michael Swanwick, "A Small Room in Koboldtown," *Asimov's Science Fiction* April/May (2007). Also published as part of Michael Swanwick, *The Dragons of Babel* (New York: Tor, 2007). For a more detailed analysis of this story, see Ekman, "Crime Stories," 49–51.

22 Lee Horsley, *Twentieth-Century Crime Fiction* (Oxford: Oxford University Press, 2005), 158–59.

23 W. H. Auden, "The Guilty Vicarage: Notes on the Detective Story, by an Addict," in *The Complete Works of W. H. Auden: Prose. Volume II. 1939–1948* (Princeton, NJ: Princeton University Press, 2002), 265.

24 Raymond Chandler, "The Simple Art of Murder," in *Popular Fiction: An Anthology*, ed. Gary Hoppenstand (New York: Longman, 1998), 508.

25 Messent, *Crime Fiction Handbook*, 17.

26 Messent, 40.

27 References to Jim Butcher, *Storm Front* (New York: Roc, 2000), are given parenthetically in the text.

28 Currently seventeen novels published of twenty-three or twenty-four planned (by October 2023), plus short stories, graphic novels, a role-playing game, a card game, and a television series.

29 References to Kim Harrison, *Dead Witch Walking* (New York: Harper Voyager, 2004), are given parenthetically in the text.

30 Currently seventeen novels (by October 2023), plus short stories, novellas, graphic novels, and a prequel novel.

31 Dennis Porter, "The Private Eye," in *The Cambridge Companion to Crime Fiction*, ed. Martin Priestman (Cambridge: Cambridge University Press, 2003), 96.

32 Porter, 109.

33 Porter, 112–13.

34 Muller's Sharon McCone first appeared in 1977; Paretsky's V. I. Warshawski and Grafton's Kinsey Millhone both first appeared in 1982.

35 Adrienne E. Gavin, "Feminist Crime Fiction and Female Sleuths," in *A Companion to Crime Fiction*, ed. Charles J. Rzepka and Lee Horsley (Chichester: Wiley-Blackwell, 2010), 264.

36 Messent, *Crime Fiction Handbook*, 17.

37 Priscilla L. Walton and Manina Jones, *Detective Agency: Women Rewriting the Hardboiled Tradition* (Berkeley: University of California Press, 1999), 30–31.

38 Messent, *Crime Fiction Handbook*, 42.

39 References to Terry Pratchett, *Feet of Clay* (London: Corgi, 1997), are given parenthetically in the text.

40 References to Paul Cornell, *London Falling* (New York: Tor, 2012), are given parenthetically in the text.

41 Peter Messent, "The Police Novel," in *A Companion to Crime Fiction*, ed. Charles J. Rzepka and Lee Horsley (Chichester: Wiley-Blackwell, 2010), 178.

42 The author intended the series to be five books in all but has yet to find a publisher for books four and five (as of October 2023).

43 In order of publication: *Guards! Guards!* (1989), *Men at Arms* (1993), *Feet of Clay* (1996), *Jingo* (1997), *The Fifth Elephant* (1999), *Night Watch* (2002), *Thud!* (2005), and *Snuff* (2011).

44 My analysis of *Feet of Clay* owes a great debt to Edward James's reading of the first six City Watch novels as police procedurals: James, "City Watch."

45 For a broader discussion on London as a historically defined setting, see Ekman, "London Urban Fantasy."

46 Messent, *Crime Fiction Handbook*, 68–69.

47 Messent, 70.

48 Horsley, *Twentieth-Century Crime Fiction*, 101–2.

49 Messent, "Police Novel," 180.

50 Messent, 181.

51 Horsley, *Twentieth-Century Crime Fiction*, 101–2.

52 Leroy L. Panek, "Post-War American Police Fiction," in *The Cambridge Companion to Crime Fiction*, ed. Martin Priestman (Cambridge: Cambridge University Press, 2003), 156.

53 Heta Pyrhönen, "Criticism and Theory," in *A Companion to Crime Fiction*, ed. Charles J. Rzepka and Lee Horsley (Chichester: Wiley-Blackwell, 2010), 48.

54 Terry Pratchett, *Witches Abroad* (London: Gollancz, 1991), 147n.

55 James, "City Watch," 212.

56 This trope presumably originated with J. R. R. Tolkien's *The Lord of the Rings*, appendix A (1954–55).

57 Messent, *Crime Fiction Handbook*, 7.

INTERLUDE II: SOME NOTES ON FOCALIZATION

1 What I mean by modernity and modern society is clarified in Interlude I, between chapters 1 and 2.

2 Gérard Genette, *Narrative Discourse*, trans. Jane E. Lewin (Oxford: Blackwell, 1980), 189–94.

3 Interested readers can find overviews in e.g., Gerald Prince, "A Point of View on Point of View or Refocusing Focalization," in *New Perspectives on Narrative Perspective*, ed. Willie van Peer and Seymour Chatman (Albany: State University of New York Press, 2001), 43–44; James Phelan, "Why Narrators Can Be Focalizers—and Why It Matters," in *New Perspectives on Narrative Perspective*, ed. Willie van Peer and Seymour Chatman (Albany: State University of New York Press, 2001), 52–56; Kai Mikkonen, *The Narratology of Comic Art* (New York: Routledge, 2017), 150–51.

4 Karin Kukkonen, *Contemporary Comics Storytelling* (Lincoln: University of Nebraska Press, 2013), 183, 48.

5 Shlomith Rimmon-Kenan, *Narrative Fiction: Contemporary Poetics*, 2nd ed. (London: Routledge, 2002), 78–84.

6 I am convinced by Phelan's persuasive argument that narrators *can* be focalizers, or, as he concludes, "as the narrator reports, the narrator cannot help but simultaneously function as a set of lenses through which the audience perceives the story world." Phelan, "Why Narrators Can Be Focalizers," 57.

7 Petter Aaslestad, *Narratologi: En innføring i anvendt fortelleteori* (Oslo: Capellen Damm Akademisk, 1999), 84–85.

CHAPTER SIX: FINDING THE FANTASTIC

1 What I mean by modernity and modern society is clarified in Interlude I, between chapters 1 and 2.

2 The Rivers of London series (also called the Peter Grant series) currently consists of nine novels, three novellas, one short-story collection, and eight graphic novels, published since 2011. There is also a role-playing game (Chaosium, 2022). This analysis focuses on the seven novels that constitute the "Faceless Man" story arc: *Rivers of London* (2011; US title *Midnight Riot*), *Moon over Soho* (2011), *Whispers Under Ground* (2012), *Broken Homes* (2013), *Foxglove Summer* (2014), *The Hanging Tree* (2016), and *Lies Sleeping* (2018). References to these novels are given parenthetically in the text. Also included are the three graphic novels that take place at various points of that arc: *Body Work* (2016), set between *Broken Homes and Foxglove Summer*, and *Night Witch* (2016) and *Black Mould* (2017), both set between *Foxglove Summer* and *The Hanging Tree*. The graphic novels have no page numbers but are divided into sections corresponding to the original comic book publications, and are referred to by section (I–V) and page in that section (1–22; occasional covers inserted as splash pages are not included in the enumeration).

3 Tolkien, "On Fairy-Stories," 125–28.

4 Clute, "Wainscots," 991.

5 Unseen people and spaces are addressed further in chapters 3 and 4.

6 Ben Aaronovitch, *What Abigail Did That Summer* (London: Gollancz, 2021), 65.

7 For a brief introduction to focalization, see Interlude II, between chapters 5 and 6.

8 Mendlesohn, *Rhetorics of Fantasy*, 115.

9 Mendlesohn, 2.

10 Mendlesohn, 273.

11 Mendlesohn, 115.

12 Mendlesohn, 149.

13 Wolf, *Building Imaginary Worlds*, 26.

14 Young, *Race and Popular Fantasy*, 153–55.

15 Borowska-Szerszun, "Ethnic and Cultural Diversity," 2–3.

16 Aleksandra Łozińska, "Spojrzenie kształtujące przestrzeń—opowiadanie Londynu w cyklu Bena Aaronovitcha o Peterze Grancie Wprowadzenie," in *Retelling: strategie przestrzenne*, ed. Dominika Ciesielska, Magdalena Kozyry, and Aleksandra Łozińska (Krakow: Wiele Kropek, 2019).

17 Remaeva, "Gorodskoye fentezi Bena Aaronovicha," 117.

18 Elber-Aviram, *Fairy Tales of London*, 190–92.

19 Kukkonen, *Contemporary Comics Storytelling*, 151.

20 For more on representations of graphic novel narrative perspective, see Kai Mikkonen, "Presenting Minds in Graphic Narratives," *Partial Answers* 6, no. 2 (2008).

21 Łozińska, "Spojrzenie kształtujące przestrzeń," 139–45.

22 Cf. Borowska-Szerszun, "Ethnic and Cultural Diversity," 9–12.

23 Ben Aaronovitch, *Amongst Our Weapons* (London: Orion, 2022), 142.

24 Giddens, *Consequences of Modernity*, 53.

25 Giddens, 17, my italics.

26 Giddens, 38.

27 Tucker, 145.

28 Giddens, *Consequences of Modernity*, 27.

29 Giddens, 57–58; Giddens and Pierson, *Conversations*, 96.

30 Tucker, 145.

31 Ben Aaronovitch and Andrew Cartmel, *Body Work*, ed. Lee Sullivan (art) (London: Titan Comics, 2016), I.10.

32 Tucker, 145.

33 Giddens's third source; see *Consequences of Modernity*, 20.

34 A. Conan Doyle, *The Sign of Four* (London: T. Nelson & Sons, 1913), 96 [ch. 6]. Variations of this appear in several stories.

35 Agnieszka Anna Jędrzejczyk-Drenda, "Magic in Fantasy: Narrative Strategies from 1970 to 2010" (PhD diss., Anglia Ruskin University, 2017), 8, 137.

36 Jędrzejczyk-Drenda, 165.

37 Giddens and Pierson, *Conversations*, 110.

38 See also Ben Aaronovitch and Andrew Cartmel, *Night Witch*, ed. Lee Sullivan (art) (London: Titan Comics, 2016), II.9.

39 Karl R. Popper, *Conjectures and Refutations: The Growth of Scientific Knowledge*, 4th ed. (London: Routledge and Kegan Paul, 1972), 50.

40 Giddens, *Consequences of Modernity*, 39.

41 Ben Aaronovitch and Andrew Cartmel, *Black Mould*, ed. Lee Sullivan (art) (London: Titan Comics, 2017), I.6, I.12, my italics.

42 Aaronovitch and Cartmel, I.19, I.21–22.

43 Aaronovitch and Cartmel, IV.6–7.

44 Giddens, *Consequences of Modernity*, 38–39, my italics.

45 Zygmunt Bauman, *Legislators and Interpreters: On Modernity, Post-Modernity, and Intellectuals* (Cambridge: Polity, 1987), 111.

46 Borowska-Szerszun, "Ethnic and Cultural Diversity," 23.

47 See also Aaronovitch and Cartmel, *Body Work*, I.13.

48 Bauman, *Legislators and Interpreters*, 3.

49 Jemisin's *The City We Became* is discussed in more detail in chapter 3.

50 Irvine, "Urban Fantasy," 200–201.

51 Mendlesohn, *Rhetorics of Fantasy*, 148.

52 Mendlesohn, 148.

53 Mendlesohn, 150.

54 Emma Bull, *War for the Oaks* (New York: Orb, 2001), 70–71.

55 Maria Turtschaninoff, *Underfors* (Helsinki: Förlaget, 2010), 106, 147.

56 Turtschaninoff, 229.

57 Nene Ormes, *Udda verklighet* (Gothenburg: Styxx Fantasy, 2010), 130–31.

58 Ormes, 115.

59 Saga Bokne, "'I Will Diminish, and Go into the West': The Departure of the Fairies in Modern Fantasy Literature," paper presented at NAES 2022: Nordic Association of English Studies Triennial Conference, Stockholm, May 11–13, 2022; see also Ekman, *Here Be Dragons*, 91–92.

60 Cassandra Clare, *City of Bones* (London: Walker Books, 2007), 244.

61 Fritz Leiber, *Conjure Wife* (New York: Orb, 2009), 224.

62 Ekman, "Down, Out and Invisible," 70.

63 Gaiman, *Neverwhere*, 110.

64 Elber-Aviram, *Fairy Tales of London*, 178–79.

65 Irvine, "Urban Fantasy," 205.

66 Elber-Aviram, *Fairy Tales of London*, 180.

CHAPTER SEVEN: MEETING THE MODERN

1 What I mean by modernity and modern society is clarified in Interlude I, between chapters 1 and 2.

2 For a brief introduction to focalization, see Interlude II, between chapters 5 and 6.

3 The series consist of nine novels and a number of short stories and novellas, published between 2011 and 2018. This analysis focuses on the first four novels: *Hounded* (2011), *Hexed* (2011), *Hammered* (2011), and *Tricked* (2012). References to these novels are given parenthetically in the text. Although there is a story arc across all nine novels, the first four form a unit of sorts. They span events that take place during a few months, after which there is a hiatus of more than a decade before the events in book 5, *Trapped* (2012), begin.

4 Viktor Shklovsky, *Theory of Prose*, trans. Benjamin Sher (Elmwood Park, IL: Dalkey Archive Press, 1990), 7.

5 Fatemeh Pourjafari and Abdolali Vahidpour, "Migration Literature: A Theoretical Perspective," *Dawn Journal* 3, no. 1 (2014): 686.

6 Homi K. Bhabha, *The Location of Culture* (Abingdon: Routledge, 1994), 9.

7 Pourjafari and Vahidpour, "Migration Literature," 687.

8 What I mean by modernity and modern society is clarified in Interlude I, between chapters 1 and 2.

9 Attebery, *Strategies of Fantasy*, 132.

10 Ryan, *Possible Worlds*, 51.

11 Since the publication of *Bird of Fire*, the situation in Arizona has changed, partly for the better, partly for the worse. As the point is to look at parallels between a description of the actual Arizona and Hearne's fictional world, I have not included updated information.

12 Andrew Ross, *Bird of Fire: Lessons from the World's Least Sustainable City* (Oxford: Oxford University Press, 2011), 18.

13 Ross, 38–39.

14 Ross, 39.

15 Ross, 42, 4.

16 Ross, 39.

17 Ross, 39.

18 Ross, 133.

19 Ekman, *Here Be Dragons*, 196–98.

20 Ross, *Bird of Fire*, 38.

21 Ross, 44, 148.

22 Pourjafari and Vahidpour, "Migration Literature," 688.

23 Giddens and Pierson, *Conversations*, 110.

24 Beck and Willms, *Conversations*, 37.

25 Tucker, 144; citing Anthony Giddens, *Modernity and Self-Identity: Self and Society in the Late Modern Age* (Cambridge: Polity, 1991), 81.

26 Andrew Gurr, *Playgoing in Shakespeare's London* (Cambridge: Cambridge University Press, 1987), 55.

27 Tanya Huff, *Blood Price* (New York: Daw, 1991), 24.
28 Glen Duncan, *The Last Werewolf* (New York: Vintage, 2012), 4.
29 Duncan, 89.
30 Duncan, 89.
31 Duncan, 5.
32 Duncan, 48–49; Huff, *Blood Price*, 88.
33 Ekman, *Here Be Dragons*, 141–54.
34 Ekman, 141.
35 Butcher, *Storm Front*, 2–3.
36 See chapter 5 for a discussion of the investigator figure and the Dresden Files.
37 Butcher, *Storm Front*, 7.
38 Giddens and Pierson, *Conversations*, 110.
39 Tom Pollock, *The City's Son* (London: Quercus, 2013); Tom Pollock, *The Glass Republic* (London: Quercus, 2014); Tom Pollock, *Our Lady of the Streets* (London: Quercus, 2015).
40 Aaronovitch and Cartmel, *Night Witch*, II.11.
41 Trent Jamieson, *Death Most Definite* (Sydney: Orbit, 2010).
42 Benedict Jacka, *Fated* (London: Orbit-Little, Brown, 2012), 3.
43 Howard's novel is discussed further in chapter 3.

CHAPTER EIGHT: MODERNIZING THE FANTASTIC

1 What I mean by modernity and modern society is clarified in Interlude I, between chapters 1 and 2.
2 Ordered by internal chronology, the novels of the series are *Last First Snow* (2015), *Two Serpents Rise* (2013), *Three Parts Dead* (2012), *Four Roads Cross* (2016), *Full Fathom Five* (2014), and *Ruin of Angels* (2017). References to these novels are given parenthetically in the text. There are also two computer games/interactive novels set in the same world: *Choice of the Deathless* (2013) and *Deathless: The City's Thirst* (2015). The Craft Sequence will be concluded by the Craft Wars trilogy, with a first novel, *Dead Country*, published in 2023. The trilogy is not discussed in this chapter.
3 Wolf, *Building Imaginary Worlds*, 26.
4 Stefan Ekman and Audrey Isabel Taylor, "Notes Toward a Critical Approach to Worlds and World-Building," *Fafnir: Nordic Journal of Science Fiction and Fantasy Research* 3, no. 3 (2016): 11.
5 Ekman, *Here Be Dragons*, 1–4.
6 For a brief introduction to focalization, see Interlude II, between chapters 5 and 6.
7 Bauman, *Legislators and Interpreters*, 4–5.

8 Collins, *From Divine Cosmos*, 6.
9 Bauman, *Modernity and Ambivalence*, 4.
10 Giddens, *Consequences of Modernity*, 36.
11 Giddens and Pierson, *Conversations*, 94.
12 Berman, *All That Is Solid*, 17.
13 Berman, 17.
14 Beck and Willms, *Conversations*, 25; Bauman, *Legislators and Interpreters*, 2–3.
15 Bauman, *Modernity and Ambivalence*; Tucker, 128; Giddens, *Consequences of Modernity*, 53.
16 Bauman, *Legislators and Interpreters*, 4.
17 Giddens, *Consequences of Modernity*, 21–22.
18 Tom Bingham, *The Rule of Law* (London: Penguin, 2011), 8, my emphasis.
19 Niall Ferguson, "The Rule of Law and its Enemies," July 3, 2012, in *Reith Lectures 2012,* produced by Jane Beresford, BBC Radio, 00:29:36, https://www.bbc.co.uk/programmes/b01jmxrx.
20 Bauman, *Legislators and Interpreters*, 4.
21 Bauman, 4–5.
22 Giddens, *Consequences of Modernity*, 56.
23 Stuart Hall, "The West and the Rest: Discourse and Power," in *Formations of Modernity*, ed. Stuart Hall and Bram Gieben (Cambridge: Polity, 1992), 186.
24 Ali Meghji, *Decolonizing Sociology: An Introduction* (Cambridge: Polity, 2021), 21. Meghji refers to Ramón Grosfoguel's "Decolonizing Western Universalisms: Decolonial Pluri-Versalism from Aimé Césaire to the Zapatistas" (2017) and also adds that in the beginning of the twenty-first century, it is "democratize or I'll kill you."
25 Quijano, "Coloniality and Modernity/Rationality," 169–70.
26 Quijano, 168–69; see also Meghji, *Decolonizing Sociology*, 19–21.
27 Mignolo, *Darker Side*, 2–3.
28 Malcolm Waters, *Globalization*, 2nd ed. (London: Routledge, 2001), 5.
29 Waters, 6–7; Tucker, 144; Bill Ashcroft, *Post-Colonial Transformation* (New York: Routledge, 2001), 16.
30 Tucker, 144; Zygmunt Bauman, *Liquid Modernity* (Cambridge: Polity, 2000), 9; Giddens and Pierson, *Conversations*, 99.
31 Ursula K. Le Guin, "From Elfland to Poughkeepsie," in *The Language of the Night: Essays on Fantasy and Science Fiction*, ed. Susan Wood (New York: G. P. Putnam's Sons, 1979), 84–85.
32 Le Guin, 93.
33 Giddens, *Consequences of Modernity*, 64.

34 Gladstone, *Deathless: The City's Thirst*, Stats > Some Helpful Terms > Craftsmen, Craftswomen, Craftsfolk.

35 See also Gladstone, ch. 2.

36 Bauman, *Legislators and Interpreters*, 5.

37 Tad Williams, *The War of the Flowers* (New York: DAW, 2004).

38 Miéville, *Perdido Street Station*.

39 *The Scar* (2002), *Iron Council* (2004), and "Jack" (2005) are also partly or entirely set in New Crobuzon.

40 Giddens, *Consequences of Modernity*, 55–59.

41 Ekman, *Here Be Dragons*, 155.

42 Berman, *All That Is Solid*, 17.

43 Catherynne M. Valente, *Palimpsest* (New York: Bantam, 2009).

44 Michael Swanwick, *The Iron Dragon's Daughter* (New York: William Morrow, 1994).

Bibliography

Aaronovitch, Ben. *Amongst Our Weapons.* London: Orion, 2022.

Aaronovitch, Ben. *Broken Homes.* London: Gollancz, 2013.

Aaronovitch, Ben. *Foxglove Summer.* London: Gollancz, 2014.

Aaronovitch, Ben. *The Hanging Tree.* London: Gollancz, 2016.

Aaronovitch, Ben. *Lies Sleeping.* London: Gollancz, 2018.

Aaronovitch, Ben. *Moon over Soho.* New York: Del Rey, 2011.

Aaronovitch, Ben. *Rivers of London.* London: Gollancz, 2011.

Aaronovitch, Ben. *What Abigail Did That Summer.* London: Gollancz, 2021.

Aaronovitch, Ben. *Whispers under Ground.* London: Gollancz, 2012.

Aaronovitch, Ben, and Andrew Cartmel. *Black Mould.* Edited by Lee Sullivan (art). London: Titan Comics, 2017.

Aaronovitch, Ben, and Andrew Cartmel. *Body Work.* Edited by Lee Sullivan (art). London: Titan Comics, 2016.

Aaronovitch, Ben, and Andrew Cartmel. *Night Witch.* Edited by Lee Sullivan (art). London: Titan Comics, 2016.

Aaslestad, Petter. *Narratologi: En innføring i anvendt fortelleteori.* Oslo: Capellen Damm Akademisk, 1999.

Allison, Peter Ray. "Shedding Light on World of Darkness, the Gothic-Punk Universe of RPG Vampire: The Masquerade." Dicebreaker, 2020, accessed October 26, 2023, https://www.dicebreaker.com/categories/roleplaying-game/feature/shedding-light-on-world-of-darkness-vampire-rpg.

Andrew, Lucy, and Catherine Phelps. Introduction to *Crime Fiction in the City: Capital Crimes*, edited by Lucy Andrew and Catherine Phelps, 1–5. Cardiff: University of Wales Press, 2013.

Anyiwo, U. Melissa, and Amanda Jo Hobson. "The Urban Fantasy Universe: Or What to Read or Watch Next." In *Gender Warriors: Reading Contemporary Urban Fantasy*, edited by U. Melissa Anyiwo and Amanda Jo Hobson, 137–60. Leiden: Brill, 2019.

Archer, Margaret S. "Introduction: 'Stability' or 'Stabilization'—On Which Would Morphogenic Society Depend?" In *Late Modernity: Trajectories towards Morphogenic Society*. Cham: Springer, 2014.

Ascari, Maurizio. *A Counter-History of Crime Fiction: Supernatural, Gothic, Sensational.* Basingstoke: Palgrave Macmillan, 2007.

Ashcroft, Bill. *Post-Colonial Transformation.* New York: Routledge, 2001.

Ashton, Cat. "Sacred Cities: Charles de Lint's Newford Books and the Mythologizing of the North American Urban Landscape." In *The Canadian Fantastic in Focus: New Perspectives*, edited by Alan Weiss, 108–119. Jefferson, NC: McFarland, 2014.

Attebery, Brian. *Fantasy: How It Works.* Oxford: Oxford University Press, 2022.

Attebery, Brian. *Stories about Stories.* Oxford: Oxford University Press, 2014.

Attebery, Brian. *Strategies of Fantasy.* Bloomington: Indiana University Press, 1992.

Auden, W. H. "The Guilty Vicarage: Notes on the Detective Story, by an Addict." In *The Complete Works of W. H. Auden: Prose. Volume II. 1939–1948*, 261–69. Princeton, NJ: Princeton University Press, 2002.

Barsalou, Lawrence W. "The Instability of Graded Structure: Implications for the Nature of Concepts." In *Concepts and Conceptual Development: Ecological and Intellectual Factors in Categorization*, edited by Ulric Neisser, 101–40. Cambridge: Cambridge University Press, 1987.

Bauman, Zygmunt. *Legislators and Interpreters: On Modernity, Post-Modernity, and Intellectuals.* Cambridge: Polity, 1987.

Bauman, Zygmunt. *Liquid Modernity.* Cambridge: Polity, 2000.

Bauman, Zygmunt. *Modernity and Ambivalence.* Cambridge: Polity, 1991.

Beck, Ulrich, and Johannes Willms. *Conversations with Ulrich Beck.* Cambridge: Polity, 2004.

Benjamin, Walter. *The Arcades Projects.* 1927–40. Translated by Howard Eiland and Kevi McLaughlin. Edited by Rolf Tiedeman. Cambridge, MA: Belknap Press of Harvard University Press, 1999.

Bergue, Viviane. "On the Fringe between Fantasy and Fantastique/Gothic Fiction: The Invention of Urban Fantasy." *Yearbook of Eastern European Studies* 6 (2016): 46–60.

Berman, Marshall. *All That Is Solid Melts into Air: The Experience of Modernity.* London: Verso, 1983.

Bethlehem, Louise. "Hydrocolonial Johannesburg." *Interventions* 24, no. 3 (2022): 340–54. https://doi.org/10.1080/1369801X.2021.2015710.

Beukes, Lauren. *Zoo City.* 2010. London: Penguin Books, 2018.

Bhabha, Homi K. *The Location of Culture.* Abingdon: Routledge, 1994.

Bingham, Tom. *The Rule of Law.* London: Penguin, 2011.

Bokne, Saga. "'I Will Diminish, and Go into the West': The Departure of the Fairies in Modern Fantasy Literature." Paper presented at NAES 2022: Nordic Association of English Studies Triennial Conference, Stockholm, May 11–13, 2022.

Borowska-Szerszun, Sylwia. "Ethnic and Cultural Diversity in Ben Aaronovitch's Urban Fantasy Cycle *Rivers of London.*" *Nordic Journal of English Studies* 18, no. 1 (2019): 1–26.

Boszorád, Martin, and Simona Klimková. "Never Mind the City Guides: The Topos of a City in Urban Fantasy (with Interpretative Emphasis on Neil Gaiman's Novel *Neverwhere*)." *Ars Aeterna* 13, no. 2 (2021): 31–42. https://doi.org/10.2478/aa-2021-0009.

Botting, Fred. *Gothic.* London: Routledge, 1996.

Bourdieu, Pierre. *The Logic of Practice.* 1980. Translated by Richard Nice. Cambridge: Polity, 1990.

Bourdieu, Pierre. *The Rules of Art: Genesis and Structure of the Literary Field.* Translated by Susan Emanuel. Cambridge: Polity, 1996.

Bourdieu, Pierre, and Loïc J. D. Wacquant. *An Invitation to Reflexive Sociology.* Chicago: University of Chicago Press, 1992.

Bradley, Raymond, and Norman Swartz. *Possible Worlds: An Introduction to Logic and Its Philosopy.* Indianapolis: Hackett, 1979.

Broady, Donald. *Sociologi och epistemologi. Om Pierre Bourdieus författarskap och den historiska epistemologin.* 2nd revised ed. Stockholm: HLS, 1991.

Budrys, Algis. *Benchmarks Continued: F&SF "Books" Columns 1975–1982.* Reading, UK: Ansible Editions, 2012.

Bull, Emma. *War for the Oaks.* New York: Orb, 2001. 1987.

Butcher, Jim. *Ghost Story.* London: Orbit, 2011.

Butcher, Jim. *Storm Front.* New York: Roc, 2000.

Carroll, Siobhan. "Imagined Nation: Place and National Identity in Neil Gaiman's *American Gods.*" *Extrapolation* 53, no. 3 (2012): 307–26. https://doi.org/10.3828/extr.2012.17.

Cawelti, John G. *Adventure, Mystery, and Romance: Formula Stories as Art and Popular Culture.* Chicago: University of Chicago Press, 1976.

Chambers, D. D. C. "Rechy, John (Francisco)." In *Contemporary Novelists*, edited by James Vinson, 1052. New York: St. Martin's Press, 1972.

Chandler, Raymond. "The Simple Art of Murder." In *Popular Fiction: An Anthology*, edited by Gary Hoppenstand, 498–508. New York: Longman, 1998.

Charnas, Suzy McKee. *The Vampire Tapestry.* Albuquerque, NM: Living Batch Press, 1980.

Clandfield, Peter. "Denise Mina, Ian Rankin, Paul Johnston, and the Architectural Crime Novel." *Clues: A Journal of Detection* 26, no. 2 (2008): 79–91.

Clare, Cassandra. *City of Bones.* London: Walker Books, 2007.

Clark, P. Djèlí [Dexter Gabriel]. *A Master of Djinn.* London: Orbit, 2021.

Clute, John. "Urban Fantasy." In *The Encyclopedia of Fantasy*, edited by John Clute and John Grant, 975–76. New York: St Martin's Griffin, 1999.

Clute, John. "Urban Fantasy." In *The Greenwood Encyclopedia of Science Fiction and Fantasy: Themes, Works, and Wonders*, edited by Gary Westfahl, 852–54. Westport, CT: Greenwood Press, 2005.

Clute, John. "Wainscots." In *The Encyclopedia of Fantasy*, edited by John Clute and John Grant, 991–92. New York: St Martin's Griffin, 1999.

Clute, John, Roz Kaveney, and Gary Westfahl. "Fantasies of History." In *The Encyclopedia of Fantasy*, edited by John Clute and John Grant, 334–35. New York: St Martin's Griffin, 1999.

Clute, John, and David Langford. "Urban Fantasy." In *The Encyclopedia of Fantasy (online)*, edited by John Clute and John Grant. https://sf-encyclopedia.com/fe/urban_fantasy.

Collins, Stephen L. *From Divine Cosmos to Sovereign State: An Intellectual History of Consciousness and the Idea or Order in Renaissance England.* Oxford: Oxford University Press, 1989.

Cornell, Paul. *London Falling.* New York: Tor, 2012.

Cox, Michael, and R. A. Gilbert. Introduction to *Victorian Ghost Stories: An Oxford Anthology*. Oxford: Oxford University Press, 1991.

Crawford, Jeremy, James Wyatt, and Keith Baker. *Eberron: Rising from the Last War.* Renton, WA: Wizards of the Coast, 2019.

de Bodard, Aliette. *The House of Binding Thorns.* New York: Ace, 2017.

de Bodard, Aliette. *The House of Shattered Wings.* London: Gollancz, 2016.

de Certeau, Michel. *The Practice of Everyday Life.* Translated by Steven Rendall. Berkeley: University of California Press, 1984.

de Lint, Charles. "But for the Grace Go I." In *Dreams Underfoot*, 321–38. New York: Tor, 1994.

de Lint, Charles. "Charles de Lint: Frequently Asked Questions." accessed October 21, 2023, http://www.charlesdelint.com/faq01.htm.

de Lint, Charles. *Dreams Underfoot.* New York: Tor, 1994.

de Lint, Charles. "The Invisibles." In *Moonlight and Vines*, 202–20. New York: Tor, 1997.

de Lint, Charles. "A Personal Journey into Mythic Fiction." In *The Urban Fantasy Anthology*, edited by Peter S. Beagle and Joe R. Lansdale, 15–21. San Francisco: Tachyon, 2011.

de Lint, Charles. "The Pochade Box." In *The Ivory and the Horn*, 287–301. New York: Tor, 1995.

de Lint, Charles. "The Sacred Fire." In *Dreams Underfoot*, 138–51. New York: Tor, 1994.

de Lint, Charles. "That Explains Poland." In *Dreams Underfoot*, 100–117. New York: Tor, 1994.

de Lint, Charles. "Waifs and Strays." In *The Ivory and the Horn*, 15–45. New York: Tor, 1995.

de Lint, Charles. *Widdershins.* New York: Tor, 2006.

Deffenbacher, Kristina. "Rape Myths, Twilight and Women's Paranormal Revenge in Romantic and Urban Fantasy Fiction." *Journal of Popular Culture* 47, no. 5 (2014): 923–36.

Del Grazia, Camilla. "Possible and Impossible Worlds: Reading Contemporary Fantastic City-Novels through the Rhetorics of Fantasy and Social Geography." PhD diss. Unpublished, Universitá di Pisa, 2022.

Doležel, Lubomír. *Heterocosmica: Fiction and Possible Worlds.* Baltimore, MD: Johns Hopkins University Press, 1998.

Donohue, Nanette Wargo. "The City Fantastic." Collection Development. *Library Journal* (June 1, 2008): 64–67.

Doyle, A. Conan. *The Sign of Four.* 1890. London: T. Nelson & Sons, 1913.

Duka, John. "The Wiz of 'The Wiz.'" *New York Magazine*, October 16, 1978, 92–94.

Duncan, Glen. *The Last Werewolf.* New York: Vintage, 2012.

Eatough, Matthew. "Planning the Future: Scenario Planning, Infrastructural Time, and South African Fiction." *Modern Fiction Studies* 61, no. 4 (2015): 690–714.

Ekman, Stefan. "Crime Stories and Urban Fantasy." *Clues: A Journal of Detection* 32, no. 2 (2017): 48–57.

Ekman, Stefan. "Down, Out and Invisible in London and Seattle." *Foundation: The International Review of Science Fiction* 94 (2005): 64–74.

Ekman, Stefan. *Here Be Dragons: Exploring Fantasy Maps and Landscapes.* Middletown, CT: Wesleyan University Press, 2013.

Ekman, Stefan. "London Urban Fantasy: Places with History." *Journal of the Fantastic in the Arts* 29, no. 3 (2018): 380–401.

Ekman, Stefan. "Map and Text: World-Architecture and the Case of Miéville's *Perdido Street Station.*" *Literary Geographies* 4, no. 1 (2018): 66–83.

Ekman, Stefan. "Urban Fantasy: A Literature of the Unseen." *Journal of the Fantastic in the Arts* 27, no. 3 (2016): 452–69.

Ekman, Stefan, and Audrey Isabel Taylor. "Notes Toward a Critical Approach to Worlds and World-Building." *Fafnir: Nordic Journal of Science Fiction and Fantasy Research* 3, no. 3 (2016): 7–18.

Elber-Aviram, Hadas. *Fairy Tales of London: British Urban Fantasy, 1840 to the Present.* London: Bloomsbury, 2021.

Elber-Aviram, Hadas. "'The Past Is Below Us': Urban Fantasy, Urban Archaeology, and the Recovery of Suppressed History." *Papers from the Institute of Archaeology* 23, no. 1 (2013): 1–10.

Ferguson, Niall. "The Rule of Law and its Enemies." In *Reith Lectures 2012.* Produced by Jane Beresford. BBC Radio, July 3, 2012. https://www.bbc.co.uk/programmes/b01jmxrx.

Fitting, Peter. "Underground Worlds." In *The Routledge Companion to Imaginary Worlds*, edited by Mark J. P. Wolf, 161–68. New York: Routledge, 2018.

Foucault, Michel. "Of Other Spaces." *Diacritics* 16, no. 1 (1986): 22–27.

Fowler, Alistair. *Kinds of Literature: An Introduction to the Theory of Genres and Modes.* Oxford: Clarendon Press, 1982.

Frisby, David. *Cityscapes of Modernity: Critical Explorations.* Cambridge: Polity, 2001.

Fryer, Jocelyn. "Rewriting Abject Spaces and Subjectivities in Lauren Beukes's *Zoo City.*" *English in Africa* 43, no. 2 (2016): 111–29. https://doi.org/10.4314/eia.v43i2.5.

Fyhr, Mattias. *De mörka labyrinterna: Gotiken i litteratur, film, musik och rollspel.* Lund: Ellerströms, 2003.

Gaiman, Neil. *Neverwhere.* 1996. The Author's Preferred Text ed. London: Headline, 2013.

Gavin, Adrienne E. "Feminist Crime Fiction and Female Sleuths." In *A Companion to Crime Fiction*, edited by Charles J. Rzepka and Lee Horsley, 258–69. Chichester: Wiley-Blackwell, 2010.

Genette, Gérard. *Narrative Discourse.* [Discours du récit]. 1972. Translated by Jane E. Lewin. Oxford: Blackwell, 1980.

Giddens, Anthony. *The Consequences of Modernity.* Cambridge: Polity, 1990.

Giddens, Anthony. *Modernity and Self-Identity: Self and Society in the Late Modern Age.* Cambridge: Polity, 1991.

Giddens, Anthony, and Christopher Pierson. *Conversations with Anthony Giddens: Making Sense of Modernity.* Cambridge: Polity, 1998.

Gifford, Lazette. "Whither Wander You? The Long History of Urban Fantasy." *Vision: A Resource for Writers* 9 (2002). http://visionforwriters.com/vision

/index.php/categories/33-fantasy/459-whither-wander-you-the-long-history-of-urban-fantasy.

Gladstone, Max. *Choice of the Deathless*. n.p.: Choice of Games, 2013. Computer game/interactive novel.

Gladstone, Max. *Deathless: The City's Thirst*. n.p.: Choice of Games, 2015. Computer game/interactive novel.

Gladstone, Max. *Four Roads Cross.* New York: Tor, 2016.

Gladstone, Max. *Full Fathom Five.* New York: Tor, 2014.

Gladstone, Max. *Last First Snow.* New York: Tor, 2015.

Gladstone, Max. *Ruin of Angels.* New York: Tor, 2017.

Gladstone, Max. *Three Parts Dead.* New York: Tor, 2012.

Gladstone, Max. *Two Serpents Rise.* New York: Tor, 2013.

Go, Julian. "Decolonizing Bourdieu: Colonial and Postcolonial Theory in Pierre Bourdieu's Early Work." *Sociological Theory* 31, no. 1 (2013): 49–74.

Gomel, Elana. "'Divided Against Itself': Dual Urban Chronotopes." In *Cityscapes of the Future: Urban Spaces in Science Fiction*, edited by Yael Maurer and Meyrav Koren-Kuik, 139–50. Boston: Brill Rodopi, 2018.

Griffin, Kate [Catherine Webb]. *The Midnight Mayor.* London: Little, Brown Book Group, 2010.

Gurr, Andrew. *Playgoing in Shakespeare's London.* Cambridge: Cambridge University Press, 1987.

Habermas, Jürgen. *The Philosophical Discourse of Modernity.* Translated by Frederick Lawrence. Cambridge: Polity, 1987.

Hall, Stuart. "The West and the Rest: Discourse and Power." In *Formations of Modernity*, edited by Stuart Hall and Bram Gieben, 184–227. Cambridge: Polity, 1992.

Hamilton, Laurell K. *The Laughing Corpse.* New York: Jove, 2002.

Harrison, Kim. *Dead Witch Walking.* New York: Harper Voyager, 2004.

Hearne, Kevin. *Hammered.* New York: Del Rey, 2011.

Hearne, Kevin. *Hexed.* New York: Del Rey, 2011.

Hearne, Kevin. *Hounded.* New York: Del Rey, 2011.

Hearne, Kevin. *Tricked.* New York: Del Rey, 2012.

Hobson, Amanda Jo, and U. Melissa Anyiwo. "Introduction: What Is Urban Fantasy?". In *Gender Warriors: Reading Contemporary Urban Fantasy*, edited by U. Melissa Anyiwo and Amanda Jo Hobson, 1–9. Leiden: Brill, 2019.

Hodrová, Daniela. *Místa s tajemstvím? Kapitoly z literární topologie.* Praha: Koniasch Latin Press, 1994.

Horsley, Lee. *Twentieth-Century Crime Fiction.* Oxford: Oxford University Press, 2005.

Howard, Kat. *An Unkindness of Magicians.* New York: Saga Press, 2017.

Huff, Tanya. *Blood Price.* New York: Daw, 1991.

Hume, Kathryn. *Fantasy and Mimesis: Responses to Reality in Western Literature.* New York: Methuen, 1984.

Höglund, Anna. *Vampyrer: En kulturkritisk studie av den västerländska vampyrberättelsen från 1700-talet till 2000-talet.* Acta Wexionensia. Edited by Kerstin Brodén. Växjö: Växjö University Press, 2009.

Irvine, Alexander C. "Urban Fantasy." In *The Cambridge Companion to Fantasy Literature*, edited by Edward James and Farah Mendlesohn, 200–213. Cambridge: Cambridge University Press, 2012.

Irwin, W. R. *The Game of the Impossible: A Rhetoric of Fantasy.* Urbana: University of Illinois Press, 1976.

Jacka, Benedict. *Fated.* London: Orbit, 2012.

James, Edward. "The City Watch." In *Terry Pratchett: Guilty of Literature*, edited by Andrew M. Butler, Edward James, and Farah Mendlesohn, 193–216. Baltimore, MD: Old Earth Books, 2004.

Jamieson, Trent. *Death Most Definite.* Sydney: Orbit, 2010.

Jędrzejczyk-Drenda, Agnieszka Anna. "Magic in Fantasy: Narrative Strategies from 1970 to 2010." PhD diss., Anglia Ruskin University, 2017.

Jemisin, N. K. *The City We Became.* London: Orbit, 2020.

Jemisin, N. K. "New Urban Fantasy. Same as the Old Urban Fantasy?" Jeff VanderMeer, 2009, accessed October 30, 2023, https://www.jeffvandermeer.com/2009/12/09/the-new-urban-fantasy-same-as-the-old-urban-fantasy/.

Jones, Diana Wynne. *Archer's Goon.* New York: Ace, 1987.

Jucovy, Kyra. "Little Sister Is Watching You: *Archer's Goon* and *1984*." *Journal of the Fantastic in the Arts* 21, no. 2 (2010): 271–89.

Kadrey, Richard. *Sandman Slim.* London: Harper Voyager, 2013.

Kelso, Sylvia. "*Loces Genii*: Urban Settings in the Fantasy of Peter Beagle, Martha Wells, and Barbara Hambley." *Journal of the Fantastic in the Arts* 13, no. 1 (2002): 13–32.

Kincaid, Paul. "Underground Adventure." In *The Greenwood Encyclopedia of Science Fiction and Fantasy: Themes, Works, and Wonders*, edited by Gary Westfahl, 843–45. Westport, CT: Greenwood Press, 2005.

Klapcsik, Sandor. *Liminality in Fantastic Fiction: A Poststructuralist Approach.* Jefferson, NC: McFarland, 2012.

Krul, Rosalind. "Young Adult Appeal and Thematic Similarity in Urban Fantasy." *New Review of Children's Literature and Librarianship* 22, no. 2 (2016): 142–58.

Kukkonen, Karin. *Contemporary Comics Storytelling.* Lincoln: University of Nebraska Press, 2013.

Lachmann, Richard. *What is Historical Sociology?* Cambridge: Polity, 2013.

Lakoff, George. *Women, Fire, and Dangerous Things: What Categories Reveal about the Mind.* Chicago: University of Chicago Press, 1987.

Lanes, Selma G. *Down the Rabbit Hole: Adventures and Misadventures in the Realm of Children's Literature.* New York: Atheneum, 1971.

Langford, David. "New Weird." In *The Encyclopedia of Science Fiction*, edited by John Clute and John Grant. June 7, 2021. https://sf-encyclopedia.com/entry/new_weird.

Langford, David. "Secret Masters." In *The Encyclopedia of Fantasy*, edited by John Clute and John Grant, 848. New York: St Martin's Griffin, 1999.

Łaszkiewicz, Weronika. "Decolonizing the Anthropocene: Reading Charles de Lint's *Widdershins*." *Acta Neophilologica* 22, no. 2 (2020): 161–72. https://doi.org/10.31648/an.5593.

Łaszkiewicz, Weronika. "From Stereotypes to Sovereignty: Indigenous Peoples in the Works of Charles de Lint." *Studies in Canadian Literature* 43, no. 1 (2018): 233–49.

Le Guin, Ursula K. "From Elfland to Poughkeepsie." In *The Language of the Night: Essays on Fantasy and Science Fiction*, edited by Susan Wood, 83–96. New York: G. P. Putnam's Sons, 1979.

Leiber, Fritz. *Conjure Wife.* New York: Orb, 2009. 1943.

Levy, Michael, and Farah Mendlesohn. *Children's Fantasy Literature: An Introduction.* Cambridge: Cambridge University Press, 2016.

Lindholm, Megan. *Wizard of the Pigeons.* New York: Ace, 1986.

Lo, Seung-Wan (Winnie). "White Capital: Whiteness Meets Bourdieu." In *Unsettling Whiteness*, edited by Lucy Michael and Samantha Schulz, 163–73. Oxford: Inter-Disciplinary Press, 2014.

Łozińska, Aleksandra. "Spojrzenie kształtujące przestrzeń—opowiadanie Londynu w cyklu Bena Aaronovitcha o Peterze Grancie Wprowadzenie." In *Retelling: strategie przestrzenne*, edited by Dominika Ciesielska, Magdalena Kozyry, and Aleksandra Łozińska, 129–52. Krakow: Wiele Kropek, 2019.

McAvan, Emily. *The Postmodern Sacred: Popular Culture Spirituality in the Science Fiction, Fantasy, and Urban Fantasy Genres.* Jefferson, NC: McFarland, 2012.

McDonald, Dean-Liathine. "Urban Fantasy: Conjuring Collapse or a Sense of Place?" *Caliban: French Journal of English Studies* 63 (2020): 237–42.

McLennon, Leigh M. "Defining Urban Fantasy and Paranormal Romance: Crossing Boundaries of Genre, Media, Self and Other in New Supernatural Worlds." *Refractory: A Journal of Entertainment Media* 23 (2014). https://refractoryjournal.net/uf-mclennon/.

Meghji, Ali. *Decolonizing Sociology: An Introduction.* Cambridge: Polity, 2021.

Mendlesohn, Farah. *Diana Wynne Jones: Children's Literature and the Fantastic Tradition.* New York: Routledge, 2005.

Mendlesohn, Farah. *Rhetorics of Fantasy.* Middletown, CT: Wesleyan University Press, 2008.

Mendlesohn, Farah, and Edward James. *A Short History of Fantasy.* London: Middlesex University Press, 2009.

Messent, Peter. *The Crime Fiction Handbook.* Chichester: Wiley-Blackwell, 2013.

Messent, Peter. "The Police Novel." In *A Companion to Crime Fiction*, edited by Charles J. Rzepka and Lee Horsley, 175–186. Chichester: Wiley-Blackwell, 2010.

Meteling, Arno. "Gothic London: On the Capital of Urban Fantasy in Neil Gaiman, China Miéville and Peter Ackroyd." *Brumal: Revista de Investigación sobre lo Fantástico* 5, no. 2 (2017): 65–84. https://doi.org/10.5565/rev/brumal.416.

Miéville, China. *Perdido Street Station.* New York: Del Rey-Ballantine, 2001.

Mighall, Robert. *A Geography of Victorian Gothic Fiction: Mapping History's Nightmares.* Oxford: Oxford University Press, 1999.

Mignolo, Walter D. *The Darker Side of Western Modernity: Global Futures, Decolonial Options.* Durham, NC: Duke University Press, 2011.

Mikkonen, Kai. *The Narratology of Comic Art.* New York: Routledge, 2017.

Mikkonen, Kai. "Presenting Minds in Graphic Narratives." *Partial Answers* 6, no. 2 (2008): 301–21.

Mumford, Lewis. *The Culture of Cities.* 1938. London: Routledge, 1997.

Ormes, Nene. *Udda verklighet.* Gothenburg: Styxx Fantasy, 2010.

Panek, Leroy L. "Post-War American Police Fiction." In *The Cambridge Companion to Crime Fiction*, edited by Martin Priestman, 155–72. Cambridge: Cambridge University Press, 2003.

Phelan, James. "Why Narrators Can Be Focalizers—and Why It Matters." In *New Perspectives on Narrative Perspective*, edited by Willie van Peer and Seymour Chatman, 51–64. Albany: State University of New York Press, 2001.

Pike, David. "Commuting to Another World: Spaces of Transport and Transport Maps in Urban Fantasy." In *Popular Fiction and Spatiality: Reading Genre Settings*, edited by Lisa Fletcher, 141–56. New York: Palgrave Macmillan, 2016.

Pleßke, Nora. "The Liminality of Underground London." In *London in Contemporary British Fiction: The City Beyond the City*, edited by Nick Hubble and Philip Tew, 161–76. London: Bloomsbury Academic, 2016.

Pollock, Tom. *The City's Son.* London: Quercus, 2013.

Pollock, Tom. *The Glass Republic.* London: Quercus, 2014.

Pollock, Tom. *Our Lady of the Streets.* London: Quercus, 2015.

Popper, Karl R. *Conjectures and Refutations: The Growth of Scientific Knowledge.* 1963. 4th ed. London: Routledge and Kegan Paul, 1972.

Porter, Dennis. "The Private Eye." In *The Cambridge Companion to Crime Fiction*, edited by Martin Priestman, 95–114. Cambridge: Cambridge University Press, 2003.

Porter, Tom. *Archispeak: An Illustrated Guide to Architectural Terms.* Abingdon, UK: Taylor & Francis, 2005.

Pourjafari, Fatemeh, and Abdolali Vahidpour. "Migration Literature: A Theoretical Perspective." *Dawn Journal* 3, no. 1 (2014): 679–91.

Pratchett, Terry. *Feet of Clay.* London: Corgi, 1997.

Pratchett, Terry. *Witches Abroad.* London: Gollancz, 1991.

Prince, Gerald. "A Point of View on Point of View or Refocusing Focalization." In *New Perspectives on Narrative Perspective*, edited by Willie van Peer and Seymour Chatman, 43–50. Albany: State University of New York Press, 2001.

Propst, Lisa. "Information Glut and Conspicuous Silence in Lauren Beukes's *Zoo City*." *Journal of Postcolonial Writing* 53, no. 4 (2017): 414–26. https://doi.org/10.1080/17449855.2016.1249576.

Pyrhönen, Heta. "Criticism and Theory." In *A Companion to Crime Fiction*, edited by Charles J. Rzepka and Lee Horsley, 43–56. Chichester: Wiley-Blackwell, 2010.

Quijano, Aníbal. "Coloniality and Modernity/Rationality." *Cultural Studies* 21, no. 2–3 (2007): 168–78. https://doi.org/10.1080/09502380601164353.

Radner, Ronni, ed. *A World of Darkness Second Edition.* Clarkston, GA: White Wolf, 1996.

Ramos-García, María T. "Paranormal Romance and Urban Fantasy." In *The Routledge Research Companion to Popular Romance Fiction*, edited by Jayashree Kamblé, Eric Murphy Selinger, and Hsu-Ming Teo, 141–67. London: Routledge, 2020.

Rață, Irina. "Trials and Tribulations in London Below." *Brumal. Revista de Investigación sobre lo Fantástico/Brumal. Research Journal on the Fantastic* 5, no. 2 (2017): 85–105.

Reid, Robin Anne. "Urban Fantasy." In *Women in Science Fiction and Fantasy*, edited by Robin Anne Reid, 307–8. Westport, CT: Greenwood Press, 2009.

Rein-Hagen, Mark. *Vampire: The Masquerade.* Stone Mountain, GA: White Wolf, 1991.

Reiter, Berndt. "A Theory of Whiteness as Symbolic Racial Capital: Bourdieu 2.0." *International Journal of Humanities and Social Science Research* 6, no. 5 (2020): 111–17.

Remaeva, Yulia Georgievna. "Gorodskoye fentezi Bena Aaronovicha: khudozhestvennyye osobennosti izobrazheniya dvoyemiriya Londona (na materiale romanov 'Reki Londona' i 'Luna nad Sokho')." In *V poiskakh granits fantasticheskogo: initsiatsiya, mediatsiya, transformatsiaya*, edited by Evdokia Antonovna Nesterova, 115–24. Wrocław: Instytutu Profesjonalnego Rozwoju, 2021.

Resnick, Mike. *Stalking the Unicorn: A Fable of Tonight.* 1987. Amherst, NY: Prometheus, 2008.

Richards, Bedelia Nicola, Hugo Ceron-Anaya, Susan A. Dumais, Jennifer C. Mueller, Patricia Sánchez-Connally, and Derron Wallace. "What's Race Got to Do With It? Disrupting Whiteness in Cultural Capital Research." *Sociology of Race and Ethnicity* 9, no. 3 (2023): 279–94.

Rimmon-Kenan, Shlomith. *Narrative Fiction: Contemporary Poetics.* 1983. 2nd ed. London: Routledge, 2002.

Ringel, Faye. "Bright Swords, Big Cities: Medievalizing Fantasy in Urban Settings." In *The Year's Work in Medievalism 10* (1995): 176–83..

Ross, Andrew. *Bird of Fire: Lessons from the World's Least Sustainable City.* Oxford: Oxford University Press, 2011.

Ryan, Marie-Laure. *Possible Worlds, Artificial Intelligence and Narrative Theory.* Bloomington: Indiana University Press, 1991.

Sawyer, Andy. "*Zoo City* (review)." Review. *Foundation: The International Review of Science Fiction*, no. 111 (2011): 74–77.

Schrackmann, Petra. "Wissen als Schwelle: Urban Fantasy für Kinder und Jugendliche." In *Fremde Welten: Wege und Räume der Fantastik im 21. Jahrhundert*, edited by Lars Schmeink and Hans-Harald Müller, 271–86. Boston: De Gruyter, 2012.

Schwartz, Ellen. "Paris Letter: January." *Art International* 16, no. 3 (1972): 46–48, 59–60.

Shklovsky, Viktor. *Theory of Prose.* 1929. Translated by Benjamin Sher. Elmwood Park, IL: Dalkey Archive Press, 1990.

Shorrocks, Anthony, James Davies, Rodrigo Lluberas, and Daniel Waldenström. *Global Wealth Report 2023.* Credit Suisse Research Institute (CSRI), 2023.

Sinding, Michael. "The Mind's Kinds: Cognitive Rhetoric, Literary Genre, and Menippean Satire." PhD diss., McMaster University, 2003.

Smith, Brady. "SF, Infrastructure, and the Anthropocene: Reading *Moxyland* and *Zoo City*." *Cambridge Journal of Postcolonial Literary Inquiry* 3, no. 3 (2016): 345–59. https://doi.org/10.1017/pli.2016.17.

Soja, Edward W. *Thirdspace: Journeys to Los Angeles and Other Real-and-Imagined Places.* Cambridge, MA: Blackwell, 1996.

Stableford, Brian. "Immortality." In *The Encyclopedia of Fantasy*, edited by John Clute and John Grant, 497. New York: St Martin's Griffin, 1999.

Stobie, Cheryl. "Dystopian Dreams from South Africa: Lauren Beukes's *Moxyland* and *Zoo City*." *African Identities* 10, no. 4 (2012): 367–80. https://doi.org/10.1080/14725843.2012.692542.

Susen, Simon. *Sociology in the Twenty-First Century: Key Trends, Debates, and Challenges.* Cham: Palgrave Macmillan, 2021.

Swanwick, Michael. *The Dragons of Babel.* New York: Tor, 2007.

Swanwick, Michael. *The Iron Dragon's Daughter.* New York: William Morrow, 1994.

Swanwick, Michael. "A Small Room in Koboldtown." *Asimov's Science Fiction* April/May (2007): 249–62.

Swartz, David L. *Symbolic Power, Politics, and Intellectuals: The Political Sociology of Pierre Bourdieu.* Chicago: University of Chicago Press, 2013.

Thieme, Tatiana Adeline. "The Hustle Economy: Informality, Uncertainty and the Geographies of Getting By." *Progress in Human Geography* 42, no. 2 (2018): 529–48. https://doi.org/10.1177/0309132517690039.

Tiffin, Jessica. "Outside/Inside Fantastic London." *English Academy Review* 25, no. 2 (2008): 32–41. https://doi.org/10.1080/10131750802348384.

Todorov, Tzvetan. *The Fantastic: A Structural Approach to a Literary Genre.* 1970. Translated by Richard Howard. Ithaca, NY: Cornell University Press, 1975.

Tolkien, J. R. R. "On Fairy-Stories." In *The Monsters and the Critics and Other Essays*, edited by Christopher Tolkien, 109–61. London: HarperCollins, 1997.

Traill, Nancy H. "Fictional Worlds of the Fantastic." *Style* 25, no. 2 (1991): 196–210.

Tucker, Kenneth H., Jr. *Anthony Giddens and Modern Social Theory.* London: Sage, 1998.

Turtschaninoff, Maria. *Underfors.* Helsinki: Förlaget, 2010.

Valente, Catherynne M. *Palimpsest.* New York: Bantam, 2009.

VanderMeer, Jeff. "The New Weird: 'It's Alive?'" In *The New Weird*, edited by Ann VanderMeer and Jeff VanderMeer, ix–xviii. San Francisco: Tachyon, 2008.

VanderMeer, Ann, and Jeff VanderMeer, eds. *The New Weird.* San Francisco: Tachyon, 2008.

Virgil. *Eclogues, Georgics, Aeneid I–IV.* c. 19 BCE. Cambridge, MA: Harvard University Press, 1999.

Wallace, Derron. "Cultural Capital as Whiteness? Examining Logics of Ethno-racial Representation and Resistance." *British Journal of Sociology of Education* 39, no. 4 (2018): 466–82.

Wallerstein, Immanuel. *The Uncertainties of Knowledge.* Philadelphia: Temple University Press, 2004.

Walton, Priscilla L., and Manina Jones. *Detective Agency: Women Rewriting the Hardboiled Tradition.* Berkeley: University of California Press, 1999.

Waters, Malcolm. *Globalization.* 1995. 2nd ed. London: Routledge, 2001.

Weber, Max. *The Protestant Ethic and the Spirit of Capitalism.* Translated by Talcott Parsons. London: George Allen & Unwin, 1930.

Weinberg, Robert. *The Ascension Warrior.* Clarkston, GA: White Wolf, 1997.

Weiss, Allan. "Destiny and Identity in Canadian Urban Fantasy." In *Literary Environments: Canada and the Old World*, edited by Britta Olinder, 109–17. Brussels: Peter Lang, 2006.

Wilkins, Kim. "The Process of Genre: Authors, Readers, Institutions." *TEXT* 9, no. 2 (2005): 1–11. https://doi.org/10.52086/001c.31906.

Williams, Rosalind. *Notes on the Underground: An Essay on Technology, Society, and the Imagination.* 1990. New ed. Cambridge, MA: MIT Press, 2008.

Williams, Tad. *The War of the Flowers.* New York: DAW, 2004.

Wirth-Nesher, Hana. *City Codes: Reading the Modern Urban Novel.* Cambridge: Cambridge University Press, 1996.

Wolf, Mark J. P. *Building Imaginary Worlds: The Theory and History of Subcreation.* New York: Routledge, 2012.

Wolfe, Gary K. *Critical Terms for Science Fiction and Fantasy: A Glossary and Guide to Scholarship.* Westport, CT: Greenwood Press, 1986.

Wolfe, Gary K. *Evaporating Genres: Essays on Fantastic Literature.* Middletown, CT: Wesleyan University Press, 2011.

Wolski, Michał. "Krwiopijca kosmopolityczny: Wpływ *Wampira: Maskarady* na współczesną kulturę wampiryczną." In *Gry fabularne: Kultura – praktyki – konteksty*, edited by Roberta Dudzińskiego and Anny Wróblewskiej, 11–29. Wrocław: Stowarzyszenie Badaczy Popkultury i Edukacji Popkulturowej "Trickster," 2016.

Young, Helen. *Race and Popular Fantasy Literature: Habits of Whiteness.* New York: Routledge, 2016.

Zahorski, Kenneth J., and Robert H. Boyer. "The Secondary Worlds of High Fantasy." In *The Aesthetics of Fantasy Literature and Art*, edited by Roger C. Schlobin, 56–81. Notre Dame, IN: University of Notre Dame Press, 1982; Brighton, UK: Harvester Press, 1982.

Zähringer, Raphael. "'Strange Tricks of Cartography': The Map(s) of *Perdido Street Station*." In *China Miéville: Critical Essays*, edited by Caroline Edwards and Tony Venezia, 61–87. Cantebury: Gylphi, 2015.

Index